Sagent

Elizabeth James

Thrall of Darkness

ISBN-13: 978-1-944969-09-7
ISBN-10: 1-944969-09-8

CONTENTS

CHAPTER 1

FALLEN STAR

It was my first time in the Drops. I'd heard about it all my life, of course: the underbelly of the grand city that orbited Earth and held the humans who managed to flee before the microbes killed them all. There were still microbes in Destiny, but not many. The number decreased the farther you got from the planet, and the upper realms of Destiny were almost microbe-free. But in the Drops, people lived short lives due to the buildup of microbes in their bodies.

There were uses for the microbes, naturally. I had a higher microbe count that most in Destiny because of my job. The microbes didn't kill everyone. In some people, too many microbes meant instant death, but in others, it had only positive changes. I was one of those people, carefully scouted in my infancy and then groomed my entire childhood to enter sagent training. The microbes gave me speed, they gave me strength, and they gave me freedom. But I was constantly aware that even though my body tolerated the microbes, at too high an amount, even I would die. One visit to the Drops wouldn't make much of a difference, though. It wasn't as if I was going to live here.

I tapped my palm chip to make sure I was at the right building. My agency had given me very detailed instructions on how to get here without attracting notice and I had followed them exactly. I would go a different way leaving, naturally, but it would be just as quick. No need to spend more time here than necessary. Everything was strangely foreign in the Drops, even though on the surface it was familiar. Streets, hovercars, tall skyscrapers, even a dome overhead. But the view through the dome was the bottom of the city above, connected by three large elevators and a mass of steel and ingenuity. In Destiny, you could see the stars. I found it extremely disturbing to look up and see metal instead of sky.

Confident that I was in the right place, I adjusted my strange outfit and went into the building. I was dressed in a kimono, or at least that's what my handler called it. It was a long, flowing robe that had an intricately tied, thick belt around my middle. It was uncomfortable, but common down in the Drops. Most of the people in the Drops were from the ancient country of Japan, and it was even rumored that some came from Korea, though that had to be a myth. The meteor carrying the microbes struck Korea and the microbes spread outward from there, so it was unlikely anyone from Korea survived. But the rumors remained.

There was a reception desk and the man stationed there seemed to be waiting for me. Not unexpected, given what I was here for. He personally escorted me to the elevator and then, to my surprise, he got in with me. I kept my eyes down. I didn't know the rules of this place or the man I was going to see, and I didn't know if my target was the type of man who allowed his guards to taste his presents. But the guard didn't do anything besides leer, and soon the elevator dinged and he held the door open while I stepped off. The guard remained in the elevator and I was alone, as far as I could see.

I took a few cautious steps forward, making sure to stay in character. He couldn't suspect that I was anything more than an escort.

"Come in," a rich voice said.

I turned to the sound and walked forward. The room was lush, decorated with expensive and rare art and furniture. Everything was black and white, with the only color coming from savage red slashes in the art. On one of the couches sat a man dressed in a black suit, leaning back and admiring me as I entered. I kept my head down, not sure how he liked his men. He let out a gasp as if surprised and stood up, coming over to me and taking my hand in his. He lifted my hand and twirled me around, examining me with pleasure in his eyes.

"What a beauty! I can't believe I've never seen you before."

I blushed. My looks were one of the main reasons I was chosen as a sagent, since blond hair was so incredibly rare and I also had the good fortune of being naturally good-looking. I still remembered the recruitment officers of the major agencies lining up to offer me anything I wanted to join with them when I was eighteen and finally eligible to become a sagent. Unfortunately for them, one company had been grooming me since birth, and I had no choice about where I would go. It was with a heavy heart that I began work with GovTech. Now, though, I worked for an agency that let me pick my own assignments, and when they had offered an assignment in the Drops, I let my curiosity take over. Looking at this man, I was glad. He was quite handsome, and seemed like a good target.

"Come with me," the man said, keeping my hand in his.

He led me to the bedroom and as soon as we entered, he drew me into a kiss. I went limp against him with practiced ease, letting him feel in control. He was a good kisser, and would probably be a gentle lover, I decided as the kiss continued. Yes, this would be a good assignment.

His hands were on the long belt tied around me when there was a noise outside the room. He pulled away reluctantly, tapping my nose and pushing me onto the bed.

"You stay here. One of my men must need something."

He vanished, and I glanced around the room. Somewhere in here was a file outlining his contact with the yakuza, an underground group who based themselves off a group of the same name from ancient Japan. The yakuza controlled everything in the Drops, yet my agency had no information on them and had never been able to infiltrate them. Any information on their workings would be valuable, and this man had been chosen as the easiest mark to gain that information.

He had long been suspected of taking bribes from the yakuza, but recently he stopped taking them and started to take a stand for honesty and openness in government, much to the chagrin of the yakuza. If we could turn him to our side, we could not only gain valuable information on the yakuza, we could gain an ally against them. I saw a green computer chip on the desk, near a stack of papers. Green was the color often used for financial concerns, but would this man really have color-coded his affairs?

After several minutes without his return, I began to wonder where he was. I debated getting up to find him. It would be out of character, but I needed him. I needed to seduce him so that I could talk to him about the yakuza and learn his secrets. Or I could just send him into a sex coma and take the green chip, hoping it was the right thing. Either way, I needed him to come back. He had only paid for an hour, and my time was short.

He appeared at the door and I let out a sigh of relief. My relief was cut short, however, when he was followed by a woman in a black kimono with scarlet herons embroidered on it. She held a gun to the man's head.

I could have leapt forward and disarmed her with only minimal risk to the man. She thought I was only an escort. But even in training I had never been in this situation and I froze a second too long. She only had to study me a moment before she recognized me as a fellow sagent. I had lost the advantage, but would she out me in front of the man?

She pushed the man to his knees on the floor, then gestured for me to also get on the floor. I obeyed. It seemed like she was going to treat me as an escort, and I was grateful. I didn't know what she wanted, but at least she wasn't going to out me in front of my mark.

"I've arranged a little surprise for you, judge," she said. "I didn't expect you to have your own company."

"What do you want?" the man said.

"I want you to submit," she said in a cold voice.

Just then the ding of the elevator sounded, and the woman

laughed.

"Right on time! Get up, you old fool. You, too," she added to me. We both stood. She tucked the weapon away, then pulled her kimono until her breasts showed and entwined herself around the man.

I've used that method before, although it works better for women. One good way to get information is to pose provocatively with someone and then blackmail them. Only this time, there was no blackmail because the judge's wife walked into the room right then and saw it with her own eyes.

She was pretty, and far younger than the judge. Beautiful ebony hair done up in a bun, with a clear almond complexion and wide gray eyes. My agency had told me that the judge treated her like a doll, having guards follow her everywhere and allowing her to do nothing on her own. She was barely allowed to have contact with other men due to the judge's extreme jealousy, even though the judge himself hired escorts like me every week. She looked stunned. Then she smiled hesitantly.

"Is this what you meant by spicing up our love life?"

The other sagent, who had her breasts bared and a victorious smile on her lips, froze and looked at the judge, who was a strange shade of red.

"Yes," the sagent said. "Your husband hired us to help you."

"I'm Amelie," the wife said, extending her hand to the woman and then to me.

I watched the other sagent, waiting to see how she would react to this turn of events. I would never have expected things to go like this and I could see the wheels turning in her head as she tried to turn this to her advantage.

"I'm Zada," she finally said. It was a false name but I expected that.

The two women turned to me and I scrambled to remember my alias.

"Peter," I said. My handler had chosen it and I had used it several times, but I knew I would never be able to use it again after this.

5

"Well," the judge said, trying to gain control of the situation. "Why don't we come to bed?"

He placed a possessive hand on my back and his wife didn't look surprised; I wondered if she knew that he took a male escort every Friday at this time. I glanced around the room and my eye fell on the green chip. Maybe in the chaos I would be able to grab it, because there was no way I would be able to talk to him now. At the least, though, my cover hadn't been blown, so I could always come back.

I wondered what the other sagent was going to do to complete her mission, then I remembered her words. She was here to make the man submit. She was probably a sagent from the yakuza, sent here to make sure he remained obedient to their cause. Now that I had met him, I knew I would have been able to turn him to our cause if she hadn't interfered. He was quite taken by me, I could tell, and would have done quite a lot to keep me in his bed, even turn against the yakuza. But now that was all theoretical, and the yakuza sagent was in control. I would have to obey her just like an ordinary escort would and pray she didn't expose me for what I was. As long as the judge thought I was an escort, I could come back later to complete my mission.

To my surprise, and probably the other sagent's as well, the wife initiated things by grabbing Zada and kissing her passionately. I felt the judge's jealousy through his hand on my back, but he didn't say anything. After all, if he had arranged this group, as we were all pretending, then there was no reason for him to be jealous. I felt pity for the wife, as she was the only one in the room who thought this was an entirely consensual affair and was acting accordingly.

After she broke off the kiss, she sighed. "I've always wondered what it would be like to kiss a woman," she said.

The other sagent grinned. "We can do a lot more than kiss," she said with a glance at the judge, who wore a closed off expression. I could tell he was a controlling man and letting his wife sleep with anyone else was going to be difficult for him, even if it meant that he wouldn't be caught with a man and a woman half naked in his bedchamber. His hand tightened on my back and he pulled me closer. I obeyed and turned to him, expecting him to kiss me. Instead, he pushed me towards his wife. She opened her arms to me and stroked a hand across my cheek.

"I've never seen hair like yours before," she confessed, reaching up to lace her fingers through my fine blonde hair. "It's beautiful. You look like you're from Destiny."

"Thank you," I said.

I didn't tell her that even in Destiny, blonde hair was a rarity, or that I was frequently stopped in the street by people who wanted to feel my hair to see if it was really that color. A lot of people bleached their hair, of course, but the texture gave it away. My hair was true blond, and anyone feeling it could tell. Occasionally it made my job difficult, but for the most part it worked to my advantage.

Then she kissed me, and I was surprised by her inexperience. She opened her mouth and allowed me to do the work, drawing her out until she moaned against me. It was no wonder she and the judge needed to spice up their love life; it seemed he had taught her nothing at all of the tricks of sex. I wondered if he were in fact a good lover, as I had assumed, and remembered our one kiss. Yes, he knew how to kiss, but he must have never kissed his wife like that. It was a shame that life in the Drops wasn't as accepting of homosexuality as Destiny was. The judge ought to have a husband, not a wife. It was a shame such a beautiful young woman had to be chained to a man who didn't – and couldn't – love her.

As soon as the kiss was over, the judge pulled me back to his side. "Yes, he is beautiful, isn't he? Like a fallen star, fallen from Destiny into my hands." He kissed my neck and I arched back to give him better access.

"So," the wife said, looking to the yakuza woman, to Zada. "What do we do now?"

CHAPTER 2
WORKING PLEASURE

I t's almost impossible to orchestrate a foursome and remain in control. Threesomes are almost as easy as couples, but once you reached four, the group tends to split up and there are too many things going on at once to properly control the situation. I had been a participant in a foursome before, but only in training, never in the real world with people who weren't also sagents. I was grateful that I didn't have to be in charge and I thankfully left that to the other sagent, who looked quite comfortable leading the group even though she couldn't have expected this.

The two women had stripped and Zada turned to us with a wicked smile.

"Your turn, boys. Give us a show. Both at once," she added, as if she didn't want the judge to get a good look at me until she was ready. He would be too busy stripping to really watch me undress and I was glad; it meant he would have to invite me back if he wanted to watch me peel off the kimono and slowly expose myself.

I tried to undress using all the tricks I knew, but the kimono kept giving me trouble. I couldn't figure out how to untie the belt – the obi, I remembered it was called – and Zada laughed.

"You've never worn a kimono before, have you?"

I blushed and shook my head. Honesty was almost always the best policy and not everyone in the Drops wore this style of clothing.

The judge was already undressed and his wife was watching him with a smile on her face. I was willing to bet that he'd never stripped for her before in his life, but his eyes were only on me. He came over and pulled at the obi gently, easily untangling it.

"I bet with hair and skin like yours, people pay to see you in the latest of Destiny's fashions," he whispered so no one could hear. I nodded; it was true. But the judge requested all of his escorts to dress traditionally so they would pass through his compound undetected by the press. His eyes were fixed on my body as he slowly pulled the layers of the kimono apart to reveal my bare body underneath. He let out a sigh, repeated by his wife, as the kimono slipped to the ground.

My body was flawless and designed to appeal to both men and women, and it was all natural. Some sagents had to have surgery to attain perfect bodies and they had tiny scars across their abdomens and chests, but mine was completely clear and they could tell. Everyone seemed to be able to tell by looking at me that I wore the body I was born with and had never been under the knife. I did have one scar on my right palm, but I was extremely skilled at hiding it. I was muscular, but not enough to be threatening, just enough to show off my abs. And my cock, which held the wife's attention, was a thick six inches, enough to appeal to any women I was seducing, but not enough to threaten any men who thought they were seducing me. The judge's eyes were on my ass, another one of my fine features that made me an ideal sagent and one of the reasons I serviced men as well as women.

When I was first recruited as a sagent, I thought that I would only be servicing women, since I was a man. But I was quickly disillusioned when my first handler, a man I despised with all of my heart, took me to bed himself to get me used to male contact. According to the rules handlers followed, a handler was not allowed to have sex with his sagent, but my first handler broke most of the rules in my training and I learned the hard way what it was like to be a sagent. He was also the one to inform me that because of my beauty, I would never be promoted to a true agent, and would always be a sex agent, or a sagent as we called ourselves.

The judge reached out to squeeze my ass and murmured in delight at its firmness as I brought myself back to the present. Zada was the only one not impressed by my body; doubtless she had expected me to be beautiful and would have been shocked by anything less. She approached me and kissed me on the lips. I submitted fully, giving her complete control of the situation. I wanted her to know that I would follow her lead in this complex dance we were about to weave, as long as she didn't blow my cover. She seemed to get the message because she pulled back and clapped her hands together.

"Now that we're all acquainted, why don't you lie on the bed?" she asked the judge, gesturing to the king-size bed covered in silk sheets and a snow-white comforter.

He wrapped his arm around his wife to bring her to the bed too, but Zada pulled the woman back.

"Not yet," she said.

The judge shrugged and sat on the bed. Zada knelt by her fallen kimono and retrieved some handcuffs. My eyes widened. The judge was not the kind of man who went in for being bound, I could tell, but what lengths would he go to in order to prevent his wife from finding out that he was cheating on her?

"I don't think those are necessary," the judge said coldly.

"You hired us to help your love life," Zada said without emotion. "So let us do the job. Lie down on the bed and stretch out your arms."

He paused and for one moment I thought he was going to reveal it all, tell his wife that the real reason there was a naked man and woman in the room was because he had hired a male escort and the yakuza had sent a sagent to intimidate him. But then he scooted up on the bed and stretched out his arms to each side of the bed and Zada cuffed him to the posts of the headboard. He could still move, but not very much. His eyes practically glowed with rage and his cock was limp.

"Peter," Zada said, turning to me. "Why don't you prepare him while Amelie and I get ready?"

I nodded and moved between his legs. She wanted him hard enough for sex and she was wise to have me do it, since it was a safe bet he would only get hard with a man on his cock. Amelie turned to her in confusion and Zada began kissing her and rubbing their breasts together. I turned my attention to the limp cock before me and licked my lips.

I started with my hand, gently stroking him until I felt him respond and heard a choked cry. I looked up at him and saw his head raised, watching me with dark eyes. I couldn't read any emotion in his face and I hoped he wouldn't hate me for participating. I needed to obey Zada because an ordinary escort would obey her in this situation, but I also needed to stay on the judge's good side. I brought my lips down to his cock and kissed him. Another choked cry and his cock began to harden and lengthen.

I let my tongue slide up and down his shaft as he hardened and soon he was completely hard and his cock bobbed towards his belly when I released it. Precum spilled from the tip and I lapped it up, spending time circling his head with my tongue and chasing the taste until he moaned and shifted on the bed. I relaxed my jaw and slid him into my throat and he gasped. I kept him as deep as I could before letting him out so I could breathe, then inhaled him again. While he was deep inside me, I let my tongue play with the base of his cock, especially a vein on the underside of his cock that twitched and pulsed as I tongued it. As I slid him out of my mouth, I pressed my tongue against that vein and his legs squeezed against my ears to keep me in place.

I glanced over at the women. Zada was sucking on Amelie's breasts and fingering her clit and the woman looked near to ecstasy, but I noticed Zada kept her attention divided between Amelie and me. I nodded slightly to indicate to her that the judge was ready. Zada pulled away from Amelie and led her to the bed, where her husband lay with his cock pressed tightly against his belly.

"Help guide him in," Zada ordered me, then assisted Amelie

11

in straddling her husband.

I held his cock and guided him inside his wife and both of them moaned as he slipped inside her, slick from my mouth. She pressed down as if longing to have all of him inside her at once and he cried out. I bet he'd never enjoyed sex with his wife before this, but he was enjoying it now.

Amelie instinctively began to move on him and he pulled at the restraints on his hands as if desperate to grab her, or grab something. He grabbed the chain on the handcuffs instead. At Zada's command, I moved to the judge's front and began kissing him while Zada took a position directly behind Amelie and began fondling her breasts and kissing the damp skin of her neck. I reached out to play with the judge's nipples, hoping I wasn't being too bold, and the judge's entire body shivered in pleasure. I moved so I could mouth his nipples, since they seemed so sensitive. He had a light covering of hair on his chest but his nipples were hairless and cherry red, and stood at attention as I nibbled and sucked my way around them before taking them in my mouth and tonguing them. He was moaning almost constantly, his entire body rocking in the rhythms of sex.

I moved back to his mouth, kissing the moans and encouraging him with my hands on his body. I tried to touch every inch of him, caressing and enticing as only a sagent knows how. I wanted him to become dependent on me so he would ask me back, so I worked hard to tickle the right places, stroke the right spots, and kiss everything I could reach. I could feel him relaxing into my touches and the woman on his cock was improving my ability to control him. I wondered if Zada knew she was making my job easier, and if it was her way of silently apologizing for ruining my mission, but there was no time to think because suddenly Zada was helping Amelie off the judge, who grunted with displeasure.

"Don't worry," she said. "You'll be inside someone soon enough."

She released the handcuffs and he sat up immediately, one hand going to his dripping cock. Zada arranged Amelie in his place and cuffed her. The judge's eyes gleamed, but Zada pulled me over the woman.

"Peter, you're going to take Amelie and our judge here is going to take you."

The judge's face twisted in shock and lust. "No one touches my wife but me."

But he didn't object when Zada pushed me into position. Luckily, my cock was hard from the stroking I'd given it while pleasuring the judge. Amelie looked up at me with a sweet, sweaty smile, her arms forced wide apart and her pert breasts trembling as she spread her legs. The judge himself grabbed my cock and guided it into his wife, though he may have done it just to feel my cock for himself. Once I was in the woman, I sighed. She felt beautiful, but I knew better than to move too soon. I prepared myself for the next step, and sure enough I felt fingers prying open my crack and something cold and moist on the judge's fingers as he stroked my hole. I was glad he was using lube, since not everyone did and I'd been ripped open more times than I could count.

Soon, though, he was pressing against me and I shivered as he penetrated me. I pressed against Amelie as he entered me and she cried out, pushing back against me and starting a slow rhythm that the judge quickly joined. I shut my eyes against the bliss. It was incredible being in the middle. I'd been trained for it, of course, but had never experienced it on an actual assignment. In training, it was mildly arousing, but this was completely different. For each thrust into the wife, I was thrust back onto the husband, and the combination had me dizzy and lightheaded. I saw Zada watching us carefully before she leaned over Amelie and began stroking Amelie's body in the same way I had stroked the judge earlier. I could not figure out her assignment – was she trying to addict Amelie to her touch? She said she wanted the judge to submit, and this was a powerful way to show her superiority, but it was also an unusual one. But then the pace increased and my mind went blank except for the constant thrusting.

The judge kissed the back of my neck and shifted slightly and I let out a cry as his penis scraped along my prostrate. Very few people were skilled enough to find the prostrate and I hadn't expected it from him, but he began pushing up against the sensitive spot every other thrust and I began to pant with the effort of holding my orgasm back. Normally it was easy, since I was faking my arousal, but he was getting me truly hot. I felt him grow hot inside me as well and I knew he wouldn't last long.

Amelie was the first of us to orgasm, and she hardly made a noise, just a surprised gasp as she clenched around me and began to pulse. The pulsations along with the pressure on my prostrate drove me over the edge and I moaned softly, feeling as though someone were yanking a long rope out of me into her willing body. My orgasm must have been the final straw for the judge because just as I moaned, he slumped against me and thrust savagely, spilling deep inside me in two firm thrusts. We all shuddered and lay there panting and out of breath as Zada watched us with a pleased smile.

Slowly, the judge pulled out of me, and I pulled out of Amelie, whose eyes were closed with a dreamy expression on her face.

"I've never felt that before," she whispered.

The judge stiffened in embarrassment and Zada's grin grew wider. Luckily, Amelie didn't see.

"Amelie, why don't you go take a shower and get cleaned up?" Zada said.

Amelie opened her eyes and nodded as Zada uncuffed her from the bed. She stood up and covered herself with adorable modesty as she headed for the adjoining bathroom and closed the door. Once she was gone, the judge turned on Zada with pure hatred in his eyes. I was surprised he managed that much emotion after what we had just been through.

"I want you out," he hissed. "How dare you do that to me, to my wife."

"Consider it a warning," she said. "If you try to escape us, we will find you."

He paled. It was a good threat. The yakuza were certainly

using their sagents effectively. The judge had turned down a bribe, and now he had been humiliated in front of his wife. The yakuza sagent had no doubt taken photos during the encounter to use as further blackmail.

She pulled her kimono back on, tied her obi with ease, and vanished out the door. I turned to the judge. I had ten minutes left and could potentially talk to him, but he would probably want me to leave.

"I'm so sorry you got caught up in this," the judge said, and I smiled inwardly even while I kept my expression steady. He didn't suspect me. "Perhaps you can come back in a few days and we can have a different type of encounter. How about Sunday, same time and place?"

"As you wish," I said, keeping my eyes down as he helped me back into my kimono and tied my obi for me. Sunday. Two days from now. I could either go back to Destiny for two days, or remain in the Drops and try to dig up information on the yakuza on my own. My agency would insist that I go back to Destiny. It was far too dangerous for me here, especially since I knew nothing about the place and barely even knew how to wear the clothing. I would get in trouble if I didn't go back. But despite that, I knew that I was going to stay. This place was too interesting to leave just yet.

CHAPTER 3

DECISION

The judge let me out an exit that he assured me no one would know about, and then I was on my own with no idea what to do. I tapped my chip as I turned towards a shadowed section of the street, hoping I would be able to stop and take stock of my situation without attracting too much attention. The path my agency had given me would at least take me past safe areas, but they assumed I would leave the building in approximately the same place I entered, because that's where his escorts normally left. They weren't normally interrupted by yakuza sagents.

I was on the other side of the large complex and unsure how to get to that side safely. I needed to check my map and there was no way to do that without stopping and drawing attention to myself. I reached the shadows and moved to the side of a building, leaning against it and hoping to look inconspicuous as I keyed the information.

"Not sure where you are?" a woman asked.

I blinked and looked at the yakuza sagent in front of me. I had been so focused on the map, I hadn't noticed her approach. I tensed, but not too much. Sagents usually went out of our way to help each other. That wasn't always the case, but she had helped me so far. I couldn't pretend to be an escort, and it sounded like I couldn't pretend to be from the Drops, either.

"This isn't where I expected to be," I said with complete

honesty.

"I'm surprised," she said, looking around. "He let you out in a dangerous area. I guess he thought you knew enough to get out of here as quickly as you could. It's dangerous to stay in one place so I'll walk you out. Where are you going?"

I started following her down the street, knowing she would take me to a safer area and then lead me in circles until I told her my destination if it was really too dangerous. I couldn't answer her yet, because I had no idea where I was going. I needed to find somewhere safe to stay, but I couldn't find it with her at my side because she was yakuza. Of course, I didn't know which neighborhoods to look in for safety because I didn't know where the yakuza was strong and where they weren't, and I had no clue who the other agencies in the Drops were or how to identify and avoid them. It was a pretty precarious situation and I thought about returning to Destiny. It would be easier.

"How did you find me?"

"Other people are watching the safer exits. They would signal me if you appeared there. I wanted to talk to you," she explained, then pulled out the green chip I had seen in the judge's room. It had to be the same one. "You left this."

I was on high alert now. Sagents helped each other, but not like this.

"I'm sure it's worthless now," I ventured. There was no way she would give it to me unaltered. She shrugged.

"It's not as valuable. I took out some information. But I didn't change anything. There's still plenty that will keep you in your agency's good graces."

I studied her. She wasn't lying, so I held out my hand. My agency hadn't taught me to wear a kimono, but they had taught me to conceal information in one, and I swiftly hid the chip.

"Where are you going?" she repeated.

"I'm not sure where I'm going," I said.

"Your agency didn't tell you how to get back? I can show you to the elevators if you want. Do you have another meeting with him?" she asked. There was no expression on her face and

I couldn't tell what she thought about that. "You should return to Destiny to wait. You're pretty obvious here. When is your meeting?"

"Soon," I said, but I hesitated about where to go. Instead of giving a location, I indicated that we should continue walking aimlessly.

I had the chip. Once I gave my agency the chip, they would cancel my second visit with the judge. He would be a valuable ally but if the yakuza was already targeting him, then even if he turned to our side temporarily because of me, he would stay with the yakuza in the long run. The chip gave them all they needed to know and it was highly unlikely I would find a more valuable chip on my second visit. There really was no reason for the second visit.

Except that the judge made my body sing. Only one other man had pleasured me to the point where I actually lost control. I wanted to see the judge again. I wanted to spend more time with him. I was scared because before, when my agency found out how I felt about the first man, they put such a high price on visiting him that I could never accept assignments to see him again. If I returned to Destiny now, I would never be allowed to the Drops again. Ever. They might even take action against the judge. I still didn't know for sure if the first man was alive or whether my agency had killed him. Sometimes it weighed on me heavily. I didn't want the same worry about the judge.

"How long have you been with your agency?" she asked.

It looked like we were in a nicer part of town and, as I had suspected, I was seeing some of the same buildings and we were mostly turning in the same direction. We were making loose circles while she waited for my instructions. If I waited too much longer, my decision would be made for me. My agency had arranged transport back on a specific elevator at a specific time so I wouldn't be hassled or targeted. I wasn't allowed to go at any other time. If I missed it, I would have to remain until they arranged another safe trip.

"A couple of years," I said. She nodded as if she expected the

18

answer.

"It's important to stay on good terms with your agency. You should go back to Destiny to wait. It's dangerous for you here," she said. "Once the yakuza find out someone like you is here, they'll come after you."

"You haven't already told them?"

"I wanted to make sure you left before I told them. I still want to make sure you're gone, even if you plan on coming back."

I came to a stop and she did, too. It was far too dangerous for me to stay in the Drops. It was too much of a risk. I couldn't even imagine how they would punish me. But I simply couldn't bear the thought of going back. Not yet. Maybe I would pretend to miss the elevator and then remain until they arranged another one. Maybe that would be all. But I couldn't go back yet. I toed the ground. I wasn't going back.

"I thought you were brand new but you're not," she said, re-assessing me. "I bet you had another agency before your current one. I guess you've just never been in a group like that."

I flushed, embarrassed that my lack of control and my inexperience with the situation had shown so clearly.

"If you go back to Destiny, will you take jobs while you wait?"

Her voice was light and curious, but I could tell it was an act. She had a reason for asking, but I wasn't sure what it was, so I didn't have a reason to lie.

"If they have some in the local area, yes. I'm not going to travel far but I'll take any they have nearby that meet my criteria."

"So you do have criteria," she said, sounding relieved. "How many jobs would you take?"

I shrugged. "It's just a couple of days. I would let my handler decide. She knows my limits."

"You're probably still working off the initial investment your agency put into you," she observed. "I assume you're working full-time. When was your last vacation?"

My eyes narrowed and I looked at her. It was completely true that I was working full-time. For sagents, full-time meant at least one assignment per day. All new sagents stayed on this schedule while repaying the enormous costs of training, and sagents who had higher costs of living, like me, remained on that schedule. But the idea of vacation was bizarre. Sagents didn't get vacation until very, very late into their careers, if at all. I hadn't realized she was that old. No wonder she recognized how inexperienced I was. My first agency had made it clear I would never get vacation, but my second agency put it into my contract: seven days a year starting after thirty years of exemplary service. More than I had ever imagined and more than a lot of sagents received. But if she knew I was at the very beginning of my career, why was she asking about vacation?

"I don't get vacation yet," I said.

"So if you stayed here a couple of days, you would essentially be taking a vacation," she said. "Even though you would be putting yourself in extreme danger."

I hadn't thought of it like that. It was true, though. I would be staying for my pleasure only, to avoid them and to see the judge again. There was almost no other way to describe it. She reached out and touched my shoulder, a move to indicate the seriousness of her next question.

"Are you willing to anger your agency and your handler, ruin your current assignment, and risk your physical safety by remaining in a place where you know your enemies are hunting you and your agency can't protect you, just to have a couple days of relative freedom?"

I very briefly closed my eyes to think, but there was no need. I already knew my answer. I pushed her hand off my shoulder.

"It's only a couple of days," I said. "I'm staying."

She stared at me, then started moving again, this time with purpose. I wasn't sure if I was supposed to follow, or if she was leaving me to fend for myself. Then she gestured for me to join and I hurried to her side.

"I'll take you to a safe place," she said. "Well, I'll take you nearby and tell you how to get there. The yakuza can't go near it. You'll be safe there."

She led me through various parts of town as I tried to keep a mental map of where we were. Walking in circles had completely thrown off whatever sense of place I had here, so I could only track where we were going from where we started walking. I would have to check my map once I reached safety and just hope it was somewhere near a safe path back to the judge's complex. I couldn't let my agency know where I was or they would just come and take me. They couldn't track me directly in the Drops because the constant, low level of microbes prevented my exact location from being transmitted. While they hadn't told me that, I overheard my handler worrying about it.

We reached a shadowed street and the sagent pointed forward into a brightly lit neighborhood. Rather than the neon lights that lit many of the neighborhoods we had passed through, this neighborhood had streetlamps with golden light glowing down. The buildings only stretched a couple of stories and were made of fauxwood planks, painted in cheerful colors with white trim. Flowers and trees lined the streets. It was a very nice neighborhood and people patrolled regularly, either for pleasure or to keep unwanted people away. She pointed to the building second on the left.

"There. Just- Whatever you do, don't lie. If you can't tell them something, say that you can't tell them. I doubt they'll have problems with you," she said, eyeing my hair and kimono. "Maybe they can teach you to wear that better, too. After you're done in the Drops, don't stay longer than you have to. Don't talk to anyone on the way out, don't go anywhere, don't do anything. Just leave."

"Thank you," I said, grabbing her hand. "If you're ever in trouble in Destiny, use these digits. They go to my chip only, not my agency. I'll help if I can."

I told her my private digits, numbers I had only given to my sister, my parents, and one other sagent before. The other sagent was dead now. She clasped my hand and nodded solemnly, then vanished back in the shadows. I took a deep breath and headed towards the well-kept neighborhood.

CHAPTER 4

BED AND BREAKFAST

The building she had indicated was a bed and breakfast and I examined it for a moment. Sky blue, though there was no sky here, with thick white curtains hiding the windows on the first and second floors. It was a warm place, a welcoming place. As I walked in, I was greeted by a young man who held the door for me and brought me to the faux-mahogany desk that dominated the entryway. As I passed through the door, my skin tingled slightly as if I were being watched, but since I probably was, I pushed it aside.

He asked for my name, my business, and how long I would be staying. I remembered what the sagent had said about lying and saw the warning reflected in the young man's eyes. It seemed odd to start by admitting that I couldn't tell the truth, but I suppose I would have to.

"The name I'm currently using is Peter," I said. He didn't look surprised and simply wrote it down. "I'm here on business and I'll be here until Sunday afternoon."

"You're not yakuza," the man said, finishing what he was he writing before looking up at me. "Why did one accompany you here?"

I was startled that he had seen her, since she had obviously not wanted to be seen.

"She was helping me find safety," I said. He continued to look at me and I blushed slightly. "We're in the same line of work and it's common for us to help each other regardless of who we work for."

"It's obvious you're a sagent," the man said, making another note on his paper. "You can speak openly. Secrets won't help win our trust. Who is your agency?"

"I don't know their name," I said honestly. "They're in Destiny. I can contact them if you like."

"No," he said. "No interference. We deal with individuals in need of protection only. If your agency could protect you, you would have asked them for protection. But you're here, which means either they can't or you don't want their protection. Which is it?"

I looked down, not sure how to answer. I hadn't even been able to express it to the yakuza, but she had understood.

"They can't protect me while I'm in the Drops," I said. "And I'm not going back to Destiny until my job is complete on Sunday."

He looked at me, pen lifted above the paper. "Are you supposed to go back to Destiny?"

"Probably," I admitted. "I'm sure I'm supposed to wait there and then return. But I'm not going back yet. That's why the other sagent brought me here. She said you could prevent the yakuza from finding me until then."

He set the pen down and folded his hands together, leaning back and studying me. "You certainly are an obvious target for the yakuza. We can't protect you once you leave here. Will you be able to protect yourself going to your job and returning to Destiny on your own?"

"She indicated that I'd be able to."

"I hadn't realized sagents looked out for each so much."

"We always help each other, but she feels in debt to me because she interrupted and nearly ruined my job earlier today, and my job doesn't interfere with hers. She's also much further in her career," I added. "I haven't been a sagent very long. It's common for experienced sagents to help new sagents."

He nodded and wrote a bit on the paper. I wondered what

notes he took and why, and how much he was required to ask and how much was just curiosity.

"Why aren't you returning to your agency to wait?" he asked, still writing.

I looked around. The room was very cheery and no one was visible. There was still a vague sense of being watched. When I returned my attention to him, he was looking straight at me.

"Do you really need to know?" I asked.

"You could be a spy for your agency," he said calmly.

I ran my left palm over my right forearm. I didn't want to tell him. I didn't really know. I couldn't lie, and I didn't think I could tell him that this was something I didn't want to talk about. I would have to say something.

"I, um, would prefer some time to myself before returning," I said quietly, not sure he would understand.

"You won't be taking any other jobs or inviting any visitors while you're here?"

"No."

He made another note and looked a little more sympathetic than he had before. I wondered how common it was for sagents to need breaks. The yakuza sagent hadn't seemed too shocked, so perhaps it wasn't unheard of.

"Are you certain that you won't need protection after your job?"

"What do you mean?"

I was puzzled by the question and I knew it showed. He made a slight note on the page, set the pen down and crossed his hands again so that he could face me fully.

"Will you return to this place after your job?"

"Possibly, if I leave anything here for safety," I said. I hadn't thought about it. "Otherwise I'll go straight back."

"I would prefer if you came here first. Are you happy at your current agency?"

My skin crawled. I hadn't expected it here, where I felt safe. I took a step backwards towards the door. No wonder I felt watched. They were waiting to get me alone where they could capture me.

"Who do you work for?" I asked, trying not to sound as be-trayed as I felt. "What agency owns this place?"

"No agency owns me, owns us," he said, gesturing to indicate the entire building. "We are completely independent and refuse to be any other way. That's why we would never contact your agency. That's why we not only protect people from the yakuza, we protect against other agencies as well."

I took a deep breath and tried to push aside the fear. I was surprised at the level of betrayal I felt. He had earned my trust quickly, and he hadn't told me anything about himself. I inched closer, though not as close as I had been. He glanced at the dis-tance between us but didn't comment.

"I felt like I should ask about your agency," he explained. "You seem to have hesitations about them. I wanted to make sure you didn't need long term protection from them."

"I don't," I said firmly. "They're much better than my first agency. They rescued me."

Again, he didn't comment but I realized my words weren't exactly reassuring. Being much better at something was not the same as being good, and the knowledge that they rescued me might make him think that I was willing to put up with a lot just because I felt indebted to them. In truth, it was a fair as-sessment. He might not know how terrible my first agency was, but he could guess, and I had not given my current agency a solid endorsement. I wanted to clarify, but suddenly found that I couldn't without lying. At the very least, he knew I didn't need protection from them. That wasn't a lie.

He wasn't writing anything down anymore but he would. The sympathy was still in his eyes and I could tell he wasn't fin-ished with his questions. I couldn't lie to him, but I was resolved not to say anything else negative about my agency. They might not be an ideal agency, but they were good. I knew they were good because I had seen a bad agency.

It took me nearly two years to gather the courage to rip out the chip in my hand and run away from GovTech, but I did it. I nearly lost my hand in the process, but my sister helped me heal, and when she recommended that I join her agency, I agreed. She loved her agency. But they hadn't assigned me to her handler, as she had requested, and I rarely saw her. I was in a completely different section and my experience was nothing like hers. Still, I had nothing bad to say. If it weren't for them, GovTech would find me and I would be enslaved again, for good this time. I would rather die.

"Have they ever hurt you?" he asked calmly.

I considered my answer. At first I wanted to say they hadn't hurt me physically, but that wasn't true. They didn't hurt me in traditional ways but they did hurt my body. And they certainly hurt me mentally and psychologically, so that wasn't an option for an answer. There had to be some way to answer, but I didn't know one.

"I would prefer not to talk about my agency," I said.

"Have you thought about leaving them?"

"No," I snapped. "They protect me."

"From what?"

"I'm done answering your questions," I said, feeling unusually vulnerable. "Either let me stay or don't."

The man looked at me, then turned to the door behind the desk. A woman came out. She seemed to be in charge, in her late twenties with a soft nose and wide lips, and expressive grey eyes. People in the Drops rarely lived into their thirties, so she was probably quite old for here. Although I wasn't surprised to see someone else, I had assumed the man talking to me was in charge. After reconsidering the two of them, however, I decided that despite the age difference, power was split between them.

"You haven't attempted to lie to us a single time," she said. "Why is that?"

"I don't normally lie," I said, puzzled. "And the sagent who brought me here said not to lie to you."

"Do you know her name?"

"Just the name she was using. It's not hers."

The woman and man looked at each other, then the woman

sighed. "She must have hidden with us once, before they found her. Unfortunately, we can only protect those willing to have our protection. We will assign a guard to you at all times," she said to me. "Do you trust men or women more?"

I considered. I didn't actually know. My handler was a woman and I trusted her, and the yakuza sagent was a woman and I had trusted her. Most of my targets were men and I was trained not to trust them. But for some reason the thought of male companionship seemed welcome.

"I guess men," I said slowly. "Right now."

"You will eat meals and sleep in this building, but you can spend your days as you like in approved areas of this neighborhood. Your guard will make sure you're in the proper areas and protected at all times. If you need anything, let him know and we'll get it for you. Anything at all," she emphasized. "Do you have any questions?"

I glanced at the floor, suddenly realizing that they would be doing more than giving me a room to sleep in. I hadn't expected that.

"I don't have any way to pay you," I started, but she cut me off.

"We expect no pay. We receive plenty of donations from former recipients of our care and from those who approve of what we do. There is nothing you could require that we will not provide. What else? I know you have other questions," she said.

"I overheard my handler say my chip couldn't be tracked here because of the high level of microbes. Is that true? And I will have to contact her soon, but I don't want her to know where I am. Is there a place I can do that?"

I looked up at the woman as I asked and she smiled. She held her hand out, no doubt for me to place mine in. I hesitated. Giving her my hand would expose my scar.

"Let me see what kind of chip you have. Most Destiny chips are untraceable here, but a few aren't," she explained, holding her hand closer to me. "I need to see it."

Reluctantly, I placed my hand in hers. Her eyes widened and

the man let out a sharp gasp as my scar was exposed, a scarlet gash across my palm directly over my chip. It wasn't a smooth cut, either; I had taken the nearest sharp object – a jagged metal shard – and torn it across my palm as deeply as I could in order to dislodge the chip that would let GovTech and my first handler track me. I only had rags to bind it before I started running and twisting through the sewage tunnels leading out of the compound where I was kept. I ran for an hour before I saw light, hours more before I was beyond the armed perimeter, and then nearly two days split between running and trying to blend in with the rest of Destiny as I traveled to the family safehouse where I collapsed and barely managed to send the emergency signal.

The woman's lips were tight but she said nothing as she held her chip against mine. I gave out no information and neither did she as our chips hummed against each other. She held hers in place a few seconds longer than normal for a greeting, but since she was scanning, I didn't worry.

"No one can track you," she announced. "It looks like this was placed about a year and a half ago. The newest software only came out six months ago and this hasn't been updated. Yours looks especially fogged for some reason, possibly because you're a sagent and your microbe levels are already high. Combined with the natural level here, it's doing a better job than usual blocking the signal."

I breathed a sigh of relief and pulled my hand back as quickly as was polite, hiding it under my other hand. I did not want my agency finding me, and I especially didn't want them hurting the people trying to help me.

"As to your other question, you're welcome to communicate from the monitor in the room we assign you. Communication from that monitor is untraceable. They won't know where you are other than the Drops," she said. "Now, there is one other thing that we'll require from you in order to stay here."

I glanced at the window, tensing slightly. I didn't think they would go through all this trouble and then give me terms I wouldn't or couldn't agree to, but I wasn't sure.

"We'll need you to return here after your job is complete to make sure that you're still okay," she said. "Then you can return to the elevator. It's not far from here."

"What if my job isn't anywhere near here? I don't really know where my job is in relation to here," I said. "I came through a dangerous area to get here and without that sagent's help, I never would have found this place. But that's also not the way I'll be coming from after my job, or at least I hope not."

"What area is your job in?"

I thought for a second. The name of the entire area was the name of his compound. I couldn't give that. But there were so many neighboring compounds that I couldn't give one of those either, because I didn't know enough.

"I can't tell you," I said. "And I don't know this place enough to tell you somewhere nearby. I only know the path my agency gave me to get back and forth, and I can't show you that or you'll know who my target is."

The woman and man looked at each other, then the man pulled up a map of the Drops on a screen and turned it so I could see.

"Find an area on the route your agency gave you that you feel isn't too close to give away your target and point to it," he suggested. "That will let us know how close we are."

I tapped my chip and my map flashed before my eyes, invisible to them. I picked out a place about three-fourths of the way along the path, then looked at the map before me. It looked very different. I carefully rotated my map until it loosely fit the outlines of what I saw before me. I wondered why Destiny's maps of the Drops were so out of date as I cleared the map blocking my view and tapped my chip again.

"I think this is right, but my map is really different," I said, cautiously pointing to the place that most resembled where the three-fourths point on my map was.

The man placed one finger where I was pointing and traced a path eerily similar to the one my agency had given me leading to the elevator.

"This is the path they advised, I assume?"

I nodded and he pointed to a spot nearly at the elevator, just a little further along the path and only a few streets over.

"This is where we are. You won't be going out of your way at all. You need to return here before you go back to Destiny."

I examined the man and woman. They didn't seem to have any ulterior motives or plans other than concern, but I didn't understand why they were insisting on this.

"We want to make sure you aren't hurt on the way to and from your job," the woman said in a reassuring voice. "We also want to make sure you aren't hurt at the job itself."

"If I didn't want this job, I would leave," I said. "They're never sending me back here again once I leave."

"What about the judge is keeping you here?" the man asked calmly.

Furious, I opened my mouth to deny it and choked. The air swelled up in my mouth and I grabbed my throat, nearly collapsing from shock. The woman was at my side in an instant, rubbing my shoulder and murmuring for me to breathe through my nose and keep calm. The man came to my other side, stroking my hair and cheek. I wanted to shove them off, but their touch was helping calm me and make my breathing easier. When I finally gasped a breath on my own without feeling like fainting, the woman chuckled.

"I was beginning to think you just didn't react the same way," she said. "But you really are an honest person, as long as no one questions your target. Or were you going to lie about why you're so attached to this target in particular?"

I shoved her as hard as I could but the force knocked me back into the man's arms and he held me still. I didn't fight my way out of his arms, instead allowing him to hold me as I continued breathing deeply and struggled to figure out what had happened.

"Why couldn't I breathe? What did you do?"

"The other sagent warned you not to lie for a reason," the

woman said. "We've made it so that if anyone knowingly lies, or even starts to say something they know is untrue, they become unable to breathe. It only works inside this building."

I paled, not even caring how such a thing was possible. A far greater fear dominated my thoughts. "You mean when I contact my handler, I won't be able to lie? I can't tell her the truth."

The man stroked my shoulder. "If you need to lie, I can let you communicate from a private room we have reserved for that before I show you to the room you'll be staying in. Is that acceptable?"

I agreed and pulled out of his grasp. I followed him down the hall and up a creaking set of fauxwood stairs. I had only seen houses like this in films. Wood was an impossible resource but this was acting like I had heard real wood did, rather than the way fauxwood did. I ran my hand over the banister, soaking in the grain and wondering if actual wood still existed in the Drops or if they just had better imitations.

He gestured me to a small room and as I entered, I felt a slight tingle along my skin. I realized that it must be whatever shield they had around the place to keep their lying method in place. But I would figure that out later. Right now, I had my handler to worry about. The room wasn't sound-proof and even though the man wouldn't listen on purpose, if things got heated, he wouldn't be able to help but overhear. I didn't know what my handler would say, and I had to be prepared to leave immediately if it meant avoiding punishment I couldn't stand.

CHAPTER 5

REPORT

I kept my eyes lowered at the proper angle as my handler's face appeared on the screen. Like me, she had pale skin, though her hair was light brown as opposed to blonde. Blonde was extraordinarily rare and neither sagents nor handlers bleached our hair. Her nose was strong and her blue eyes were narrow and wide-spread. My first handler had pale skin and light hair like mine, too. I didn't know if they paired me with people who looked like me because they thought I would relate to them better, but after my first handler, I developed a fear of people who looked like me and my second handler hadn't done enough to help me get over that fear. I didn't think this conversation was going to help, because she looked absolutely furious.

"Where are you?" she demanded. "Why haven't you left the Judicial Compound?"

I opened my mouth to explain that I was safe when I hesitated, her second question sinking in and puzzling me. I glanced up at her even though I was supposed to keep my eyes down. There was another person almost off the screen, a dark shape nearly invisible to me. I met her eyes cautiously, wanting her to see my sincerity.

"I'm not in the Judicial Compound," I said, letting my honest confusion show. "I'm safe, though. It didn't go as planned. I'll report. Why do you think I'm still there?"

"Report first," she said.

"No," I said, still meeting her eyes and knowing that refusing to answer plus looking at her, on top of not being in Destiny right now, was going to make my life miserable. "Tell me why you think I'm there first."

She looked genuinely surprised that I refused to answer and tilted her head slightly towards the other shape, not enough that most people would notice. Whoever it was must have given her permission because she answered my question.

"We assigned two guards to make sure you arrived and left safely. They're still waiting at the compound for you to leave," she said. "Where are you?"

I shouldn't be angry, but I was. If they thought I would be in danger that I couldn't deal with, they shouldn't have sent me.

"Why? Why not just send someone else if you didn't think I could handle it?"

"I will answer any further questions after your report," she said coldly, glaring at me.

I took a deep breath and averted my eyes as required. It was going to be bad for me when I returned. Very bad. Still, nothing they did compared to anything my first handler had done to me, so I would face it. It would pass, and things would get better again. Maybe I would get to see my sister again in a year or two if I didn't do anything like this again.

Very briefly, I explained about the yakuza sagent interrupting my session with the judge and taking control. I didn't mention the chip at all. I didn't want her to know I had it. If something went wrong on my second visit, I would give it to her. I did emphasize quite heavily how much the judge was under my control, and how easy it would be to turn him in a second session. I explained when the second session would be and how he had let me out a back exit to protect me from the yakuza. Then I stopped and waited for her to speak.

I could see her skin flushing with rage as her body trembled slightly. But I also saw very sincere concern and fear in her eyes. Maybe she was trembling from both. She leaned forward.

"You do have the authority to make verbal agreements for

further visits," she conceded. "But it is entirely up to me to determine whether or not to keep that verbal agreement. It is far too dangerous for you to stay in the Drops that long. You've missed your window, but I'll arrange for safe passage on another elevator as soon as possible while the guards head to your location. Where are you?"

This wasn't good, and I wasn't sure how to explain everything to her.

"If I go back today, or even tomorrow, the yakuza will be watching for me," I said. "I'm staying here until after the visit on Sunday. By then, the yakuza will assume they lost me and if they still do have people watching, they won't be watching as closely."

She stared at me in shock.

"You don't make that decision. I haven't even decided whether or not to allow you to return to the Drops on Sunday and given your current behavior, it's almost certain that I won't. You're definitely not staying in the Drops that long. Now where are you?"

I was quickly running out of ways to divert the conversation. To my surprise, there was a spark from the console that visibly flared in front of the screen as I scooted back. I hadn't expected the equipment to be unstable. My handler looked likewise uncertain.

"I need a window two hours after the visit on Sunday," I said, trying to keep calm as another spark flared. "I'll stay safe until then."

My handler nodded. "You'll have a window. Identify yourself as usual. You can find your guards at the compound when you come to your senses. They'll protect you."

There was another flare and the screen went completely dead. The door opened and the man walked in, unsurprised to see me scooted quite far from a dead console. I was shocked that he just walked in on my private communication, even if it was finished.

"I apologize about the interference," he said. "It seemed like you needed help getting out of the conversation."

"You listened to me?" I said, wanting to be more outraged than I had the strength to be.

"It's important to us that our location not be revealed. I have the means to cut communication if you had started to give our location. I can do it much less dramatically, of course," he said. "But I thought something like that might help close your conversation in a less suspicious manner."

"Thanks, I guess," I mumbled. He had saved me, though. I had no idea my agency already had people down here who could track me down. I thought I was safe because they couldn't track my chip.

He led me back out to the main room and into the basement. I paused before going down the stairs, but he explained that having a room upstairs was too dangerous. After all, if I could see out, others could see in. The basement was the only safe place for guests who were truly in danger. I wanted to add that it was also the easiest place to trap people, but something about him was very reassuring. I trusted him, just as I had when I first entered. I still knew almost nothing about him, but I knew he wasn't deceiving me.

The basement was just as brightly lit as the upper floors and it was an odd reminder that all light in the Drops was artificial, since sunlight didn't reach here directly. There was enough ambient light that day and night were usually clear, except in the central neighborhoods or where light pollution was a problem, but sunlight rarely hit the Drops. So the basement didn't seem like a basement the way it might have in Destiny. And just like all the other rooms in the house, it was warmly upholstered. The main door opened into a living area and the bedroom was visible through another open door. I could see plush, plaid couches and large tables and nightstands, white tablecloths with red stitched embroidery along the edge, and a full bed with blue and yellow cleverly quilted together. The walls looked like raw wood planks, though obviously they couldn't be. As I walked into the bedroom, I noticed two doors. One led to a bathroom with a cream-colored toilet, sink, and small shower. I had never seen a shower that wasn't glass, but it looked otherwise normal. The other door led to a stairway leading further down.

"It leads to an escape route," the man said. "If anything should happen, go through here. All the doors leading to this room will take a long time to break through, so you should get a good head start. I'll give you a path from here to the elevator."

He brought me back to the main door, where another man waited with a nervous smile. He looked at me hopefully and for a moment I stiffened. I was used to targets waiting for me and turning to look at me hopefully. They were never disappointed. That hint of hopefulness put me on guard, and I turned to the first man, unable to believe that he would require me to take targets when he seemed so opposed to that idea.

"This is Ari," the man said. "He'll be one of your guards."

I relaxed, a little embarrassed.

"I believe Kim will be your other guard, but he's off duty right now," the man continued. "Only one will be on duty at a time, but we want to give Ari and Kim some flexibility in their schedules as well. One of them must be with you at all times. They'll answer all of your questions and help you with everything. Is there anything you need before I leave?"

"The guards from my agency," I said. "I don't know who they are."

"We'll be looking for them. You'll be safe."

"If they find me after my job, if they're following me, do I still come here afterwards?"

"Yes," the man said without hesitation. He took my hand and squeezed it. "That's part of the deal. You must come here afterwards. Even if you think you're putting us in danger. Even if you know you're putting us in danger."

I nodded. He squeezed my hand again and left. Ari smiled hesitantly at me and extended his right hand. I didn't extend mine. Ordinarily when people met, they shook right hands and exchanged basic information through their chips. For people who were complete strangers, it was only your name. If you were in a social situation where you didn't necessarily know someone but you all had similar interests or all had a mutual friend, you would share more information. At more intimate events such as a wedding where people from different families might be meeting for the first time but anticipated knowing each other for a long time, much more information would be shared. In this situation, though, where he ought to know that I hadn't given my real name, there was no need to even make the gesture.

His smile faltered. He looked around twenty, probably close to my age, though life had treated him a lot better even if it had dumped him in the Drops. He wore his thick black hair in a stylish sweep to one side, and his brown eyes sparkled with life. He was attractive, though not enough to warrant being genetically tested to see if he could tolerate the levels of microbes needed to make him, among other things, a sagent.

"Have I offended you in some way?" Ari asked.

I considered my answer. I wanted to say no, but that wasn't true; he *had* offended me. He reminded me too strongly of a target and made me afraid. He also attempted to greet me in a way that put unnecessary strain on me, since he should have known that I wouldn't have revealed any information and I hated greeting people that way because keeping my scar a secret in those handshakes was so difficult. But he couldn't possibly know why I had taken offense to anything he had done. I shouldn't have judged him harshly for doing what most people would do in his situation.

"Nothing you've done is offensive," I reassured him. "I apologize for my reaction."

"There's no need to apologize," he said. "You're entitled to your reactions. But please tell me if I can do something to keep from offending you."

His answer was odd, since I wasn't entitled to my reactions, ever, and I was the one who needed to adjust, not him. Every emotion I felt and displayed was designed to be catered to that of my target and while he wasn't my target, he was currently the main person in my life and they always filled the role of my target. Usually my handler filled that role. This was actually the only time other than training or when I was between agencies or jobs that someone other than a target or my handler filled that role. And in training, I was still technically acting to please my handler, even though my immediate target was the person or people training me.

"Have you eaten yet?"

"No," I said. "I have a very strict diet though."

I had eaten several hours before leaving for the Drops to give myself time to digest and pass the food, and I hadn't eaten anything since. I was trained to go up to twelve hours without getting hungry, but it wasn't healthy and could easily affect my all-important weight. I hadn't seen a scale in the bathroom, I realized. I would have to request one. If my weight was affected in the slightest while I was out of my agency's control, my punishment would double.

Ari assured me they could get anything I wanted by tomorrow morning and I made a list. I ate very basic food and he seemed surprised, encouraging me not to leave anything off. Then he listed the food they currently had available, none of which I recognized. He explained that it was all local food and tried to give descriptions. It all sounded good, but Ari didn't know the most basic information like sugar or calorie counts for anything on the list and there were seven categories I had to be extremely careful about.

I wondered if it were better not to eat anything than risk something with unknown ingredients. In Destiny when I ate something unknown with a target, I just sent the general contents and portions to my handler and she told me how much to exercise to work it off. But now, I couldn't send her anything and even if I could, it was unlikely I would recognize the contents to tell her. I couldn't over exercise to work it off or I risked losing weight, and I had been taught how to handle my body if I didn't eat. I hadn't ever skipped a meal before and it would cause a temporary drop in weight, but since I wasn't being weighed in the next two days, it wouldn't be a problem. I would adjust my exercise and diet over the next two days and be fine by the time I returned.

Ari was displeased when I told him my decision not to eat, but rather than pressure me, he just asked if anything he said could change my mind. When I said no, he accepted it. The rest of the night went without incident. I requested a scale and even with my exacting requirements, he provided one in minutes. I was not the first sagent they had helped, after all. I reluctantly asked if he could show me how to take off a kimono and he did, being careful not to touch me. I showered, dressed in the night-clothes that appeared in my room while I was in the shower, along with several kimonos, and got into bed.

Although I was aware of Ari stationed by the door, I felt alone. I often slept with guards in the room. I shut my eyes and my day flashed by in a confusing blur of colors and emotions. Blue and yellow touching but never mixing on my quilt. Dread and fear at the thought of returning to Destiny. A black kimono with scarlet herons. Betrayal at the thought that this place was owned by an agency. Pink enraged skin on my handler's face. Gasping in pleasure as a real orgasm hit me. A midnight sky pierced by white stars.

I turned on my side and struggled to calm my mind, but it was hopeless. Sleep was a long way off.

CHAPTER 6

IN DANGER

My weight was down the next morning, but less than I had worried. It would drop more in the evening. Ari brought my breakfast to my room while he ate something that smelled good, but didn't look like any breakfast I'd ever seen: a medium bowl of meat, rice, and several kinds of vegetables topped with an egg that he poured bright red sauce on and thoroughly mixed before eating. I hesitantly tried it when he offered. It was extremely spicy, but not in the way I was used to thinking of spicy. This was more an overwhelming combination of flavors that overloaded my tongue in an imitation of spiciness. It was delicious and I wondered if I could figure out the ingredients. It didn't look too complicated and from the ingredients I knew, it would be within my diet if I limited it to small portions.

I felt bad about my poor reception to him the night before, so I attempted to be friendlier, but all of my attempts fell flat. We had no common points of reference. I tried talking about the weather, the most universal topic of small talk I knew. He had no idea what I was talking about and I realized there was no weather in the Drops. I tried talking about sports, a topic that I wasn't interested in but was well-versed in since it was so popular among all ranks of people. But after feeling him out on every single sport I knew, from football to cricket, without him realizing that I was talking about sports, I gave up. Either they had a completely different vocabulary here, or they didn't have sports.

He knew what I was doing, luckily, and attempted to respond in kind, but his conversation starters were as meaningless to me as mine must have been to him. He asked if I had any pets, but I'd never heard that word and wasn't even sure if pets was an object, a condition, or something abstract like a dream or fear. I hadn't faced this problem with the judge and wondered if it would come up when I met with him a second time. I planned on talking to him and if we had this much trouble communicating, I wasn't sure I would be able to turn him as easily as I had thought. After we ate, I got ready for the day, which included a two-hour workout. I warned him in advance how long it would take so he wouldn't get bored, then began stretching my muscles.

I rotate between seven daily routines, but most of them rely on weights or equipment. It doesn't really matter what order I do them in, as long as I maintain my weight and muscle tone; I mostly rotate routines to prevent myself from getting bored.

Since I had no equipment here, I chose a routine based heavily in balance and yoga where the main challenge wasn't repetition or strength, but rather getting into a pose and maintaining it. It would help clear my mind, too. I was balancing on my right hand in a particularly challenging position when a flash of pain radiated from my palm to my elbow. I collapsed, clutching my hand to my belly and wrapping around it. It took all my strength not to scream.

Ari raced to my side, prying my arm from my protective embrace. I couldn't believe I had damaged myself. I did that pose all the time. I had never been hurt before. Holding my weight up with one hand shouldn't have been difficult, but my hand was throbbing. I could feel Ari rubbing against my palm but my eyes were shut and I was curled in the fetal position to hide from the pain.

"You're fine," he said. "Nothing's hurt, nothing's broken, nothing's wrong at all. Is there some sort of trigger in your chip that could be going off?"

I struggled to think. It was possible. I remembered my handler mentioning something like that. She had warned me that if I were ever in danger and she couldn't find me, she would have a way to contact me. Some way to let me know that I needed to get in touch with her immediately. I wouldn't have dreamed that it would be something like this. I forced the pain to the back of my mind as I had done so many times before, as my first handler had taught me, and managed to stand.

"I need to contact my agency."

He led me to the main floor without a word. The woman was at the main desk and Ari had a brief, whispered conversation with her. Then she took my left hand and brought me to the second floor hall I had gone to yesterday. I started to go in the same room, but she pulled me to a different room. I felt the familiar tingle along my skin and was silently grateful I wouldn't have to worry about telling the truth. I could barely think as I entered my handler's contact info and added my code to let her know it was me. Less than a second after I hit the last number, her face appeared in the screen and the pain stopped.

I couldn't help but shudder and rub my hand as the pain continued in my mind, even though it was gone from my body.

"Sorry," she said unapologetically. She was looking at my surroundings carefully and I realized why I was in a different room. The owner didn't want my agency to know I was in the same place. "Things have changed. You're in danger. We've contacted the judge and your visit is cancelled. You need to return immediately."

"What?" I looked up at her, shock from my pain and confusion momentarily making me forget the rules forbidding eye contact.

"He was not your primary target," she informed me. "Your primary mission has just been accomplished. Now you need to leave. Immediately."

I stared at her blankly. She was growing visibly angry at my confusion when what she wanted was obedience. But the pain was still clouding my thoughts and having my hard-earned few days of freedom snatched away so suddenly was like the heartache I felt every time my sister left. Especially since I would be punished, even though I hadn't gotten any reward.

"Where are you?" she asked in a much gentler voice, switching tactics. Apparently she realized that the chip had caused me a great deal more pain than she had anticipated. "Are you hurt? Let me send a guard to get you."

"I'm okay now," I said, remembering to avert my eyes. "I'm safe. I'm sorry. I'll go to the elevators right now."

"Good," she said, again in the gentler voice. "You're in very grave danger. I don't want you to be hurt."

"Yes," I whispered. "I'll be there soon."

She ended the call and so did I. I sat there for a few moments in confusion, leaning forward to cradle my head in my hands. What did she mean, the judge wasn't my primary target? And how did I accomplish something else when I hadn't done anything? My heart thudded in panic and I leapt up. I opened the door and crashed into the owner. She put a hand on my shoulder to slow me.

"Do they know where you are?" I asked, trying not to sound panicked.

"No," she assured me. "Whatever other mission she was talking about is, it has nothing to do with us."

I resented that she had listened even as I relaxed at her answer. I took a deep breath and forced my heart to slow. It took a few seconds longer than usual. I shut my eyes and tried to make sense of the situation.

"My agency wouldn't lie about me being in danger," I said. "They might cancel the visit and order me back, but they wouldn't lie about that. She wouldn't lie about that."

"Why would you be in danger?" she asked. While her voice was as gentle as my handler's, hers was sincere. The difference was noticeable.

I considered. The most obvious answer was that they had information that someone knew where I was. My agency might not know where I was, but someone did. I shivered at the thought that GovTech knew where I was. No, if GovTech knew where I was, my handler would have told me specifically so I would know exactly who to look for. I didn't have to worry about that. But it had to be another agency in Destiny, and many of them had worse reputations than mine. Several of them knew about me and had followed my career since my Transition Day, and might try to steal me now that my agency couldn't directly protect me.

"Another agency knows where I am," I said cautiously. "But I don't know who. I need to go back. I don't want another agency to take me."

She placed her hand on my cheek and stared at me for a long moment. I didn't move, knowing that I wouldn't be allowed to leave unless she agreed. Finally, she nodded.

"You will go straight to the elevators. Do not talk to anyone or stop for anything," she said. "If you ever need protection again, you will always be welcome here."

Very shyly, I leaned forward and kissed her cheek, the way I had once done with my mother. A faint smile appeared on her lips and she stroked my hair. I withdrew from the caress after only a few seconds, unused to any physical contact that wasn't sexual. Since my family had known all my life that I would be a sagent, the minimal physical comfort I got as a child stopped completely when I reached puberty. It wasn't just done for my sake. Since my parents were both sagents, it probably wasn't in their nature to dole out that sort of physical affection.

She helped me get back into my original kimono with some concern. I would have been happier in something else, too, but there was very little choice. If I had been coming from the judge's, I planned to say that the judge had given me a kimono or come up with a similar lie to explain the different outfit I planned on wearing. There was no way I wanted to walk around in an outfit that the yakuza knew about. But now I had no option. I had no money, so if I wore something else, my agency would know that someone had helped me. They would insist on knowing who. If I didn't tell them, I would be punished and even though the owner had offered to give me the name of someone who didn't mind being used in situations like this, I refused. She didn't know what my agency might do and I couldn't tell her.

Ari reached his hand out instinctively and this time I accepted it. He was already shaking my hand before he remembered that he shouldn't have tried. He wished me well and I responded in kind. The man and woman who owned the place were both there. They looked uncertain about letting me leave, but I assured them that I wanted to go and since they knew it was the truth, they agreed. They both hugged me and gave me the safest route to the elevators, followed by the second safest in case something happened. Both routes took me near a yakuza neighborhood but they clearly described it so I would know to be on guard. High-ranking yakuza, they said, always wore a dragon pin in this part of the Drops. If I saw someone with that, I was to run.

I agreed, nervous and frightened by the suddenness of everything. I lingered for a moment longer than I needed, but when the owners looked at me as if about to order me to stay, I left. My eyes were inevitably drawn up to the missing sky, to the wretched mass of metal filling what should have been a glorious sunrise. I took a deep breath. I would be back in Destiny soon. I just needed to focus on that and let everything else fade into the background.

This neighborhood was easy to navigate; the next one had a few tricky turns into alleys that were barely visible. The transitions between neighborhoods were stark, usually a literal wall or at least a dramatic shift in building style. I had noticed it earlier as well. Often there was a strip between the neighborhoods with a few commercial buildings that served multiple neighborhoods, and I entered one of those nervously. This strip lay along the yakuza neighborhood and there were plenty of openings into the yakuza side. The yakuza were likely to frequent this commercial area. However, they probably wouldn't be looking for me.

I knew how to move without attracting too much attention and so far hadn't drawn any unwanted eyes, but if someone were specifically looking for me, they would notice me. I entered a mostly empty area. There was an outside café with one man sipping a drink and reading a book and a few people walking by. The man at the café wasn't wearing a kimono and I eyed him cautiously before drawing near. He was quite handsome and dressed as a businessman in a tailored suit. I had seen a considerable number of men and women dressed like that on my way into the Judicial Compound. He looked out of place here, but not in the Drops in general.

I started walking on the other side of the street when I saw someone else who wasn't in a kimono and I paused. She was quite far down the street, but I recognized her walk with dread. I could always tell agency enforcers. I tried to convince myself that she wasn't there for me, she wasn't one of the guards my agency had sent to find me, but I couldn't. She was looking for me. She was moving slowly, searching each side of the street carefully and questioning each person who passed. I needed to get out. If I returned to Destiny on my own, the punishment wouldn't be bad. But if I were brought back by one of the guards, I didn't even want to imagine how bad it would be. I had to avoid that at all costs.

I turned to go back and felt a strange clenching in my heart. At the end of the street, I saw the other guard, working his way towards me. At their current slow pace, the woman would reach me first in five minutes but if either of them spotted me, they could both be here in two. There were no exits they wouldn't notice into the safe neighborhood except directly into residences. I couldn't risk going into the yakuza neighborhood. I eyed the man at the café table. Perhaps he lived nearby. Perhaps he would be willing to hide me for a few minutes in exchange for something, anything.

Very quietly, I crossed the street and slid into the shadow of the café so I could observe him before talking to him. I had very little time, but I needed to know what to offer him. He was, as I had noticed before, very attractive, with black hair in a sideswept fringe that angled over his wide, black eyes beautifully.

But what caught my eye was the dragon pin on his lapel. My hands curled into fists. Of course he was yakuza. My only chance of escape. He hadn't seen me; I could still run away as I had been instructed to do. But I would run straight into the arms of the guards. What would be worse?

I saw movement down the street and flinched. The yakuza's eyes flew up to me. I knew he was shocked because of how tense his body became, but his expression never wavered and the hand holding his drink didn't tremble. He had exceptional control over his body. He didn't make any movement towards me, as if wondering what I was doing. I stared at him, too frightened to do anything, until movement from the other direction caught my attention. I was running out of time. I had to do something.

He set his cup and the book down and approached me. I didn't move. He stopped about two feet in front of me. My back was against the wall of the café or else I would have shrunk backwards.

"Are you hiding from someone?" he asked. His voice was as lovely as his face. "Not from me, I hope. You're failing, if you are."

I couldn't speak. He turned to look down the street and his eyes narrowed as he must have recognized the walk of an agency enforcer. He glanced the other way and seemed startled to see another one. He turned back to me and pinned me with his eyes, still keeping that wide distance between us.

"Do you need help?"

"I need to get past them," I said as calmly as I could.

"What do I get out of it?" he asked. To my surprise, his eyes never left mine. Normally a question like that would be accompanied by a leer, or an inspection of my body of some kind. He hadn't glanced at my body.

"What do you want?" I whispered, eyeing the street nervously.

"I want you, of course," he said with a chuckle.

"How long do you want me?" I asked, still focused on the street. My handler wouldn't be pleased if I were late, but she would have to accept that I needed to stay safe. It was still better than being brought back by the guards.

My attention snapped to the yakuza as he closed the gap between us without warning, pressing one hand on my chest and the other against my cheek. I forced myself not to react. I had to stay on this man's good side if I wanted to stay safe. He looked amused by me and I didn't know how to express how serious the situation was for me.

"I don't want a favor from you," he said. "I want to claim you for the yakuza. I want you to belong to us."

I shivered. This was the worst possible position I could be in. He hadn't leered at me, so I didn't think there was any way I could seduce him into helping me. The guards were within a block or two and if I went into the main courtyard of the café, they would see me, or at least the woman would. Running from them wasn't an option.

"I have an agency," I said firmly but quietly. I didn't push him, though. I didn't want to draw attention in any way.

"It looks like you're about to claimed by someone," the man pointed out. "You're terrified of them. You're only scared of me. We won't hurt you."

"I'm not about to get claimed by anyone," I said, wishing I could just shove him and run. "They're from my agency. I just don't want them to find me."

He looked behind him. The woman's figure was just visible and I shivered again. It was too late. I was hidden behind him but if he moved, I would be visible. She would find me. And he had no reason to stay unless I was willing to join the yakuza. He turned back to me and stroked my cheek. I knew he could feel my heart racing under his other hand, even though I was trying to keep it under control. It wasn't worth too much effort.

"Are they going to hurt or kill you?" he asked.

"No," I said, hoping it was the truth.

He stroked my cheek again, then very slowly edged into the shadows away from me. I stayed frozen in place. He moved skillfully enough that the woman didn't seem to notice him as he moved to the front of the café, where he ordered another drink and then openly walked back to his table. I could see him tapping the chip in his palm but didn't have time to wonder why, because the woman was standing directly across the street, turning in my direction.

CHAPTER 7

THE PODHOUSE

Her gaze landed on me and chilled me to the core. She saw me. She knew me. I recognized her, too. She had been assigned to protect me several times. She locked on to me and began striding purposefully towards me. Unlike the yakuza, who had given me space, she came right up to me, grabbed my arm, and yanked me out of the shadows, dragging me several steps towards the other guard and away from the yakuza. She was grinning. It wasn't a pretty sight.

"I guess the glory's all mine. You've been causing a stir. Whoever finds you is allowed to take quite a few privileges with you," she said in a low voice, running her eyes up and down my body. "In quite a few ways. With everything you've been doing, no one expects you to resume working for months, if not longer."

She jerked me closer and I shut my eyes, trembling. "I can do anything I want to you, honey. And I have a big imagination."

It was hard to think clearly with her threats looming in my mind. I wouldn't return to work for months? My breathing quickened and my pulse raced. Her hand tightened around my upper arm until it bruised. She turned and took a step towards the street, towards Destiny. Towards pain. I dug in my feet. I would not go back. She looked at me in disbelief as I turned to the yakuza, who was pretending to read while watching everything. He was too far away to hear what we were saying but he was watching.

"Help," I whispered. It didn't matter if he heard. He just needed to see my lips form the word. Really, he just needed to see me look at him and say anything.

Before I could react, he was between me and the guard and my arm was free. I stumbled away, nearly falling as I tried to put distance between me and the guard. The yakuza and the guard were arguing. Then the other guard appeared close to me and reached out to grab me. Someone snatched me from behind. I was too stunned to fight back. I was pushed against the building and then a woman in a kimono rushed in front of me to ward off the other guard. I realized it was the yakuza sagent from before, but was too numb to feel surprise. I should have felt surprise. But I couldn't. The yakuza man and sagent were keeping the guards off for the moment, but eventually the guards would start fighting rather than arguing, and guards from my agency were more than willing to kill for me.

There was movement in the street and I flinched. Ten people appeared and at first I thought they were agency, but there was something distinctively smooth about their run that I had never seen. They filled the street and cut off the area, then surrounded the agency guards. I slid to the ground in a crouch as the yakuza and sagent came to my side. He asked me something but I could barely hear it. Zada put her fingers against my neck to check my pulse and I realized I had let it race completely out of control. I wasn't surprised when she tapped my wrist twice, hard, the signal sagents and handlers give when our vitals need serious, immediate readjustment.

I slowly calmed my heart, taking my time. Too sudden a shift would cause damage. The cortisol released by my intense reaction had also done some damage and I signaled my microbes to repair as much as they could. Time would do the rest. I worked on expanding my breathing and in less than two minutes, my body was functioning again.

As soon as I looked up, the yakuza hauled me to my feet. He rushed me through the chaos of fighting into the street, not letting me look back as he took me straight into the yakuza neighborhood. The sagent was behind us. The yakuza's pace slowed considerably once we were inside the neighborhood, and he let go of my arm, letting me follow instead of dragging me. We came to an immense podhouse near the center of a very nice housing area, and he gestured for me to go inside. I entered a little hesitantly, and was relieved when it was a perfectly ordinary if expensive entry room, and there were no other people.

I paused a few steps inside and looked around. It really was quite ordinary. It looked like any of the mansions I had been to; at least, the mansions of people who were truly wealthy and not just money-wealthy. There was a subtle difference, but sagents knew it intimately and I more than most. Those with true power had monetary wealth, but they also had many, many other forms of wealth, whether political or military, loyalty, charisma, or that unnamable quality some people just seemed to be born with. They were the best allies, the ones to please. And the best targets, in my experience at least, because they didn't need to dominate or hurt in order to fill some deficiency in their lives.

The style was unique, I noticed. Dragons must be important to the yakuza because they were everywhere. There was an interesting blend of old and new, with crisp silver hardware against ebony doors and trim, but soft white walls, the largest holding a tapestry featuring a dragon soaring across water at sunset. I wondered if it was supposed to be Earth. The other walls were full of the ebony doors, all leading to various pods. Podhouses had a central hub built into the city floor, but the adjoining rooms were only connected through doors and could be detached, shuffled, and reattached however and whenever the owners desired. This podhouse had looked enormous on the outside, and probably had several staffmembers devoted to shifting rooms.

The door shut behind me and I turned to see the yakuza and the sagent. The sagent excused herself and left through one of the doors, leaving me and the man alone. He put his hand on my neck, probably checking my pulse again, but kept it there as he stared into my eyes. I hadn't realized how flattering it was to have someone look at me and not stare only at my body.

"You understand what you agreed to when you asked me for help, don't you?"

I nodded, unable to voice the words. This man at least seemed decent, and the sagent had helped me twice now, so maybe I would be able to tolerate the yakuza. Of course, I had thought that about my last agency, too. I had thought there was no possible way they would be worse than GovTech. And they hadn't been, not for a long time. They were strict from the beginning, but that was understandable. Things just seemed to deteriorate no matter what I did, no matter how hard I tried to obey. And when I thought of months of punishment, months of being in so much pain that working wasn't even an option, I knew that anything was better. Maybe the same thing would happen here and in a year and a half I'd be running away again. But at least I'd get peace for now.

"I was hoping you would join us," he said. "I designed a suite for you. I wasn't expecting it to be in use yet, but it should be ready in a minute or two. Once it is, I'll explain what we need to do."

He tapped his chip and I knew people were finishing the room and the building staff were moving the room into position. I rubbed my wrists together and my mind flooded with the thought of the agony that had driven me out of safety in the first place. If my agency could make me feel that much pain, what else could they do to me through my chip?

"Excuse me," I said as quietly as I could while still getting his attention. I kept my eyes down, reading his physical cues to let me know that he was looking at me. "The guards, um, they can't tell my agency. And I need, um…"

I came to a stop, unable to explain. I had no idea of my position in this place except that I was at the lowest rank and he was one of the highest since he wore the pin.

"Tell me what you need," he said, placing one finger under my chin and forcing me to look at him. "Tell me as clearly and directly as possible."

"I need to remove my chip before my agency finds out," I said, frightened at being so bold to a superior.

He gestured for me to stay still and left through one of the doors. I looked at the tapestry again. I had seen tapestries before, but this was very finely woven, perhaps the most beautiful I had ever seen. I approached it carefully and looked at the water. The water covered the entire bottom half of the image. We were taught in school that most of Earth was covered in water like this. It was called ocean. I had always wanted to see it for myself.

I heard a footstep and realized I had moved without permission. I rushed back to where I was supposed to be, but he didn't look upset. He was looking at the tapestry, too.

"It's a copy of one from Earth," he said. "This was made right after people abandoned Earth. It's not a true replica. An artist recreated it from memory. It's been in the yakuza's possession ever since."

My eyes widened. I had never, to my knowledge, seen something so ancient. To see it hanging so casually like this was astonishing. Perhaps the material at the bed and breakfast really had been wood.

The yakuza gestured for my right hand. He had a chip machine and even though I had asked him to remove my chip, I was now reluctant. Showing him my scar would let him know that I had a history of running away, and getting a new chip was not to be taken lightly, not just because it was highly illegal. Most people had one chip their entire life, and the only time they got a new chip was if they committed a felony and wanted to illegally wipe their slate clean. This would be my third chip. There were other people who had two, but I had never heard of anyone with three. I felt like I had failed because I needed yet another clean start. I didn't know what I was doing wrong, but I couldn't seem to live for more than a few years as an adult without needing to run away and start over.

I extended my right hand palm up, keeping my eyes down so I wouldn't see the usual surprise at my scar. If he was surprised, I didn't feel it when he took my hand and placed it on the chip machine. There was a sharp pain and I shut my eyes. It was out. I relaxed a little and opened my eyes to see him put my old chip in one section and another chip, my new chip, in the machine. I held my hand open again and there was another sharp pain. Then he let me draw my hand back. I tapped my chip hesitantly. It was completely empty. I tapped it again, bemused. I had never felt anything like it. The yakuza smiled, and I realized he could see what I was doing. I blushed and stopped.

"I'll transfer your information over as soon as possible, and give you new information as well to help you get adjusted," he said. "I noticed you were bruised. Do you need anything?"

I was surprised he noticed, or remembered. The guard hadn't bruised me too heavily, but since my body was still recovering from shock, it would take longer than usual to heal. Normally it would be thirty minutes at most, but I was putting it at a low priority so it might be hours. It did hurt a little.

"If you have any pain medicine, just a low dose, I would appreciate it," I said politely.

He tapped something into his chip, then opened one of the doors and led me into a hallway lined with doors. In such a large building, there must be plenty of halls. The halls were probably stationary and had a set number of rooms that revolved around them. At least, that's the way I would do it. He took me to the end of the hall and gestured for me to open the door. As I entered the suite, soft lights glowed to life.

The suite had a stark, plain beauty rather like the judge's rooms, and I wondered if that was the style in the upper class of the Drops. In Destiny, the style for personal quarters was to fill rooms with as much furniture and knick-knacks as possible to show off one's wealth. The bed and breakfast had followed that general theme, but it was a middle class neighborhood. Here, though, everything was about clean, smooth lines. The suite was almost completely open, with partial partitions into living, dining, sleeping, and bathing areas. There were no doors and not even the bathroom was completely divided from the rest, though it was angled to be unseen.

There was a very simple and elegant queen bed with pale green sheets, bed stands with sleek lamps, and a black dresser topped by a white square vase holding a single red rose. In the living area was a large bookshelf filled with red and green books with names in gold script that I couldn't quite make out, a white chaise, an entertainment center at least twice as large as my current one, and a large empty space that had to be for workout equipment as I didn't see any. In the dining area was an ebony table and two chairs. I could just see into the bathroom, and the simplicity and beauty seemed to continue into there. I was grateful for the bathroom; some podhouses had shared bathrooms, which could get complicated with the pods constantly fighting for access.

"This is mine?" I asked in awe, forgetting for a moment that I wasn't allowed to initiate conversation.

He seemed pleased, but I silently reminded myself not to break any more rules. Agencies were always flexible with new sagents, but I didn't want to press my luck. I needed to save that flexibility for when I really needed it, not for something like this.

But he simply smiled.

"There are quite a few matters for us to discuss. Why we don't we get started?"

CHAPTER 8

THE CONTRACT

He gestured for me to sit across from him at the table, and I noticed several dozen papers stacked on the table with small writing. There were two stacks, one in a language and alphabet I'd never seen before. There were also two pills and a glass of water, which he gestured for me to take, explaining it was a low dose pain medication. I thanked him and took the pills, then set the empty glass to one end of the table. I could feel it working already as the throbbing along my arm began to lessen.

The man sat and moved the stack in the foreign alphabet in front of him, and after I sat, he moved the stack that I could read in front of me. I blinked. It was a legal agreement between an agency and a sagent. Me. I looked around uncomfortably. I had already committed myself to this, but I didn't know who my handler would be and until I knew that, I wasn't really ready to sign anything. I had also never seen an actual contract before. At both of my agencies, they simply told me the terms and I signed a single sheet of paper with vague language on it. He extended his hand to me.

"We haven't been properly introduced," he said, smiling. "My name is Junsu Lee. You will call me Lee. You will call everyone by their last name unless given specific instructions otherwise. My technicians said that there are some strong protections on your chip so they're still working on getting the information from it.

Until then, what is your name?"

He had already seen my scar and there was literally nothing in my current chip, so I shook his hand with less worry than I ever had before. I met his eyes as we shook, as was proper, then lowered them again.

"My name is Gabriel," I said, giving him my childhood name. It was the name I called myself and I rarely gave it out. He seemed to expect more and I blushed. "My family never really had a last name. I'm sure there's one on my chip that's official, but I don't know what it is."

"Will you mind going by the last name on your chip?" he asked. "Calling someone by their first name in our culture is extremely intimate. You'll need a last name so people can address you properly."

"That's fine," I said. It wouldn't be any different than going by any other name. I glanced around the room, wondering if my handler were going to show up or if they were going to make me sign first, and then let me find out.

"What are you nervous about?" he asked. When I started to turn my head and avoid the question, he chuckled. "No evasions. Tell me clearly what's bothering you right now."

"Who is my handler going to be?" A sliver of fear escaped into my voice, but I couldn't help it. My handler would have absolute control over every aspect of my life. I needed to know what kind of a person he or she was. I needed to know how painful this would be.

"What makes you think I'm not your handler?" Lee said, voice ripe with humor.

I met his eyes again and let a small smile cross my lips at the joke.

"Handlers don't talk to sagents this way," I said.

"Which way?" he teased.

"Like we're human."

The smile on Lee's lips faded. Alarmed, I thought back on my words. Had I said something wrong? He was friends with handlers, I realized. Of course he was. I should have known that. And

I had said something negative about handlers.

"I'm sorry," I said, returning my eyes to their proper position. "I shouldn't have spoken so rudely. I didn't realize-"

"No," Lee interrupted. "Don't apologize until you understand why you're apologizing."

I couldn't look up at him because I was confused and frightened. My fingers curled into my palms until I forced them flat again, forced my body to relax again. I didn't know what was going on, but I was out of the flexibility they would allow me, and I hadn't even met my handler yet.

"Why did you ask me for help?" he asked. "Look at me while you answer."

I reluctantly looked up at him. He looked troubled, but his midnight eyes swept mine up and held them in place. I found my usual reluctance to speak fading, even though I was normally terrified of talking to anyone except targets, and even with targets I only liked talking about very specific topics. Talking about this subject shouldn't be easy, but his eyes were reassuring.

"I knew I would be in trouble when I got back," I said. "I wasn't supposed to stay here. Then my handler ordered me to come back today. I thought if I could get back on my own, I would be, well, I would get through it. If those guards brought me back, though, it would be bad. Except when the guard grabbed me, what she said-"

I drew in a sharp breath and felt the sharp prickling of tears. "It didn't matter how I got back. My handler had already decided. Anything was better. I won't go through it again."

Lee glanced at my right hand. "This was your second agency. What happened with your first agency?"

I lowered my eyes. He was comforting, but what GovTech had done was so inhuman that I could only face it alone. I also had to be careful what I said because I didn't want him to tell my new handler that I had run away from both of my previous agencies after spending less than two years at each of them. He or she would likely start off so strict that when things turned bad, it would become so bad so quickly that I wouldn't be able to stand it, and it would be far more difficult to run away here.

"I left them," I said, wondering if he would let me leave it at that.

To my surprise, he did. Or he seemed to, until he turned his hand over and motioned me to put my right hand palm up in his. I did, slowly. He traced one finger along the jagged scar, then wrapped his other hand on top of mine as if embracing my hand and my scar. It was an odd gesture of acceptance.

"I will ask for more eventually," he said. "But not today. Will you be offended if I call you Gabriel for now?"

"I would like it if you call me Gabriel," I said without thought, then blushed when I remembered what he had said about it being very intimate. He chuckled.

"Well, Gabriel, I assure you that your next handler will treat you like a human," he said, and I lowered my head at the reminder of the insult I had given. "I will do my best to understand you and help you reach your potential as a sagent and beyond. I don't know what your other handlers have been like, but I suspect I will be quite different from either of them."

My brow creased. He had to be kidding. He wasn't a handler. Handlers didn't smile, or laugh, or look at you like they cared about you. They didn't look into your eyes when they met you; they examined your body to make sure you were taking good care of their property. But I could tell he wasn't lying about being my handler. Maybe he was just new to being a handler, and would fall into the habits all handlers had before long.

He sighed and gestured to the papers.

"These are just the empty forms right now," he explained. "I want to discuss your current arrangement to make sure we're not giving you anything less than you're receiving right now, and then see if we need to make adjustments. I've heard that in Destiny, new sagents aren't able to negotiate some of their terms and agencies tend to take advantage of them. What are the terms of your contract?"

I thought. I wasn't even sure what types of things were in a contract. I had never heard of a sagent who had ever seen a contract before, let alone negotiate one. Contracts were discussed, though, by many sagents in both of my agencies, by the sagents I occasionally met from other agencies, by my parents and sister, and from what they said, by the sagents they knew. It was a point of contention between sagents and agencies, but since sagents were completely controlled in all ways by their handlers, there would never be any way to change it. Suggesting it resulted in punishment, death, or vanishing, and my parents impressed on me from an early age never to discuss it with anyone other than a sagent. This didn't seem like a trap, though.

"Have you forgotten the sections of the contract?" he asked.

I nodded, grateful for the excuse. He pointed to the first section of the papers in front of me. It used jargon that made almost no sense and I looked back at him, still confused.

"It is hard to understand," Lee acknowledged. "Lawyers like to write like that. I should get you a lawyer but I want to get this signed quickly. Do you mind if I summarize what it says and ask you for details, then we work out a suitable arrangement?"

I was shocked at the mention of getting me a lawyer. Sagents didn't deserve legal representation for something as minor as this. If we committed a crime as part of a job, or were falsely accused of a crime while on a job, then we were protected, but we weren't protected at any other time. Generally, we just remained in agency compounds where we couldn't get in trouble anytime we weren't on jobs. It was another reason I had put myself at risk staying in the Drops, but a very small reason.

"You can summarize it," I said.

"All right. The first section involves amount of work. My other sagent said you were working full time, which is normal for new sagents. Unfortunately, your timeline for that will be reset as the yakuza will be making a new investment in you. I don't have the exact figures yet as there are still a lot of unknowns, so that will be filled in later. What was the cap on your full time at your previous agencies?"

When I looked puzzled, he explained. "The cap is the maximum time you'd be working full time before you'd transfer to

61

normal working hours."

"There's no cap," I said, confused. "I've never heard of that. You work until you pay back your investment, and then you work as much as it takes to repay your living expenses every month. I was told that because of my living expenses, I would always work full time."

He stared at me in shock. "That's ridiculous. Besides, I would think the high prices you could command would more than make up for any expenses you might possibly incur. Do you have a lot of living expenses?"

"I must," I said. "They don't seem more than my sister's, but my handler told me comparisons between men and women aren't accurate."

He looked very skeptical and glanced at the contract. "A two-year cap is standard. I guess I need some more basic info on you. How old were you at your Transition Day, how long was your training, how long did you work full time at your first agency, and how long did you work full time at your second agency?"

He wasn't asking my general age for Transition Day, since everyone was eighteen. Transition Day was triggered when the last qualifying student in the school district turned eighteen. It was held that day, since occasionally another student had their nineteenth birthday the very next day. It was a brutal process even though the school and government officials tried to make it as comforting as possible. In my district, only fourteen students qualified, including me. We were weeded down through three genetic tests: one at age ten, one at fifteen, and one on Transition Day itself. The tests ensured that we were genetically compatible with the microbes and were unlikely to die when the microbes were introduced into our systems. The initial pool of students identified at age ten was over forty students, but by fifteen only twenty-five were still compatible, and on Transition Day, there were fourteen.

After the genetic test, we passed through a full body scan to make sure we were microbe-free. Then we were strapped down in pods and knocked out while the microbes were injected into us. When we awoke, everything was different. Microbes affected everyone differently. Two students never woke up. One student's lungs were crippled and she was sent to the hospital, where she would be on life support until her parents could say goodbye. The rest of us were healthier, stronger, and faster. Any physical or psychological ailments were gone, from chronic headaches to poor eyesight to depression. We passed through another body scan to test the results, and were sent to our agencies.

I glanced at Lee cautiously. I was a little scared of how young I was. My first handler had been delighted at my youth, and taken pleasure in breaking me. I was broken now, but still young. Nothing Lee had done or said indicated that he would take advantage of me, but that might change.

"Transition Day was my birthday. I trained for eighteen months," I began, but faltered when his eyes narrowed and he leaned forward.

He didn't say anything, but I knew what he was thinking. Two years was the absolute minimum for training and the average training time was three. I was positive it was the same in the Drops. But my handler pushed me well past my limits, and skipped portions of training that he taught me himself in my bedroom at night, even though the highest and most sacred rule in all training was that a handler could never touch a sagent in lust.

Before I was a sagent, when I grew scared of my inevitable fate as a sagent, my parents always reassured me of that rule. But my first night, the night of my eighteenth birthday, my handler, James Acron, entered my small room and disillusioned me of that myth so thoroughly that I never recovered. I tried to tell other handlers, but they all laughed. Acron was the best, they said, and he would never break the law. Especially that law. No handler would break that law. I was punished by them for my lies, then punished by Acron for trying to tell the truth. Only my parents and sister had ever believed me.

"I worked full time for them for six months, two weeks and three days before I- I left," I said, catching myself before I said I

63

had run away. "I didn't have an agency for almost a month. I've worked full time for my second agency about a year and a half."

"What does full time mean for you?" Lee said, carefully spacing his words. He was extremely angry, I could tell, and I hoped he wasn't angry at me. I hoped my answer would be adequate.

"Officially, I take at least one job a day," I said. "But handlers decide jobs, so it's rare that I only have one job unless I have to travel for it. I usually have three."

His eyes were now completely blank and his anger was gone, replaced by an expressionless mask that put me on high alert. I couldn't read him at all. Acron had looked like this sometimes, right before he did something terrible. I trembled.

"How many days a week did you work like that?"

Again my brow creased. The question didn't make sense but I would answer. I had to answer or he would hurt me.

"All of them."

"Is that the standard definition of full time in Destiny?"

"Yes," I said. I didn't know if I should expand, so I didn't.

"My sagent indicated that you would receive vacation. What are those terms?"

"After I serve thirty years to my handler's satisfaction, I'll get seven days vacation per year," I said, wondering if he would be pleased or displeased by my agency's generosity.

"Is that standard in Destiny?"

"Oh, no," I said. "That's very good."

Abruptly his mask shattered and he slammed back in his chair, rising like a viper and stalking back and forth. I shrank in my chair, waiting for him to strike. He hissed words in a foreign language and occasionally looked at me. I shouldn't look at him, knew it would get me in trouble, but I was terrified and needed to know when to brace myself. He stopped, and I flinched. I didn't know if I should apologize, if I should get out of the chair and prostrate myself as Acron always demanded, if I should stay still and keep my mouth shut. I just knew something was about to happen.

"Why are you scared?" he demanded.

I shrank even more but knew I had to answer as honestly as I could, even if I would be punished more.

"You're going to hurt me," I whispered.

"Get up," he commanded. I obeyed as quickly as I could. He gestured for me to come to his side, then clutched me to him. His hands clasped behind my back and his chin rested on my shoulder possessively. I kept tight control over my body, making sure that my vitals didn't spike again out of fear. I didn't want him to feel how frightened I was. I tried to soften my body, but I couldn't.

"I am not angry at you," he said, voice still angry. "I'm furious that you have been taken advantage of, abused, and mistreated for years, and yet none of these things are the reason you left your agencies."

Puzzled, I sensed his body language. There was a latent attraction in his body, but there had been since he first saw me. He was attracted to me, but it was within the limits of what was acceptable for a handler to feel towards his sagent. There was no lust driving this embrace. He was holding me to comfort me, something I hadn't felt in well over a decade. The owner of the bed and breakfast had touched me like this, but not embraced me. And while her touch caused me to shy away, this embrace invited me in. Hesitantly, I tilted my head towards him until my forehead rested against his neck and my cheek lay on his shoulder. I allowed my body to relax a little. I shut my eyes. His hands unclasped and one settled at the base of my spine while the other stroked my back in a slow, smooth rhythm.

My eyes prickled with tears but I couldn't cry. I remembered how I used to cry before I became a sagent. I wished I could cry like that. But it had been trained out of me. I suspected my training in that regard was more thorough and ruthless than any other sagent. When Acron began raping me every night, he always gagged me to prevent me from screaming, but he also began teaching me to be silent. Part of being silent was controlling crying, something sagents learned to do anyway.

Sagents were taught to cry artfully, on command only. Never genuinely. Most learned it fairly late in training. I learned it in the first two weeks and the one time I slipped up and let a tear fall in the wrong place at the wrong time, the results were so brutal that it never happened again.

"Put your arms around me," Lee instructed.

I obeyed cautiously, still unsure if this would lead to something. It was much more comfortable having my hands resting on him than hanging at my sides, and I allowed myself to relax a little more fully into him. His arousal was not increasing. It seemed he just wanted me to be comfortable. Was he new to being a handler or was this actually who he was? I was frightened to know the answer. I wanted desperately to believe that he would always be like this.

I held him tighter and my legs weakened. I had been through so many shocks today that my body was starting to go out. My microbes were keeping everything running so far, but I would need help soon. My arm was throbbing again and my pulse was rising. I was starting to have difficulty controlling my body even with my training. I gently pushed away from Lee and lowered my eyes. He was very considerate but I still didn't know if I was allowed to ask for things. Still, my health depended on this and that was something he was required to know.

"I need a doctor," I said. "I need some anxiety medication and I might be dehydrated."

"I was going to take you to be examined after we signed the contract," he said, glancing at the forms. "I can't technically give you anything else until you sign."

"Where do I sign?" I asked, walking to the table. "That's all sagents do. You're my handler. You make the terms and tell them to me."

"That is not how we do things here," he said sharply. But he must have seen how much weight I put on my hand as I leaned on the table, because he sighed. "You can sign and I'll fill in the terms to my liking, and in a way that will be fair to you and your experience. Here."

I scrawled the mess of loops that I had been told was my signature even though it had no resemblance to Gabriel, and he frowned at it.

"This is your signature?"

"That's how my parents taught it to me," I said. "I don't think Gabriel is the name on my birth certificate. That's my real name but I never learned what it was, just how to sign it. They said I would have to know how to sign it for legal documents but nothing else."

He signed his name neatly beside mine, then we both signed the copy in the foreign language. He wrapped an arm around my waist and I flinched, then realized that once again, he wasn't doing anything wrong. He knew I was feeling weak, and was helping to support me. I flushed slightly as he led me to the door and glanced into an iris scanner I hadn't noticed before. He was probably taking me to the doctor, but I was still nervous to leave the safety of this room.

CHAPTER 9

PHYSICAL EXAM

This time we exited into a gleaming white, tiled hallway. We walked towards where the entry room had been, only now when we walked inside, it was a large medical lab. To the right were a large variety of machines and tools I had never seen before, and rows of labs. Despite the large area, only a few people were moving around. Lee took me to the left, to a row of examining rooms. At the far end, I saw larger rooms that I suspected were for surgeries, large scale testing, and other devices for more serious ailments than I would hopefully ever need.

He took me into the nearest exam room and shut the door. It was spacious, with the usual exam table and chair where they would take most of the tests. The normal equipment was all there, plus a more comfortable chair for Lee to sit in. He helped me sit in the exam chair before sitting himself.

"She'll be in shortly. Ananti is my doctor," he added. "I trust her completely. Be as open and honest with her as you can. She won't judge you. If you need me to leave at any point, you can ask me or indicate it to her."

I nodded, though I would never dare. Still, it was beyond generous to offer. For him to assign me the same doctor that he used was strange, since I had always been taught that sagents required different doctors who specialized in our unique biology. Perhaps since everyone in the Drops had microbes, sagents weren't that unusual.

The was a rap at the door before it opened; a pale woman with ebony hair walked in with her hand already extended. I hesitantly took it. She didn't even react to my scar, smiling at me and already examining me, I could tell.

"My name is Ji-eun Ananti," she said. Her voice was warm, like honey melting in the sun. "Please call me Ananti. I understand we don't have a last name for you yet. May I call you Gabriel?"

She blushed a little as she said that, and I realized how awkward it must be to call me by my first name. Lee didn't react to it, but he was also my handler and had the right to call me anything he wanted. I nodded shyly, glancing at Lee to make sure I was doing all right so far.

"Well, Gabriel, we're going to do a full physical on you, but let's make you comfortable first," she said with a smile, barely stumbling over my name this time. "I'll need some basics before I can give you anything. I'm sure you've done this a million times. First, I'll need you to undress."

I was relieved when she untied my obi for me and I didn't need to immediately reveal that I didn't know how to undress in these clothes. Lee carefully picked up my kimono, folded it, and set it on the floor beside him. Afterwards, for the first time, he examined my body. This was the first time he had seen me naked, and while he didn't take long, it was a thorough examination. There was approval in his eyes when he finally looked up at me again and I relaxed, not even aware how much I needed that approval.

Ananti helped me sit and adjust my wrist into the pressure clasp and my finger into the pulse and oxygen register, then asked my height and birthdate as she waited for results. She hesitated and asked me to confirm my birthdate.

"You're twenty-one?" she asked, glancing at Lee.

I also looked at Lee, wondering what was wrong. He just gestured for me to answer and I confirmed. She jotted down the answer and continued to check measurements. The chair took my weight and I was nervous about that, especially when she wrote down the results and then asked my usual weight. She appeared surprised when I told her.

"Are you aware your weight is off?" she asked.

"Yes," I said quietly, glancing at Lee to see how angry he was. He just looked concerned.

"How off?" Lee asked. "Which way?"

"Down, three-tenths," she said.

I sat up straight in horror. It was only one-tenth that morning. I knew my daily variation and even with the strain I had been under, I should have kept my body under better control than that. Acron had raped me for hours once over a one-tenth drop; I had known I would probably get to two-tenths by this evening but anything beyond that was utterly unthinkable.

Lee stood up and placed his hand on my shoulder. I flinched and looked up at him. He didn't look angry.

"Your schedule is off," he said. "Your system is completely disrupted. As long as you continue to weigh yourself twice a day and we communicate about your diet and exercise needs, you don't need to worry no matter how much your weight varies over the next week or so."

I blinked. He smiled reassuringly, patted my shoulder, and sat down again. I looked at the doctor to see if she had heard Lee, but she just smiled at me as if it were completely normal.

"Let's get you on the exam table," she said, helping me stand. "Your oxygen levels are lower than I'd like and your blood pressure isn't where I would like it, either."

She helped me recline on the table and pressed the button that changed it from a hard surface to one that would conform to my shape. I was still sitting up and able to see Lee, but relaxed in a cocoon of comfort. Ananti took my arm and I turned it so she could insert a needle and start the flow of liquids into my system. Sagents had no allergies or diseases, so she didn't need to ask if I had an intolerance to any medication, and now that she knew my stats, she could start anything she wanted without worry. I was used to doctors giving me medication without warning, never telling me what they were doing or why, so I was surprised when she didn't add anything besides the basic saline solution.

"What symptoms do you need help with right now, Gabriel?" she asked.

"My heart will be racing soon," I said. "I can't control it much longer. I'll hyperventilate soon. My body's under too much stress."

"Do you have a preferred medication?"

At my puzzled look, Lee came over and placed his hand protectively on my shoulder again.

"I doubt he's had any input into his medical care before," Lee said. "Just give him something that will help without knocking him out too much."

She nodded and retrieved a needle, inserting it into the tube connected to my arm. I took a deep breath as the medicine hit me. I let it completely fill my body before I allowed my microbes to relax and let the medicine take over. I continued to take deep breaths as the medicine made me heavy and limp and I gratefully gave the job of calming my panicked body over to the medicine and gave my microbes a rest.

I watched Lee and Ananti talk, but even though I could hear blurs of noise, I couldn't really make out what they were saying. Ananti approached me and placed something cold around my upper arm. I recognized it instantly: an arm scanner. I absent-mindedly moved all of my microbes out of the way of the scanner as I always did, and felt the scan flash through my arm. The light on the scanner blinked green, as it always did. Only this time, Ananti and Lee looked not only confused but alarmed. Lee shook me. I focused on him and forced my microbes to help me draw my senses to him.

"Gabriel, can you hear me?"

"Yes," I managed, the word slowly escaping.

"You said you went through Transition Day. Is that true?"

"Oh," I said, shocked at the mistake I had made. I had cleared all of my microbes out of my system for the arm scan, so that the scan would show that I was microbe-free, because that was what I always did when traveling through Destiny to avoid detection. But they knew I was a sagent, and expected microbes. They needed to see them, and see them at the proper level.

"I'm sorry," I said. "Do the scan again."

Lee stared at me in disbelief, and continued to stare at me as Ananti snapped the arm scanner on again. This time, I allowed exactly the right number of microbes into the scanned area. The scanner flashed red, flagging me as having microbes, and Ananti and Lee turned to it in shock. Scanners all worked in the same way: the initial result came back in seconds and either flagged the individual or didn't. They were used throughout Destiny to make sure no one from the Drops ever snuck in. Detailed results giving the exact microbe count came back in a few minutes and revealed whether a person was from the Drops or a sagent, since sagents' microbe count was always within a very narrow range.

Unlike other sagents, I could manipulate my microbes so I could pass arm scanners easily. I couldn't, however, pass full body scans, and both of my agencies had forbidden me from even going near them, training me to kill everyone who attempted to get me close to one. Most sagents got flagged by scanners, grabbed by security and taken into custody, then quietly released when their detailed results came back. But apparently my results were slightly higher than the range expected for sagents, and both of my agencies feared I would be dumped in the Drops if I were ever caught in a scanner I couldn't fake.

I relaxed against the soft bed and allowed the medicine to calm my body. It was incredibly tempting to fall asleep. They might test me again to see if their results were correct so I directed the exactly correct number of microbes to remain where the scanner would be placed and let the rest disperse however they wanted to replenish themselves. I shut my eyes and sank into darkness.

CHAPTER 10
NEED TO KILL

"Gabriel."

I vaguely heard the name and recognized it as my own, but it wasn't quite enough to draw me out of the warm darkness surrounding me. Everything was safe. Everything was calm. My body was gone; I had nothing to worry about. I was alone in my mind, surrounded only by myself, and no one could touch me. I was finally free of the part of me that belonged to other people. I luxuriated in the feeling. I could hear voices, but there was nothing they could do to me.

"That barely registered. Shouldn't he respond to his name?"

It was a woman's voice, but a neutral voice. She wasn't a threat.

"I doubt he goes by it much."

A man's voice. Also neutral.

"It's me, Lee," the man said.

The name meant something, but I didn't know what. It was a positive name. I liked the person attached to the name. He would keep me safe while I floated here in emptiness.

"Your handler," he added.

My eyes snapped open. He wouldn't keep me safe. I had to be attached to my body because he controlled my body, and he would hurt me if I weren't in my body to protect myself. I quickly scanned my body, but everything was exactly how I had left it, except for a strange heaviness that seemed to seep into every

73

blood vessel, every muscle, every nerve. I hoped it was an after effect of the medicine. I released the microbes in my arm, since they wouldn't test me anymore and I was conscious if they did. I scanned my body again, but even my scan felt slower and heavier than usual.

Lee rested his hand on my cheek, stroking me gently.

"Your response to my name was better than your response to my title," he said in a softly scolding voice. "I'm not here to hurt you."

I realized there was something on my forehead, no doubt documenting my brain activity. That was why the woman – Ananti, I remembered – had commented on my lack of reaction to my name. They had seen my positive reaction to Lee's name and obviously seen my violent reaction to the word handler. I tried to relax and look at Lee, reassuring myself that what he said was true. As strange as it was, and as temporary as it might be, he appeared to be a kind person.

Ananti had been looking at her computer screen the entire time. She asked how I was feeling without glancing at me, and I scanned myself again, puzzling over the heaviness.

"I feel odd," I said, not sure how to explain it. "Slow. Heavy. Is that the medication?"

"No," she said, eyes fixed to her computer screen. "We put some trackers in your system. I'm sure you're just feeling them."

For the fourth time, I scanned myself, this time directing my microbes to do a thorough search specifically looking for anything that wasn't supposed to be there. They found nothing and I was puzzled.

"There aren't any trackers," I said. "Are you sure it's not the medication?"

Ananti finally looked at me. "No," she said. "We attached them to your microbes."

"You can't do that," I said, frightened. "No one can do that."

Her eyes returned to her screen as I turned inward to examine my microbes. It was true. Each and every microbe was weighed down with a tracking device. The microbes themselves

74

were so incredibly small, I didn't know how it was possible to create a device small enough to hide on them, but there they were. I had one microbe try taking it off, but it couldn't. I had that microbe take it off another microbe and destroy it. It succeeded with no negative repercussions. Without thinking, I sent all the microbes to tear the devices off each other and destroy them. In less than ten seconds, they were gone. I ran another scan of my body to ensure that they were all gone, and the scan felt normal. They were gone. I looked at Ananti defiantly.

She was staring at the computer screen in absolute awe, then turned to me.

"You can control individual microbes?" she asked.

"What?"

I was startled. Suddenly I realized that my actions in getting rid of the tracking devices had been fully documented. She had seen my first attempt with a single microbe, and then my full assault before the trackers were gone. She had also seen me scan my body several times before I realized there were trackers. She had also, I realized, seen that I could control the level of microbes in my arm, since I had been artificially keeping that number low. And if she had given me exactly the right number of trackers, that meant she knew exactly how many microbes I had.

I had to kill her. My training snapped into place. No one could know about my microbe count. A red haze slipped over my gaze and my focus narrowed around her even as my awareness of my surroundings expanded. I was supposed to kill Lee, too, but I didn't want to. He was my handler, so perhaps I didn't have to. Without shifting my gaze from Ananti, I searched the room for a weapon with my other senses. I didn't like killing with my hands, even though I could. I was still in the exam room, and there weren't many options.

Lee's hand pressed into my chest and I stared into his eyes. I didn't see a man, or even my handler. I saw a potential target ringed in the scarlet edging my vision. I didn't want to kill him but I would if I had to. Especially if he prevented me from killing Ananti. She was my target, not him. I would let him live if I could.

"I've seen that brain pattern before," Lee said. "I see it in your eyes. Why do you need to kill us?"

"You know how many microbes I have," I said. "I have to kill you."

Ananti edged toward the door. I would have to kill Lee to prevent her from leaving. I didn't want to kill him. Lee called for her to stop and she did. He kept his hand on my chest, very loosely keeping me pinned. I could easily kill him, and he knew it. I inhaled his fear.

"You have to kill us? Including your handler?" he asked. "Including someone your handler explicitly told you to trust?"

I hesitated. My eyes left his for a second to look at Ananti. She was terrified. I looked back at Lee.

"I have to kill her. I don't want to kill you, but I will if you get in my way."

"Are you allowed to hurt your handler?"

"No," I answered instantly.

"Then what gives you the right to kill me?"

I stared at him. The contradictory nature of this situation was threatening to collapse on me. I had to protect my handler. I had to obey him. I had to do everything and anything he wanted. But at the same time, I had to kill anyone and everyone who even suspected my microbe count was unusual, no matter who they were. It had been trained into me by both of my agencies, ingrained so deeply it wasn't even an option, it was instinct. But it couldn't be instinct this time, because it conflicted with my other instinct to serve my handler and I didn't know which should take precedence.

Normally if I didn't know which rule took precedence over another, I would ask my handler, but I couldn't in this case. I already knew his answer. But didn't that give me my answer? Shouldn't his answer be my answer? My confusion was pushing me out of the mode I needed to be in to kill. I couldn't kill unless I was primed for it. My body shifted back abruptly, my microbes retreating from their heightened state as I blinked at Lee in confusion.

"I don't have that right," I said in response to his question.

I sensed Ananti relaxing and coming back to the computer screen. Lee's hand on my chest traced up to my collarbone, then along the curve of my neck to stroke along my jaw. Though it would have been highly sensual in most circumstances, it wasn't now. He tilted my head to one side, then the other. He seemed to be looking for something and I was passive in his hands.

"Who taught you to do that?" Lee asked, sitting beside me. The bed adjusted to his weight and he leaned over me, caressing my cheek and gazing at me with extreme concern.

"My agencies," I said. "No one's supposed to know."

He shook his head. "No, I mean who taught you to react like that?"

"Oh," I said, realizing that he was asking about my ability to kill, not the specific trigger.

My mind fled back to how Acron had taught me, how he had laid an unconscious body on the floor and told me he would stop only when I killed the man, then he raped me, tortured me, taunted me, did everything in his power to hurt me until something inside me snapped and I killed the man without thinking. I tried to turn on Acron to kill him, too, but at his command, my strength left me, and I was helpless again. He controlled me utterly.

"Your first handler taught you, didn't he?" Lee asked. I nodded. "How many people have seen you like that?"

"Well, the people I kill," I said, puzzled. "And him. And once there were two women from my first agency. I wasn't supposed to know they were watching. They were in another room behind a mirror, but I could feel their body heat."

"Anyone at your second agency?"

"No," I said. "They only asked me to kill one person and I didn't do it."

"But I assume your second agency knows about your microbe count," Lee said. "Why didn't you kill them?"

"Because I hate my first agency," I snarled. "If they didn't want anyone to know, then why should I care if my new agency knew? But my new agency also didn't want anyone to know," I added, a little slower. "So they emphasized that I should take the precautions my first agency had taught me."

"If you did kill both of us, how were you planning to escape?" Lee asked. "Where were you planning to go?"

Those were very good questions, ones that hadn't even occurred to me. The bed and breakfast would take me. They would protect me. But this was a podhouse, and at least some of the rooms were protected by iris locks. I couldn't control the rooms and couldn't leave or enter most of them. There was no chance I would ever get out of this building.

"I didn't think of that," I admitted. "I just knew I had to kill you."

"Yet you were fully capable of rational thought," Lee mused. "And aside from your eyes, there were no physical changes. It was also temporary, which is unheard of. Does it feel different when you're like that?"

Some of those comments seemed to be directed more towards Ananti than to me, as they didn't really make sense, but I considered his question. It always did feel very different, but it was hard to put it into words.

"It feels like something shifts inside me," I said, unsure how to describe it. "But it's instant. Everything is different. I don't see the same. I don't think the same. I sense things differently. My microbes work differently. My body works differently. I don't really know how or why."

Ananti came around from her computer screen to stand beside me.

"How aware are you of your microbes, Gabriel?" she asked.

"I guess more than most sagents," I said, after glancing at Lee to make sure I was allowed to answer. "I know it's unusual that I can get around the arm scanner."

"Not in comparison," she said. "In your everyday life, how do they factor in?"

"Well, when I'm working I obviously use them a lot since

that's how I control and manipulate my body. It's habit at this point, though," I said. "But I do use them deliberately a lot. When I'm hurt, I use them to heal, and sometimes I need to prioritize injuries. When I need to hide, I can use them to blend in unless someone's looking directly at me. When I'm passing an arm scan, I push them out of the way. I think that's it."

"So it's safe to say that you're always aware of them," she said. "You manipulated an individual microbe before. Could you pinpoint every individual microbe in your body if you needed to?"

"I don't know why I would need to," I started, then glanced at Lee and realized I needed to answer more directly. "But yes, I could."

"What do your microbes do when you, er, shift into that different way of thinking?" she asked, clearly trying to use the terms I had used instead of other terms that she knew.

"They become aggressive," I said. "It's like they unfold somehow, and new parts of them are exposed. They move to different areas in my body that force me to think and feel differently, but I've never really thought about it before."

She nodded and I could see excitement in her eyes. I looked at Lee, but he just appeared concerned as he stroked my cheek.

"Is there any risk that you'd be trapped like that?" he asked softly, and I realized why he was so concerned. My value would go down dramatically if I were stuck in that state.

"No," I assured him. "I can't do it for more than five minutes or so. My handler had to give me really specific triggers on each mission so I would be primed at the right time. It's not a natural state for me."

He nodded and slipped the device off my forehead. I barely noticed it. Lee and Ananti were acting like I had done something unusual, but when I shifted, he recognized my brain pattern without any problem. And Ananti was deliberately using my words instead of vocabulary she was more comfortable with, which meant she was used to talking about this. So why was I so strange?

I couldn't ask, of course. I was a sagent and they were in

charge of me. If they thought it was something I needed to know, they would tell me. The significance of my microbe count had always been a mystery to me, even though it seemed like something they should tell me since it was so essential to me. When I started at my second agency, I had hoped they would tell me. It was one of the reasons I fought my instincts and let them take the body scan. They hadn't told me anything, though, just reinforced that I shouldn't let anyone else know. I lowered my eyes and waited for them to ask more questions.

Lee stood up and helped me up. My body was fully back under control, and I was able to stand without problems. He kept his arm around my waist, and while I was slightly more comfortable about his intentions, I checked his arousal just to make sure. Again, he was only trying to assist me, not take advantage of me.

"We've been experimenting with microbes in the Drops a lot longer than Destiny has," Lee said, rather cautiously, holding me against him while tilting my head to look into my eyes. "We have easier access to them and they aren't feared the same way. Because of that, we know that there's a concrete limit to the number of microbes a person can have in their system, based on height, weight, and other variables, and once they pass that limit, something happens to them."

I was stunned. He was telling me things that were clearly not common knowledge, or at least knowledge that I would have as someone from Destiny. Why was he telling me? I tried to focus on what he was saying, and not just the fact that he was saying it.

"We haven't figured out what makes people react differently, but until you, everyone who hits that point or goes above it reacts in one of two very specific ways that involve significant physical and mental changes," he said, and I shivered. "You'll see one of the ways for yourself shortly. We use them as guards."

"I don't understand," I said. I shouldn't speak, but I was confused, and if he were talking to me like this, he would probably allow questions. "I thought it was unusual that I responded well to the microbes on my Transition Day. Do a lot of people respond like this and we just don't hear about it?"

He shook his head. "What were you told was the cause of your high count?"

"I wasn't supposed to know about it," I said. "There was a mistake, and one of my teachers gave me the scan after the injection instead of the government employee. When we were waiting after, she came up and mentioned that I had responded well and my count was high. She was killed later that day for telling me. I didn't find out right away, but my handler told me."

"You didn't get that many microbes because you responded well, Gabriel," Lee said. "You were purposefully given that many microbes and because you responded well, you survived. The government should have scanned you? And your agency knew? One of them was responsible, then."

"My agency was a branch of the government," I offered.

"You have no loyalty to them at all, do you?" he asked, but he didn't sound angry. "Well, we'll need to figure out how many other people they experimented on like that. You may have been the first, especially if they didn't realize how unusual you were. The people here with that many microbes are not made that way on Transition Day. Their stories are sadder."

He began caressing my hip; again, his motive was pure.

"For a long time in the Drops, crimes were punished with microbe injection, since everyone knew microbes turned people into mindless monsters. The victims were then run out in the streets to be killed. We yakuza took them in," he said with an edge of anger. "People should not be destroyed like that. We gave them lives again. The practice was stopped nearly a century ago, but of course they're still alive and we still care for them as we always have. Few people outside the yakuza have seen them, though there are still plenty of stories. We guard them well."

"People don't live that long," I said, again confused. "And what do you mean, mindless monsters?"

"They have the same lifespans as sagents," he said, surprised. "You do know how long you'll live, don't you?"

I was silent. I had learned that people with microbes lived considerably longer, but I had never thought about it in practical terms before. I knew that vacation in thirty years was very good, because in terms of my overall life, thirty years wasn't much. But at this point, it was all very abstract. Every day seemed to take forever; it was hard to imagine surviving more than two years. I tried to think of other sagents and how long they lived. I had no idea how old my parents were. Old enough to have me and my sister, old enough to earn maternity and paternity leave for two children, even though one of them was working full time almost the entire time as part of the arrangement, but I didn't know how old they were, since we didn't age the same way. I didn't know how old anyone was. We just worked until we were killed or vanished.

"I never thought about it," I said. "No one ever talks about age. But you said monsters. Am I a monster?"

My voice trembled. Perhaps that was why my handlers had always been so strict with me. Maybe that was even why Acron felt safe abusing me. Who would believe a monster?

"No," Lee said emphatically. "You are not a monster. You'll know the difference immediately. There are two types, but you won't encounter one of them for a long time, if at all. The other type, however, serve as bodyguards for us. They're called Meat."

"That's a terrible name," I said, wondering how anyone would be fine being called Meat.

"I agree," Lee said quietly. "I avoid calling them that, but you need to know what they're called. I've asked mine to stay out of sight, but now that you know, you should meet them."

CHAPTER 11
MEDITATION

O nce we were back in my room, Lee gestured me to take off my kimono. I hadn't met the bodyguards yet and was nervous. I stripped quickly and managed to get it off, though not with enough grace to do my job. Luckily, it was just my handler and he didn't comment. He would eventually have to teach me to dress and undress in the kimono, but clearly this wasn't the time.

He led me to the dresser and opened the middle drawer to reveal ordinary Destiny clothes. At his silent command, I dressed in what looked like the most comfortable clothes that complemented my complexion. Being in the form-fitting denim pants and long-sleeved azure shirt relaxed me immensely. I felt like I finally had some sort of comfort to hold on to. I hadn't realized how much I needed it. Everything was changing and nothing was safe. Lee was now familiar to me, but only because he was the only consistent point I had over the past day. I wondered how long it had been since I asked him for help from my agency's enforcers. Everything blurred together and I didn't know how long I was unconscious.

"Can you stand one more shock today, or should I wait until the morning to introduce you to my bodyguards?" Lee asked.

I wasn't quite sure how to reply. The choice was his, not mine, but he also hadn't worked with me to know my limits. I considered. It sounded like it was night. I would undoubtedly have a job tomorrow, probably an easy one, but if I were shaken before my job, it would affect my performance. I couldn't fail my first job.

"Today," I said, keeping my eyes down and trying not to sound demanding.

If it were one of my previous handlers, they might do the opposite of what I said to emphasize that they were in charge. Lee just nodded, and tapped his chip. The door opened and two men came in. Or I thought they were men.

I tried to hide my shock, not wanting them to think it was disgust. They were men, but distorted. Everything about them was larger, from their height, which must be over seven feet, to their bulk, at least three times as thick as me. They were all muscle. Even under their loose-fitting black uniforms, I could tell how muscular they were. It was their faces, their eyes, that struck me, however.

Their faces were identical and looked as if they had been smashed against a wall. Their eyes had white pupils. I couldn't stop staring. It wasn't contacts. It fascinated me. They were not human. They were something else, distorted by the microbes into new bodies. I could almost feel the form their microbes had taken to turn them into this. I knew I could replicate it in my own microbes, but I would be terrified to do so.

"Hi," I said hesitantly. I didn't extend my hand. I was frightened to touch them, afraid they would change my microbes, plus I had nothing on my chip.

"They can't speak," Lee said. He placed a hand on my shoulder. Intended to comfort, I noticed. He hadn't touched me in any way other than comfort since I met him. I wanted to relax into the knowledge that he wouldn't hurt me, but he could change at any time. He was a handler, after all.

Lee gestured to them. "They can't communicate at all, but they obey commands and protect their assigned yakuza fiercely. You learn to tell them apart," he added. "Sagents have an easier time distinguishing individuals because their microbe count is closer. Most people don't bother."

I looked at them again. I could feel a difference, now that I was looking. Their microbes were different. I wondered how I could sense their microbes so clearly. Sagents could instantly recognize each other, but I had never been able to sense anyone else's microbes before. Perhaps it was because their microbes were so concentrated, and different than mine.

"What are their names?" I asked, realizing he hadn't actually introduced me.

"They have none," Lee said with a shrug. "They can't communicate, and it's hard to tell them apart, so no one bothers giving them names."

I tried not to keep staring at them but it was hard. I wondered if they hated being indistinguishable to people, if they secretly resented having to serve as bodyguards.

Hesitantly, I extended my hand to the one on the left. He didn't seem to notice. There was a glazed look in his eyes. I suspected he knew everything going on in the room, and he was choosing not to interact, but Lee's hand squeezed my shoulder.

"I told you, they can't communicate. I've tried."

I finally tore my eyes away to turn to Lee, keeping my gaze down. Asking him a question and changing the subject was inappropriate. But he had already allowed so many infractions that perhaps he wouldn't mind another.

"What is the other type?"

Lee sighed. "This is enough for now. I'm leaving one with you to watch you and keep you safe. He won't do anything to you."

"Aren't they your bodyguards?" I asked, briefly glancing at him.

"I only need one if I stay in the complex. I want you to have protection."

I wondered why I needed protection, and why he would risk being in danger to help me, but I didn't dare ask any more questions. I had pushed my luck too much already.

Instead, I lowered my head and nodded obediently, trying to look as submissive as possible. A flash of irritation crossed his face, and I mentally braced myself, but he simply told me what time he would come in the morning and left.

I glanced at the bodyguard. He stood near the door impassively. I felt incredibly awkward as I crossed the room to look at a clock. To my surprise, there were still quite a few hours of the day left. Lee must really think I was out of my depths and confused. It was true, but I wondered if he would do something to me for not taking a job tonight. If the yakuza was making a new investment in me – and it certainly seemed that they were, if they gave me a suite and were prepared to take care of any of my needs – then I was starting over and I needed to get to work soon.

I sat on the couch, then scooted to the chaise to be more comfortable. The entertainment system looked too confusing to attempt, so instead I closed my eyes and began to meditate. I had learned meditation from my sister when I was between agencies. She said it would help my healing, and I believe it did.

I focused inward on my breathing until I was completely calm. Then I let my awareness of my body expand into my microbes. They were always buzzing, ready to do anything I asked, and I stilled them. It had taken a long time to learn how to do this, and even longer before I realized that my sister didn't, and couldn't, do this. I never told what I did, or how I quieted my thoughts and relaxed my body. She probably assumed I was just good at focusing.

With my microbes silent and swaying through my body rhythmically with my breath, I focused deeper. When I truly relaxed, my mind was frequently flooded with beautiful images of Earth. I remembered my Transition Day, when I first experienced the visions. They frightened me then, but now they were almost comforting.

This time, I saw a large expanse of ocean with rolling hills of water rippling over the surface. I wondered if there would be a dragon like in the tapestry. But it was only the ocean, and the feel of a breeze on my body, a scent like salt and heat washing through my senses. As always, my microbes hummed. They weren't active, but they seemed to recognize the visions, and made me long for the visions to be real.

As I meditated and allowed the scene to sweep through me, I realized that my microbes were shifting and multiplying. I observed from my relaxed state. The new microbes began humming in tune with my existing microbes. This had happened once before when I was in lower Destiny.

I was in the Drops, I realized suddenly. The atmospheric microbe count here was extremely high. I couldn't let the microbes in or I would die. But I couldn't stop the process. I was trapped in my own mind. I mentally reached out for help, and a hand dropped on my shoulder. Startled, I came back to my senses. It was the bodyguard. He lifted his hand immediately and retreated to the door. I stared in shock. My body was slowly revving up to its ordinary state; the additional microbes were now a part of me. I couldn't even tell them apart.

The bodyguard was impassive, and I wondered how he knew to touch me, and draw me out of my trance. More time had passed than I anticipated, and I needed to sleep if I were to function properly tomorrow. I went through my evening routine and glanced at the bodyguard before getting into bed. I didn't feel nervous with him, but I couldn't relax. I fingered the soft silk of the sheets. This would be my room from now on. It felt unreal.

CHAPTER 12

DOMINANT AND SUBMISSIVE

L ee entered my suite without announcing himself, but I was sitting on the chaise, so I wasn't worried about being somewhere I wasn't supposed to be. He was a few minutes early and I made a mental note to always be prepared earlier than I needed to be. I stood and smiled at him. I continued smiling when another man followed him in, despite my panic. It was another sagent, and he was a dominant.

Dominant sagents are extremely rare. They openly controll situations instead of using the tricks we all learn for controlling in secret. They also used those tricks, of course, but they mostly made use of other tricks the rest of us couldn't get away with. Some sagents, like the woman I encountered on my mission, could be dominant in certain situations like when I met her, but it was clear she was also submissive. And some, like me, couldn't be dominant in any situation. I had encountered many dominants before, but never a dominant who was also a sagent and I was frightened.

He read me as easily as I read him, of course. In one glance, he knew exactly who I preferred given the body weight and muscle mass I maintained, the hairstyle I kept, the millions of other things I did to appeal to the class of men and women I wanted to appeal to. This man appealed to people in power, to politicians, businesspeople, mostly men, I noticed. He exuded confidence, power, and wealth, and those who wanted to associate with those qualities would be drawn to him.

It only took a passing glance to notice all of this before I looked back at Lee, who approached with the sagent at his side. I stood in exactly the correct manner as they approached, wondering why the sagent was here.

"Smith is here to walk you through a few basic skills," Lee said in answer to my unspoken question, placing his hand on the other sagent's shoulder. Obviously a false name, but a generic name from Destiny that might be intended to reassure me. "I prefer to know what my sagents can do before I send them out."

Lee pushed Smith forward, giving him permission to take the lead. Smith was a dominant, but still a sagent. With his handler's permission, though, he altered from a passive sagent into a sparkling, bright man who could sweep anyone up into his smile. He was exactly the type of man I preferred as a target, and I was surprised Lee had judged me so well. I smiled shyly in return and when he wrapped his arms around my waist, I realized there would be no real seduction. I placed one hand on his shoulder and one on his wrist, looking at a specific point in the air between us with a blush as if having second thoughts about being so close to him, but so overtaken by his charm that I couldn't resist myself.

I let my eyes travel to his lips as I slowly leaned into him, and my neck curved back as my eyes continued up his face to meet his just as my lips pressed on his. He reacted as any man would, cradling my head and neck and pulling me into the kiss. I let my eyes shut as if in bliss and rested one hand on his chest, using the position to check his heartbeat and other vitals.

The sagent kissed me thoroughly, which I hadn't been expecting. I wasn't planning on holding back, since I knew Lee was testing me, and it wasn't the quality of kissing that surprised me as much as the length. The sagent kissed me even after my ability to kiss had been determined. I didn't understand his motive, but I also didn't question him. Perhaps it was just that he was dominant.

When he finally pulled away, I appeared out of breath and

dazed and completely taken by him. My heartbeat was up high enough to fool the average person, though not as high as it would be during sex. Sagents have to be very careful to start low so we don't overexert ourselves, and we have to account for a natural rise in blood pressure as well. I let out a soft moan and stroked his cheek, letting my eyes do all the talking. They were one of my best features, because I could control my microbes to express almost any emotion. Lee wouldn't be able to see, but the sagent would report it to him.

"Stand next to the bed," the sagent murmured. "Face me and strip."

I let a shiver of pleasure run through my body as I pressed into him before untangling myself to obey. I carefully maintained the illusion of a lovestruck human desperate to obey as I mentally mapped the situation and swayed towards the bed. Lee was on the other side of the bed. He was sitting down and observing fairly close to the bed, but once I turned to face the sagent and strip, Lee would be behind me. That would be an interesting challenge, though not one I hadn't faced before. I stood by the bed and turned to the sagent. I raised my eyes to him obediently. He nodded.

It's impossible to strip for a fellow sagent. Stripping requires a constant awareness of what turns the other person on and a continual adjustment of moves to heighten that experience. Sagents don't find each other sexually appealing. Occasionally we'll be turned on during sex, but it's rare. Stripping is usually taught in front of an ordinary person, but tested in situations like this, since on jobs we might need to strip blindfolded, or with the person behind us. We need to know how to do it. We need to sense arousal without seeing it.

I'd never done it like this, of course, but I could. Lee was not immune from sexual arousal the way sagents were, after all. After my experience with Acron, my parents and sister taught me the appropriate range of arousal handlers could feel for their sagents, and what to do if a handler felt more. Lee's reactions were in the upper end of that range, but I felt safe with him. And because he was interested in me, I could read his body and strip.

As I stripped, I kept my eyes on the sagent, made my entire body echo the sentiment that this striptease was for the sagent alone, but he and I both knew that the moves I made followed Lee's interest and Lee's awareness of my body. I wondered if Lee knew it, too. Did he want me to strip for him? He had to know that sagents couldn't strip for each other and I wouldn't have been able to strip with no one else here. Or had the sagent suggested it without Lee's permission to see what I would do? I didn't let my uncertainty show. I was just grateful that I was in Destiny clothes, and confident at least in my ability to strip with them. I couldn't have done this with a kimono. When I was finally naked, the sagent – also naked at this point – pushed me onto the bed with more force than I was used to, though I made no indication of that.

Again, there were very few preliminaries, but this time I forced them. A lot of targets wanted to rush things and part of my job was to slow it down so I could lure them better. I suspected that was why he was doing it, to see how well I could handle a rush from a physically larger and more aggressive man.

I let the initial rush happen as he laid his body on mine, but I carefully positioned myself under him so when he landed on me, his hips couldn't make contact because my knees and thighs were angled just right. His chest did make contact and his lips met mine. I kissed him and let my hands travel along his sides, then his back, touching every point that would release the precious chemicals in his brain to build intimacy and increase arousal. My touch was light and hesitant, as it ought to be for a submissive, but I used enough pressure in the right places to trigger him.

He moaned and pulled away from my kiss, writhing against me in an attempt to press his hips further down just as all men did. I gently pressed one of his shoulders, not commanding but suggesting that he turn over, and I licked my lips. I've never had a man misunderstand that. Smith might not have recognized the move from training, since I had found it on my own, but he certainly understood what it meant.

He grabbed my hips and flipped us so I was straddling him, but again he used more force than he needed. I didn't react and simply made sure my movements were appropriate as I gently rested above him, hips far above his as I didn't want him to pull me down on him. It didn't happen often and I usually didn't fight when it did, since the position gave me so much control, it was worth losing the preliminaries, but this was a test and Lee would want to see all of my abilities. I couldn't let Smith rush me.

I was keeping careful watch on my outward emotions and signals. As far as anyone could tell, I was completely caught up in the moment, dazed from passion, heart racing and already hard. Inside I was carefully calculating every move. Normally, I wouldn't be so calculating. Normally, I would let my inner thoughts reflect my outward emotions more and let my entire self be caught up, but this was a test. I couldn't afford any weakness. I had to appear perfect, and I had to act perfectly.

I nuzzled Smith's neck, then began licking him, again enticing him and stroking all of the spots we were trained to identify. I had found several spots on my own and I could tell from his short gasps that he wasn't expecting those. Most of what he was doing was probably acting, but I felt a few tremors in his body that couldn't be acting. It was hard to recreate that small a physical reaction.

I worked my way down his body, teasing with my tongue and hands, playing with his body the way we were taught to do, devoting the same time and care to him as I would to a typical target because Lee was watching, and Smith would be reporting the quality of my actions. I didn't want to overdo anything because I didn't want to mislead them. I didn't want to oversell my abilities. I could do more, yes, but since I didn't for most of my targets, I wouldn't for Smith.

When I finally reached Smith's penis, he genuinely gasped and I was surprised. Then I remembered that most of the strokes I did from the belly button down were ones I had discovered on my own, ones he wouldn't know how to handle. I felt bad for pushing him out of his comfort zone, but Lee wanted to see what I could do. I would have felt more comfortable on an actual target, but it did make sense to match me with a sagent, who could recognize my actions for what they were.

I slid my tongue over his penis as he shuddered, again a genuine reaction, and then I moved into the motions we were taught in training. His heartrate was higher than I would have let mine be, but his body clearly had different limits. As I lavished attention on him, he reacted as he was supposed to, moving his hand to my head at the appropriate moment to push me further onto him, thrusting against me with apparent abandon. He was excellent. I could barely tell he was acting except for the careful positioning of his hands to occasionally check my reactions. I was careful to give him exactly the reactions he wanted to feel: I was extremely turned on, desperately passionate, ready to beg him for more.

He tried to end my blowjob early a few times, as many men did, but I carefully held him in place with well-placed strokes of my tongue that left him paralyzed. Unless I only had a short time or I didn't want a man to fuck me, I never allowed a man to orgasm at this point and many men, especially dominants, were unaccustomed to being forced to wait. I had to entice them to wait while still giving them the illusion of being completely in control of the situation. If I knew they were going to be brutal to me, I had to keep them in this position for as long as I could. That wasn't the case now, though, so as soon as I had shown off my skills, I allowed him to pull me up and wrestle me under him.

Somewhat to my surprise, he immediately pulled me into the second best position for a submissive: lying on my back beneath him. This gave me the ability to kiss him and use my arms and legs freely, letting me continue to seduce and manipulate him even as he fucked me. I had expected him to push me onto my knees and try to take me from behind to see how well I could negotiate into this position. But he just gave it to me, though yet again he pushed me into it with an odd show of force. I adjusted my movements and anticipated his next moves.

CHAPTER 13
AROUSAL

I couldn't understand why Smith was using so much force with me, unless he were testing me to figure out how much force I could tolerate. I could take quite a lot more than he was giving, but that didn't mean I liked it. Did that mean most of my targets would be forceful with me? Or was it just that he was a dominant?

He kissed me again once he was over me, and started running his hand up and down my cock, then against my balls, slowly working his way back to my opening. He was using all of his tricks, too, though he didn't have to, as he wasn't trying to prove anything, and I made sure to respond appropriately. After all, many men knew to stroke these areas even if they didn't know where exactly to put pressure, so I had to demonstrate that I knew how to shut my eyes and bite my lip and moan and toss my head and press myself against him and pull him forward with my palms – never my fingers, that was too aggressive – and catch my breath and gasp at exactly the right moments. Everything was an art.

He coaxed me open. There was no lube, but he was going to be gentle and he was slick. He pressed against me, not entering yet, and laid one hand on my cheek, gazing into my eyes. A lot of men liked looking into my eyes as they penetrated me so I looked back, careful to emit passion and lust and everything he could possibly want. As he entered me slowly, I tilted my head up but kept my eyes fixed on his, knowing he wanted to see them. I gasped and allowed a flicker of pain through my eyes, replaced immediately with satisfaction and pleasure. He smiled, as if pleased by my abilities.

He kissed me lightly, then leaned against me and began thrusting into me as I curved against him. Then he struck my prostrate and I barely kept from reacting. It happened frequently with targets, who rarely knew what they were doing, but a sagent knew what he was doing. That was an unlikely accident. He rubbed against it again, as if trying to arouse me.

I squeezed his shoulders lightly to let him know that he was in the wrong place. He hesitated and readjusted so he could look at me. I kissed him and invited him in again, but again his thrust was designed to pleasure, not to test, and again I squeezed him, this time with more force. What was he doing?

He pulled back a little further this time, stopping his thrusts completely as he stared at me while resting on his elbows. I wasn't sure whether or not to stay in character. I needed him to stop and there was no real way to tell him that in character, since he wasn't taking the hint. Why wasn't he taking the hint, though? I stroked his back, starting to allow him back, hoping he would understand this time, and felt another tremor in his body. That didn't make sense. He should be in complete control right now.

Although I had been closely monitoring his heart and a few other body functions, I hadn't bothered monitoring his arousal, since I assumed that his arousal, like mine, was entirely fake. Sagents learned to pretend to be aroused, learned to control the rigidity of our penises and even our orgasms with the same precision we controlled our heartbeats. We learned how to emote passion and arousal even while we felt nothing. So I hadn't bothered checking his actual arousal levels. I had accidentally raised them a few times, but now I tested them.

My eyes widened. He was turned on. Legitimately aroused. He seemed to be in control of his arousal, unlike targets, but he was still undeniably aroused by me. This wasn't an act for him.

I lay there paralyzed for a moment, unable to maintain my act, until his eyes clouded with worry and he leaned even further back. His arousal lessened. I took a deep breath and tried to pull myself together.

I wasn't sure how I was going to do this. He was going to be using sagent tricks on me to get me to lose control, even while I was using those tricks on him. But no one had ever used those tricks on me before. Lee had probably chosen him because Smith knew how to recognize them, but I had never felt them before. I was going to lose control, and he was going to hurt me. I had to fight the instinct to shrink away from him.

Instead, I returned my hands to his shoulders, did my best to smile enticingly, and tried to pull him back down. It didn't work. Lee was standing next to us, I realized.

"What happened?" he asked Smith softly, though he was mostly looking at me. Again, I didn't know if I should stay in character. When I saw that Smith wasn't, I allowed my body to leave its aroused state as well, matching Smith's slow pace.

"He was uncomfortable with what I was doing," Smith said, sounding confused. "I slowed down. Then he scanned my arousal, which he hadn't done the entire time, and freaked out."

"Why weren't you scanning his arousal?" Lee asked me. "Shouldn't that be your primary concern?"

"He's a sagent," I said, just as confused as Smith seemed to be. "Sagents don't feel arousal for each other. His other stats gave me the info I needed."

"From what I could see, you were doing a superb job arousing him," Lee said, glancing at Smith for confirmation. "And you were just as aroused, at least as far as I could tell. What were your observations, Smith?"

"He was doing a lot of things beyond what we were trained to do," Smith said. I was pleased and looked to Lee for approval, but didn't get any. "I don't know why he's surprised I was so aroused. And while I know some of it was acting, especially at first, every signal he gave confirmed that he was turned on as well."

"Isn't that what I'm supposed to do?" I asked, knowing I

shouldn't interrupt but puzzled why they were even discussing this. "Sagents are trained to act aroused and that's what I did. That's what I thought you were doing. I only hesitated because you were doing things to me that a normal target never would."

"You mean I was trying to give you pleasure," Smith said. "Surely you've had targets able to do that before."

"Not with your level of skill," I shot back. "And if they do it's usually by accident, not on purpose."

"Surely the sagents who trained you had my level of skill," he said. "Even if you'll never use it in the field, training you how to deal with it is a standard precaution."

I hesitated, unsure how to respond. I wasn't sure what kind of training he was talking about. I wasn't sure what he meant by dealing with it. His language was so vague, in fact, that I had no clue what he was talking about at all. I glanced at Lee, but he didn't seem about to step in on our conversation, so I would have to say something.

"I don't know what you mean," I said honestly.

"When they trained you to imitate arousal based on actual arousal, and how to control your arousal," he said. "You must have had experienced sagents teaching you who pushed you so you would know how to control extremely strong lust."

Lee leaned forward. "You were trained to handle lust, weren't you?"

"Sagents don't feel lust, or arousal," I said, repeating what Acron had told me many, many times. I suddenly realized I had never heard anyone else say it. Other people said that it was unusual for sagents to feel arousal while working, but no one ever said it in the same terms that Acron had.

"It's not usual on the job," Lee acknowledged. "But what about your first time? Sagents chosen for that task are highly trained to give the new sagent the most pleasurable experience possible. I know you enjoyed that."

I fought a shudder, thinking of the door opening on my first night and Acron entering. I hadn't realized why he was there at first, thinking only that he had forgotten to tell me something.

I still hadn't really understood, even after he told me he wanted to introduce me to a few basics and started kissing me. But when he had me lay down, when he forced a gag into my mouth and ordered me to stay still, when he stroked my body and laughed when I couldn't control my responses, when he brought me to arousal and then penetrated me against my will, something inside of me died that could never be revived.

Lee placed his hand on my shoulder and I flinched, coming back to reality with a start. I forced the memory back into my mind, deep where it couldn't hurt me.

"Your first time wasn't with a sagent, was it?" Lee said softly. "Who was your first time with? How were you hurt?"

I lowered my eyes. I couldn't tell him. He was unlike any handler I'd ever heard of, but he was still a handler. Handlers stood by each other, just like sagents stood by other sagents. Agency didn't matter as much as career. Lee didn't like how my agency had treated me, and he might not approve of what my handler had done, but he would still side with my handler over me. I was only a sagent.

"It was your handler," Smith said, sounding appalled. I looked up in horror, trying to indicate that he should stop talking before he completely alienated Lee. "How could a handler do something like that to you?"

Lee continued to look at me, though I couldn't look at him. I didn't want to see the walls going up, the disdain as he realized I had allowed myself to be taken advantage of. I kept my face as expressionless as possible. I couldn't lie and deny it, but I wouldn't confirm it either.

"Why didn't the sagent assigned to your first time recognize what had happened?" Lee asked. "Why didn't you tell them?"

"I had learned how to fake it by then," I said softly. "And she wouldn't have believed me. No one did. Trying to tell people just made it worse."

Lee's hand on my shoulder tightened. "Learning to imitate arousal takes time and training. The first sexual encounter takes place late in the first two months. He couldn't have done anything to you until you were there at least six weeks. Even if he delayed your first official encounter after that, you couldn't learn that quickly."

My heart sank. Of course he didn't believe me. Of course he believed Acron. Rules were rules and of course Acron would follow them. He was the best trainer in all of Destiny, after all. Why would he break the rules, especially that rule? And even if he had touched me in lust, he would certainly follow all of the other rules and wait until the appropriate time. Breaking one rule didn't mean he would break all of them, after all. Now Lee would punish me for lying to him. I didn't think his punishment would be bad, as Lee seemed like a fair person, but to be punished for this yet again would be a slap in the face.

"Are you going to explain what happened?" Lee asked.

"No," I said. "You understand the situation."

"Clearly, I don't," he said, caressing my shoulder. "Do you think I won't believe you? Do you really think I'll take someone else's side when you are my sagent – mine – and he's a handler who has deeply hurt you? Tell me what happened."

I cautiously met his eyes. There was no judgement. He wanted to know. Well, if he really wanted to know, then I would tell him. I would make him understand the pain, humiliation, and futility of my situation in training.

"My first time was my first night there. I didn't want it. I never wanted it from him. He had to tie me up at first so I wouldn't fight or scream. At least until he taught me not to fight and to stay silent," I said, forcing the memories down so I would be able to continue. "Sometimes he wanted to see me in pain. Sometimes he wanted to see me enjoy it. I had to learn what to show him because if I didn't, he hurt me more and made my days miserable too. It was hard enough surviving with just a few hours of sleep. I did anything he wanted to avoid more."

Lee was furious but Smith's reaction caught me off guard. I had nearly forgotten about him until he lunged forward and smothered me in a full-body hug. Frightened, I tested his arousal. There was none. He kissed my cheek and held me close, stroking me in ways that were not ways we were taught to do. They served no direct purpose in seducing. But they were reassuring. Very hesitantly, I relaxed underneath him and moved my hand against the back of his neck to embrace him. Not fully, but a little.

Lee stood up and looked down at us, his gaze softening for a moment.

"Smith, please remain here while I deal with some business. Gabriel," he said, and I was surprised he used my real name in front of another sagent, "You are allowed to take comfort. You will certainly not be punished for anything. You are very safe here. And if Smith chooses to tell you his real name, he is welcome to do so."

CHAPTER 14

PUSHBACK

Smith cuddled against me. Lee left the room, and I was frightened. I tried to shy away from his grasp, but he wouldn't let me. He did lift his head and torso so he could look into my eyes, but he was pinning me down and still embracing me with gentle hands and arms.

"I guess if I know your first name, you should know mine," he said with a warm smile. "I'm Sora."

Sora was a beautiful name, though not one I'd ever heard before. Hearing it quieted me for a few moments as I studied him and applied the name. It made me far less nervous about him. It was easier to think of him as a person now, not as a sagent, not as a dominant. I had never known the name of a dominant before. I rarely knew the names of other sagents. Really, I only knew my parents' and sister's names, and my parents had shifted their names several times growing up, so I never had a firm grasp of them. They each had a name that they defined themselves by, because occasionally I would hear them refer to each other by something that wasn't the name they instructed us to use. It was rare to know the name someone referred to themselves as, and I was honored to know how Sora identified himself.

"I'm sorry I pushed you," he continued. "I didn't understand why you were reacting, so I kept going. Something like this never would have occurred to me. If someone did that here, in the yakuza, we would have listened. You wouldn't have been ignored. The bastard would have been strung up and executed."

He was telling the truth, or at least he thought he was, and I was reassured by his confidence even as I doubted that it would actually happen. The sagents might think it would happen, and the handlers might let them think it would happen, but in the end, the handlers would stick together. Except that Lee hadn't sided with the handler. He hadn't sided with Acron. He sided with me. I didn't know what to make of that.

"You really weren't turned on by me? By anything I did? Do you find me attractive?"

He was disappointed, but there wasn't any jealousy or threat, as there might have been with a target who suspected me of acting. He had no authority to hurt me, so I could answer truthfully. Plus, I didn't think my answer would disappoint him too much.

"You were a sagent, so it didn't occur to me to think of you as handsome, or to even allow my body to be in a state were arousal was an option," I said. "But I did think you were exactly the type of man I like as a target. And looking at you now, well, if you weren't a sagent I might think you were handsome."

"But because I'm a sagent you're not allowed to think that?" he asked with a hint of laughter in his voice. He sounded eager to get me and my thoughts away from my first handler, and I would let him. "You're allowed to have the usual range of emotions. But if you weren't interested in me, at least that explains why you stripped for Lee instead."

I blushed deeply as his eyes twinkled.

"You easily could have stripped for me if you'd checked. You didn't. But you did such a good job acting like you were stripping for me that I doubt he noticed. I won't tell him," he said, leaning down to kiss the tip of my nose. "But if I ask again, I want you to strip for me only."

I hesitantly ran my hand over Sora's back, finding a secure grip on his shoulder. He felt like a good source of stability. I was unsure how to feel about him flirting with me like this, but it wasn't threatening, and Lee wouldn't punish me for it. After all, he had told me to take comfort. I didn't know if that meant having sex or not, but surely Lee realized that I didn't find comfort in sex. He must have meant companionship.

I had never had companionship. Even being with my sister didn't count because there were so many secrets we couldn't share. We couldn't talk about our current lives, so we simply reminisced about times that weren't quite so bad. It was bittersweet for me because she was happy, and I couldn't let her know I was miserable. I had to act even with her. But there was always love between us, and that's why I needed to see her as often as I could.

Sora suggested we shower and I agreed. I was covered in the scent of sex – not to mention the physical traces all over my body – and I longed to be free of it. When I entered the partially hidden bathroom and started the water for the shower, however, Sora was right beside me, testing the water's heat. I blushed.

"Um, do you want to shower first?" I asked.

"You've never taken a shower with someone before?" Sora asked in an amused voice.

"It's just that-"

"I'm a sagent?" he interrupted, finishing my thought.

"I don't know my status in this agency and I don't know yours," I said, trying to explain why this felt wrong. "I don't know anything about this place."

Sora rubbed my back, then pushed me into the shower with as much force as he had used during the test. He looked annoyed as he got under the water as well and slid his hand up to caress my neck. Or hold me still. I couldn't tell.

"Why don't you give any pushback?" he asked. At my blank look, he seemed to think for a moment before rephrasing his question. "Maybe you call it something different. But when I use too much force on you, why don't you push back against me so I know what you're comfortable with?"

I blinked. He had been using force on me on purpose as part of the test? I had never heard of pushback, or even the idea of it. Targets did what they wanted, and it was my job to look like I enjoyed it. I did feel better knowing that his forcefulness wasn't a preview of the targets I would have here.

"I'm a submissive," I said, not exactly knowing how to explain. "You're a dominant. It's my place to accept whatever you choose to do."

"I can be submissive too, you know," he said. "And you could learn to be dominant."

"No," I said firmly. "I can't. And even if you were acting submissive, everyone would still know you're a dominant. It's who you are."

He kissed my neck and licked the water running down it. It was erotic, and I wasn't sure if I was ready for that. Normally, I would allow it, but he wasn't a target or my handler. I turned my head just slightly to break his contact. I suppose it was pushing back in a way, and he seemed to take it the same way because he chuckled.

"Now you have a spine," he murmured, reaching to tousle my hair under the stream of water.

He reached for the soap and began cleaning, and he luckily didn't attempt to clean me. When we both had washed our bodies and hair and removed every trace of sex, he turned the water off and handed me a towel. He went with unerring precision to where the extra towels were. His room must be set up exactly the same as mine, and I was amazed that the yakuza could afford to house multiple sagents like this. My suite was beyond incredible. I had assumed both that it was temporary and that it was meant to entice me to serve the yakuza better, but now I realized that this suite really was mine, and I wasn't alone in receiving such luxury.

After we both dried off, we returned to the main suite to dress. Lee was waiting for us there. He and Sora exchanged a significant look, and as I tried to figure it out, Sora kissed me on the cheek. He dressed quickly and, after another glance at Lee, left. I dressed more slowly. I didn't know if I would be working or not, so I didn't know which clothes to wear. He didn't stop me as I pulled on Destiny clothes, my preference.

"I wish I could spend the day with you," Lee said. I could hear real regret in his voice. "I'm hosting a fundraiser, however, and that is going to take most of my time today. Smith will be helping me, or I would ask him to stay with you instead. Will you be okay spending today alone?"

"I'm not alone," I pointed out, gesturing to the bodyguard. "Is Sora working?"

Lee smiled. I could tell he was pleased that I knew Sora's name. I realized with a start that it was Sora's first name, which Lee had said was extremely intimate.

"Yes," Lee said.

"Will I be working?"

"No."

"What jobs will I have today?" I asked, a little nervous.

Lee sighed and shook his head. "None, Gabriel. You're new. You're recovering. I don't want to push you."

"You're not," I assured him. "I want to work."

I did. I had almost never gone a day without working in the last three years and it would be strange and frustrating to be alone while I could be working.

Lee stared at me. I tried to express my eagerness and my readiness through my eyes, using my microbes to triple the force of my gaze. He softened.

"I don't think you're right for the job," Lee said, but he didn't sound quite so reluctant. "I'm speaking to guests from Destiny. I don't want you recognized."

"I could look at the names and tell you if I know any of them," I said helpfully.

Lee shook his head again, but he would let me. Almost all men gave in to my eyes when I was determined.

"All right, Gabriel. I'll let you look through the names, but if you recognize anyone, if you're in any danger, you have to tell me."

I eagerly agreed. I needed to start earning back my investment, and I wouldn't stand not working. I needed to feel in control again, and I felt in control when I worked. Lee called up the names and we began looking through them together.

CHAPTER 15

RECOGNITION

I tried to ignore the hostile looks of the prostitutes around me as we filed into the conference room where important men mingled with each other and waited for their entertainment – for us. Prostitutes and sagents always had a wary relationship, since both did essentially the same thing, except sagents lived lives of luxury and prostitutes barely scraped by on what they could make selling their bodies. Occasionally, a successful prostitute was recruited to be a sagent, but it was rare, almost as rare as a sagent becoming a true agent and leaving the sex behind.

But the prostitutes wouldn't out me, because they were being paid not to, and money was a powerful bargaining chip whether in Destiny or the Drops, and besides, we felt some strange kinship with each other. Or at least I felt some kinship with them.

My job tonight was simple. Seduce one of the men, and convince him to invest in yakuza property. It didn't matter which man, and most of them were already thinking of investing. I glanced over at Sora, in the other group of prostitutes. My group had been groomed to look like we were from Destiny, wearing Destiny fashions and with hair bleached and dyed. My hair, of course, was natural. Sora's group was dressed in fashions from the Drops: mainly kimonos. There were an equal number of men and women in both groups. Quite a lot of variety for the men the yakuza was trying to woo.

We entered the main room as two units, my group first. There were some appreciative whistles and then Sora's group entered. They received even more whistles, and for a moment, I was disappointed my entrance wasn't as grand, but I stifled that jealousy quickly. Jealousy was useless in a sagent.

As the groups dissolved and merged into the group of businessmen in dark suits carrying half-empty drinks – clearly the yakuza had already wined and dined them – I started scouting for my target. Then I saw him, and although my exterior remained the same, my mind and heart stuttered. It was Acron.

His name hadn't been on the list; he must have given a fake name. How did he find me? I keyed in an emergency code on my chip but before I could give any explanation, Acron was at my side, taking my hands, preventing me from continuing. Lee wouldn't know what was going on, but I hoped he at least understood it was an emergency. I couldn't see him.

"Keep your palms open," Acron murmured. "Come with me."

He led me to a wing of rooms designed for the purpose of seduction and went in the first one. It was a beautiful, lush room, not at all like the sparse rooms I was used to at Destiny parties like this. Acron didn't care; his eyes were locked on me and my body.

As soon as the door closed behind us, he pinned me to the wall with my hands overhead, palms wide so I couldn't send any messages. I wouldn't dare, now that he was here. I couldn't disobey him, and my head spun. He leaned into me and inhaled deeply.

"My sweet, sweet boy," he said. "How I've missed you."

I fought a tremor, but couldn't entirely hold it back. He grinned the way he used to grin before punishing me.

"I taught you better than that," he said. "Have you forgotten everything? Should I tie you up, or will you prove that you remember how to be a good boy?"

I didn't want to do anything he said, but I certainly didn't want to be tied and gagged while he abused me. I relaxed into his grip to indicate that I wouldn't fight. One of his hands slid down my body, tracing behind me to grab my ass. He pulled our groins together. He was hard.

His face had changed since I'd seen him last, and not for the better. Stress etched across his features, but as he gazed at me, some of that stress faded. His hand on my ass pulled me closer. I was terrified. Where was Lee?

"Keep your palms open," Acron said, lowering his other hand to his side.

He shifted, and suddenly there was a blade pressing against my inner thigh. He had often raped me while physically threatening me, and it wasn't the first time he'd used a knife to subdue and frighten me, but I had new fears now. I had run away from him, the ultimate disobedience. Would he scar me and make me useless now that I wasn't his, or would he try to kidnap me and bring me back to Destiny?

There was a soft knock at the door. The blade pressed closer and nicked the cloth of my pants. I could feel the cold steel of the blade.

"Not a word," Acron hissed.

Another knock, and the door opened despite the lock Acron had set. Lee walked in, but I couldn't feel any joy. The blade was still against me and Acron could kill me if he wanted.

"Excuse me," Lee said. "This prostitute doesn't have permission to be here. He's been banned from the grounds."

Acron smiled. It seemed warm and sincere, but I knew better.

"I don't mind at all if he stays," Acron said.

"I apologize, but he must be escorted to the street. I'll find another partner for you."

I hid a gasp as the tip of the blade pierced my skin. He pressed firmly and I couldn't react. If I reacted, he would make it worse. Right now, it was only a small cut. If he wanted, he could slash and do damage that I couldn't hide. I was bleeding now, but the way our bodies were angled, Lee couldn't see.

Acron leaned into me, his lips brushing my ear.

"I'll find you again, darling," he whispered. "Now that I know where you are, you can't escape."

He quickly and fluidly inserted the knife into me up to the hilt, then withdrew it. He must have hidden it, and I was still at an angle that Lee wouldn't see. Acron moved away from me and I lowered my hands, which had still been over my head. I couldn't grab my thigh because Acron was still too close. Instead, I watched Lee escort him out. I felt helpless; I had no way to tell Lee who Acron was without injury to either me or Lee. I was also worried about the replacement prostitute. Would Acron take out his anger on the next man? As Acron walked toward Lee, I deliberately and obviously tapped my chip. Lee saw, but didn't react. He led Acron out.

Alone now, I grabbed my thigh. The cut was extremely deep, but hadn't severed any muscles. It had severed at least one major vein, however. There was already a growing pool of blood under me. I didn't know how Lee would react to my obvious tap. I didn't know how else to warn him that Acron was dangerous, and that I needed help.

There was another knock at the door and I flinched as the door opened. Had Acron killed Lee and come back for me? But Sora entered, and I gasped in surprise.

"Is everything all right?" he asked, closing the door softly behind him.

"Lee might be in danger," I said. "He's with someone dangerous."

Sora immediately tapped something complicated into his chip. I relaxed against the wall. Lee would be safe. Sora approached me and appeared puzzled by the puddle at my feet. Then his eyes rose and he saw the dark stain on my clothing.

"Are you all right?"

"No," I said. I wished I was able to cry, but I had been trained so thoroughly never to let a tear drop that I couldn't. I moved my hands and Sora saw my injury. He looked stunned, then tapped something into his chip. It looked like a medical emergency call, if his codes were the same as mine.

Sora then came close enough to touch me, and he reached out to grab my shoulder. I flinched, the memory of Acron still fresh in my mind. Looking extremely concerned now, Sora pulled me off the wall. I staggered. He examined my injury and a slow rage filled his eyes.

"Take off your outfit," he said.

I knew he wasn't mad at me, but it was still frightening having a dominant ordering me in such an angry voice. I cautiously took off my clothes, finally revealing the injury. I looked down to see how bad it was. Just a clean slit in my skin, I saw with relief, although blood streamed down my leg. Sora had a different reaction.

"What happened?" he demanded as he examined the area. "How dare someone hurt you! We need to get you to the doctor now. Can you walk?"

I staggered forward and he caught me. I could walk, but I needed to lean on him quite heavily. He led me towards a large curtain that I was surprised to see concealed a door. After being half-carried down a hallway, Sora spoke quickly into his chip in a different language. A light over a door to the right started glowing, indicating that it was now connected to another room. As we staggered through, I nearly sobbed in relief. It was the medical wing, and Ananti was waiting to assist me onto a table. She adjusted the table into a bed and I shut my eyes.

Sora stroked my cheek.

"I have to go back, but you must tell Ananti what happened. I don't know when Lee will be here to see you. He can't let anyone know something happened. But he's not ignoring you," Sora said, no doubt trying to reassure me.

I knew that Lee's responsibilities as host took precedence over his role as my handler. I just wanted to make sure he wasn't hurt, or that a prostitute wasn't hurt. Surely Ananti would tell me if either of those things happened. Normally, I wouldn't dare expect such information, but she was different. The yakuza were different. I was starting to accept that I had a right to knowledge.

Sora left and Ananti finished inserting the IV into my arm.

A flow of medicine entered my bloodstream and began relaxing me. I could tell it would help slow the flow of blood while also encouraging blood production, since I had lost quite a bit of blood. She moved to my thigh and examined the wound, gently wiping away the excess blood.

"It won't scar," she said.

I already knew that. Acron had left a smooth cut that would heal easily. He knew the healing abilities of my microbes. I hadn't been able to heal my hand because the injury was so jagged and infected, but this wouldn't be difficult. The scar, anyway. It was hard for me to control blood loss despite my microbes. I was only able to ensure that my microbes didn't spill out with my blood. My microbes were part of me; I couldn't afford to lose any.

"We may have to give you a blood transfusion," she said, still examining the wound. "It should have stopped bleeding by now. Can your microbes do anything for it?"

"Not really," I said, lowering my eyes to avoid looking straight at her. It wasn't the answer she wanted and I didn't want to appear disobedient.

"Have you tried?" she asked. "Surely stopping the flow of blood is something you can do."

My brow crinkled. It should be something I could do. I could control every aspect of my body, including my pulse. Why couldn't I prevent an injury from healing like this? A doctor had once suggested I might not be able to, so I had never tried. I hesitantly reached out with my microbes to the wound. Shocking pain. I hissed and withdrew my microbes as far away as possible from the agonizing wound. It had barely been hurting, but now I could barely stand the pain. It felt as though my microbes themselves had absorbed the pain and no matter what I did, I couldn't rid them of it. The microbes emanated pain as they flooded my system and my senses.

"What's happening, Gabriel?"

I heard the question from a distance but couldn't answer. A strong flow of medicine rushed into my system but even though it numbed my body, my microbes were still on fire. I shifted and writhed to try to calm them.

Another flow of medicine and to my surprise, it melted against my microbes and stopped the pain. I relaxed and took several deep breaths. I could barely move because of the first medicine, but I was still conscious. Ananti leaned over me and placed a finger under my eye, examining me carefully. I wondered what she saw, if my iris were white like the guards or some other inhuman color.

"Can you hear me?" she asked.

I blinked, because I couldn't quite speak. The medicine had relaxed me too much, and even my microbes were being lulled to sleep. They were almost out of my control, but I knew I could shake off the fogginess and reawaken my microbes at a moment's notice. I just didn't know if the pain would return.

"Gabriel," she said. "There was a poison on whatever stabbed you. It's interfering with your microbes. See if you can locate the poison in your microbes and get rid of it like you did the trackers before."

My eyes widened. A poison targeting microbes? How had Acron gotten it? Why had he used it on me? Had he hoped to reduce me to so much pain that I couldn't fight as he ran away with me? But no, he hadn't expected to see me there. So why did he have it?

I shoved the questions aside and focused on my hibernating microbes. I analyzed one, and found a point of pain in it. The microbe couldn't get rid of it, but when I had another microbe try to remove it, the pain vanished. Just like the trackers. I had all of my microbes gently assist each other. While I had been violent with the trackers, now I was slow and careful, because I couldn't stand much more pain. I had a high tolerance usually, and could fake an even higher tolerance, but the extraordinary pain combined with the shock of the last few days was almost too much. I had to be careful while freeing myself.

When I was finally finished, I scanned myself. I was safe. Ananti was next to me, holding my hand while watching her monitor. I realized that she had attached an arm scanner at some point and I hadn't even realized it. That was not good. I had to be aware of my body at all times to prevent people from knowing my microbe count. This pain had really undone me.

"Gabriel, I want you to blink once for yes and twice for no. Do you understand?"

I blinked. Her lips curved into a small smile of relief.

"Are you in any more pain?"

I blinked twice. She looked even more relieved, but still worried.

"Do you know why your microbe count is higher than it was last time we measured?"

I blinked once, thinking of my foolish meditation and the guard who had stopped the influx of microbes before they killed me. Or mutated me. Or whatever too many microbes would do to me. I had always thought too many microbes simply meant death. Now I knew there were other options.

Ananti nodded. "The drug I gave you will help you sleep for a few hours while you recover. You're going to be fine. Just rest."

For the second time in as many days, I allowed myself to relax and lose consciousness in Ananti's care, but I missed Lee's soothing presence.

CHAPTER 16

AWAKENING

I awoke cradled against a man's chest, and only my training and a lingering slowness from the medication kept me from bolting. The man was asleep; I could tell by his breathing. I was too frightened to open my eyes and see Acron. He had found me.

The embrace truly frightened me as well. I had never slept in the same bed as anyone. I may have gone to my parents as a small child, as many children did, but I had no memory of it. On long-term assignments, it was usual to sleep with your target, but I wasn't allowed to go on any assignment longer than 12 hours. The arms around me were terrifyingly strange, but as I lay there and listened to Acron's breathing, it wasn't as threatening as I first thought. My cheek was against his chest, and one of his hands curled over my back and tangled in my hair. It was a very possessive pose, and I almost enjoyed it. How could I possibly enjoy anything Acron did to me?

My microbes finally churned to life and I could sense them sparking against the microbes in the body beneath me. But that didn't make sense. Acron had no microbes. I sharpened my senses, and suddenly the man's scent registered. This was not Acron. It was Lee.

I cautiously opened my eyes. Lee lay under me, arm curled around me, face peaceful with sleep. He was beautiful. I could sense his microbes and to my shock, I sensed far more than I expected. I expected some, since he was from the Drops, but if I was sensing him correctly, he had just as many microbes as a sagent, yet he wasn't a sagent. Was he an agent who also handled sagents? That didn't make sense. Agents had more freedom than sagents, but Lee would still have to devote most of his time to his own assignments, not to being a handler. Even with the seemingly looser standards of the yakuza, it couldn't work.

Lee's breathing changed and he turned his head to me. I was careful not to allow the tension I felt to show. My body was relaxed, but I was still prepared to bolt. The hand wrapped around me ruffled my hair as his other hand rose to feel my forehead.

"How do you feel?" he asked.

"F-fine," I replied. I couldn't control the tremor in my voice. But I was starting to learn that while Acron and even my latest handler would punish such a lack of control with severe measures, Lee would accept my weakness. Yet the woman sagent I met had been superb. How could Lee be kind to weakness and still produce good sagents? I was always told that handlers had to be strict to get good results, that it was for my benefit in the long run. Everyone told me that, from my parents to my sister to my handlers. Sora was an excellent sagent too. How did Lee do it?

Lee examined me carefully, his hand tracing to my neck and checking my pulse. But his other hand continued to pet my head and tangle in my hair. It was an affectionate gesture, and I didn't have any idea how to react. My parents had never done anything like this to me, even though I sensed that this was the type of thing most parents did.

"You've never slept with anyone, have you?"

"No," I said. My right hand was on his chest and I used it to check his arousal. Considerably higher than normal, but still in a safe range. He enjoyed lying with me, and it was more than friendly enjoyment, but it wasn't at the point where I felt threatened. I had never felt someone interested in me who didn't take advantage of me.

"You still don't feel safe with me?" Lee asked, placing his hand over mine.

I was shocked. Had he noticed me checking his arousal? There was no way to tell unless you were a sagent. It wasn't anything that involved movement; it was a way that you sensed the person's microbes. Most sagents did it without realizing that they were manipulating their microbes. In fact, almost all sagent training was geared towards learning to use your microbes, even though that was never stated. Since I was the only sagent I knew who could control microbes consciously, the training came easier to me than to others. But how could Lee tell?

"Are you a sagent?" I blurted out, unable to help myself.

Instantly, I shrank from his touch. He might allow certain transgressions, but surely not this, which was an unprovoked, personal question. His hands tightened on me, and I couldn't hide an element of stiffness in my body.

He looked disappointed.

"You should know that I won't punish you for questions, Gabriel," he said, stroking my hair again. "I know you're more alert with targets than you are with me. I know you wouldn't ask them questions like this. But with me, you can ask anything without fear of punishment. The worst I'll do is refuse to answer."

Very cautiously, afraid it was a trick, I raised my eyes to meet his.

"Will you answer that question?"

Lee turned his head away and his body tensed. I instinctively brushed his neck in a way designed to relax him. I used it on targets sometimes if they had second thoughts. I saw a smile cross his lips and felt embarrassed. He was my handler; I shouldn't use tricks on him.

"I will answer," he said, looking at me again. The tension in his body remained and I almost told him he didn't have to. It was clearly a painful topic. I couldn't contain my curiosity, however, so I let him continue.

"When I was very young," he began, then stroked my hair. "I was twenty-one, just like you."

I blinked in consternation. People didn't live long in the

Drops, so twenty-one shouldn't be that young. But he had microbes, I remembered. They extended life.

"I was kidnapped by a different Family. They injected me with microbes, and tried to sell me as a sagent, but I used my new strength from my microbes and killed them. My Family rescued me before their reinforcements could come."

I couldn't contain my shock. I had never heard of anything like that even being considered. Kidnapping someone and injecting them against their will? I could tell that wasn't the whole story, but I didn't have the right to ask any other questions about the incident. The pain in his voice was probably obvious to anyone, and as a sagent, I could hear betrayal and regret. I could also hear the way he pronounced Family with a capital F and wondered what it meant. I considered, then decided I could ask about that without inflicting more pain.

"Who is your Family?" I asked, putting the same emphasis on the word that he did.

Lee stroked my head again.

"There are five Families in the yakuza. There used to be six, until I was kidnapped. The other five Families joined together to demolish the Family who hurt me. I was the younger son of the leader of my Family, but it's been several generations since then. Now, the man I call my nephew heads the Family," he said. "But even he defers to me because of my place as a direct descendent of our Family line."

I had thought his previous comments were shocking, but this revelation stunned me. I had known he was high-ranking, of course. And I knew he was important because of the quality of party he had hosted. But I had no idea he was anywhere near being the head of the group now controlling me. Handlers never had that much power. It was one of the reasons they enjoyed controlling sagents, or so I had found. They were restricted by the agencies, and lashed out at us. But if Lee were the son of the ruling Family, then he could probably do whatever he wanted.

I wondered if that were why he was kind to me and, from what I'd seen, Sora and the woman. He was in control of his life and had considerable influence over his agency, his Family. He had no need to control me.

He smiled and kissed my forehead, then pushed me slightly. I rolled off him immediately and stood. He stared at me for a moment and I couldn't interpret his gaze. I had always been able to interpret the way people looked at me, since it often saved my life, or prevented pain. But I couldn't read Lee, and it frightened me. I didn't show my fear, however, since he would be disappointed again. The unknown look on his face was quickly replaced by a smile as he stood.

I looked around and realized we weren't in my room, though this had very similar decorations. It was about the same size, too. There were personal pictures, however, and small trinkets that indicated that someone had lived here a long time. Was I in Lee's room?

"This is my room," he said as if in answer to my unspoken question. "I brought you here while you recovered. You fell into a much deeper sleep than Ananti expected, and we were worried you might slip into a coma."

My eyes widened slightly. Healing my microbes had taken a lot of energy, but I hadn't realized it had taken enough to make me vulnerable. Now that my recovery had been mentioned, memories flooded back. I unconsciously felt my thigh while thoughts of Acron filled my mind. The wound was fine and would heal easily, and Lee was safe. Acron hadn't hurt Lee. But Lee also didn't know who Acron was, and I was scared to tell him. Not scared of Lee, but scared of admitting the reality that Acron knew where I was, and could hurt me whenever he wanted.

"I, um," I started, then clasped my hands and stared at the ground. Instincts were hard to break, and I had very little experience volunteering information.

"Yes?"

His voice was gentle, and he didn't seem angry at my hesitance.

"The man was Acron," I whispered.

Lee didn't react, and for one horrified moment, I thought he was in league with Acron to hurt me. Then I remembered that I had never said Acron's name before, and Lee genuinely didn't know who I was talking about.

"Acron is- was my first handler," I said in just as small a voice.

Lee gasped. He stared at me in disbelief, then I felt rage building up in him. He started pacing, shaking his head and staring towards the door with a look of murder. Even though his anger wasn't directed toward me, it was still unnerving. If I had any doubts that Lee would side with a fellow handler over me, those fears vanished. Lee was firmly on my side.

"I had him," Lee muttered. "I could have killed him."

He glanced over at me. I had no idea what to do, so I shrank from his gaze. I was partially responsible, since I hadn't told him who Acron was. I was too frightened, and then in too much pain. I should have told him as soon as Acron left the room. I had told Sora that Lee was in danger, true, but I should have more specific.

"We know who he is now," Lee said, stopping his pacing to look at me. "We can protect you."

I thought of my previous agency. I stayed with them partially because of how well they protected me. I had no fears with them, because they valued me and wouldn't let me be stolen. Why had they sent me to the Drops when Acron was here?

Suddenly, I remembered my handler telling me that the judge wasn't my primary target, and that I was in extreme danger. Had they been trying to lure Acron into the open and used me as bait? I had assumed that my handler would tell me if GovTech knew about me, but what if she hadn't? What if she had been confident about my safety with two enforcers to guard me? She undoubtedly knew that telling me about Acron would terrify me to the point of being unable to return. It was true. If I had known that Acron was in the Drops, or anywhere near me, I never would have left the bed and breakfast.

It would also explain why he had a poisoned knife. He didn't know where I was, but he always liked to be prepared. He might have also heard that the yakuza had taken me, or just reached that conclusion on his own. Maybe that's why he was even there, pretending to consider an investment, but secretly looking for me. And now that he knew where I was, there was no way to hide. The yakuza could protect me when I was here, and probably when I was in yakuza territory, now that they knew what Acron looked like, but what about when I left to do a job? I would have to leave eventually; surely there wouldn't be enough demand within the yakuza for me to earn back their investment.

"You don't believe we can protect you," Lee observed. "The yakuza control the Drops, Gabriel. Nothing will happen to you."

"How do you know? What about when I leave?"

Lee looked at me oddly. "Gabriel, no one from the Drops leaves. Even though you can pass the scanner, I would never send you someplace I can't follow."

I stared at him. It felt as though the floor vanished beneath me and Lee was at my side in an instant. I wouldn't go back to Destiny? My life was in Destiny. My parents, my sister, how could I live without ever seeing them again? I thought about living under the grotesque metal sky down here, unable to see the stars. I couldn't stay here. I didn't belong here.

"Surely you realized that, Gabriel," he said. His arm wound around my waist and I was grateful; I might not have been able to stand without his support.

"My family," I said, unable to keep from raising the last pitch and making it into a question. He sighed.

"I can arrange for your family to visit if they must," he said. "I didn't realize your family was still part of your life. Most families cut ties once their child becomes a sagent."

"My parents are sagents, too," I said softly. "And my sister was at my agency."

"Your entire family are sagents?"

He sounded puzzled, and slightly shocked. It was extremely rare for two children from the same family to tolerate microbes; the only reason my parents were allowed to live together and raise us was because my mother and father had somehow snuck away and she became pregnant. Sagents were sterile, but somehow my parents weren't with each other. With that and our blonde hair, my sister and I were treasured and highly sought after. Acron had emphasized that my uniqueness was why he needed to be so harsh with me. It was why he broke the rules.

I realized that now that Lee knew about the unique circumstances of my birth, he might also take advantage of me, and I shied away from him. I felt wobbly but I would rather stumble than feel his body harden, his smile vanish, and that look come into his eyes that I had seen in both of my handlers. I was valuable. Too valuable. No leash was short enough.

"I guess we both have unusual family histories," Lee finally said. "May I tell Ananti about your parents?"

All of my previous doctor visits flashed before my eyes. Every time, they grilled me with questions about my parents, my sister, my microbes. They drained my blood for study, sometimes taking so much I would be weak for days and my weight would drop considerably. The first time it happened, and I was put on a liquid diet until I recovered, Acron was brutal. The second time, I tried to eat solid food without anyone knowing, so I wouldn't lose as much weight. But Acron found out what I was doing, and it was worse. The third time, I tried increasing the amount of liquids I was taking. Again, he found out. After that, I had no hope and just accepted the punishment for losing weight.

Lee had been extraordinarily kind about my weight loss so far, but what would he say when I lost weight after this introductory period? Would he punish me for being weak after having what felt like all of my blood drained away? Or would he accept my weakness and give me time to recover?

"Tell me what you're thinking," Lee commanded.

Hesitantly, awkwardly, I explained. "Whenever I get blood drawn, I lose weight," I said softly.

"You think Ananti will draw your blood if she knows?" he asked. "How much did they take? I can't imagine how having blood drawn could possibly affect your weight unless they drained you dry."

"It felt like it," I said. "I would always faint and be weak for days. It was worse at my first agency. My second agency only did it three times and didn't punish me much for losing weight."

The first time it happened with them, I was sent on an assignment that I didn't want, but compared to what Acron had done to me, it was nothing. My handler was actually surprised at how easily I accepted the job that I vehemently opposed earlier, but she didn't know what Acron's punishment had been, and she wouldn't have believed me if I told her. She didn't believe that he had done anything except frighten me, and that I had run away because I was a foolish child, not because I was being abused. My sister and parents believed me, at least.

And Lee believed me. I looked up at him. I could tell he wanted to touch me but he wouldn't, not unless he had my permission. My permission. I had never been free to give my permission. My body wasn't mine, after all. It belonged to my agency. I used it and maintained it, but it was not strictly mine. People could do what they wanted with it, including and especially my handlers. How was Lee so different? Was it because he had almost become a sagent?

"Ananti won't take any blood," Lee said. "I still want to tell her, though. Can I?"

I nodded quickly, afraid he would change the terms. I knew he wouldn't, but deep down, I couldn't fight my instinctive distrust of handlers. He was not like them, and I shouldn't be mistrusting him just because of my other handlers. But it was difficult.

CHAPTER 17
SCHEDULING

"**W**hat are my jobs for the day?" I asked.

Knowing my assignments would help me feel more grounded. And taking a job would help me feel in control. I knew Lee wouldn't send me on painful jobs, so I could look forward to feeling the only control I ever felt in my life as I manipulated my targets.

But Lee was staring at me with that blank look again. I shifted under his gaze. I had no idea what he was thinking or feeling. He was using his microbes to hide his thoughts, I realized. It was a sagent trick, and he couldn't do it as well as a sagent, but it was still a reminder that he had microbes and was eerily similar to me. Except that he was the handler, and I was the slave.

"Your job for today is to establish a routine," Lee said. "You will make a list of anything and everything you are accustomed to having, including workout equipment, personal products, and food. Once you're finished, I want you to go through your morning routine and document everything you do and how long it takes."

I nodded. He would need to know my habits and what I was used to. Very practical.

"Then, I'm sending Sora to show you around the building and give you retina access to areas that you may need. I may join you if I have time."

I nodded again. I was beyond shocked that I was being given retina access, but it would probably just be my room and the doctor.

"You and Sora can have lunch," he continued. "I've sent files to your chip on the Drops that I want you to read, understand, and memorize after lunch. We should have all of your information off your old chip by then, and you'll have your personal files back."

I hesitated, remembering one file that I didn't want opened. The man who gave it to me made my body sing, and I trusted him. I didn't know if he was still alive, but he had given me the file and said that as long as the file was unopened, I could go to him for protection. If I opened it, he said I could read it, but if anyone else opened it, the file would erase itself. I had never opened it – and I certainly hadn't told my handler about it; she was mad enough about my infatuation – and I didn't want it erased now.

"Excuse me," I said, casting my eyes down out of habit. Lee waited for me to speak. "Some of the files on my chip were private. Will the technicians be opening everything?"

"No," he said. "We respect your privacy."

I sighed in relief.

"I'll have dinner with you, and you need to get a full night's sleep."

"But what jobs will I have?" I asked again, puzzled as to why he would leave that out.

That blank look again.

"None," he said. "I'm not risking you until we can track your former handler better."

"But aren't there agency jobs for me?"

Lee hesitated. "What do you mean?"

"You know," I said, blushing. I didn't like agency jobs, but I had already guessed that I would have to do them for a while. I knew Lee wouldn't risk me out of the complex. "Requests from people in the agency."

"I'm the only one who gives you jobs," Lee said. "Why would

you even know about requests from other people?"

"No," I said, annoyed that I was having to explain something that was better left unspoken. I was frightened of challenging him like this, but annoyance won out. "Agency jobs are when people in the agency request my services for themselves."

Lee's eyes widened.

"Do they know you're a sagent, or are you spying on them?"

"They know," I said.

"Your handler allowed others in the agency to touch you?"

There was a distinct note of jealousy in his voice that surprised me. I instinctively checked his arousal, but he wasn't aroused; he was protective.

"No one in the yakuza will lay a hand on you," Lee said. "I can't believe sagents are treated like this in Destiny. Why haven't you all risen up in protest?"

"I think people did, once, but they all vanished," I said. "Everyone who disobeys vanishes. My parents taught me how to avoid vanishing."

I lowered my head. "They'll think I have vanished. Their handlers will never let them visit. They'll be told I'm gone."

"Wouldn't they just say you're dead?" he asked in a gentle voice.

"No," I said. My eyes grew warm and once, there might have been tears, but not anymore. "If I'm dead, I can't be used for leverage against them. They have to think I might come back."

The blank look again, then Lee reached out to take my hand. He didn't take it, though, just left his hand extended as if giving me the choice. I cautiously took the hand, and Lee pulled me into an embrace. A comforting embrace.

"Who have they used against you like that?" he asked, his breath brushing my hair.

"Anyone I care about."

"Your family, then," Lee murmured. "Anyone else? Do you have any friends?"

I was confused for a moment, then realized that Lee might expect me and Sora to be friends. Was it allowed for a sagent to have friends here? Relationships between sagents were strictly forbidden, in part to prevent the type of revolt that Lee had mentioned.

"No," I said. "One of my targets. I–"

I blushed, glad he couldn't see. I could have prevented the blush, but I didn't need to.

"I liked him. I disobeyed so I could see him again. They might have killed him, I don't know."

"The judge?" Lee asked in a puzzled voice.

I almost laughed. From his perspective, that was exactly what had happened with the judge. And in fact it was, though the circumstances were completely different.

It had been one of my first jobs for my second agency. They hadn't cracked down on me yet, and I had a lot of flexibility with my jobs. Having sex with him was the first time I had even imagined sex could be pleasurable. I was supposed to find out what his connection to the government was, and whether or not he was a double agent. As our time shortened, I just wanted to keep him in bed instead of talking to him, and I did.

Before I left – with nothing to show for the job – he gave me a file on my chip. He told me that if I ever needed protection from anyone, I should find him. If the file was unopened, he would protect me. He stroked my cheek gently and told me that if I chose to read it, he would understand. He would let me read it, but if anyone else accessed it, it would self-destruct. He kissed my cheek and I left. I didn't mention the file to my handler, but I did tell her that I could gain information if I returned.

A week later, he was amused at my return. He asked if I had read the file, and was almost disappointed that I hadn't. I couldn't figure out why, still couldn't figure out why, but we spent our time together in the best way possible. Faced with the prospect of returning with no information for a second time, I reluctantly initiated conversation. He kissed me, whispered his job title to me and what he did for the government, then tugged me under him yet again. I don't know if he knew I was a sagent, but he did know why I was sent, and I was grateful.

My handler noticed that I was in too good a mood, and quickly found out why. I didn't say anything, but she knew. She grilled me for information he might have told me that I hadn't shared. I had of course told her everything he said and I knew nothing else except the file, and nothing she did could make me admit to having that file. It was then that she started being stricter with me. I had less freedom in selecting my jobs, and I had more of them. The punishments started. Sometimes I wondered if it was worth it, but it was. It gave me hope.

And then, I felt almost the same with the judge, and disobeyed again to see him. In doing so, though, I put myself in danger, as opposed to last time, when I had returned to her between trips. I openly disobeyed this time, and that was intolerable. I thought of the enforcer who grabbed me to try to drag me back, and the threats she made. I couldn't believe my luck in being taken by Lee and the yakuza. The man and woman at the bed and breakfast were wrong to protect me from the yakuza, even though that's what I had wanted. I knew, intellectually, that the yakuza was a criminal organization, but they had only been kind to me.

Lee was watching me now, his neck curved to gaze down at me. I had, of course, kept my face in a pleasant smile while drifting off in my thoughts. I probably looked as unreadable as he did to me sometimes.

"It wasn't the judge," I said, remembering what we were talking about.

"But it was also the judge, wasn't it?"

This time I couldn't hide my blush, but I allowed it just as I had allowed the first. It was getting easier to control my reactions when I could choose to show them sometimes. I wasn't forced to reject everything my body did; I could allow it to express itself and control it freely.

"Yes," I said. "He's probably going to be killed."

"He won't be," Lee said. "And if you want, you can see him again. You'll have to be under guard the entire time, since he does have contact with your agency."

"I can… see him again?"

I backed out of his arms. "You would let me see someone that you know I can't control?"

"By the time you see him, you'll know how to control yourself," he chided. "Sagents shouldn't need to control their targets; they control themselves and encourage their targets to make a mistake."

I considered. What he said was true, even though it was the opposite of everything I'd ever learned. I never forced a target to do anything, except in the rare cases when I was hired to kill someone. I just, as he said, encouraged them to do what I wanted. And I was very persuasive. So he would train me, then let me see the judge again. While in my previous agencies that would be a threat so I knew not to disobey or they would take away something I wanted, with Lee I suspected it might actually happen. I considered the ramifications.

"You want me to complete the other sagent's job?" I asked.

Lee laughed. "That is one bonus. Once he knows you work for me, I have no doubt he'll be more loyal to the yakuza to have the chance to see you. But I wouldn't ransom either of you. You can tell him whatever you want. I won't consider it a job, I'll consider it a reward."

I shook my head slowly. Rewards were ransoms, in my experience. I had never gotten one before. I had tried to grab a reward by staying in the Drops, but it failed.

Lee gestured for me to dress and I realized someone had changed me into sleeping clothes. They were so comfortably fitted that I hadn't even noticed I was wearing them. Lee was in similar attire and we dressed together, I in Destiny clothes and him in the same type of casual suit he had been wearing when I first saw him. The dragon pin was already on his lapel and he noticed me staring at it.

"My Family – your Family now, too – is known as the Dragon Clan. Once you read about the Drops this afternoon, you'll have a stronger sense of what life is like here."

He led me outside and pulled me in front of the retina scanner. With a few buttons, he entered my ID into the computer, allowing me access to the room. I was too surprised to react until it was done.

"I shouldn't have access here," I said, knowing my protests were useless now that the computer had entered my ID.

"In an emergency, you may need to reach me," he said, leading me back to my room. "You'll have access to most areas. You can't leave the building, however."

I shivered, thinking of Acron waiting outside. There was no chance of me running away.

We reached my room and he entered my information as I looked into the retina scanner. The door slid open. Before I could enter, Lee kissed my cheek.

"Stick with Sora. I don't want you getting into trouble," he said, then walked away.

I jumped into the room before the door could shut on me. A guard was waiting. Despite their size, they were very unobtrusive. I wondered if they used their microbes to blend in. I didn't have a chance to ask, however, because there was a polite rap on my door.

CHAPTER 18

TRANSACTION

"Sora's fast," I muttered as I opened the door.

But someone different was there, someone who looked vaguely like Lee and wore the same type of suit, also with a dragon pin. His dragon pin was larger, though, and more elaborate. Higher ranking? Or did Lee just not like wearing such a large pin? I realized that I hadn't met a single other person who was in the yakuza. I had met Ananti, and the two sagents, I supposed, but they didn't strike me as yakuza. This man did.

"May I come in?" he asked.

It almost sounded like he were making a joke, but if it was, I didn't understand it. I backed out of the way and gestured him in. Once inside, he looked at me the way I was used to men looking at me. I didn't need to check his arousal; he was attracted to me and not in a safe way. Just looking at his eyes told me that. I tried to reassure myself that Lee had said no one in the yakuza would lay a hand on me.

Despite my internal misgivings, externally I was greeting him with a warm smile. I wasn't quite sure how to treat him. Not as a target, but also not as a handler. Those were the only types of people I knew outside of family. Then I thought of other handlers I had met. There were strict rules for how to behave around a handler who wasn't yours, but still potentially had power over you. I would follow those.

We both sat on the couch on opposite ends, facing each other. Aside from a few pleasantries, nothing had been said. He was friendly enough, and seemed extremely curious about me. Most of the yakuza probably were, but did this man have Lee's permission to be here? I thought about summoning Lee, but Lee must have known this man was here. The knock had been so quick after I entered.

"You're exceptionally beautiful," the man said, again running his eyes over me. "A good acquisition for this Family."

I kept my eyes down, as I had been doing since he entered.

"I'm honored to serve this Family," I said, hoping it was the right response.

The man grinned. "Do you know who I am?"

I quickly glanced at him to confirm that I didn't know him, then shook my head.

He extended his hand for a handshake. He probably wanted to exchange information from the chips but mine had no personal information, just a few things about the Drops that I was to read later. I awkwardly met his handshake, hiding my scar easily but not having any information for what was supposed to be a reciprocal gesture.

He gave me his name and address, both of which I filed away in my memory. My chip would keep the information, of course, but my parents had trained me to memorize everything in case my chip were compromised. His last name was Lee and I wondered what I was supposed to call him if they were both Lee. The significance of the name took a second to sink in and I glanced at him again. Was this really the nephew who ran the entire Family?

"It's considered polite to share at least your full name and address," the man scolded, but it was friendly scolding. "Lee hasn't taught you any manners."

"There's no information on my chip, sir," I said, still not knowing what to call him.

He looked amused. "Destiny has different naming customs, I know," he said. "You may call me Lee-sama. It's a term used to indicate that I'm a higher rank than you. So you still don't have your chip restored? It's taking longer than usual. Well, why don't you just tell me your name?"

I hesitated. This was clearly the head of this Family, one of five Families in the yakuza. I didn't know the ranking of the Families, but it hardly mattered; this was one of the five most powerful people in the yakuza. But at the same time, my handler hadn't given me permission to tell my name to anyone. I couldn't lie, but I wasn't ready to just tell him, either. Names were important. Names had power. His name especially had power, but for me and all sagents, the lack of a name was our power. Already too many people knew the name I called myself. I wasn't eager to expand that circle.

"As I said," the man said, voice growing dark rapidly. "It's polite to share your name."

Suddenly I became aware of the guard behind me. He was reassuring me somehow, through the vibrations of his microbes spinning into mine. He thought it was fine to share my name, so I would.

"Gabriel," I said. "I don't have a last name yet."

The man smiled again, that dark anger hidden. He extended his hand again, not to exchange information this time, but to hold my hand. I sensed the guard's assurances and took Lee-sama's hand. The man stroked the back of my hand.

"We're investing a good deal of money in you," he said. "And we've lost a potential ally because of you."

I thought of Acron and inwardly shuddered. Still, I was extremely reassured that even Lee-sama was putting my life above a potential ally, as he called Acron. It seemed the yakuza really would put my life and safety first.

"Thank you for your generosity," I said. "I'm overwhelmed by your kindness."

It was hard not using my sagent tricks on him but he wasn't a target. He was the boss of all bosses.

"You could do more to show your gratitude," he said, and I blinked. That was a definite sexual invitation, practically an order given that it came from someone with his rank. Instantly, the guard's acceptance turned to shock and disgust. Clearly this was not something I was supposed to be doing, or at least Lee-sama wasn't supposed to be doing it. I again considered tapping my chip for Lee, but it would be too obvious. I couldn't alienate the person who held my life in his hands. If I disobeyed him, he could override Lee and send me straight to Acron.

He leaned towards me and tapped his cheek. There was no question what that meant, and no chance to protest. I cautiously slid across the couch so I could reach him, and leaned to kiss his cheek. He turned at the last moment to meet my lips with his. I wasn't surprised, and didn't really react except to open my mouth to him and let him taste me. He kissed me deeply for a very long time. Although I didn't use my usual tricks, I did make sure he enjoyed the kiss thoroughly. Luckily, he was a good kisser. Otherwise it would have been miserable. When he was finished, he ran a hand through my hair.

"So beautiful," he murmured. Then he stood. "I'm sure I'll see you again, Gabriel. Obey your handler, obey me, and you'll be safe here."

"Thank you, Lee-sama," I said, rising to show him to the door. The threat was hardly veiled. If I obeyed him, he would protect me. If I didn't, that protection would end. This was more what I had expected. Lee was too kind and considerate for what I had been expecting from the criminal yakuza. Lee-sama had the transactional approach I was used to.

After he left, I went to the guard.

"Could I have done anything else?" I asked softly. For some reason, I needed his approval. He couldn't tell Lee, but I would feel guilty unless he accepted my actions. Lee said no one would touch me, and I had let someone. I failed Lee by causing his promise to be broken.

The guard lifted his hand and rested it on my shoulder for just a moment before withdrawing. I could sense nothing from his microbes. But that had to be acceptance.

CHAPTER 19
DIFFERENT CUSTOMS

The rest of the morning went smoothly. As I went through my routine, I entered everything I was used to having, and how long everything took. I knew my schedule very well, as Lee had likely known, so it wasn't too difficult. The only hesitation I had was when it came to my hair products, which were extremely expensive. Lee would want to know them, so I added them, but also added a note that they weren't really necessary. Blonde hair required upkeep, but I could get by.

I didn't want my debt to the Family to be too large. I didn't want Lee-sama to have any more reasons to come and visit me, and if my debt were too big, I would have no reason to deny him. Not that I did now. But still.

It was strange having both Lee and Lee-sama. How did people survive in this world without first names? And if Lee-sama meant that he was higher ranking than me, why did Lee let me call him Lee? I wasn't equal to him. Maybe it was just to prevent confusion, since there couldn't be multiple Lee-samas walking around.

More than anything, I worried that I had made a mistake allowing Lee-sama to kiss me. The guard's reaction to the request had been so extreme, and his forgiveness wasn't certain. He had touched me; he had reacted. But was he absolving me of blame, or was it some sort of warning?

There was a knock at the door, and I checked the viewer

before answering this time. It was Sora. I allowed him in. As I smiled and escorted him to the couches to sit – almost exactly where Lee-sama had sat – he seemed amused.

"I'm not a target, you don't have to be so formal," he said. "Or have I done something to put you on edge?"

"No, of course not," I said, trying to relax. I needed to give some reason for my actions, but couldn't mention Lee-sama, so I smiled as flawlessly as I knew how. "I'm not used to acting any other way."

"You never had time to relax, or be with friends?"

"I saw my family sometimes," I said. "My sister. But there were always others present."

"Do you want to talk about your sister?"

I considered, then shook my head. It was time for lunch, and I was feeling hungry. My eating schedule was considerably off, and I was eager to get my weight under control.

"I would prefer to have lunch," I said.

Sora asked for my list of foods and scanned it, nodding to himself. He tapped instructions into his chip and I knew food would be arriving shortly. But to my surprise, he stood up.

"Let's go."

"Where?"

I was completely puzzled. Unless we were going to his room, perhaps. That would make sense. His room must already have his food, and mine was being brought there. I politely requested a minute and checked to make sure I looked good. I realized suddenly that I hadn't been fully made-up when Lee-sama saw me. I wondered if he knew how comparatively disheveled I had been. But after a few minutes, I was coiffed to perfection, and I allowed Sora to guide me out of the room. I wasn't quite as elaborately made up as I would be for a job, but I felt much more confident.

The hall was creamy with ebony doors dotted along it, but it also contained a large double door and that was where Sora led me. He instructed me to hold still for the iris scanner to register me. There was no way this was Sora's room. The door opened and I was shocked to see a cafeteria-like room with long tables and benches. Even more shocking, it was filled with at least two dozen people, most wearing kimonos, the rest wearing suits like Lee wore, several of whom wore dragon pins.

In both of my agencies, I occasionally met others from the agency who weren't sagents outside of agency jobs, but only a couple, and usually by accident. Sagents were kept hidden away, isolated from contact with the rest of the agency. As everyone in the room either openly stared at me or eyed me surreptitiously, however, I knew that my appearance was now openly known by the yakuza. I had never felt so exposed.

Outwardly, I accepted everything calmly, though I did hesitate when I entered the room. Sora led me through the room as I kept my smile pasted, and I glided the way I was taught to do when people were watching. None of these people were targets, but like Lee-sama, I couldn't afford to ignore them, either. We sat at a booth in the corner. Although almost everyone could see us, we could also see everyone, and it was a small bit of comfort. I hated worrying about people watching me without my knowledge.

"I didn't realize you would be so on edge here," Sora said. He had smiled and waved at a few people as we walked through. "This house is the center of the Dragon Clan, so even though almost no one lives here, they all live nearby and come here for work or to socialize."

"What are we doing?" I asked, careful to keep my relaxed smile. Sora was close enough and observant enough to know I was nervous, but I didn't want anyone else knowing.

"We're eating," he said.

True enough, as soon as he spoke, a young man in a grey shirt and black pants came over with two plates. Compared to my bland plate, Sora's was incredibly colorful and exotic. The server left, and Sora explained what was on his plate. He ate more than me, of course, since he had a larger frame and higher weight to maintain, but I wondered if I could include smaller portions of the bizarre foods he described. He encouraged me to try some of the food and I did. Cautiously. The lettuce in red sauce – kimchi – was a little sour for my taste, but the small strips of faux meat – bolgolgi – were delicious. I couldn't eat much faux meat and maintain my weight, but I would ask Lee about replacing the items in my meal with the local fare. He could help me figure out replacements that would maintain my weight.

As we started in on our own meals, he picked up two sticks and deftly started plucking food from his plate and putting it in his mouth. I couldn't help but stare, and I couldn't hide my confusion, but I turned it into an expression of admiration so no one would think I was confused. I had noticed quite a few people watching me, or at least casually glancing in my direction every so often.

"These are chopsticks," Sora said after a few bites, setting them down. "Don't tell me you've never heard of them."

"No," I admitted. "I mean, I'd heard that people in the Drops didn't have the same manners, but I didn't know there were different utensils. How do you have a fork for me if you use those?"

"We use regular utensils, too," Sora said. "But most people prefer these. Once you learn to use them, they're quite easy. Do you want me to teach you?"

"Here?" I asked, scandalized. Of course I wanted to learn, but in private, not in front of people who weren't sagents or trainers.

"I guess not," Sora said, glancing around. "What kinds of interactions are you used to having with people in your agency? You didn't eat with them, I take it."

"Only agency jobs," I said. "Sometimes I would see another sagent, or another handler, but otherwise just my handler and people directly involved with a job."

"How could you possibly be so isolated?" he asked, sounding as puzzled as I felt about his view of normal. "How can your agency protect you if no one knows you belong to it?"

"Oh, I guess the enforcers knew who I was," I said. "But that was often because of agency jobs."

Those were the worst agency jobs. It was usually three or

four enforcers who pooled their money to get me for an hour or more. Once an entire night, twelve hours. It was the longest job I'd ever had, and the only reason Acron permitted it was because I wasn't leaving the agency compound and he knew the enforcers in question. He knew how cruel they were.

"You keep saying agency jobs," Sora said. "What are those?"

I considered. Lee hadn't been feigning ignorance and his anger hadn't been false, though I hadn't suspected him of deception. I was still hesitant about accepting his kind nature, but it was hard to resist trusting him and his motives. If Lee didn't know what agency jobs were, then Sora wouldn't either.

I briefly explained an agency job in the fewest words possible and Sora's eyes went wide.

"No wonder you're not comfortable in front of everyone like this," he said. "But no one here would hurt you. And even though most of them are attracted to us, to all sagents, none would dare touch us without our permission. It's safe for our faces to be known, so that if we're ever in trouble outside, they know who to protect. They can't mark us, so there's no other way to tell that we belong to the yakuza."

"What do you mean, mark?"

"All yakuza are marked with a tattoo of their clan over their heart. The higher ranking the yakuza, the more elaborate it is, and members of the actual family have tattoos covering their backs and arms as well."

I thought back to the morning, dressing with Lee. I had noticed that his skin was darker than I might expect, but I assumed it was shadows. I had purposefully not looked at him when he changed, not wanting him to think that I was in any way attracted to him and risk inviting some sort of advance from him. An unnecessary step, probably, but an ingrained one.

"The ink is special," Sora continued. "Each Family uses a different ink that has a slightly different frequency, but the ink emits some sort of wave that can be read. Once you join a yakuza Family, you belong to them your entire life."

"But we're not marked?"

"No, not usually," Sora said. "We have to go places yakuza aren't allowed sometimes, and often we don't want people knowing we're yakuza, and some people don't like tattoos, so it would reduce our usability."

I thought of the bed and breakfast. If they had the technology to prevent people from lying, they could certainly keep the yakuza out. They would still need to be careful of ordinary people hired by the yakuza, and they were careful, but it was a safe bet that any true yakuza would be physically unable to go near.

Another sagent entered and, as had happened when we entered, everyone's attention was drawn to her. She scanned the room and fixed on us. It was the first yakuza I had met, who had given her name as Zada, and I wasn't sure why she was here.

CHAPTER 20
DECEPTIVE COSTS

Zada smiled at me as she crossed the room and sat down beside Sora and across from me. Instantly I felt outnumbered, even though I shouldn't. She extended her hand. I took it, wondering what information she would give me. She gave me her address. It was the same as Lee-sama's, and I guessed it was the address for this podhouse.

"You look comfortable, but you're not, are you?" she said without preamble. "You've barely touched your food. You need to eat or your weight will be off, and I'm sure it's already off a little."

Obediently, I began eating, and also projected more confidence than I had been. She laughed.

"Don't overdo it. No one expects you to be perfectly comfortable here yet. We barely know you, and you don't know us. A lot of people here are curious about you, you know," she said, gesturing to the room where many of the eyes were turned towards us. Towards me. "They know you're from Destiny. People from Destiny are extremely rare here."

She looked pretty curious herself and I wondered if that was why she was here. As a fellow sagent, she did have some right talking to me. Did Lee send her, or had she come on her own? Would Lee approve of me talking to her?

"What's the biggest difference between Destiny and the Drops so far?" she asked.

"The sky," I said without hesitation. "It's terrifying to look up and see metal instead of stars and the sun."

She and Sora were both silent, both expressionless, and I knew they were hiding whatever they really thought. Then Sora smiled. A forced smile.

"You get used to it," he said. "So it's true? You can look up and see nothing except the sky?"

I nodded as I finished my food. "Sometimes it's cloudy, of course," I added. "And in lower Destiny there are problems with pollution, so on a bad day, the sun looks like a reddish orange blur and you can stare straight at it without hurting your eyes. Sometimes there's light pollution in upper Destiny, too, in the cities, so the sky just looks kind of washed out and grey, day or night."

They were staring at me in awe and I lowered my eyes. I wasn't used to people looking at me like that, like I was interesting for more than my body. They were fascinated by what I said, I could tell. They had never seen the sky, and I tried to figure out what it would be like to have never seen the sky. They had grown up under this metal monstrosity and had never even seen a star, let alone spent their childhoods wishing on them, wishing to be anything other than a sagent. But maybe that wouldn't be their wish. Things did seem to be better for sagents here.

I wondered about that. Was Lee treating me differently than them? He had been kind to Sora, but what if that were a show? Maybe this whole thing was an act to make me cooperative, and everything would change in an instant. But how to find out? There were subtle codes that we all knew to indicate our situations, but would they translate in the Drops? After all, I had barely been able to communicate with Ari at the bed and breakfast. I hadn't had that same problem yet, but I would eventually.

"You get used to it," Zeda said, echoing Sora. She also forced a smile. "You can set your entertainment center to stream images of the sky from one of the satellites. A lot of people keep it on when they aren't watching something else. It can be comforting."

What an odd concept, I thought, but it did make sense in a way. I was grateful for it, because I could just pretend I was looking through a window and maybe recapture the feel of Destiny. I hesitated briefly before speaking, deciding to take a chance and use coded language.

"It's nice to see the sky," I said, emphasizing the word "see." That indicated a contract, which sagents talked about between themselves, but which no one could openly say. I was indicating to them that I had seen my contract, implicitly asking if they had seen theirs.

They looked confused. There must be different codes here. I was curious, though, if Lee treated them the same way he had treated me. He had been willing to give me input in my contract. Had he let them? But there was no way to ask directly.

"It is nice," Sora said, responding to my comment and not the code. "I can help you set it up in your room when we return."

"Look," Zada interrupted, leaning forward. "What are you trying to say?"

I pasted a smile on my face. "Nothing."

She and Sora exchanged a skeptical look. She shrugged as she finished her food, then stood up. Sora stood as well, so I did too. Sora and Zada started leaving the room. I was supposed to stay with Sora, but Zada put me on edge. She had saved my life and helped me, but I didn't know her. I trusted her as far as I would trust another sagent: with my life, but not with my heart or mind.

To my surprise, she accompanied me and Sora as Sora showed me around and locked my iris settings in far more doors than he should have. There was a library, the kitchen, a gym, his room, which greatly surprised me, and then Zada's room. I stared at them in shock when Sora said I would have access to her room. Maybe Sora's room made sense, but certainly not hers.

"The three of us are Lee's personal sagents," she explained. "You are free to come and talk to me whenever you want."

My brow furrowed. "What is a personal sagent?"

My first thought was that a personal sagent was a sagent

assigned to please only one master, but Lee was my handler. And unlike Acron, he would never make unwanted advances on me. I was more and more sure of it.

Zada smiled, and gestured me and Sora to enter her room. The answer must be secret, then. Otherwise, she would have explained in the hallway. I stared at her room in surprise as we entered. While my room, and Lee's room, was a sleek black-and-white with accents of color, her room was a glow of lilac with green highlights. The fauxwood looked like honey and perfectly complemented the pale, subdued purple walls and lamps. In terms of layout, her room was mostly similar: an open concept, but both the bathroom and the gym equipment were completely out of view. She also had a large closet that appeared to be full of colorful kimonos. Women's clothes almost always took up more room than men's; my sister also had a large closet that my clothes would never be able to fill.

Once we were seated in honey chairs with white cushions that appeared nearly pink in the halo of purple lamps, she explained.

"Lee is the handler for all three of us," she said.

I had thought as much. I wondered if they felt that I would steal attention from them. In Destiny, handlers only had one or two sagents assigned to them. Three would be very unusual. Suddenly, I was struck with the fear that Lee would send me to someone else, since he already had two sagents. What if the other person were like Lee-sama, like all of the other people I had ever met? What if this were just a fluke and reality would hit with a reassignment?

"Will he send me to someone else?" I asked, struggling to hide my fear.

"No," Sora said emphatically. He must have heard the fear. "Lee can easily manage three personal sagents."

"But what's a personal sagent?" I asked again.

"Lee is in charge of training all of the sagents for the yakuza," Zada explained. "He gets to know everyone during training, and slowly matches them with handlers that will best suit them. By the time training is over, all of the sagents have been matched and most have already transitioned into their handler's care full-time. But he chose both of us, and you, to be under his exclusive supervision."

"Does that mean we help with training?" I asked, again trying to hide my fear. I had been used for training enough times to know that it meant pain and punishment.

"No," Zada said with a frown, as if puzzled by my reaction. "Well, I guess he does sometimes," and she tilted her head towards Sora, "but I don't and you won't have to."

"He's more likely to put you in training than ask your help with it," Sora said.

I bristled slightly. "I'm fully trained."

"Not in all areas," Sora said, raising an eyebrow.

I thought of my experience with him and how badly I had failed Lee's test, and blushed. Maybe I wasn't as trained as I thought. There was a buzz at the door followed by its opening. Zada didn't look upset that the person hadn't waited for her permission, and at the sight of Lee, I decided that Lee didn't wait before entering his sagent's rooms. He hadn't waited for me, either.

Lee smiled at us, then held his hand out to me.

"I'll be taking him off your hands," he said. I noticed he didn't use my name. Perhaps Zada wasn't supposed to know my real name, just as I didn't know hers. But why, when he had been pleased that Sora and I knew each other's names?

I stared at his hand for a moment, wondering if I could possibly avoid it. Then I remembered that this was Lee, and an extended hand did not mean pain. I took his hand, but all three had seen my hesitation.

We left and returned to my room, where he took my lists and quizzed me about what I needed. He paused at the hair products.

"Why are these optional?" he asked.

I looked down. "They're very expensive."

"If these are your only other needs, it doesn't matter how expensive they are," Lee said. "You cost far less than my other sagents. Are you sure you aren't forgetting anything?"

As I shook my head, I wondered exactly how expensive the hair products were. Both of my handlers emphasized that my costs were extremely high, and that was why I had to work full time. My sister was considered a bargain, but my second handler explained that men and women were completely different. Had she lied in order to force me into full time? I had never considered it before. After all, it had never occurred to me that my handler might lie about something important before. But now that I suspected I had been used as a lure for Acron, I was rethinking everything she had said and done.

"Is there anything else you want?" he asked, still looking at my list of needs.

"Um," I started, then stopped. It still felt wrong to request things from my handler. He waited. "I was wondering if I might replace some of the food I usually eat."

Lee smiled. "You like the food here? We can work it out. What did you like?"

I relaxed at his easy acceptance, and explained what I had and hadn't liked. He asked several questions and studied my current food carefully. He was just getting to know me, so he didn't know my exact nutritional requirements yet. After a few minutes of questions and tapping his chip, he nodded and explained a meal plan that included bulgogi for dinner and the meal the man at the bed and breakfast had eaten for breakfast. It was called bibimbop, and Lee hadn't pressed me about where I had tried it. The plan sounded wonderful.

Then he studied my preferred exercise equipment. He looked at the list of routines I had, and what I used on the equipment. I waited nervously. Perhaps this was where my costs were.

"There's newer equipment more streamlined to your needs," he said, looking up at me. "Perhaps you don't have it in Destiny. Would you feel comfortable using different equipment if it included everything you need?"

"I don't need anything newer," I said, keeping my eyes downcast.

"It's not a major expense," Lee said. "I would prefer you having top of the line equipment."

Still keeping my eyes down, I nodded. If he wanted it, then I would do it. No matter what it added to my costs.

He tapped a few more things into his chip and nodded, then went to the table, pulled a tablet from his jacket, and started writing.

"Come here, Gabriel," he said. "I'm updating your contract with your costs and I want you to be a part of it."

I obeyed. He showed me an electronic copy of a contract, and I again felt a shiver of uncertainty to be seeing my own contract. I still wondered if Sora and Zada had seen theirs.

"I looked up your hair products," Lee said. "Here are your total costs."

I stared at the number. There were several zeros and I wondered how much that amount meant. I vaguely remembered spending money as a child, but everything was purchased by my parents' agencies, and once I became a sagent, everything was covered by my agencies. Sagents were allowed anything we wanted, as long as we worked to pay it off. My parents taught me early to have simple tastes so I wouldn't cost as much, not that it worked. But I had never had a concept of money.

Lee wrote another number with another zero on it.

"These are Sora's costs."

I blinked. I didn't know money, but I did know math, and if I were an entire zero lower than Sora, it was far less. Significantly less. Either Sora had extremely high costs, or my handlers had both lied to me. I expected that from Acron, but not my second handler. She had indeed lied about my costs.

"With your costs, you only need to work full time for one year to pay back our investment, and you'll only need to work a four-day week once you're part time. Unfortunately," he added, "I don't think it's appropriate to send you in the field yet."

I nodded, thinking of Acron. I tried to fight the feeling that Lee was lying to me about how long I would work full time, and I was a little curious what a four-day week meant. Surely it couldn't meet I only worked four days a week, even though that was the most logical explanation. But that would mean that three days a week were vacation, and that much vacation was impossible.

"You won't complain about being put back in training?" Lee asked.

"What?"

"You're untrained in one of the key aspects of being a sagent," he said. "If you can't handle what your targets might do to you, you can't handle a job."

I lowered my eyes. I could feel the heat in my cheeks that meant I was blushing, but I didn't stop it as I nodded, knowing I had no choice. I caught the look of annoyance on Lee's face. I wondered what I had done to annoy him. He seemed to look annoyed whenever I was being the most obedient.

"I don't think you'll be comfortable joining the other sagents in training," Lee said. "Even though you could teach them a lot. Instead, I'll train you individually with help from a few others. I know you enjoyed the judge. Would you want to train with him?"

I was confused and a little lost, and he seemed to notice.

"We often ask for volunteers in the community to assist us in training. It's considered a great honor, and we only invite those in the yakuza or those who know how to maintain secrecy. The judge has participated twice in the past. He will almost certainly accept another invitation."

"Will he know it's me?"

"Not until he arrives. Shall I set something up, or would you prefer a member of the yakuza?"

I looked down again, considering. My heart instantly knew what I wanted, and I suspected Lee wouldn't judge me no matter what I chose, but I still hesitated. I didn't want the judge to be killed, and further contact with me might well be a death sentence. There had to be enforcers from my agency watching his compound for anything out of the ordinary. Even if they didn't follow him into yakuza territory, they would capture and interrogate him when he returned.

"I don't want to put him in danger," I said slowly, ignoring my heart.

Lee nodded. "I understand. I'll make sure that he isn't in danger from your former agency and invite him here."

I looked up at him, startled into meeting his gaze. He had a slight smile on his face that widened when I met his eyes. I wanted to explain the danger, since he clearly didn't understand, but he winked at me and stood up.

"Read the material on your chip. Memorize it and practice the advice. You'll have to demonstrate your knowledge tonight."

"A job?" I asked, puzzled.

"No," Lee said. "Not that kind of demonstration. Read your chip and you'll know what I mean."

He left and I glanced at the guard. It was a different one than the one who had been interacting with me, and I wondered if this one would be as communicative. I smiled shyly at him before heading to the chaise to read in comfort.

CHAPTER 21
PRACTICE

The Drops are a fascinating place. Much of the knowledge I gained from my chip was entirely new, and contradicted most of what I knew. To my surprise, people didn't die young because of the microbes. There was a significantly higher infant mortality rate, since not everyone could adapt, but it seemed that the low level of microbes in the people of the Drops gave them some of the same benefits that sagents enjoyed. Instead of barely reaching thirty, as I had been taught, most people who survived infancy lived to be over a hundred, nearly two decades longer than the average lifespan in Destiny.

There were sports, to my relief, and I just didn't know the terms. I memorized them gratefully, since it was such an easy topic of conversation. Other small talk items included light pollution, also a problem in Destiny but for different reasons, and animals. Pets, they were called, and I remembered Ari asking me about them at the bed and breakfast. Almost no animals had made it into Destiny, but there were apparently many living in the Drops. I hadn't seen any in my wandering, but they lived primarily in residential neighborhoods and aside from the one I currently lived in, I hadn't been to any neighborhood that primarily housed people. Even the bed and breakfast was in a fairly urban area.

I wondered about the pets, and how they escaped Earth after the meteor hit and people began to realize what microbes did.

As people scrambled into Destiny, a city half-built and devoid of life, no one had been allowed to bring animals for fear that they would carry microbes. Those animals, those pets, were left in the Drops. Far enough away from Earth's surface to survive, but posing no threat to the pure, sprawling city of Destiny in synchronous orbit around the now-hostile planet.

After learning the history of the Drops, the information Lee had given me turned to more practical matters. I quickly memorized the maps Lee provided and mentally compared them to the maps my former handler had given me. I couldn't understand the difference, unless somehow, no one who knew the Drops had ever left. No one from the Drops was permitted in Destiny, of course, but people from Destiny often traded legal and illegal goods and traveled back and forth. It was strange that no accurate maps had left with them.

I read about the yakuza with great interest, though I wanted to know more than the files contained. And finally, I read about the even more practical matters such as etiquette in sharing information, dressing and undressing in traditional clothing, and how sagents were used and viewed in the Drops. Since the Drops were considerably smaller than Destiny, having initially been used only as a platform to build Destiny, there was a greater chance of a sagent being outed. However, sagents still worked even when people could recognize them. Sometimes it even worked in their favor. I wondered if Zada was out, since she hadn't bothered hiding her role during our first encounter.

I studied the instructions on dressing and undressing again, then went to my wardrobe. There were no kimonos, only Destiny clothing. But surely Lee wouldn't give me instructions if he didn't want me to practice. I looked around and my eyes landed on the guard. He knew the room better than I did.

"Excuse me," I said, moving to a few feet away from him. "Do you know if there are kimonos here?"

The guard was expressionless, but I could feel his microbes pushing me to the left. I studied the wall and realized there was an almost invisible closet. It was obvious once I knew it was there, but very cleverly hidden so as not to detract from the clean lines of the room.

"Thank you," I said with a smile at the guard.

There was slight surprise on that impassive face. Maybe he hadn't known I could feel his microbes, and hadn't expected me to find the closet. I hesitated, wondering if perhaps all of the guards communicated through their microbes. I could do it if I wanted, but I was still afraid of turning into one of them if I tried doing what they were doing. I resisted the urge, and opened the closet instead.

At least a dozen kimonos filled the closet, most in somber colors but a few in bright shades. All of them would look good on me, I decided, but people probably preferred darker, more muted colors. I pulled out a dark green kimono with patterns of fans on it and laid it on the bed, studying it. After analyzing all of the parts and pockets and hidden features of the kimono that I had just learned about, I held it up to see how it folded together, then tried it on.

With the kimono draped over my body, I looked at the obi. This was the challenging part. There were a few hidden pockets in the obi, but its main purpose was to keep the kimono in place. Tied properly, it couldn't be accidentally undone. Apparently, most people had other ways of securing their kimonos but since sagents didn't stay in their clothes, a kimono and obi were the only things they wore, so tying the obi was important. Lee's instructions had indicated that practicing would only be useful if I practiced while wearing the obi, so I wrapped the obi around me, then attempted the complex knot I had read about. It fell apart.

I tapped my chip and read the instructions again, then tried again, with no more success. But this was going to be extremely important, so I kept trying, constantly checking the instructions, checking my actions, and finally it held. I gingerly tugged it to test it. It fell apart. With a moan, I sank into the bed. I was making progress, I assured myself. It was just going a lot slower than I wanted.

The door buzzed and I tensed, wondering if Lee-sama could

possibly be back. When the door opened without my permission, however, I relaxed. Only Lee would do that. And it was Lee. I remembered that he was supposed to have dinner with me and I glanced at the clock. I had spent the entire afternoon reading the files on the Drops and then practicing. I slid the kimono off and laid it on the bed. I was in Destiny clothes underneath, since I hadn't stripped for my practice, and I suddenly wondered if having clothes on under the kimono made it harder for me.

Lee approached and fingered the kimono with a smile.

"I'm glad you found this. You picked a lovely color. How are you doing?"

I kept my eyes down, realizing that this was probably what he intended to test me on. Lying would only compound the punishment for failure, however.

"Not very well," I said. "I managed to tie the obi but it won't stay."

I braced myself, wondering what the punishment would be. Nothing bad, I didn't think. Certainly nothing I couldn't handle. Actually, I had no idea what kind of punishments Lee would give. He hadn't punished me for anything yet.

"It's difficult to get the hang of," Lee said. "I'll help you after we eat."

Puzzled, I glanced up at him. He was still looking at the kimono, not at me. Then he did look at me with a smile, and gestured to the small table where we had discussed our contract the last time. It didn't seem like he was going to mention the punishment yet. Maybe he was going to wait and actually test my ability before deciding on a punishment. That would make sense. He wouldn't necessarily take my word for my inability to do something. He would want proof.

I sat across from him cautiously. The catering unit in the wall hummed as our plates were delivered, and even though I stood to retrieve them, he gestured for me to stay seated and he brought me my plate. As we had discussed earlier, there was a portion of bulgolgi and it comforted me. He had actually done what we agreed on. His food looked exotic and, like Sora, he encouraged me to try it, but it was too spicy for me. He ate with chopsticks and while I was tempted to ask for lessons, I didn't want to fail at those lessons and then fail at tying the obi as well. I would wait for a lower-risk opportunity.

We ate in silence for a few minutes, then Lee smiled.

"Do you have any questions for me?"

I considered. I had several, though many seemed like questions I didn't deserve answers to, but one involved food and that seemed appropriate enough.

"The food here is very different than in Destiny," I said hesitantly. "But I've had Japanese food before. Why is that?"

Lee's smile froze and I tensed, realizing I had asked the wrong question. It hadn't seemed like an intrusive question. It seemed like a perfectly innocuous, conversational question. Lee gestured for me to relax, chopstick in hand.

"I expected to tell you this, Gabriel, but not from this direction," he said, shaking his head. "Most of the food in the Drops is Japanese, because many of the people in the Drops are from Japan. But this part of the Drops, and my Family in particular, are not Japanese and neither is the food you like. It's Korean."

I stared at him. That was impossible. Korea was the site of the meteor strike, the site of the microbes' first impact. Korea was devastated by the microbes. People in nearby Japan were the first ones to flee to Destiny, but had stopped at the Drops, I knew from school, because they didn't realize how deadly the threat was, and the city of Destiny itself was unfinished. No one was sure it could actually sustain life. So the Japanese people inhabited the Drops and remained, even after the rest of the planet began swarming in an effort to reach Destiny, never mind Destiny's potential problems.

There was no way anyone could escape Korea in time. Once the meteor hit, the microbes started killing instantly. History class had taught me that it was absolute chaos and fear, and since no one knew how the microbes were spread, anyone suspected of being in contact with microbes was killed. That meant anyone from Korea would have been killed. Didn't it? Or had someone adapted, even then? Had someone from Korea become like a sagent, mingled with the others, and hidden in the Drops?

Lee smiled at me humorlessly. "I'm not sure what you learn about Korea in Destiny. What they teach here is bad enough, but they have to temper it because they know there are descendants of Korea in the Drops. Korea was where the meteor hit, but plenty of people escaped with the Japanese to the Drops. Maybe they carried microbes with them. Maybe they didn't. We'll never really know. Microbes don't make a person evil," he added. "You should know that. And you can't spread microbes through touch. Only by environmental exposure or deliberate injection. The Koreans who escaped did nothing wrong."

I considered. It was true. It was just such a shocking notion that someone could survive such close expose to the meteor itself without being permanently damaged. I kept my eyes lowered, as was proper, but studied Lee as much as I could. His ancestors were Korean. In Destiny, Korea was distorted into a thousand myths that I knew were impossible and wrong, but since no one knew the truth about the destroyed country, I didn't know what else to think. Koreans were incredibly powerful and could blow up distant parts of the world with a thought. They were masters of technology and lived among robots who were just like humans. They had a strict culture that valued obedience and militarism but at the same time, some of the most beautiful art and music was said to come from Korea. I had even heard a rumor that there were two Koreas, though most people didn't believe that.

I wondered how much Lee knew about his ancestor's home. More than me, certainly. More than anyone in Destiny, since no one in Destiny would believe that Korean food even existed. But records of Old Earth were notoriously faulty, and the ones down here probably weren't any better. In the mad scramble for survival, a lot of information was lost. The survivors had immediately copied down everything they knew, and most of Destiny ran on that knowledge. The first few generations in Destiny frequently faced problems when finishing construction of the city, since the slightest lapses in memory on the part of the scientists and engineers who came to Destiny translated into billions of dollars of wasted money, and often lost lives as well. Old Earth's scientific knowledge was reclaimed, but historians were always highly skeptical of anything that wasn't technical in nature.

We didn't learn Old Earth's history in school anymore, though my parents had, because the government decided there were too many gaps, too many ways that the biases of the first survivors had manipulated that history. The resulting narrative was causing too many problems for Destiny, so our history started with the meteor now. I wondered if children in the Drops knew more about Old Earth, and if their records were better.

"Why wasn't that on my chip?" I asked, hoping it was an acceptable question.

Lee smiled and gestured for me to finish eating. I obeyed as he answered. "I didn't know what your reaction would be, so I wanted to tell you in person. You seem very curious. That's good. I can give you more information if you want."

I hesitantly met his eyes and nodded, then resumed eating. He was nearly finished, I noticed. I sped up so we would finish at the same time. Oddly, he slowed down. I matched his pace, wondering if there was a reason he was lingering over the last portions of his meal. He leaned his chopsticks against his plate and I wondered if he was finished, and just not going to eat everything, in which case I was also finished, but his lips curled in a smile.

"Take your time eating, Gabriel. We're not in a rush."

I blushed and continued eating at the fastest pace I thought he would allow as he slowly scooped up his last few bites. He finished before me and I stopped when he did, but he gestured me to continue. Very uncomfortable, I tried not to scarf down my food, and instead paced myself. He clearly didn't want me rushing, but I had never been allowed to eat at my own pace in the company of someone else before. It was nerve-wracking.

Lee took my plate and returned it to the catering unit along with his plate, sliding the door shut and flicking it on to send the empty dishes back to the kitchen. After a brief whir, the unit quieted again. Lee stood there for a moment before turning to me. He gestured towards the bed where the kimono was neatly laid out.

"Let's see how far you're getting," he said. My heart sunk. Now it was time for punishment.

CHAPTER 22

IMPROVISATION

Before I could lift the kimono, he gestured at my Destiny clothes.

"It will be easier with nothing underneath," he said. "And I want to see how your thigh is healing."

I lowered my head as I quickly undressed. I had completely forgotten the injury Acron had given me the night before. It was probably gone, since I healed so quickly, but Lee didn't know that. I paused halfway through undressing, realizing Lee might have wanted me to strip rather than simply take my clothes off, but a quick glance confirmed that he simply wanted me naked, no matter how I got there. He didn't need me to prove that I could undress in Destiny clothes. I had already proven it once with Sora.

Once I was undressed, he approached and I angled my thigh so he could see where the injury had been. He laid his hand on my inner thigh and I hid a tremor. Not well enough, I realized as he glanced up at me. Oddly, it wasn't a tremor of fear. Or at least not entirely fear. I was afraid of him touching me like this, in such an intimate place, and he was lingering, too, stroking lightly along my skin because there was no mark where the dagger had been but he seemed to want to make sure he wasn't missing it.

It was mostly a tremor because I wanted him to touch me. I didn't think it was sexual longing; it was longing for comfort. He was touching me to check that I was safe. He was protecting me. No one had done that for me before. Even my parents and sister hadn't checked on my injuries like this. They were always concerned about how any injuries would affect my potential value as a sagent. Lee seemed genuinely concerned that I might still be hurt. The way his hands traced over my skin, barely enough to caress the surface, but not enough to bump against any bruises, told me clearly that he had my interests in mind as he checked me thoroughly.

"You've healed," he said slowly. "Do you always heal this quickly?"

"Yes," I said. "It was a clean cut."

Lee's eyes flicked to my palm briefly and I flushed, curving it out of his sight. No matter how comforting Lee was, I wasn't up to talking about running away yet. Lee went to the bed and picked up the kimono, sliding it over my shoulders and draping it around me. He placed the obi in my hands and gestured for me to begin as he sat on the edge of the bed to watch.

I took a breath and mentally reviewed the instructions, then carefully wound the obi and began tying the knot. I didn't go quickly, because I would mess up if I did, and I didn't try to look pretty while I tied it, because I wasn't at that level yet. I just needed to accomplish the basics to avoid punishment. Then the bar would be raised each subsequent time. I had the knot halfway done when Lee lifted his hand to stop me. I froze.

He approached and placed his right hand over my left hand, gently tugging the obi to the opposite side of where I was bringing it. I reviewed the instructions in my mind in a panic. I had been overlooking that step. I had been skipping it and that must be why I was having so much trouble with this.

Lee sat back down and gestured for me to continue. My heart pounded, but I didn't let my anxiety show. I mentally reviewed where I was in the process and continued at a slightly slower pace, wary of skipping another step. I finished with a complete knot and put my hands at my sides. Lee gestured and I approached. He tugged the knot firmly, and I braced myself for it to fall apart. It held. Somehow, that one step was indeed the cause of all of my problems.

"Good," he said. "Now show me how to strip."

I took a few steps back, again hiding my nerves. I had read about how to undress, but since I hadn't successfully tied the obi, I hadn't had a chance to practice this. I smiled shyly, letting one hand trace from my cheek down my neck, then pulled against the opening of the kimono as the instructions said. I continued following the instructions, for the most part, but I of course read Lee's body as well and I discovered several strategies that weren't in the instructions but worked quite well, such as turning my body to hide my exposed chest, then twisting back just as I released the knot in the obi. Lee had a faint smile as I improvised and when I was naked, he nodded in approval.

"You learn very quickly, and have good instincts. Keep practicing the more mechanical aspects of tying the obi, but I don't think anything else will give you trouble."

I nodded, pleased to have done so well. There was no mention of punishment, so perhaps there would be no penalty for my mistake in tying the obi, or perhaps my skill in improvising while stripping outweighed that mistake. It was one reason I learned to improvise: sometimes when I overperformed in one area, Acron was less likely to punish me for underperforming in other areas.

Lee gestured for me to dress in Destiny clothes and I obeyed. He didn't seem to care how I dressed, so I simply put my clothes on without making a show and then sat beside him on the edge of the bed as he patted the spot beside him. With Acron or a target, that would have been an invitation to more, but with Lee, I was pretty sure it just meant he wanted to sit next to me. I sat obediently, looking at his hands because I wasn't allowed to look directly at him unless he were addressing me. He took my hands in his.

"I have news about your old chip," he said.

I glanced up at him briefly, puzzled. It was taking an extremely long time to transfer the information, but then again, I had never transferred information from one chip to another, so maybe it was a complex process. My first chip was lost, probably destroyed, and I started my second chip fresh. Luckily, my sister and parents had all of my important information and transferred it to me once I had my new chip, so the only things I lost were my personal additions: a few playlists, some books I had loaded, and other random bits of data that had appealed to me over the years. My parents taught me to keep everything truly personal in my head, since my agency could technically access everything in my chip, so I never relied on it the way many of my schoolmates did.

"Something happened," Lee admitted, sounding reluctant. "When your chip was first removed. It self-destructed. We've been trying to extract data from it, but the technicians have given up. There's nothing left."

I gasped, my mind instantly going to the one file I cared about, the one file I couldn't lose. Thoughts of the other information I lost flitted through my mind, especially since my family wasn't here to fill in the gaps, but nothing mattered as much as that one file. The man had said that no one else could read it; was it possible that removing my chip had triggered something in that file to prevent anyone from reading it, and the entire chip was destroyed? What would he think if I saw him again, without the file and without having read the file? I supposed I didn't need his protection anymore, but I did want his regard. I rubbed my palm nervously.

"Do they know why?" I asked, uncertain if I really wanted to know. If that file had destroyed the chip, then it had probably also alerted the man to its destruction. He would think I was dead. But perhaps, I thought, perhaps he was already dead, and it didn't matter anyway.

"Do you have any theories?" Lee asked.

I glanced at him again. He was expressionless. I lowered my gaze.

"I had a file on my chip," I said nervously. "I wasn't supposed to open it."

"No," Lee said, stroking my hand. "It wasn't that. It was something in the design of the chip itself, nothing on the chip. Is that the file you asked about earlier? What was it?"

I shrugged, hoping he would let it slide. He hadn't pushed on several other important issues, so maybe this would be another one.

"What else was on your chip?" Lee asked, and I relaxed slightly. He was going to move on to something else. Something related, but he wouldn't push when he knew I didn't want to talk.

"Just what's on everyone's chip," I said. "I didn't keep much of my own stuff there."

"You're sure your agency didn't have information they didn't want anyone else to know?"

"Well, my medical history would have been on it," I considered. "And my microbe count. No one was supposed to know that."

"They had to realize if your chip was removed, the person removing it would surely find that out," Lee said. "What else? Your family history, I'm sure. You do have an unusual family history. Is that something they wouldn't want people to know about?"

"I don't know," I said. "I never actually had access to a lot of what was on my chip. I knew it was there and could see it, but not access it. If there was something in my family history other than what I've told you, I don't know what it is. I haven't kept any secrets from you."

Lee's lips quirked and my eyes darted towards him. He caught my chin in his hand and gazed at me, lips curved in a half-smile.

"You haven't kept secrets, perhaps," Lee said. "But you also don't share them."

I blushed, thinking of the file I had just refused to talk about, about hiding my hand so he wouldn't ask me about running away, about all of the things I didn't want him to know about me. I was keeping secrets from him. But I would tell him eventually. I just didn't want to tell him yet.

Lee stroked my cheek, his eyes amused. "Why don't you tell me a secret about yourself, then, Gabriel," he said in a soft voice. "What is something that no one knows about you, that you've never told anyone else in your life?"

CHAPTER 23

FATAL SECRET

I ducked out of his grasp without thinking and turned my head away from him. Then I froze, realizing I had just deliberately pulled away from my handler when he was touching me. That was not allowed. I couldn't even imagine what Acron would do. Lee grabbed my chin again and forced me to face him. He was expressionless.

"You realize your mistake," Lee said. "Your punishment is to answer my question honestly."

My eyes widened. I was tempted to bolt from his hands, from the bed, from the room. There was only one thing I had never shared with anyone before, and I couldn't tell him. I told my sister and parents almost everything, and I confided in my handlers more than I liked, though not always by my choice. Some things I let slip in coded conversations with other sagents I knew I'd never see again. Only one thing had I kept secret, sacred, telling no one, barely even acknowledging it to myself. He could not know.

"I can't tell you," I whispered. "I'll tell you about the file."

"No," Lee said. He stroked my cheek again. It was meant as a soothing gesture, but it wasn't helping. "You'll tell me the secret you're thinking of, the one you don't want to tell me. The one that made you openly disobey me like that, because I doubt many things could cause you to pull out of your handler's grasp without considering the consequences. Whatever secret it is, I need to know, so it doesn't affect you in the future, so no one can blackmail you."

"No one knows it," I said, a little desperate. "No one ever will know it. I've told no one, I never will."

"You'll tell me."

It was a command and I stared at him in dismay. This was my punishment and I should be grateful it wasn't physical punishment. If I had turned my head when Acron was touching me, he would have tortured me for days. But he probably would have also forgotten the conversation that caused me to disobey, and there would have been no follow up. I suddenly found myself longing for that kind of punishment instead of this, which would inevitably end my relationship with Lee. He would never look at me the same way again, my career would be destroyed, my life would be over.

I lowered my eyes. "I'll take whatever punishment you give me."

"Your punishment is to tell me," Lee repeated sharply. "I'm not going to punish you in any other way."

I glared at him, then instantly lowered my eyes again. I was making things worse. Glaring wasn't open disobedience, but I could still be punished for it. Lee ran his thumb across my cheekbone.

"Does this have to do with your first agency?" he asked gently. "I know you ran away. I know you tore your chip out. You won't surprise me with anything."

Heat flushed my cheeks. Of course he knew. It was obvious what had happened, even though I wasn't ready to talk about it. I wondered if I could share that secret and pretend it was the one I didn't want to tell him. Could I get away with it? Did I want to get away with it? I would feel guilty every time I looked at Lee if I lied to him now. I couldn't lie, even if it were my only escape. He was my handler, and I respected him. I never had any problems lying to Acron or even my second handler, but Lee was different. I would never lie to him.

"No," I said. "It isn't about them."

164

I took a deep breath. If this were to be my punishment, so be it. It would be worse punishment than Lee intended but since there was no way to tell him that without telling him the secret itself, there was no way to get him to back down. He had set the punishment. I would obey. I met his eyes, more frightened than I had been in a long time, almost as frightened as when I had been running from Acron, clutching my bleeding palm with only a vague idea of how to escape.

"I don't want to be a sagent," I said simply.

He blinked in surprise, then his brow furrowed. I knew it wasn't anything like he was expecting. He had said I couldn't surprise him, but I had. It would probably take a few seconds for the implications of my statement to sink in, and I lowered my eyes. I didn't want to see his eyes change, see his disgust and disbelief. I didn't want to see his dismissal.

What would happen to me now? I would remain a sagent, of course, but he would know I didn't want to be one. He would be hesitant to use me for anything important, and I would be trapped in the type of meaningless jobs I had come to despise. Brief missions, hopefully, to men or possibly women that I would sleep with and steal information from, but the emphasis would always be on the sex. I didn't think Lee would deliberately give me any brutal targets and this shouldn't change that, but it would just continue to be the sort of bland existence I had scraped by on for the past two years. I honestly couldn't fathom the thought of more than a few more years of this, but I would survive. Perhaps, in time, Lee would trust me again. He had an extended lifespan as well, I remembered. Maybe in a few decades he would put this behind him and trust me.

"If you don't want to be a sagent," Lee said, clearly not quite understanding that concept yet, "then why are you one?"

"I was purchased at birth," I said, still unable to meet his eyes or see what he thought. "My parents negotiated for my sister to have the right to choose, but they weren't allowed to negotiate on me. I was always going to be a sagent."

Lee inhaled sharply and took a moment before asking his

next question.

"If you don't want to be a sagent, then what do you want to be?"

I lowered my head further, ashamed that I had no good answer.

"I don't know anything else," I whispered. I didn't want to add that I had never let myself consider any other options, because there were no other options for me. Dreaming of being something else would give me false hope and might interfere with my job. Perhaps that was why he was asking, I realized.

"I don't need anything else," I said, looking up at him and clutching his hands, hoping he knew how earnest I was. He was expressionless again, but I could tell he was masking very strong emotions. "I'm a sagent. I will always be a sagent. You don't need to worry about me doing my job."

Lee stroked my cheek again, very slowly. It wasn't sensual, but it also wasn't comforting as most of his touches were. Or if he meant it to be comforting, he wasn't expressing it well. He seemed to be focused on shielding his emotions, and I realized that in his previous touches, I had felt comforted because he was using his microbes to convey comfort. Unconsciously, I was sure, since all sagents used microbes unconsciously, and Lee probably had even less experience using his microbes than sagents, but feeling the difference in his touch now, I was positive. He manipulated his body every bit as much as I did. But nothing about his previous touches ever indicated that he was lying or conveying anything he didn't actually feel. Maybe his microbes just strengthened his existing emotions and desires.

"When did you realize you didn't want to be a sagent?"

I looked to the side, unwilling to look at him once again. I knew what he wanted me to answer. He wanted me to say that my first handler had scarred me, that I had been so abused it made me hate being a sagent. Because that was something he could fix. He was already fixing it. But it wasn't my answer, and there was no way to fix my answer.

"I've never wanted to be a sagent," I said.

I thought back to the day when I fully realized my future. My parents had never hidden it from me, and there was no moment of revelation on their side. My sister and I always knew what their jobs were, why they weren't both home, why one of them was always working and what that person was doing. We never knew specifics about their jobs, of course, but we knew if they were on a long-term assignment or a series of short assignments, and we could tell that even though the remaining parent missed and longed for the other deeply, there was no resentment or jealousy. Sex with others was simply part of the job.

My life at home was completely unlike any of my friends and my parents were raising me with very different values. But my parents also raised me to value privacy, and to never speak about anything that happened at home and with our family to anyone else. The few times I mentioned things about my parents or revealed my morality on subjects like sex, my friends and their families thought I was joking. I lived in a good neighborhood, with quality people, who would never dream of giving their bodies to others in exchange for anything besides love. They taught their children very strongly not to experiment with sex, and never to trade sexual favors no matter what they might gain. My parents taught me the same, of course, but they also taught me that preserving my body was temporary, until my agency took control of me. My agency would be my everything, they taught me, and I had to keep my body perfect until they took me.

My sister had other dreams and aspirations, but when she was tested for microbes and realized that she could become a sagent, she counted that among her dreams and eventually freely chose it. No one forced her, my parents hadn't pressured her one way or another, and all agencies were free to bid on her. But my parents never allowed me to dream about anything else. When I was very little, I would sometimes talk about the usual jobs kids wanted: Earth explorer, doctor, athlete. My parents would quickly dismiss those ideas, telling me in no uncertain terms that my future was already determined. They never specifically said I would be a sagent, but it was inferred.

And then, when I was eight, I finally asked my father if I was going to be a sagent. He said yes without hesitation, without any indication that he had worried about this moment, even though it was a pivotal moment for me. He didn't say anything else, just returned to cooking dinner for me and my sister as I thought about what I knew about his life and my mother's life. All of the things they had modeled to us over the years, all of the things they had taught us. And I compared it to everything my friends knew, everything their parents modeled. I realized I didn't want to be a sagent. I wanted to be like my friends. I asked my father if I had a choice, and he said no just as simply. I never asked again, and never allowed my discontent to show.

They began telling me more about life as a sagent after that, about the rules handlers followed, the rules sagents followed. Some of it comforted me. Some of it terrified me. They seemed to understand the terror, but always assured me that my handler would take care of me. They always assured me that I would be treasured. But even then I had my doubts, because it was clear how little power I would have as a sagent if I wasn't treasured. They taught me to hide my feelings, to hide my opinions, to keep from vanishing, all without realizing that they were teaching me that being who I was somehow made me incompatible with being a sagent. If I expressed myself, they told me, I would vanish. But what was I, unless I was myself? I would learn, they told me.

And in time, I did learn. I became what they wanted. I became a sagent. But I had never been able to destroy my identity the way they said was the safest. I couldn't even hide myself very well all the time, though they assured me it would get easier throughout my lifespan. My agency wanted my body and an obedient, intelligent mind, my parents told me frequently. They didn't want me, so I had to convince them that I didn't exist.

Everything they told me was in stark contrast to my education and my friends, all of which encouraged me to explore who I was, to embrace my individuality. I often had trouble reconciling the two, and it was one reason Acron had been so rough with me. My parents had explained it as they helped me recover from his abuse. He wanted to help me get rid of myself, but I couldn't. My second handler hadn't even noticed me inside my body until I disobeyed, and though her punishments were less severe than Acron's, her intent was the same.

I knew what they were doing wasn't bad, for a sagent. Sagents didn't survive long if they were independent and free-spirited, so it was up to the handlers to break their spirits early. I thought mine had been broken by Acron, but I had run away. I thought it had been subdued by my second handler, but I had run away again. Now Lee knew for sure that I existed, he knew I didn't want to be a sagent, and he would be obliged to get rid of me. His previous plan had probably just been to strengthen my ability to guard against myself, not destroy me, but now he had no choice. I was a threat to my value.

CHAPTER 24
SHARING SECRETS

Lee was silent for a long time, stroking my cheek idly and seemingly deep in thought. I wondered what his plans for me would be. What restrictions would he place on me, and how would this change things? Would he still bother training me, as he was planning, or just send me into the field, since he knew there was no point? I wasn't sure which I would prefer. If he trained me, it meant he had faith in me still, but if he didn't, I could start repaying my debt faster, and would feel less in debt to the yakuza. I thought of Lee-sama and knew the less debt I incurred, the better. But I would rather be in debt than lose Lee's faith.

I had never really cared about what someone thought of me before, not like this. Normally, I cared about their thoughts only to prevent myself from getting hurt. I needed to stay on everyone's good sides to avoid pain, so I was constantly aware of what impression I made. Even with my family, I never worried, because I assumed that they would always love me no matter what happened. But with Lee, I was actually, genuinely frightened that he no longer valued me. If he no longer thought I had any value, if he thought there was no point training me, then it meant I didn't have any value other than monetary.

"You pose an interesting puzzle, Gabriel," Lee finally said. "I'm not sure what to do with you."

I didn't dare look at him. He wasn't condemning me, not yet.

A puzzle wasn't negative, after all, though it certainly wasn't positive. And he hadn't decided on a course of action, so he hadn't ruled out anything.

"Until I decide how to deal with this in the long term, we'll continue as normal," he said. "Are there any other secrets like this that I need to know?"

"No," I said quickly, unsure whether or not his decision to delay was a good sign or not. I needed to reassure him, though.

Lee squeezed my chin and I met his eyes. He was still expressionless, but I could see an edge of pain in his dark eyes. I was startled. Had I hurt him somehow? Had I disappointed him so much that he was hurt?

"I want you to take the rest of the evening to think about everything else I need to know about you," Lee said. "Tomorrow morning, I'm going to have breakfast with you, and you're going to share your secrets. All of them. I won't hurt you. The rest of the day will be busy, so you need to get sleep tonight as well. Can you do that?"

I nodded, and he released me. He patted my shoulder, and I felt a flicker of comfort and reassurance. Then he left.

I got ready for bed slowly, going through my routine automatically. Tomorrow, I would have my usual products, but there was still an element of strangeness to everything as I washed my hair with unfamiliar shampoo, brushed my teeth with unfamiliar toothpaste. If Lee were letting everything continue, then he would give me everything I requested. He wouldn't hold anything back as punishment. He hadn't mentioned any punishment, but he hadn't ruled it out, either. He hadn't decided. I would just have to wait and see.

As I lay in bed, I tried to think of what Lee would ask me in the morning. I would have to tell him about Acron and my first agency. About running away. I would have to tell him about my second agency, and the man who had given me the file. I shivered, thinking of the people I had killed, and the one person I had refused to kill. I might have to tell him about that. If I didn't tell him, and he found out later, I would be punished for sure. I needed to tell him everything he might possibly find out about, so that nothing would surprise him in the future. Did that really mean everything, though? It would take a long time to tell him everything, but I would take that time if necessary. I knew, without question, that he had no more patience with me. From now on, I would face punishment. And while his punishments weren't physical, they were devastating.

When I opened my eyes, I took a long moment to examine my body before getting up. The extra microbes I had gained didn't seem to be doing anything different than my original microbes, but as I scanned my body, I realized I had heightened awareness of my body, and of the room around me. Once I learned to control my new microbes, I would probably have increased control as a sagent as well. Perhaps it was good I would be training before returning to the field, so that I could accustom myself to my new microbe levels.

He would be coming late in the morning, after my workout, so I went through my usual morning routine, then considered what to wear. He hadn't specified and Destiny clothes were my preference, so I pulled those on. I prepared myself as if I would be going in public, because I wasn't sure what my day would hold. Lee had said it would be busy, but hadn't specified. So I prepared myself as if I would be on display, which took quite a bit longer than if I were just going to see my handler. I always had to look good, but handlers were used to a certain level of informality. Lee hadn't really seen me fully made up. Only when I had been working the party, and he had only seen me beforehand briefly to make sure I was ready. This would be his first good look at me when I was fully prepared, and I took my time as I styled my hair and patted makeup on my cheeks.

Once I was finished, I waited on the chaise for only a few minutes before Lee came in. I hadn't meant to cut it that close. I stood and bowed slightly, keeping my eyes lowered as I waited for his reaction. He studied me, then reached out and touched my shoulder. I looked up at him and he smiled.

"You look beautiful," he said. "Are you ready?"

"Yes," I said. I wasn't, not really, but I had no choice. He seemed to be in a good mood, and I was pleased that my appearance had helped. I would do my best to keep him in this mood, no matter how many secrets I had to share.

Lee led me to the table and our breakfast appeared. He served me, though I tried to preempt him again, and we ate in silence. After he put the plates away, he led me to the couch and set me beside him. He relaxed into the couch, and pulled me against him. I tensed and checked his arousal, but it was the same as always. I leaned against him. He probably knew this would be uncomfortable for me and wanted to put me at ease, but didn't realize that physical contact like this while talking about Acron wasn't a good way to do it. Still, he wasn't trying to hurt me.

"Start when you're ready," he said. I gulped. I had been hoping for more direction than that.

"How much do you need to know?" I asked nervously.

"Everything," he said, squeezing my shoulder. "No secrets."

"I mean, how much detail?" I clarified. "There's so much."

"Whatever you feel comfortable sharing," he said. "But don't keep anything back."

He really wasn't helping. He was probably trying to give me flexibility, but I wasn't used to flexibility. I wanted rules. I wanted him to ask me direct questions, so I could answer them, and not have to worry about leaving things out. I didn't want to have to think of things myself. I wasn't used to thinking for myself. I was used to taking orders.

Hesitantly, I told him about my first night with GovTech. He already knew the basics, but he didn't stop me. I told him about Acron coming into my room, and then about my efforts the next day to get people to listen to me, and how those efforts had backfired. I told him about the next few weeks, when I attempted to resist Acron, before I gave up hope. But I didn't go into much detail as I didn't like to remember it. I gave simple, declarative statements of what I tried, and what they did, what he did, in retaliation. Lee didn't say anything, but I could feel his support as he held me. It wasn't as uncomfortable being held by him as I thought.

I told Lee about the rest of my training in just a few sentences, as it passed with a blur for the most part. Once I gave up, once I broke, everything fell into a pattern of learning and abuse. There wasn't much to say. My transition to full-time was merciless. Normally, sagents were eased into work through agency jobs, which I could tell Lee didn't like from the way his hand tightened on me, but I was thrown into a real job with a brutal target Acron knew I couldn't fully handle, leading to immediate punishment. And then it was just about escaping punishment and pain. I gave a few details, a few specific jobs that I thought Lee should know about, including the people I had killed, but mostly passed over my time at GovTech as quickly as possible.

When I reached the night when I snapped, I paused. Lee rubbed my shoulder. I wasn't looking at him, nor was I at a good angle to do so. I didn't want to see his reaction to this. I could feel his support and knew he was on my side against Acron, but I didn't want to risk seeing the opposite in his eyes.

"That night," I said slowly, "Something happened. I don't know what. After he left, as usual, I just couldn't do it anymore. I started walking. I was allowed to walk, though anyone could grab me if they wanted. I stayed hidden. And I saw a grate leading to the sewer, and realized I could escape. It had never occurred to me before."

I blushed and pressed against him. "I don't know why I never realized it. But I knew they could track me. There was a trash heap nearby with metal shards, so I ripped my palm open and took out my chip, then went into the sewer and ran. I didn't know where I was going, but there was light and I followed it. But when I got there, there were bars. I could see Destiny beyond, but there were bars blocking me."

I shook my head, remembering my desperation. "I starting slamming into the bars, using my microbes to weaken the metal, I did everything I could to get through and finally, finally they broke. I got through. I'd been in the sewers for hours, and I ran for hours more before I reached the city. And then I had to blend in, even though my hand was bleeding. I finally made it to one of my family's safehouses and told them where I was."

Lee's hand on my shoulder was soothing and I took a moment before continuing. "My sister found me first, and helped me with my hand. It was infected and I was close to death. I nearly lost my hand. My parents eventually came. Between the three of them, they healed me. I knew I needed an agency to protect me, and my sister liked her agency, so I approached them. We requested her handler. But agencies get to pick, and they assigned me to a completely different part of the agency. I barely saw her after that."

I took a deep breath, and continued my descriptions, telling him about my life at my second agency. I told him about my disobedience and the file with a blush, and I could tell that he was curious about the file. I hesitated before telling him that the man had offered me protection, but I did. I didn't mention that his protection would be gone now that the file was gone, even though I was keenly aware of it as I spoke. I didn't need anyone's protection other than Lee's, I assured myself. But Lee hadn't made up his mind about me, and there was no guarantee what he would decide. I might need the man's protection if life here became unmanageable.

"What are you thinking, Gabriel?" Lee asked, and I gave a start. I had stopped talking when I considered the implications of losing the file. Just briefly, but he noticed. And he had said no secrets. I shut my eyes.

"If I need help from him, in the future," I said, unwilling to specify why I might need help, "I don't think he'll give it to me anymore."

"But you don't know if he's alive," Lee said slowly. I shook my head. I didn't know, but I could find him if I needed to. Without my agency's interference, I could theoretically track down any of my targets. "What is his name?" Lee continued. "What was his job?"

I hadn't mentioned specifics, just as I hadn't with any of the jobs I had talked about. They were private, between me and my agencies, and he hadn't pushed. This was private, too, though for different reasons. I didn't want Lee to find him and prevent me from contacting him if I ever did run away. But if I lied or hid knowledge from Lee now, then the chances of me having to run away rose exponentially. If I told the truth and trusted him, as I had been doing, perhaps I wouldn't need to run away. Very cautiously, I told him. He nodded and patted my shoulder, then seemed to be waiting for me to continue. There would be no immediate consequences to that information. I was relieved.

I told Lee how my handler cracked down on me after my disobedience was discovered, and then I reached the job I didn't want to tell him about, the one my handler forced me to take. Tricked me into taking, really. She offered to give me another job with the man I adored in exchange for doing a job for her, a job I wouldn't receive information about until after I agreed to it. I briefly told Lee about how she tricked me, how she made me agree, how she knew I would agree to anything in exchange for seeing him again, and then I stopped.

"They wanted me to finish the job before I could see him. I was supposed to kill someone, and bring back her chip. Her hand, too," I added, my lips twisting. "I didn't kill people like that but the target insisted on more proof than just the chip. I had already agreed, so I had to do it. But when I tracked her down, when I faced her, my instincts didn't trigger. I couldn't do it."

I remembered the moment, when I had cornered her in an alley, when I came out of the shadows and she held up her hands to defend herself, which should have triggered me to attack. But I couldn't, because her arms were full of microbes. She was full of microbes. She was a sagent. They had sent me to kill a sagent. I approached her without attacking and her fear lessened, though she knew why I was there. She knew I had to kill her.

"Why couldn't you do it?" Lee asked gently.

"She was a sagent," I whispered. "I talked to her. She knew how to escape, if I could buy her time. She insisted that I take her chip, and her arm. She told me she would survive, that she knew a doctor who could help her before she bled out. So I- I cut off her arm, and took it back."

Lee squeezed me tightly as I shivered. "I thought it was over," I continued. "I begged my handler not to do that to me again and she agreed. But the next day, I was called to meet with the target again. The sagent was there. Her body. She had been killed, and they knew I hadn't done it. My handler knew I hadn't done it."

"That was it," I said. "My other assignment was taken away. All of my assignments were taken away for a while, and I had almost no choice after that. She would give me a few preselected jobs and I could pick between them. I was used in training, for a month or so," I added, realizing suddenly that he might want to know this, since he might potentially want to use me in training as well. "But I got through it, and was back to regular jobs. I saw my sister again a few months later. And then, it's just been regular jobs until she asked if I would be interested in going to the Drops for a job."

I shrugged. "I was curious. She knew I would be. She knew I would take the job. I didn't know why she gave me the job for a long time, until Acron showed up here. But I'm pretty sure she sent me here as bait, to lure him out. Maybe the goal was to catch him and keep me safe. I don't know. But she didn't warn me about him."

I told Lee about the judge, and very briefly about Zada, though he already knew about that. I mentioned that she had helped me find a safe place but gave no specifics. I wouldn't betray the people at the bed and breakfast, even if it potentially alienated me from Lee. They would protect me. I still had some protection if I ran away. I told him about how my handler had used my chip to contact me, and then how the enforcers had surrounded me and I turned to him. Then I stopped. He knew the rest.

Lee waited a few moments, then leaned and brushed his lips against my head. I was surprised, but there was nothing sexual about the gesture.

"Thank you, Gabriel," he said. "That helps me more than you know."

I wondered how, and if, he would use it as blackmail against me. He now knew what I did and didn't like, and had a ton of information that could make my life miserable. But he wasn't like that. I didn't know what his ultimate decision about me would be, but I didn't think he would hurt me. My life might become unbearable again, I might need to run away again, but he would not deliberately hurt me.

"And Gabriel," he added, shifting our positions so that I met his eyes. "I realize the previous times you've run away, you've acted impulsively. But you've had plenty of cause. If you ever feel like running away might be an option, you will tell me, and give me a chance to change your situation."

"Yes," I whispered. So he knew I was worried about having to run away, but he thought he could fix it so I wouldn't want to run away? I wasn't sure what to make of that.

"I mean it, Gabriel," Lee insisted. "If you're unhappy at all, you need to tell me."

"I will," I said. He did mean it, I realized. He wanted to know. But there was always a certain level of unhappiness in a sagent's life, so I would have to figure out specifics. I still had to make sure he knew I was reliable as a sagent, that I could handle my job. I needed him to trust me, and he wouldn't, if he knew how miserable being a sagent made me on a daily basis.

CHAPTER 25

UNEXPECTED TARGET

L ee stroked a hand across my cheek and looked pleased. I knew that despite pouring my heart and past out, I still looked flawless. My eyes had probably grown a little red while speaking, but my body had been under control the entire time, and I looked perfect now. I wondered if the additional microbes helped with that. Lee circled me, and I wondered if my clothing were appropriate. He hadn't mentioned that I was in the wrong clothes, but now I wondered, as he tugged my sleeve gently.

"Choose a kimono and change into it," he said. "You'll be wearing traditional garb today."

I nodded. He hadn't mentioned that my current clothes were a mistake, and I was grateful. I went to the closet and chose a pale blue kimono with white dragons on it. It was a lighter color than most of the others but it was beautiful. Lee didn't say anything when I pulled it out. I set it on the bed and quickly undressed, then reached for it. Lee stopped me and I froze, wondering what I had done wrong.

"Show me how to dress," he instructed.

I relaxed. I hadn't messed up. He just wanted a display. I remembered what I had learned about dressing and added a bit of improvisation, but as I tied the obi I started to make the same mistake I had made before. I caught myself quickly and covered well, but he noticed. I didn't think it detracted from my display, however. When I was dressed, he tugged the obi to check its security and nodded.

"Keep practicing," he said simply. "Now come with me. I'm not sure whether you should think of this as training or as a job, given your history with each, but I'm bringing you to a target that you will seduce. However, I will be coaching you if you need it."

I nodded, confused. Still, it wasn't my place to ask questions. He had told me what I needed to know and if I needed help on the job, he would apparently be there as a coach. I followed him out of the room into a new hallway. He led me through several doors until we were back in the entrance hall. I hesitated and he glanced back, returning to my side and taking my hand.

"We're not going far, and we'll be very well protected," he assured me. "We know everyone to watch for."

I briefly wondered who he meant besides Acron, but then I realized my previous agency would be looking for me as well. I wasn't quite as worried about them, but only because I had never really seen how cruel they could be. I had only seen flashes of it. They had never fully turned against me, as they would if they retook me now. I swallowed hard, but followed Lee without a word. He wouldn't let anything happen to me. I was too valuable. I hoped.

We went through the neighborhood and I looked around curiously. This was my first chance to see a residential area, and I wondered if I would see an animal. A pet, I corrected myself. I scoured the area as we walked. There were several people walking around, though many of them walked with the smooth glide I recognized from the people who had shown up to defend me from my previous agency's enforcers. They were there for my protection, or for the general protection of the neighborhood. The others were probably locals, dressed in kimonos and a few suits. But no signs of animals as we walked.

We turned to a large, traditional house and I caught a glimpse of a small object darting across the steps. I gasped and took a few steps forward, straining to see it as long as I could.

Lee glanced at me, puzzled, then looked after the animal with a small smile.

"You've never seen a cat before, have you?"

"A cat?" I repeated. I hadn't seen it well enough to identify what kind of animal it had been. I supposed once you knew all of the types, it was easy to spot. I thought of the pointy-eared creatures I had heard about in stories, and the huge, immense creatures that used to roam Earth.

"It was so small," I said.

"I hadn't realized you would be so curious," Lee said, clearly amused. "I'll introduce you to some of the neighborhood pets later today."

I couldn't hide my delight as I beamed at him, wondering what kinds of animals I would be meeting. Did the pets belong to a person, I wondered, or the entire neighborhood? His wording was unclear, because the notes I had read indicated that individuals owned pets but he was implying the neighborhood did, but perhaps I would be meeting the famous pets in the neighborhood. I didn't know how it worked. As we entered the brick building, I cast a final glance in the direction the cat had gone. My curiosity had never been rewarded before, I didn't think. It was always punished. No matter what decision Lee reached about me in the future, he would always be a better handler than my previous handlers. I would never regret turning to him.

We entered the house and were surrounded by guards, but since Lee didn't tense, neither did I. The guards seemed to be from two different groups: some were probably yakuza, but I didn't know who the others might be. There was a clear uneasiness between the two groups, though, even though they were mingled. They might work together, but they clearly didn't trust each other. I was led to a small room with only two guards, one from each group. One of the walls was clear and looked into a bedroom with a man, and I realized it was an observation room where Lee would watch me seduce the man inside. I wondered why I was here, as I had never been in one of these rooms before. Then the man in the attached room turned, and I recognized the judge. I paled and turned to Lee, who was watching me closely.

I wanted to say something but felt frozen. This was Lee's decision, not mine. He had indicated that I could see the judge again, but I hadn't actually expected it, certainly not so soon. It was too dangerous. I looked at the guards and realized who the second group of guards were, and why they didn't fully trust the yakuza. The judge had worked with the yakuza for most of his career so they wouldn't be on bad terms, I didn't think, but they were officers of the law and the yakuza were criminals.

"Is this all right?" Lee asked, taking my arm and staring at me. "Look at me."

I met his eyes and nodded hesitantly, then glanced at the guards. "Is it safe?"

"He can't hurt you," Lee reassured me.

I shook my head. "No, will he be safe? They'll be tracking him. They'll know."

"We know the risks. He doesn't know who you are yet, but he knows the risks of coming into yakuza territory right now. In addition to his own people, our people will be protecting him for as long as he needs it. He's a valuable asset."

I nodded. The yakuza wouldn't want to lose such a powerful political ally. They would protect him. Lee took my hand and led me to a sliding door leading into the bedroom. My task was to seduce the judge, and it wouldn't be hard. I also knew, now, that I would be learning how to control my lust, since that was what I had struggled with last time with the judge. I wasn't sure how Lee would coach me, but I would do my best. My new microbes would help, I was sure.

We entered the room, and I kept my eyes politely averted. He had seemed to like how submissive I was last time. I heard him gasp as he recognized me and did glance up briefly to see his reaction. He was shocked, and angry. That wasn't good. I had thought he would be pleased to see me. He would be harder to seduce if he thought I had tricked him. Luckily, I could still sense a high level of arousal from him, in addition to that strange anger. Harder, but not impossible.

I waited, though, because Lee was there and I wasn't allowed to act until he gave me permission. From his stance, I knew that he didn't want me to do anything. He seemed surprised by the judge's reaction, and there was silence until the judge finally spoke.

"I knew you must have him," the judge said. "But how dare you bring him to me?"

"If you're opposed to training my sagent," Lee began, but the judge appeared puzzled and gestured for him to stop.

"Training?"

"That is why you're here," Lee said. "My invitation was clear."

"He's fully trained."

"Not to my standards," Lee said.

The judge studied me, then Lee. He wasn't angry anymore, but he did seem confused.

"That's really why I'm here? Why he's here? You didn't want me to see him for any other reason?"

"What other reason are you thinking?"

The judge glanced at the wall leading to the observation room. From this side, it appeared a normal wall. It was impossible to tell that there were people on the other side, but he clearly knew we were being watched. Lee strode across to the edge of the wall, flipped a nearly invisible switch, and returned to his place at my side.

"It's private, but they'll worry if we take too long."

The judge nodded.

"I'm sure you know his agency has been searching for him. They're desperate," he added, eyeing me curiously. "They've been hounding me for any information. I thought perhaps you were trying to send a message to them."

"No," Lee said. "I've taken too many steps to keep him hidden. They probably know the yakuza found him, but they know nothing of the yakuza. I invited you because he enjoyed you. There's a risk, of course, because I know his agency is in contact with you, but I believe you'll keep his presence here a secret."

"You stole him," the judge pointed out. "Why wouldn't I want to return him to his agency?"

I shifted, frightened, and glanced at Lee. It hadn't occurred to me that the judge would want to tell my agency where I was. But Lee placed his hand on my shoulder as if to reassure me.

"Ask him what he wants before you act," Lee said simply. "You can ask after I leave, if you think my presence will influence his answer. But if you have been in contact with his agency, then I doubt you really believe he's better off with them."

The judge considered me as I shifted again, shyly meeting his eyes and wondering if he would ask. A small smile curled his handsome lips.

"You enjoyed me?" he asked.

I let myself blush, knowing my seduction was starting. Would it be good to speak, or seem too embarrassed to speak? I threaded my fingers together and looked down as if overcome with shyness. I wasn't sure what words he wanted, and silence worked just as well. The judge chuckled.

"Well, I have no complaints helping you train at all. But your agency has given me a message for you, in case I ever found you. It's best if I give it to you after we train, I think," he said, then looked at Lee. "But don't let him leave without receiving the message."

Lee nodded, then went to the wall and flipped the switch again, reopening communication between the rooms. He glanced at the judge.

"For now, no specific instructions. Your past performance indicates that you'll do what you need to do. After this, I'll come in and give him instructions."

The judge nodded, and Lee left the room. The judge turned to me with a wide smile and gestured for me to approach. I obeyed, falling into his arms and tilting my head to gaze into his eyes. I was actually looking forward to this.

CHAPTER 26
LOSS OF CONTROL

I leaned against the judge and inhaled deeply, sensing what he wanted me to do next. I let one hand trace up his arm, against his shoulder, gently brushing against the little places that would start arousing him as I went. I stroked his neck and his chin, tilting my own head back as I invited him to kiss me with my body and my eyes. He didn't resist, wrapping his arms tightly around me as his tongue tangled with mine, dominating my mouth. I invited him deeper.

We kissed for a long time as I stroked him inside and out, sparking the sensitive spots in his body that I could already feel putting him into overdrive. He was hard against me and I was pleased. I had been worried at his anger, but he wasn't angry at me. He just thought Lee had tricked him. We broke out of the kiss with a gasp and I placed my hand on his chest. Time to move to the bed, but I'd see if he wanted anything first. Men often did, and I would give him anything he wanted.

I had no requirements with this, so I wasn't required to follow any pattern or force anything. As with Sora, I normally spent time sucking men off before letting them fuck me, but if he wanted to skip that kind of foreplay, I would let him. It wouldn't make a difference in the kind of training Lee wanted. I wouldn't really get aroused until he was inside of me, so anything before that was for his benefit only. I'd certainly give it to him, though.

The judge stroked my cheek and winked at me.

"Have you learned how to undress in your kimono yet, gorgeous?" he asked.

"Perhaps you could help me a little," I murmured.

I thought it was the right choice. The judge enjoyed being in control and enjoyed touching me, and this would give him a chance to do both. He would have enjoyed watching me strip, too, but this was more intimate.

I gently guided his hand to the collar of my kimono. I had never stripped with someone in a kimono before, nor had I read about how to do it, but I could figure it out. And if I messed up, then he could help me for real. This was training, I reminded myself. It wouldn't be the end of the world if I wasn't perfect.

With the judge's help, I removed the kimono. He did very little; I guided his hands in the motions I would have taken myself, letting him see me and feel me at the same time. He enjoyed it. His eyes gleamed with lust as he eyed me, and he stroked my skin a good deal more than necessary when sliding the fabric to the ground. I pressed against him as I was finally exposed, not letting him get a good look at me yet. I leaned into him and stood on my tiptoes, pausing with my lips beside his ear.

"May I undress you?"

The judge stroked my nude back and caressed my ass as he murmured yes. I began stripping him, lingering on his skin just as he had lingered on mine. He felt luxurious, and I showered him with kisses as I went. He was already hard, and now I was, too. I was enjoying the feel of him against my skin and pressed against him when he was nude, kissing him fiercely so he would know how turned on I was.

He pushed me to the bed, pressing me backwards onto the mattress. I laid back and let him gaze at my body. During our last encounter, he hadn't gotten a good chance to admire me, not really, and I could tell he was enjoying it now. I stretched, watching his eyes to see what to flex to best appeal to him. After a long moment, he leaned forward and slid his hands up my torso, then lowered himself on me and kissed me.

We scooted to the center of the bed and he kept me under him, on my back. A good position to be in, for me, and I was content as we kissed and he stroked me. A tingle ran through me as I felt the beginnings of true arousal. I wrapped a leg around him, crooking my knee to give him access to me. I didn't usually rush things, but if I were legitimately turned on just laying here with him, I wasn't sure how long I could hold on when we did more.

The judge shifted until I felt him at my opening. I took his hand and slid one of his fingers into my mouth, swirling my tongue against his sweetly salty skin. He let out a soft moan, then gripped my hips and entered me with a gentle thrust. He slid into me quickly, burying himself in my body as I arched my back and cried out in pleasure. True pleasure, though it was identical to what I would have done even if I didn't enjoy it. Then he began thrusting into me and the tingle of true arousal spiked. I gasped and clutched him, digging my fingers into him for a moment before quickly flattening my hands. I was never allowed to grab my target, ever. But this felt so incredibly good.

As he thrust into me, I felt my control of the situation slipping. I wanted to enjoy this, not control it. I wanted to allow the pleasure to spill through my body and mind. I gripped him again to pull him closer and his lips met mine. I tried to regain control by twisting my leg around his waist, pushing myself into a slightly less pleasurable position so the sensations wouldn't swamp me, but he adjusted his position as well. As he kissed me, my mind fluttered past control and I let him take over fully.

Luckily, his body couldn't last any more than mine could and before my lack of control became apparent, he came inside of me, and I gratefully allowed myself release as well. The orgasm rocked me even more out of control and I gasped and arched back against him, even though I wasn't allowed to do that at this point. He kept kissing me as our bodies seemed to melt together, and I was out of breath. I tried to reclaim control over my body, reigning in my racing heart and pacing my breathing to match his. I had expected the pleasure to vanish after my orgasm but it was lingering. My body was back under my control, though.

Feeling confident again, I led him through the steps after sex, of kissing and smiling and stroking to take him down from his orgasm gently and build the relationship between us, cementing the chemical reactions that were bonding us in his brain. If there were any information I needed from him, I could get it. He would tell me anything, but I hadn't been sent to get information, just seduce him, so I concentrated on locking him to me. By the time he pulled away from me, I had secured a place in his mind. He sat up and I sat beside him, leaning against him and intertwining our fingers.

There was a buzz and the judge kissed my cheek. Then Lee walked in.

"A word?" he said to me, then smiled at the judge. "Thank you. I'll speak to him while you clean up. If you wish, I would like him to try again after some instruction. You are welcome to assist."

The judge grinned. "I'm not sure what he isn't doing right, but I'd be happy to help a second time."

He stood and went to an adjoining room as Lee flipped the switch to give us privacy. I lowered my head and wondered if he would punish me or just instruct me.

"Do you know where you failed?" Lee asked.

"Yes," I said with a blush. "I know the things I did wrong. I didn't do them on purpose."

"I know you didn't," Lee said. "You lost control, little by little. You regained it quickly, but you can't lose control of your body. Ever."

I nodded, keeping my eyes down.

"There are several strategies for maintaining control," Lee continued. "But there is one that I think you would understand best."

I listened as he described a way of allowing myself to feel the pleasure while remaining in control of my actions. Although he didn't discuss microbes directly – no handler did – it was obviously what he was teaching me to do. And as he spoke, I understood how I could use my microbes to create that separation. It never would have occurred to me that it was acceptable to feel pleasure. Lee wasn't trying to take that pleasure away, or even reduce it. He wanted me to feel it. But it couldn't affect my actions.

"I understand," I said when he finished. "I can do it."

"Good," Lee said. "There's a shower, and when you're ready, you'll try again. You won't lose control this time."

I agreed, though I couldn't help but wonder what would happen if I did lose control. He said it as a declarative statement, not an expressed wish. I could not fail. He flipped the privacy off and sent me into a second adjoining room which contained a small bathroom. I used the toilet, then got into the shower and quickly but thoroughly scrubbed my body. After, I went to the small mirror to redo my hair and face. Since we often shower with a target after sex, sagents learn how to make ourselves beautiful with and without makeup. We need to look perfect at all times, and we do. So it took only a moment to get ready. I was nowhere near as perfect as when I had entered in full makeup, but my natural state could be just as beautiful if I altered it correctly.

I exited the bathroom and saw the judge speaking quietly to Lee. They turned as I approached, and the judge whistled appreciatively, eyeing me with desire. Lee seemed pleased and came up to me, placing a hand on my shoulder and leaning close.

"Do what I taught you. I gave him some advice to make you lose control faster, so be prepared."

I nodded and Lee left the room. I shyly looked up at the judge, who held out a hand to me. I was more than ready to try again.

CHAPTER 27

SECOND CHANCE

The judge moved faster this time, kissing me for only moments before drawing me to the bed. I obeyed him and wondered what Lee had told him. The judge laid down on the bed and brought me over him and I wondered what all he would want. I would give him everything. I kissed down his body. He was quickly growing hard and enjoying himself, and he placed a hand on my head to guide me to his cock. I obeyed and caressed him with my tongue. To my surprise, a shiver of pleasure went through me as I took him into my mouth. I hadn't expected pleasure from this.

When I did this to Sora, I held back, because I usually held back on my targets, but I didn't want to hold back now. I wanted to feel the judge and let him feel me so as I touched him with my tongue and hands, I triggered far more places than I had with Sora. I curled my tongue around his shaft to caress exactly the right place to make him groan, I grazed my fingers against his balls at exactly the right moment to make him pant, I slid him into my throat at exactly the right speed to make him clutch my hair and try to force me faster. And I enjoyed it. Pleasure was spiking rapidly throughout my body, but I wasn't out of control yet, not yet at the point where I needed Lee's instructions. Then the judge pulled away from me and dragged me up on the bed. Preliminaries were over; now we would see if I had learned or not.

As he pulled me up, he turned so I was on my knees. I attempted to negotiate positions to one that gave me more control, but he countered my moves skillfully and I decided it wasn't worth the fight. I had already seduced him, after all. I didn't need to do anything else, and if he wanted this position, I would let him have it. I adjusted myself under him and he caressed my back before reaching to stroke my length. I gasped in pleasure, though I also would have gasped if I were in control. Time for my lessons.

As he stroked me, I shuddered, nearly out of control before I was able to direct my microbes to buffer me from my body just enough to put me back in control. The judge knew exactly what he was doing as he stroked me, but even as I felt like I was drowning in the pleasure, my microbes kept my body under control. I had done this so many times, trained for it so much, that they knew what to do even as my mind reeled. Then he entered me, and I strengthened the buffer before my pleasure became too evident.

As he thrust into me with far more skill than the usual target, almost as much precision as a sagent, I had to keep increasing the buffer. But I found myself curling into him and improvising new ways to increase the pleasure I was allowed to experience. I was incorporating my natural reactions into my calculated movements, and I could tell the result was sending him into a heightened state of bliss. I wanted to extend my pleasure and I slowed against him, using everything I knew to entice him into slowing down as well. He did, and I knew he would last precious minutes longer. Minutes that I intended on thoroughly enjoying, even as I remained in absolute control of my body.

Finally, though, I allowed our pace to pick up again, and in a matter of moments, he exploded into me. I was monitoring him far more closely than usual, and came at almost the exact same time, after doubling my buffers in preparation. It was a good thing, because I nearly blacked out from the sheer enormity of my orgasm, but my microbes kept my body reacting exactly as it should. I could barely think as we went through the motions of ending sex, as he pulled out and I cuddled against him, but slowly my mind returned, and I hadn't lost control.

I didn't think I could have done it without the new microbes I had gained. They allowed me to double my buffer at the end. I would have lost control without them and I was grateful as I nuzzled him. I didn't kiss men after sucking their cocks as many men didn't like it, but the judge pulled me into a kiss and I returned it happily. My body still hummed, and I wasn't entirely ready for this to end. He was still wrapped around me when there was a buzz and I reluctantly sat up. There was a longer pause than last time before Lee entered. He looked pleased, but the judge didn't let go of me as he had last time. He kept an arm around my waist, holding me against him still.

"Good job," Lee said to me, then looked at the judge. "Thank you."

He eyed the judge's arm around me. "Do you want to deliver your message to him now, or should both of you clean up first?"

The judge kissed my shoulder and finally let go of me. "After."

Lee gestured for me to stand and I pulled out of the judge's reach. Normally, I would never leave a target like this, when he clearly wanted me to stay, but a handler's commands were absolute. I went into the bathroom again and cleaned myself again before making myself beautiful. I didn't need to seduce him a third time, I was certain, but I also didn't like walking around when I wasn't looking my best.

As I went through the quick steps to enhance my natural beauty, I wondered what message he had for me. When I returned to the room, the judge was dressed again and Lee handed me my kimono, indicating that I should dress quickly. I obeyed, though I tried to look as good as possible while doing it. I slowed slightly as I tied the obi, careful to remember the step I tended to skip, and while Lee noticed it, I doubted the judge did. When I was dressed, Lee placed a hand on my shoulder. He used physical contact far more than I was used to from a handler, and he didn't use it to hurt. I was still getting used to it.

"The judge will deliver his message in private," Lee said. "If you don't want to tell me what it is, I won't push."

I glanced at him, surprised. He nodded at the judge, and left the room. The judge flipped the switch for privacy and gestured for me to approach. He took my hands, but didn't embrace me. His face was deadly serious. I kept my eyes lowered and adopted a similarly serious expression, hiding my fear. It didn't seem like this was a message I would like.

"Your agency has set certain deadlines if you don't return," he said. "They wanted you to know about them if possible, to inspire you to return."

His lips twisted at that and he seemed to hate what he had to say.

"I wouldn't tell you but you should know. You're better off here, you really are, but you should have the choice."

I glanced at him quickly. He sighed.

"On the first day of next month, if you haven't returned, your mother will vanish. A month after that, your father. A month after that, your sister. If you show up, it won't happen. I'm sorry."

My heart went numb and I glanced at him again, desperate to see some sort of deception there, some sign that he had made this message up. There was none. This was a real message from my agency, and they meant it. Even if I never received this message, they still would be willing to vanish my family. If I were capable of this type of disobedience, perhaps my family was, too. They were too dangerous for any agency to keep. Even if I returned, it was no guarantee of their safety, however. I was trembling and controlled myself quickly, using the same trick Lee had just taught me about using my microbes as a buffer. These emotions were just as strong as the pleasure I had felt earlier, though they were as negative as the previous ones had been positive. No wonder the judge had waited until now to tell me.

The judge stroked my cheek.

"If you need help, I'll give it," he said softly. "If you want out of the yakuza, but don't want to return to Destiny, I can protect you."

"You would be killed," I said. But he smiled.

"I'm harder to kill than you might think. But if you wanted to come with me, I would treat you well. You would be mine alone, but I think you would enjoy that, wouldn't you?"

I let myself blush. Other men had proposed similar things to me over the years. None had offered me protection, except the one man who reminded me of the judge so much, but many men and some women had wanted me to stay with them, in their beds, as theirs alone. I knew how to react, and I went through the response automatically as my heart reeled from thinking of my family.

A finger on my lips brought my attention back to the judge. He had a soft smile and had stopped me mid-sentence. I couldn't even remember what I had been saying. He was studying me.

"I know what you're supposed to say," he said. "And you're doing a wonderful job. But I'd rather know what you really think."

I studied him, gazing into his eyes though it wasn't allowed with a target.

"Thank you," I said quietly. "It means a lot to me, and I won't forget your offer. But for now, I can't accept."

The judge nodded slowly, and I lowered my eyes again. He stroked my cheek. "My offer stands any time," he said. "If you ever change your mind, I will protect you."

He leaned forward and kissed my cheek. "What's your name, beautiful?"

"Peter," I said.

The judge grinned. "I mean your real name."

"Peter is my name with you," I said, a little uncomfortable. It was rare that my targets knew I was a sagent, and that I was lying to them. I didn't want him to doubt me, because my job was to keep him seduced. I considered, then I glanced up at him briefly, letting myself blush. "It will never be my name with anyone else."

The judge's grin broadened and he chuckled. He pulled me

into an embrace and kissed me, on the lips this time, and I happily submitted. He kissed me deeply, then let go of me with a sigh and reached to flip the switch. There was a buzz and Lee entered quickly. He looked between us, then touched my arm.

"Are you ready to leave?" he asked me. "We'll leave first. The judge will be well-guarded as he leaves the area."

I nodded and glanced shyly at the judge. "Thank you," I said, meaning so much with my thanks. Thanks for not just the offer, or giving me the message, but also for the pleasure he had given me, and the knowledge that I was allowed to experience that pleasure. The judge smiled, and then Lee led me out.

CHAPTER 28

JUDGEMENT

Lee pulled me to a stop outside the building. The guards weren't surrounding us, though I could tell many of the people in the streets were guards. But they weren't close, and we had some privacy.

"We'll discuss your training at the end of the day, after you've had time to reflect on what you learned. In the meantime, do you still want to meet some pets?" he asked. "I know his message couldn't have been good."

I considered. Part of me wanted to hide and sob at the thought of what would happen to my family, but I wasn't capable of crying, so I would just end up more miserable than I was right now. I had already decided that I wasn't going back. Nothing would change that decision. It was likely that even if I returned to my agency, my family would still suffer. Maybe they wouldn't vanish, but they would be punished. My return was meaningless, and I didn't want to ponder the consequences of my decision yet. Maybe a distraction would help.

"I would like that," I said, feeling very bold in making my desires so clearly known. He seemed pleased by my response and patted my hand before leading me down the street in the opposite direction we had come from, farther into the neighborhood.

We hadn't gone far when I spotted a dark shape on the stairs of a house with a large porch. I gasped and looked at Lee, who led me towards that house. I was eager to meet the animal, the pet, but he slowed me down. We stopped several feet away and I stared at it.

I thought it was a cat, because it had large ears, but I wasn't positive. There were also dogs, but the files Lee had given me hadn't discussed how to identify them, so I was relying on the myths and stories I had heard growing up. No one in Destiny had seen a cat or dog in hundreds of years.

The pet stared at me with golden eyes. The pupils were slits, but they looked natural on the animal. Its ears were aimed at me, but then one of them tilted towards the street where a group of people had burst into laughter. The sight of one ear moving and not the other was bewildering and I wondered at the animal's strange biology. It was completely black, but I could tell it wasn't skin. I remembered that some animals were covered in hair. Cats were probably one of those animals.

Lee took my hand and led me forward slowly. The cat rose to its feet and Lee stopped me. I wondered what the rules were for approaching a pet, because clearly there were rules. Lee would have to give me a whole new set of instructions for dealing with animals.

Lee crouched and pulled me down as well. He extended his hand palm up towards the animal and I imitated him. I wondered if the animals were dangerous. The cats on Earth were fierce; there were stories of enormous cats roaming the wild and even killing humans. But this cat was so small.

The cat walked towards us and went to Lee first, sniffing his hand and then butting its head against him. He rubbed his fingers against the animal's head, between its ears, and I heard a strange rumbling sound. It had to be coming from the cat. The cat rolled its head back and forth under Lee's fingers and clearly enjoyed the touch, but then it looked at me. I tensed as it approached me, wondering if I was supposed to rub my fingers on its head or let it sniff me.

"She's going to sniff you," Lee said softly. "Just let her do it. If she accepts you, you can pet her. If she hisses, just pull your hand back slowly. She's friendly and won't bite."

I hid my fear. So cats were dangerous, though not this one. The cat drew close and I could sense her nose right against the tips of my fingers. Then, unexpectedly, her entire head shoved against my palm. I pulled back in fear and she cocked her head at me. Cautiously, I extended my arm again and touched her head. She was covered in thick, dense hair that was luxuriously soft. I stroked it, and it was much shorter by her ears. She liked it and twisted her head just as she had for Lee. I couldn't hold back my smile as I felt her body rumble with that strange noise.

"She likes you," Lee said with a laugh.

The cat flopped onto her side and rolled onto her back, exposing a fluffy tummy. Cautiously, I rubbed her tummy the way I had rubbed her head. The hair on her belly was much longer than on her head and was silky against my fingers. The rumbling sound grew louder, and I could feel it vibrating through her body. I wondered if I could ask about it. Probably. It wasn't in Lee's file, so I wasn't expected to know it.

"What is that noise she's making?" I asked shyly, still petting the cat.

"She's purring," Lee said, sounding amused. "Cats purr when they're happy."

"So she's a cat?" I asked, pleased that my guess was correct.

Lee chuckled. "When you see a dog, you won't have any confusion. They're very different, in appearance and attitude."

"Are they dangerous?" I asked, glancing at him in worry.

"Some are," he acknowledged. "So are some cats. Don't approach any animals you don't know. I know most of the animals in this neighborhood. This cat lives here and I know her owners."

The cat rolled back to her feet and bolted. I stared in shock where she had been, but Lee just stood up.

"Cats do that," he said. "She probably heard something. I know the neighbors feed her, so maybe one of them just put food out for her. They have excellent noses."

I got to my feet as well, standing carefully in the kimono. I hadn't moved around in it much, and I was wary about exposing too much in public. Sagents have to protect our bodies carefully, since we're only allowed to show ourselves when on a job. Lee offered me his hand as I stood and I took it, since ignoring it would be rude. But I managed to stand without his help for the most part. Nothing showed, at least.

Lee led me back to the podhouse and I looked around for more pets, but didn't see any. Either they were rare, or I didn't know how to spot them yet. I tried to keep focused on the pets because I didn't want to think of my family, but eventually I would have to face the reality of their fates, and as we entered the podhouse again, I gave a mental sigh. No more distractions, unless I had more jobs. I suspected I wouldn't have any, though. Lee seemed to want to give me time to adapt. Today, though, I wanted more jobs so I wouldn't have to think.

We went to my room and he went to the table, gesturing for me to sit. I obeyed.

"Are you ready for lunch? It's a little early, but not too much, and I'd like to talk. I'll be busy after lunch."

"Of course," I said politely. Lee sent the order to the unit and soon was placing a dish in front of me. He let me try his food, as with previous meals, and while they were quite spicy, one was delicious. He made a note and promised to add it to my diet after calculating what to replace. He assured me the cooks could make it less spicy and I smiled shyly. I hadn't commented on the spiciness, but he must have been able to tell.

We ate in silence for the most part, even though he had said he wanted to talk. I knew what he wanted to talk about, though, and was grateful he was waiting. I wouldn't have an appetite once I started talking. All too soon we finished. I was careful to pace my eating from the start so we finished at the same time without me having to speed up partway through. Lee didn't comment and may not have noticed. He took my plate and returned it to the unit, then sat across from me again. He stretched his hand across the table palm up and at his command, I reached out and put my hand in his. He stroked his fingers against my palm, and my scar.

"You can refuse to answer this, Gabriel," he said seriously.

"There won't be any punishment if you don't want to tell me what message your agency gave you. But if it's something that puts you in danger, then I would appreciate hearing it."

I stared at the table, then at his hand holding mine. He squeezed my hand and I knew he was serious. I wouldn't get in trouble if I didn't tell him, but there was no harm in telling him. I didn't want to keep secrets from him. He couldn't help my family, but maybe just sharing their fate with him would lessen the sorrow.

"My family," I said softly. "Next month my mom will vanish, then my dad a month later, then my sister after that. They're claiming that they'll be fine if I return. But I know my return won't matter."

Lee drew in a sharp breath. "I'm so sorry, Gabriel," he said, squeezing my hand again. "Is there anything I can do?"

"No," I said, keeping my eyes fixed on his hand. My eyes prickled and if I weren't a sagent, I would be in tears. I shut my eyes and forced myself to stay composed.

"I'm surprised the judge didn't offer to protect you himself," Lee mused. "He's quite taken with you."

I opened my eyes with a start, then blushed as I saw him observing me closely. He smiled.

"So he did try. I gave you permission not to tell me the message from your agency, but you should have told me what he said outside of that."

He was still smiling but my heart was thudding. I hadn't even realized I had disobeyed him. His standards were so different than what I was used to. I could keep some secrets, but not others. It was easier when I wasn't allowed to keep any secrets and didn't have to figure out the exact rules in every situation. He didn't seem upset, and I didn't think the punishment would be bad.

"What did he tell you?" Lee asked.

"He told me if I wanted to leave the yakuza, he would keep me safe from you and from them," I said as honestly as possible. "He assured me he would be safe, and so would I. He wanted me for himself."

"What did you say?"

I looked down. "I politely declined, but he ignored me. I had to speak to him very plainly. I know I shouldn't have. I told him I didn't need help right now."

"But you left it open for the future?"

"Yes."

Lee sighed. "You won't need it, Gabriel. I will do everything in my power to make your life comfortable so you won't need to run again. Did he say anything else?"

"He wanted to know my name. My real name. I told him my name was Peter, and I wouldn't use that name for anyone else."

"I'll keep that in mind when choosing your aliases," Lee said. I glanced up at him and he was smiling again. I relaxed. "But you should have told me, if only so I knew to be careful about your future names. I realize I may not have been clear about what you were and weren't required to tell me, Gabriel. I'll be more clear in the future. But keep in mind that you are not allowed to keep secrets from me."

I nodded, wondering if that meant he wouldn't be punishing me. He had to do something, didn't he? He was excusing me a little, but I had still kept a secret from him. Lee squeezed my hand and sighed again.

"Your workout is normally two hours. Tomorrow, you'll do three. Choose a routine and extend it. I'll adjust your diet accordingly."

"Do I need more muscle?" I asked, puzzled.

He stared at me in surprise. "That's your punishment," he said.

I considered, but didn't understand how it was punishment. It was just doing a little more exercise than usual. There was nothing painful about it. He shook his head.

"Some would think doing three hours of physical exertion a punishment. I suppose you don't, but perhaps at the end of three hours, you will."

I nodded, though I knew I wouldn't. He let go of my hand and stood up.

"I need to go. I don't want you alone, not yet, not now. Sora will be with me. You know my other sagent as Zada, I believe. Would you feel safe with her?"

She wasn't as familiar as Sora, but I had nothing against her, so I nodded. But she knew me as Peter and I didn't want to use that name with anyone else. Could I be bold enough to ask for a new alias? I took a deep breath and he waited, clearly knowing I wanted to say something.

"Um, could I have a new alias? For use here."

"Of course," Lee said without hesitation and I relaxed. "Only Sora, Ananti and I know your real name. I'll input your new alias into your chip."

I hesitated. He clearly didn't know that Lee-sama knew my name, and he had said that I couldn't keep secrets. He was deep in thought, eyeing me, probably considering a name, and then his eyes narrowed.

"Does someone else know your name?"

"Yes," I said. "I didn't have another name to give, so I told Lee-sama."

"Lee-sama?" Lee asked, sounding confused and a little worried. "Who do you call Lee-sama?"

"His name was Eric Lee," I explained, and Lee's eyes narrowed further as his lips tightened. "He told me to call him Lee-sama."

"You've spoken to him?"

"Yes," I said, suddenly realizing that Lee didn't know anything about the encounter. "He knocked on my door right after you left yesterday. I thought you saw him."

"What did he say to you? Did he touch you? I can't believe you hid something like this from me," Lee hissed, and I shrank back. He was angry, and for once, his anger was directed at me.

"He wanted to know my name," I said, wondering what the punishment for this would be. "The guard seemed to think it was fine so I told him, but then he wanted me to kiss him, so I did. I didn't know how to refuse. He said I would be safe if I obeyed him, and then he left."

Lee stepped away from me and crossed his arms, pacing and glancing at me. He was indeed angry.

"He kissed you?" Lee repeated. "He threatened you? And you said nothing to me?"

I didn't know what to say, so I remained silent. Lee stopped and glared at me.

"I suppose you're used to people treating you like that, aren't you?"

He seemed to be waiting for a response so I nodded, because it was true.

"Even though I told you no one from the yakuza would touch you?"

I lowered my head. "I know I shouldn't have let your promise be broken," I whispered. "I couldn't see how to refuse."

"You let my promise be broken?" he repeated. "No, Gabriel. You are not responsible for this and I won't let you blame yourself. He kissed you. He made sure you couldn't refuse. That is not your fault. It's mine. I didn't realize he even knew where you were. But it is your fault that you didn't tell me. Did you tell anyone?"

"The guard saw it," I said. "But I didn't tell anyone."

Lee shook his head. "Four hours, your short routine. No breaks. You'll need to get up early to keep on schedule."

Another hour in addition to my previous disobedience, but this would be much more difficult. My short routine was quite punishing, which he knew because he knew my routines. It only took an hour because it was so intensive. The thought of repeating it for four hours did indeed seem like punishment, though nothing compared to my previous agencies. I stared at the ground and nodded.

He tapped a finger against his lips.

"Your name will be Byul, for now," he said. "I'll update it to your chip immediately. Zada might choose to give you her name, as she rarely uses that particular alias. You can give her any name you like."

He approached me rapidly and I barely managed not to flinch. I expected him to do something to me, hurt me in some way. People only approached me like that when they wanted to harm me. But he wrapped me in a fierce hug.

"If anyone ever touches you without your permission, you must tell me. Is there anything else I need to know? Anything at all?"

I wracked my brain for anything I hadn't told him, and drew a blank. Did that mean he knew everything, or was I just forgetting something? I wasn't sure, and it frightened me. His patience was gone, and his punishments were significant now, though nothing I couldn't handle.

"I don't think so," I said. "But I will tell you everything in the future."

"Good," he murmured, then pressed a kiss against my head. He let go of me and went to the door, glancing back. "Zada will be here soon. If you need anything, contact me. I may not be able to leave, but you can always contact me. No matter what."

"I will," I promised, though I hoped I would never need to. Then he left, and I was alone with the guard. It was the second guard, who had shown me the closet, and I smiled at him before going to the couch and staring at the entertainment system. Perhaps Zada could help me set up the sky on the vast screen, because I missed the sky deeply. Was my sister looking at the sky right now? Would she even know why she was being vanished? Or would they just take her? I shuddered and hoped Zada would be here soon.

CHAPTER 29
CHOSEN DESTINY

W hen the door buzzed, I checked the viewer first to make sure it was indeed Zada. Of course, I would have let anyone in, even Lee-sama. But I wanted to be prepared if it were him. If it were him, I would send a message to Lee before letting him in. But it was Zada, and I let her in with some relief. She smiled at me warmly as she entered, and I smiled back cautiously. Then she extended her hand. I didn't think she'd mind as I checked my chip quickly to see if my new name had been input. It had, and Lee had given me a last name as well. I shook her hand and let her see my full name and address, as was proper. This time, she showed me her name as well, although I could tell it was still her alias: Mei Zada. I hadn't realized Zada was a last name.

"Byul Park?" she said, sounding amused. "That's a cute name. It means star, you know. It suits you. But I doubt you'll keep it long."

"I wanted a new name," I said shyly, but she patted my arm.

"It's a good name," she assured me.

It sounded like a compliment so I took it as one, and smiled at her. She kept her hand on my arm and squeezed me gently.

"Lee said you just received some bad news. Is there anything I can do?"

I looked down, then at the entertainment center. She couldn't do anything about my family, but she could help.

"Can you show me how to set up the sky?" I asked, and she nodded and went to the center.

"Do you know how to use this?" she asked. "I've heard technology is a little different in Destiny."

"I haven't tried," I said, coming beside her.

She showed me how to turn on the different parts of the center and I was glad I hadn't tried on my own, because everything was different. All of the parts were there, but scrambled. The power and main control buttons that should have been at the top of the remote were at the bottom, which would have taken me a while to find, and the order of things was dramatically different. I filed everything away as she taught me how to operate everything and suggested a few channels on the television and radio that she thought I might like. She turned on the main screen and hit a few buttons, and suddenly I saw a night sky filled with stars.

"This looks into space," she explained. "It's day in Destiny, just like here, but this channel is always night like this."

She preset the channel on the remote and went to another channel of a blurred blue sky with the aurora of the sun glimmering along one edge. I sighed at the familiar sight. I would never see it again for myself.

"This is upper Destiny, I'm not sure where," she said. "It changes every day to a different spot in Destiny. We're not really allowed to use their equipment, so we can't stay in one place for too long. Sometimes this channel is down completely."

She preset this channel as well, and glanced at me. "I know you've never seen this, but you might like it. It's a view of Destiny itself."

The screen changed and I gasped. It was Destiny. The satellite must have been orbiting along with the city, or else orbiting the city itself, and the entire structure was on display as it showed the city sideways. Destiny looked like a blooming flower, with four petals spread outward along the pale fuzz of the atmosphere and the stem dropping down. The petals were the four districts of upper Destiny, and the center of the flower was lower

Destiny. Below, in what would be the receptacle, was another bulge that was the Drops. And then metal continued downward off the screen.

Destiny wasn't connected to the Earth, but parts of it stretched down almost to the surface. At first, people wanted to cut off everything below lower Destiny, including the Drops, to protect against the microbes. But the scientists warned that changing anything risked sending Destiny out of orbit and crashing down to Earth. If the science of Earth had been fully preserved, perhaps they could have figured out how to cut at least the lowest parts, but scientists in later generations remembered only the warnings. Besides, every fifty years a group of explorers was sent down the long metal structure to Earth in order to see if the microbes had vanished, and Earth was habitable again. None had ever returned, but children dreamed of being Earth explorers, the first to rediscover their planet.

I could see a sphere in the haze below Destiny that had to be Earth and I looked at it curiously. I had seen pictures of old Earth, but had never seen Earth as it was now. It glowed blue, as I always imagined. My attention was drawn back to the city, though, sparkling and very slowly circling on the screen. The satellite must be orbiting the city.

The tall ebony towers of the fourth district stood out starkly and my eyes instinctively went to the neighboring district. I reached out to the screen and even though I didn't touch it, I felt the buzz of electronics under my fingertips as I traced the outline of my beloved district.

"This is my home," I said to Zada. "This isn't close enough to see the neighborhoods but this is my district."

"We call that the dream district," she said.

"You have names for our districts?"

"Many people watch this all the time," she explained. "Most parts of Destiny have a name if they're large enough for people to see. There are people who devote their lives to watching Destiny."

I was disturbed at the thought of all of the Drops watching

my city, fantasizing about it the way we fantasized about Earth. But they had no knowledge of Destiny and Destiny was considered a perfect place, I knew from Lee's files. It wasn't, not by a long shot, but the people in the Drops still idolized it.

"Why is it the dream district?" I asked.

Zada pointed to the fourth district, with its distinctive towers. "This is the spire district," she said. "You can tell why. On the other side the buildings are just as sharp, though not as large. We call it the claw district. But between it lays the dream district, because it looks so soft and inviting. It would be a dream to live there."

She looked at me with desire in her eyes, but not desire for me. "What is it like?"

"I don't know enough about life here to compare it," I said honestly. "It's all residential, a good district for families. That's why my parents brought us there. They have the best schools and the safest neighborhoods. There's hardly any crime and the best air, no microbes. It's the safest place in all of Destiny. I've never gone there as a sagent."

At the thought of my parents, my heart clenched. They had done everything possible to give me a good life and help me become a good sagent, and I had failed them. They told me over and over again that I needed to hide myself, destroy myself, so that I wouldn't be tempted to disobey. They told me that Acron's actions, though regrettable, were in some ways necessary if I was to learn how to be a sagent properly. I couldn't be me and also be a sagent, and I had done everything to obey them, but I couldn't. I couldn't get rid of my thoughts and feelings and desires, even though I wasn't allowed to have them, and now they were going to vanish.

I took a deep breath. My sorrow was showing, but I wasn't controlling my outward emotions as tightly as I would in public. My handler was allowed to see my emotions, and I didn't mind if Zada saw them, since she also belonged to my handler. I couldn't lose control, but I didn't have to hide too much.

Zada added a preset for this channel and handed me the remote. "Those are the three sky channels. There's a fourth, but it's been down for over a week. I'll show you if it comes back up. Do you want to keep this on?"

"Yes," I said, not wanting to lose the sight of my home. I wouldn't ever see my sister or parents again, but at least I could still see Destiny.

I went to the couch and sat down, staring at my city. Zada sat next to me.

"May I call you Byul?" she asked. "You can call me Mei. That's my preferred first name. I change last names all the time but usually keep Mei."

"I thought you weren't supposed to use first names," I said, thinking back to Lee's files to remember the exact rules. There were a lot of rules and I hadn't fully understood all of them. There were a wide variety of titles for people, based on their relative rank and their relationship to you, and I had memorized them as much as possible, but knew I had more to learn. Some of the titles for people were Japanese, some Korean, and some entirely new, according to the files, and some were used in some parts of the Drops but not others. It was a lot of information to take in, and I had planned on studying the files in more depth today.

"You can use a first name when you know the person," she said. "It indicates a certain level of intimacy, but not sexual intimacy. Just personal closeness."

"You can call me that," I said. "What will my targets call me?"

"If you're in public, probably your last name," she said. "In private, they'll use your first name or a title of some sort. You can tell how they feel about you by the title they use."

"I'm not usually in public on jobs," I said.

"What kind of jobs do you take?" she asked, and I could tell she was trying to help me move beyond my sorrow and following the train of conversation I was suggesting. She didn't want to pry and if I wanted to talk about jobs, she would let me. But did I? It was better than thinking about my family.

"Short jobs," I said. "Twelve hours was my longest, and it was an agency job."

Mei's eyes narrowed. "Sora told me about those."

I shrugged. "Some are fine. Some aren't. But those are the only longer jobs I take. Mostly it's like the job you saw. I have an hour or two to seduce my target and get information, then I return to a safe point, send my information, and go to my next job."

"How many jobs a day do you have?" she asked, sounding scandalized.

"As many as my handler gives me," I said. "I have some choice. I only work twelve hours, so sometimes I can't do as many because travel is involved. The job you saw was my only job that day because it takes so long to travel to and from the Drops."

"You only work twelve hours?" she exclaimed. "What do you mean, only? How do you possibly manage twelve hours when your jobs are just a couple of hours long? You must work three jobs a day!"

"Usually, yeah," I said. "But my previous agency was fifteen hours a day, so this was much better."

She shook her head. "No wonder you stayed in the Drops."

"Why did you help me?" I asked, thinking of the bed and breakfast and deciding to be blunt. She was a sagent, after all, and she hadn't understood my codes earlier, so bluntness would have to do. "I mean, the yakuza has treated me well so far. They seem to treat you well. You don't seem to mind working for them. Why did you help me hide from them?"

"Lee is a good person," Mei said. "Most of the yakuza are good people, even if they are criminals. Just don't ever ask what someone does for a living unless you really want to know. But not all of them are. As soon as you entered the Drops, you were spotted. Lee wasn't informed, though he should have been, so I didn't know to expect you. They were going to kidnap you, to force you into the yakuza against your will. I don't agree with that."

She looked away. "When they take someone like that, they tattoo you to make sure you can't escape. It limits your usefulness but ensures your cooperation, since you would be killed without their support. That's what happened to me."

My eyes widened and I thought about how she hadn't been able to go near the bed and breakfast even though Sora had said sagents didn't have tattoos. So she really had been hiding there and the yakuza had forced her into service.

She shrugged. "Once I told Lee about you, he took over, but I couldn't be sure who would find you. If you chose to join the yakuza, I had no problems. But I didn't want you to be forced into it, so I helped you find protection. And you found Lee, and made your choice, and you're free of that abusive agency as well. It turned out for the best."

Had it turned out for the best? The best for me, certainly. But not the best for my family. Their three lives were far more valuable than my one life. They wouldn't be in danger if I hadn't disobeyed, if I hadn't asked Lee for help rather than go with the enforcer. My sister would be living her happy life, not knowing what her agency was capable of, and my parents... well, I never really knew what they did or who they worked for. I suspected at least one of them worked for GovTech, since that agency had bought me at birth, but I didn't know which. I did know that they worked for different agencies because they had met on a job – they were assigned the same target. They told me and my sister about it sometimes, but only in the most general of terms. I suspected something like what had happened with Zada had happened with them: one of them took charge and they both got what they wanted because they cooperated.

After that, they managed to sneak away and meet up, and after a long time, years of sneaking, my mother became pregnant. Since sagents were sterile, it took a long time for them to realize what was wrong with her and why she kept gaining weight in her belly only. They pressed her for information and she admitted to seeing my father, and both agencies were too intrigued by the thought of two sagents having a child to really punish them. But when I was born, and my parents weren't allowed to negotiate for my freedom, they decided not to have any more children. After my transition day, they were split up, but they still saw each other sometimes. Their agencies didn't try too hard to keep them apart, since they were still hoping for more children.

Mei was looking at me curiously but didn't press, instead turning to the image of Destiny floating on the screen. I did, too.

"What do you call the first district?" I asked. "You gave names for the other three."

"The shadow district," she said. "There aren't any towers, and everything is dark. It's not like the others at all. At night, you can barely see it."

"That's the agriculture district," I said. "It's mostly fields of plants and faux meat. They grow everything for Destiny there."

"What do you call it?" she asked.

"The first district," I said. "We don't have names really, just numbers. It's first because it was inhabited first. People started in lower Destiny, but they wanted away from the microbes. The first district already had a lot of fields planted, luckily, and for a long time, people stayed there. As society reestablished, they needed a place besides lower Destiny for banks and financial centers, so they went to the second district. Then, people wanted more space to live, and started developing the third district as residential only. And then, the new businesses and all the cutting-edge technology companies decided to expand into the fourth district. It was the least developed and the air filtration was barely functioning when they started, but now it has the cleanest air in all of Destiny."

"I thought your district had the best air," she said.

"We have the fewest microbes," I corrected. "So it is the best. But not the cleanest. Clean air comes straight from the atmosphere, and microbes are more likely to get through in the fourth district than anywhere else. It's high risk, but a lot of people are willing to take it."

I glanced at her, suddenly remembering where I was, and how many microbes there were here in the Drops. The risk of possibly encountering a couple of microbes probably didn't sound like much to her, since everything was saturated with them. Not at a lethal level, but they were still everywhere. She had a slight smile on her face.

"I can't imagine living in fear of the microbes," she said. "They can be dangerous, but they're not deadly for most. Is it true that there are scanners everywhere?"

"Most large buildings have a metal detector for weapons and arm scans for microbes. It's pretty standard. A few buildings have full body scans because there are so many people moving through. Sagents get caught all the time, even though we're pretty good at avoiding the scans. I've never been caught, but my sister seems especially prone to getting scanned. Seems to happen to her at least once a month. Do you have scans in buildings here?"

"No," she said. "Doctors will scan because they need to know your exact level to cater their care, but other than that, it's only the elevators. They're extremely thorough. They have full body scanners and also check with arm scans. How did you get through?"

I shrugged. "Bribes, I assume. I was taken down individually on a private elevator. There were only two of them to please on the way down, and they weren't allowed to remove my clothes. Going back, I had a place to go and a person to contact, and they would get me around the scanners again."

She shook her head. "Seems like a lot of trouble for a simple job like yours. You must be a high-value sagent. Why did they use you for a job like that?"

"There was another part of my job I didn't know about at the time," I said cautiously. "Specific to me."

"Is that why you left them? Because they told you the rest of your job?"

"I didn't really leave them," I said, looking at Destiny again. "But I needed Lee's help, and I was willing to join the yakuza to get it."

"Do you regret that decision?"

I was silent. Did I regret it? I thought of my sister, and the way her mouth quirked when I said something funny but she wasn't supposed to laugh. My dad, and the way he was always there to comfort me when my fears were overwhelming. My mom, making sure my jacket was straight before I went to school, her touch on my infected hand as she applied the antibiotics and assured me that I wouldn't lose it. She wouldn't allow it. They wouldn't be killed. Vanishing didn't mean death. It meant something far worse.

That was what the enforcer had threatened me with when she said I would be unable to work. That would have been temporary, though, so not really vanishing. Vanishing meant a permanent state where you were in so much pain, under so much torment, that you were unable to work. Eventually, you died. That was the fate I was dooming my family to. But did I regret turning to Lee? Somehow, despite everything that was going to happen to my family because of that decision, I didn't. I should, but I didn't. It was an unsettling self-discovery and I wasn't quite sure what to make of it, but there wasn't a trace of regret when I thought back on that decision. Whatever the outcome, I would accept it.

CHAPTER 30
PUNISHING MISUNDERSTANDING

As I started the fourth repetition of my short routine, my body ached and I fully understood how this was punishment. I was going to be sore the rest of the day, and while it wasn't painful, exactly, it was exhausting. I paused to get some water. At dinner with Lee last night, he had amended the punishment so that I could take breaks to get water, but for nothing else. I tried to drink slowly to rest my body, but I couldn't take too long.

The first time through, I was slower than usual because the equipment – which had been delivered yesterday while Mei was still here – was different than my usual equipment, and it took me a few moments to find the parts I needed. But by now, I had everything memorized and as I placed the weights back to their starting settings, I decided I never wanted to do this again.

There was very little to do while I worked out, and I spent much of the time thinking of anything that had happened that Lee needed to know about, that for some reason I hadn't mentioned. I didn't want any secrets from him anymore, but I couldn't think of a single thing. I could go into more detail on a lot of things for him, but I was pretty sure I had covered everything. He probably knew this would inspire me to think about potential secrets. It was probably why this was physical punishment and nothing that required any mental exertion. When Acron really wanted to torture me, he would pair physical pain with all sorts of tests. He would give me long lists to memorize while torturing me, and if I messed up the slightest detail, he would hurt me more. I had an exceptional memory as a result, but he knew exactly what the limits of my memory were, and if he wanted me in pain, he knew how to do it. I would be desperately trying to remember what he wanted, even while my body was in agony. I doubted Lee would ever do something like that to me.

He had been firm but gentle last night, walking me through the experience with the judge and talking to me about controlling my body. He made sure I fully understood what I had done so I could apply it to other situations, and he was pleased that I had already used his instructions to hide my grief over my family. Well, not exactly pleased. But he was glad I was a quick learner.

As I switched out weights, I took a brief moment to shut my eyes and lean against the equipment. Not a break, exactly. Just a pause. I thought that was probably okay. If he really wanted to make sure I was working nonstop, he would be here watching me. I was a little surprised he wasn't, actually. This was my first real punishment, and he wasn't even here to make sure I obeyed him. My two previous handlers would have been watching me for sure. Acron would have added on more punishment if I paused like this. Even my second handler would have scolded me and extended the punishment by however long I paused. I quickly moved into the next part of the routine. Maybe the room was being recorded, and Lee would find out that I had paused.

Luckily, the physical exertion was just enough to distract me from thinking about my family, the one subject I was trying to avoid. Last night was tough. I barely got any sleep and the little sleep I did have was marred by nightmares. My lack of sleep was making this punishment worse, but I was used to going without sleep from my time at GovTech. I could go three days and two nights without sleep, and even though I was barely functioning at the end of that time, it was reassuring to know that if I needed to skip a night, I could. I had gone longer than that, of course, since Acron always pushed me farther than I was capable of going, but the results were disastrous. At the end of three days, I was exhausted and not thinking as clearly as I needed to think to survive; after that, I could barely think at all.

I wondered if I would have jobs today, or more training, or if Mei or Sora would spend time with me. Mei and I had avoided any difficult subjects yesterday and at my request, she quizzed me on small talk until I felt comfortable discussing the random topics of conversation that people tended to use as icebreakers. When I was on a targeted mission as with the judge, I didn't need small talk. But if I were on a mission where my target didn't know I was coming and I had to seduce them, small talk was essential. Mei taught me how to turn the small talk to my advantage, and which subjects appealed to which types of people. I would probably make mistakes at first, because I still made mistakes sometimes in Destiny and I had grown up there, but a poor choice of discussion didn't ruin a mission, it just delayed it.

Pets were a favorite subject for everyone, Mei informed me, and if I met someone who didn't like pets, I should avoid them. There were also some people who liked dogs better and some who liked cats, and that preference was a good indicator of personality. My own stated preference would often impact people's opinions of me, so I had to be careful about it. It seemed strange, but there were indicators like that in Destiny too. She had pulled up pictures of cats and dogs for me to see, but I suspected I needed to see them in person to really understand the difference. They seemed quite similar in the pictures except the dogs were a little bigger.

I paused while shifting the weights a final time. My legs and back ached, but I focused on finishing quickly. No more pauses, just a final push and then I was done. I let out a sigh of relief as I returned the machine to its starting position and went to take a shower. Normally, I didn't linger in the shower, as speed was necessary when showering with a target or between jobs, but today I did linger as the hot water steamed into my sore muscles. I didn't know what I'd be doing, so I prepared myself as if for a job and was reassured by the familiar products. Everything had been delivered when Mei was here, and she had helped me put things away.

I returned to the main room and considered what to wear. Lee had given no instruction. He knew I preferred Destiny clothes, and had never once said wearing those clothes was a mistake, but I always seemed to have to change into kimonos. Maybe I should just start with one. I took out a deep azure kimono and practiced putting it on and tying the obi several times until it came smoothly. Then I went to the chaise and collapsed. I urged my microbes to ease the tightness in my muscles. I had stretched before and after the workout, of course, but I wasn't used to such intense, extended physical exercise. I heard the door buzz and bolted to my feet just as Lee entered. I bowed to him and he studied me.

"How do you feel?" he asked.

"Tired," I said honestly, keeping my eyes down. I wasn't sure whether he wanted to hear that I was in pain, or if he wanted me to pretend like it was nothing, but this was the honest answer. He seemed to value honesty.

"Come here," he said. I obeyed and stood before him, head and eyes down. He placed a hand under my chin and lifted my head. I cautiously met his gaze. In all of my training, I had been taught that looking into your handler's eyes was a challenge. You had to project obedience at all times. But Lee seemed to want to look into my eyes as often as possible. I needed to get used to it, and to find a way to do it that didn't challenge him.

"Is there anything you need to tell me?"

I gulped. Had he been watching? There could be no secrets.

"I paused several times," I said.

"You took breaks?"

"No, I just... towards the end, I stopped for water more and took more time changing the weights. I'm sorry."

"Did you spend more or less than four hours working out?"

"I don't know," I said nervously. "I didn't know I was supposed to time it."

Lee seemed puzzled. "I told you four hours. Why wouldn't you time it? How did you know when to stop?"

"I did four repetitions," I said, wondering if that were the wrong thing to do. "They take me an hour so I did it four times."

Lee sighed and let go of me. "I specified four hours for a reason, Gabriel. I knew you would slow down. I had assumed you would get through three, maybe three-and-a-half repetitions in four hours. I didn't mean for you to do it four times."

I stared at the ground. I had been trying so hard to obey, and I had somehow misjudged everything. Now, I would face the same punishment tomorrow to make sure I could understand the proper directions, plus additional punishment for disobeying him.

"You probably went for at least thirty minutes longer than you had to," Lee said. "Let that extra time be your punishment and next time, listen to what I'm telling you to do. I seem to give different orders than your previous handlers, and I don't want you accidentally punishing yourself unnecessarily."

"I apologize," I said, staring down. "I'll do it right tomorrow."

"Gabriel," he said in annoyance. "What did I just tell you?"

"To listen to what you say," I replied, wondering why he was annoyed. I wasn't protesting or trying to get out of it.

"And what did I say about your punishment?"

I paused, then thought back to his words. "The extra time I spent was my punishment for not listening," I said slowly. "You don't want me to do it again tomorrow?"

"No," he said. "You've completed your punishment. But you do need to learn to listen to me better, and not jump to conclusions based on what your previous handlers would do. Can you do that?"

"Yes," I replied instantly, not wanting him to change his mind. Was that really it? A little extra exercise that I had already done? That was all the punishment for misunderstanding his instructions? I would have to listen to him carefully, because it never would have occurred to me that he didn't want more. I would have done the same routine tomorrow without a direct command, because I would have assumed he wanted it.

Lee stroked my cheek, observing how I looked.

"Is there a reason you're not in Destiny clothes?"

"I wanted to practice," I said cautiously, wondering if it was a mistake. "You always request that I change. I'm sorry."

"You didn't make a mistake," Lee assured me. "I was just curious. When you're on your own time, you can wear whatever feels most comfortable. I would probably have you change no matter what you were wearing. Did the practice help?"

"Yes," I said, still cautious. I wasn't in trouble. Was he warning me that I should wear Destiny clothes? Was he indicating that I wasn't able to or shouldn't choose my own clothes? Did he just want me to be comfortable as long as possible? Probably the latter, but I feared one of the first two.

"Show me," Lee said. "Strip first, then dress again."

I obeyed as he sat on the couch to watch. I was careful to be perfect and for the first time, I managed the obi without any hesitation. I was quite pleased when I was dressed again, and there was approval in Lee's eyes.

"Good job," he said. "How are you doing with everything I taught you about the Drops? I know some of that will take a while to memorize."

"I'm getting through a lot of it," I said. "I'm still having trouble with the titles. There are a lot of them."

"Hmm," Lee said. "Those are probably the most important thing you need to learn. You don't necessarily need to know which title to use for someone else, since you're clearly from Destiny and very few people will expect it of you. But you need to know what people are saying about you. That's vital. Focus on the names for males. Those are the ones people will use for you. Once you feel comfortable with those, shift to names for females. What are some possible names you might call Sora?"

I went through the information in my mind. "He outranks me, right?" I asked hesitantly.

"He's older than you," Lee said. "You should assume that everyone older than you outranks you."

I listed four titles that were used by young men to address older men, then hesitated and added two more that also indicated a family connection. He wasn't family, but we shared a handler, so he was close.

"Why did you hesitate?" Lee asked. "Those are the two most appropriate."

"He's not family."

"It does mean brother, of a sort," Lee said. "But not brother in the sense of family. It means friend more than anything, or someone you admire as you would a brother. I'll go back in the files I gave you and indicate which are biological family only. Most have this looser meaning."

"Thank you," I said shyly.

If he thought terms that denoted friendship were the most appropriate, then did that mean he wanted Sora to be my friend? I wasn't sure how to react to that. I wasn't allowed friends, especially not other sagents. My agencies only barely tolerated me seeing my sister, and limited our time together. They also kept us under watch as we talked, and though we occasionally passed coded messages, we mostly just avoided any real subject. Mei seemed quite friendly with me as well. But maybe he just meant the admiration part, since I did admire Sora's superior skills as a sagent. That made more sense.

"You don't have any jobs today," Lee said. "But I want you to stay active. Mei will stay with you most of the day. Sora will be with me."

I nodded, though I wondered why Lee seemed to rely on Sora more than Mei. They were equally skilled, as far as I could see.

"Tomorrow, I may ask for your help in training," Lee said, and he sounded almost cautious, although it was his right to demand it of me. I shrunk slightly, thinking of all the ways I had been used in training. Not all of them were bad and I didn't think he would hurt me, but training was always punishment and I wasn't sure what I had done. Could I ask? Probably. I would try. If I was already getting punished, then one question wouldn't add too much more.

"What have I done wrong?" I asked softly.

"Nothing," Lee said. "It's not punishment. But you know much more than my sagents. I want them to learn from you. You won't be hurt in any way, and no one will do anything to you. I may ask you to do things to targets in front of them and explain what you're doing, but no sagent will touch you."

I glanced at him, puzzled. That wasn't like any training I had ever heard, but thinking back to my own training, that was a common technique. An experienced sagent demonstrated and explained moves and strategies while we watched and took notes. I had just never been used like that, because training had always been punishment. Perhaps this wouldn't be as bad as I thought.

"You really train all the sagents?" I asked, not sure I was allowed to ask for more information.

"Yes," he said. "I have seven right now. Three are about to finish, two are midway through their training, and two are brand new. I've selected handlers for most of them and those handlers will be present for training as well."

That was a lot of sagents to handle, but Mei had indicated that Lee trained all of the sagents for the yakuza. That wasn't a lot of sagents for the Drops. But most sagents in the Drops wouldn't be with the yakuza, I realized. Most would remain with the government. I wondered how it was determined who worked for the government, and who worked for the yakuza. Was the yakuza actually allowed to bid on sagents like other agencies?

"You look like you have a lot of questions," Lee observed with a faint smile. "You can ask them, but not now. I need to leave. Have breakfast, relax, and Mei will be here in about two hours. If anything happens, contact me immediately. I'll either come, or I'll send someone in my place. You won't be in public, but there is nothing wrong with how you're dressed. Try wearing the kimono today. You'll need to get used to wearing it casually."

I nodded obediently and he took my hand and squeezed it.

"Even if you feel uncertain about whether or not to contact

me, you should contact me. If I don't think it's important, I'll send someone else. You aren't distracting me at all."

"Yes," I said, wondering if I would be bold enough to contact him unless I knew for sure I was in danger.

He squeezed my hand again and left. I ate my breakfast and enjoyed sitting down, since my body still ached. I had just put my dish into the machine when the door buzzed. I checked the viewer. It was Lee-sama.

CHAPTER 31
CONTRACT NEGOTIATIONS

I took a deep breath. Lee-sama was outside and I had to let him in. I keyed a message to Lee, because I knew for sure he would want to know about this. I didn't use an emergency code, but I did indicate it was urgent. Then I opened the door, and greeted Lee-sama with more deference than I had used on his previous visit. Now that I knew about how the yakuza worked, I understood how absolute his control was. The Dragon Clan wasn't the most powerful or the largest, but all of the other Clans deferred to it nonetheless, partially because of Lee and his connection to the old dynasties, partially because all sagent training was done here. Lee was a big part of the Dragon Clan, but this man was higher ranked than Lee. I had to be extremely careful with him because I suspected there was an element of resentment between him and Lee that might cause him to lash out against me.

Lee-sama came in and as the door shut, he gestured for me to approach. He observed me with a grin.

"You're much prettier than you were," he observed, and reached to clasp my shoulder. "And in such a pretty outfit. Come here."

I obeyed and he embraced me, immediately pulling me into a kiss and grabbing my ass. He caressed my body greedily while his tongue plunged down my throat. I wasn't entirely sure how much to give him, and simply made sure he enjoyed himself.

He pushed me backwards and I let him steer me to the bed. He pushed me onto the bed, and I wondered if I should allow this. I could sense that the guard was disgusted by this, but the guard wasn't doing anything to stop it, and I couldn't think of any way to stop this. I could delay it; I was quite skilled at that. But most of my delays involved intimacy in some way.

He ran his hands down my chest and pulled my kimono open, then ran his fingers across my nipples. I let myself shiver as if in pleasure and clenched my hands, which were visible to him, as if his touch were unbearably good. I needed to delay him, and if he were focused on teasing my body, he might wait to fuck me. And as I had anticipated, he lowered his mouth to my nipple and swirled his tongue around it. I felt the usual physical response, since I was fairly sensitive, but it didn't turn me on. Still, he needed him to think it did, so I moaned softly and arched my back, pressing against his tongue. He pressed his teeth into my body and I wondered if he were going to bruise me. Well, I would just heal myself. It was unlikely any marks he left would last more than a few hours.

He lifted his head and clasped my hands. "Have you already contacted Lee?" he asked.

"Yes," I said, unwilling to lie. Maybe this would dissuade him, but he just grinned.

"He's completely occupied for the next forty minutes," he said. "He might be angry, but we have plenty of time."

Forty minutes was a long time to stall, I thought with an edge of panic. Twenty, maybe. Thirty was pushing it. I had never delayed anyone for forty minutes before, and with someone this determined to take me, I had never managed above ten. Most people wanted to savor me and didn't mind the delay, but if they really wanted to fuck me, there was only so much I could do.

I let my body respond as he continued sucking along my skin. He was indeed leaving marks along my chest, collarbone and neck. But I encouraged him, giving every indication that I was enjoying this, because I could deal with a few bruises. If he fucked me, though, I would get in trouble.

But he spent only a few minutes sucking on me before he flipped me onto my belly. I tensed. This wasn't good. I looked back at him and licked my lips. I was going to be a little bolder than usual, but it was required.

"Can I taste you?" I asked in as seductive a voice as possible.

He stared at me. He was hard, and without a word, he stood up and gestured me to get on my knees. It was a very submissive position, and one I was quite used to. I got on my knees and stroked to the waistband on his pants. He was in a suit and I felt very comfortable undressing him. I would have been more hesitant if he were in a kimono, and I was glad I knew how to take my time with this, teasing and arousing him as I went, but soon enough his cock was in front of my face and I leaned forward and extended my tongue. He let out a grunt as my tongue wound around him, then I began using all of my tricks to entice him into staying in this position but delaying his orgasm. Maybe I should bring him to orgasm here, but he would probably still fuck me even if I did. Men who wanted to dominate me usually had no problems getting it up multiple times, and he was likely the same.

I let him fuck deep into my throat as he grabbed my hair and thrust against me. I couldn't breathe, he was thrusting so hard, but I knew how to handle it. He was rough, but it was nothing compared to many of the men I'd been with. I kept him satisfied as he fucked my throat, needing to keep him here as long as possible. I could feel him starting to lose control when there was a buzz at the door. He paused, withdrawing enough for me to catch my breath. Since the door didn't immediately open, I knew it wasn't Lee.

Lee-sama smirked and I opened my mouth for him again as he entered me, but there was another buzz, then a muffled voice.

"I'm coming in," a man said, and then, without warning, the door opened and an older man in a suit entered. He didn't seem surprised to see me on my knees with a cock in my mouth. Lee-sama looked annoyed as he pulled out of me.

"You're not welcome, Kim," Lee-sama warned.

"I need to speak with the sagent about legal matters."

"He's occupied. Come back."

Lee-sama was getting soft from the conversation, and I did nothing to help him keep his erection even though I would if he were a target. I was grateful he wasn't the type of man who got off from other people watching, because otherwise he might start fucking me harder.

"This is urgent," the man said. "Unless I speak with him about an issue in his contract, he can't work for us."

Lee-sama cursed. "Are you serious? Lee doesn't make mistakes in his contracts."

"His costs were not fully calculated when he signed, and a mistake arose when Lee did input them. If we want to keep him, I need to talk to him."

My heart fluttered. Was that true, or was he just saying it to get Lee-sama out? If there was a problem with my contract, if I couldn't stay here, then Acron would find me. I used my microbes to buffer my fear, but I realized I had accidentally allowed my body to leave its highly aroused state. Lee-sama could probably tell I was afraid, and no longer into this. He cursed again and withdrew completely, pulling his pants back up before grabbing my chin.

"We'll continue when he's done," Lee-sama threatened. "Don't go anywhere."

I didn't say anything, because that wasn't in my control, but he seemed satisfied because he left with a glare at the man. Kim. It was a last name, and one of the more common ones, I had learned. When Lee-sama was gone, Kim waved for me to stand.

"Take some time to recover," Kim said. "I'll be here a while. Lee sent me."

He gestured towards the bathroom and I obeyed, then washed out my mouth and pulled my kimono back on properly. I tried to be quick, because I didn't want him to wait, but I wasn't too quick, because I did want him to stay. As long as he was here, Lee-sama would stay away. Once he left, I would be back on my knees.

"Is there really a problem with my contract?" I asked nervously when I returned. He did indeed have a stack of papers, and he brought them to the table. I sat across from him and my heart sank. It was my contract. There was a problem. I needed to resolve it quickly or else I would lose the protection of the yakuza. I would do anything to stay away from Acron.

"Not a problem, exactly, but your signature is void at the moment," Kim said, and I flinched. I hid it, but I was terrified.

"What do I need to do? Do I need to sign again? Do I need to do something?"

"You signed without knowing what you were signing," Kim explained. "Unless you fully understand the agreement, it could be argued that you were coerced into signing."

"Why does that matter?"

He stared at me oddly. "You have to understand the terms to sign something."

That wasn't true, but maybe he was just saying this to kill time and protect me from Lee-sama.

"So I just need to sign it again now that Lee input my costs?" I asked hopefully.

"I need to walk you through everything," Kim said. "Lee would have sent for me when you signed but I guess you needed medical attention and couldn't take the time."

"Are you... a lawyer?" I asked cautiously. I had only met a lawyer once, when someone suspected me of murder. I had indeed killed the woman and the lawyer had demanded a personal price in addition to the price he charged my agency that I then had to work off. He wasn't the worst target I ever had, but he was quite rough with me in exchange for his services and I dreaded the thought of repeating it. I had never seen a lawyer outside of that, because sagents weren't allowed to talk to lawyers.

"Yes," he said. "My job is to represent you and make sure you get what you need. If there are any terms you don't like, tell me and I can negotiate on your behalf. We may not get everything that you want, but I'll push for it. Some terms, though, are non-negotiable. Is there anything you want going in?"

"You can negotiate a contract?" I asked, confused. "Don't I just sign it?"

"Lee told me you might not understand," Kim said with a sigh. "I'll tell you if I think you need to push for more. Ready?"

I nodded, and he put the first page in front of us and began explaining the terms being outlined. As we went through every single page, I was amazed at everything that was covered, and also by what Lee had given me. I was getting vacation immediately, and a lot of it. I could accumulate one day a month, and if I didn't use it, it rolled over to the next month and then stayed for two years. Kim recommended saving vacation for a longer break once I had enough. In addition to vacation, I was also allowed sick days. I had to stop him and ask what those were, because I'd never heard of them, and I couldn't believe such a thing existed. Sagents didn't get normal diseases and Kim explained that it was mostly used after a difficult job or if I were injured while working. I didn't know how to get him to understand that I was injured on every job, and just had to keep going. I doubted I would ever use a sick day, but I was amazed it existed. I was also only working six days a week and despite my opposition, he said he was going to push for five.

"Many people get a two-day weekend," he explained. "It's a standard amendment. Given your costs, he should allow it."

"I don't want more time off," I said nervously. "What am I supposed to do if I'm not working? I have to work. I'm full-time. I don't even want one day off. Can you take that out?"

Kim laughed. "Pick up a hobby," he recommended. "Read some books, watch some movies. You'll appreciate the time off before long. I'm asking for two days."

It didn't take me long to realize that it didn't actually matter what I wanted. He thought he knew best, and my protestations made little impact. He kept saying he would demand more freedoms for me, but I didn't want more freedom. I didn't know what to do with freedom. I was a slave. I was a sagent. I was shocked enough by the things Lee was allowing me, including a monthly allowance that didn't need to be paid back. If I lived within my means, then I wouldn't be charged for anything. I wouldn't have to work it back. And after I paid off their initial investment, which he said would take two years, one at full-time and one part-time, I would start earning a portion of my profits. It took him quite a while to explain that concept to me, since sagents didn't use money and I didn't understand why I would want to earn it, but it was added to my monthly allowance and rolled over just like the vacation days. I could save up for a big purchase, he suggested, but I couldn't imagine anything I would ever want.

Nearly three hours passed as he went over the terms, having to explain a lot. Sometimes he got annoyed at my ignorance and insistence on stricter terms, but mostly he was amused. He asked about conditions in Destiny several times and seemed amazed at how sagents were supposed to be treated. I was in disbelief, because this couldn't be my real contract. Maybe Lee had sent him here with a fake contract just to kill time, but why? It didn't make sense and when I finally signed it, I did so as if in a dream.

"Do you understand what you're signing?" Kim asked before handing me the signature page.

"I think," I said. "Are you sure this is all right?"

"These are your rights," he said. "I know you need a functioning contract at all times, so you may have to sign one more time if we get any of our amendments. But you're fully covered by this, and fully protected. Do you have any other questions?"

My mind was reeling with the confusing terms, but I remembered the cause of this interruption and glanced at the door.

"Is Lee-sama still here?"

"You call him Lee-sama?" Kim asked. I wondered what he was supposed to be called. Lee had seemed surprised, too. "I'm sure he told you to call him that, didn't he? We'll check, but I doubt he stayed this long. The other sagent is supposed to be here by now, and he won't try anything once she's here. She has quite a bit of seniority and even if he orders her to leave, it's unlikely she will."

"She'll disobey someone?" I asked in disbelief.

"She'll obey Lee's command to stay with you," Kim corrected. "Lee's orders take precedence over his. But you're so new that you can't really stand up to him yet. It's safer for you to obey him, and just let Lee know any time you see him so he or someone else can stand up for you."

"Thank you," I said shyly. "How do you want me to repay you?"

He looked puzzled, then laughed. "Sagents at the yakuza do not pay for services like this with their bodies. You shouldn't even offer. Your body is to be used on jobs only. Remember that."

I blushed and nodded. We stood up and checked the hall. Mei was leaning against the wall looking bored, and Lee-sama was nowhere to be seen. We opened the door and Kim was replaced by Mei, who smiled at the lawyer before turning her smile to me. I noticed her eyes lingering on my neck, where one of Lee-sama's bruises was probably visible. He had left quite a few in visible places and I hadn't covered them the way I would if I were leaving, because I had assumed he would be back.

"You got your contract worked out?" she asked, and I was amazed at how easily she said the word. Sagents vanished for saying that word. But here, it was openly talked about, and even negotiated. This was a strange place, with strange freedoms, and it would take a long time for me to adjust.

CHAPTER 32

FRIENDSHIPS

My body still ached from my morning workout, and Mei and I mostly sat and talked about things. She showed me how to access movies and was surprised when I told her I didn't watch them. I always read about them, because I often needed to be able to talk about them, but I didn't have time to sit and watch something for over an hour. She insisted on watching a movie, and I reluctantly agreed. I had to admit it was rather fun. She chose an action-adventure about a group of explorers who snuck down to Earth and found it filled with an advanced species of humans who had adapted and survived. They were strangely mutated and seemed to be based on sagents, as they seduced nearly all of the human explorers. It was fascinating and I found myself wanting to watch more. Seeing my interest, Mei recommended several other films and some books as well.

We then went for a walk around the podhouse, though I was incredibly nervous to be in public where anyone – including Lee-sama – could approach me. I took several minutes to prepare, making sure that all of my visible body was flawless before reluctantly leaving the room. Mei insisted, saying Lee had wanted me to stay active. Laying around all day after my workout would have been a mistake, but I would have preferred being active in private, as would happen at my old agencies. When we finally returned to my room, she offered to help me download some books to read. I was about to respond when a message flashed in my chip. I opened it immediately, as messages meant orders, and I needed to respond quickly or face punishment. But it wasn't from Lee. It was from Sora, and the message was strange.

"What is it?" Mei asked.

"I got a message from Sora," I said, puzzled. "Am I supposed to be doing something right now?"

"Not really," Mei said. "It's a day off for you. For me, too. What did he say?"

"He asked how I'm doing," I said in confusion. "Why does he need to know? Are you sure I'm not supposed to be doing something? Why isn't Lee contacting me if he's concerned?"

"It's possible Lee's busy, but I think Sora's just making sure you're doing okay," Mei said.

"What am I supposed to say?"

"Well, how are you?"

"Good, I guess, but what does he want me to say?"

"Tell him you're fine," she said. Now she sounded puzzled. "I know you understand how small talk works. He's just checking on you."

"Is he allowed to check on me?"

Mei stared at me. "Do you never chat with your friends in Destiny?"

"Chat?"

"You know that word," she said. "I know you know it."

Then she paused. "You do have friends in Destiny, don't you? People you care about and talk to?"

"Sagents aren't allowed to have friends," I said. "We have to stay isolated to maintain our value."

"Well, you shouldn't have too many friends or it might impact your neutrality," she said. "But surely you had some."

"I saw my sister every couple of months," I offered, though that wasn't what she meant.

Mei shook her head. "The three of us share a handler. That gives us the right to be friends. Sora and I are quite close. He seems to like you a lot, so I'm sure he wants to be friends with you, too. He's just checking on you. You don't have to respond, if you don't want, but just a word or two is fine."

I considered the message on my chip. Lee had seemed to want me and Sora to be close, perhaps even friends. And small talk was a way to develop relationships. Maybe that was how friendships developed. It had been years since I'd had friends, and I barely remembered what friends did with each other, but I could handle small talk. I entered a brief message and sent it. Then I considered Mei.

"Do you want to be friends with me?"

Mei chuckled. "We've spent two days together and I've saved your life twice. You don't already consider me a friend?"

I was silent, and she laughed.

"All right," she said. "I guess it takes more than that for you, since you don't have any friends. You did growing up, right?"

"Yeah," I said. "But it's been a while. I guess one of them also became a sagent, but I've never seen him. He went to another agency. I forgot about him."

"You need a union in Destiny," she said. "The way you're treated is unspeakable."

"What's a union?"

She explained, and I was surprised. I had never heard of collective bargaining, but it sounded like a great way to do things. It also sounded like exactly the reason sagents were so isolated. If we banded together and refused to work unless we got better conditions, the agencies would have no options. It was unlikely there would be sagents willing to be scabs, as she called them, who would work when no one else would. Every sagent I had ever met wanted better conditions, though no one ever dared complain. The agencies would completely lose control.

"The only reason we have a union here is because of Lee," Mei added. "He organized us, both in and out of the yakuza, and helped us get rights. We're an official class of people in the government, and we have unique rights. Anyone with the correct microbe level gets the rights that he fought for."

It had to be because Lee had almost been a sagent and he had those microbe levels. When he fought for rights for sagents, he was also fighting for himself. Had conditions for sagents in the Drops been similar to Destiny before that? Probably. I wondered if there were anyone capable of leading the sagents in a unified revolt in Destiny. Sagents were so scattered and so restricted that it would be almost impossible to unify them. But all of them wanted protections. All of them would help.

"We talk to each other sometimes," I said. "About how we're treated. No one likes it. We use codes so our handlers don't know."

"Is that what you were trying to do the other day?" she asked, and I nodded. "What were you trying to say?"

"I wanted to know if you'd seen your, um, contract," I said nervously, uncomfortable saying the word out loud. "I've never known a sagent who's seen one, but Lee showed me mine. We all want to see them to know what we're required to do, or if our handlers are making things up. But anyone who says the word vanishes."

"You know, if every single sagent in Destiny started disobeying at the same time, they couldn't kill all of you," she pointed out, but I shivered.

"Vanishing isn't dying," I explained. "It means you'll be tortured and you'll eventually die. They would do that to all of us, at least until we obeyed again. Almost every sagent vanishes at some point, when their value gets too low, but they'd vanish everyone if we disobeyed."

She reached out to place her hand on my shoulder in a comforting gesture.

"I'm sorry you had to live there, Byul. I'm glad you're here now."

"Yeah," I said, thinking of my sister and parents. My eyes grew warm and I pulled out of her reach. "It doesn't matter."

There was another flash on my chip and again I instantly checked, but it was Sora again with another puzzling message.

"Is Sora allowed to talk to me right now?" I asked. "I thought he went with Lee to work."

"He's probably taking a break," she said. "Why?"

"You're sure we're not supposed to be doing anything?"

"We're allowed to do anything we want," she said. "What did he ask?"

I entered a quick response and glanced back at her. "He asked what I was doing."

She looked at her chip and I saw her concentrate briefly, probably sending a message of her own. I wondered what she was doing, if she was reporting me in some way for talking to Sora. But she smiled at me.

"I told him he was making you nervous," she explained. "He'll leave you alone for a while. But at some point, you're going to have to get used to him. He's very chatty. You can always ignore him."

"He messages you, too?" I asked, surprised.

"He's already checked in on you a couple of times," she said with a shrug. "He's working, but it's just training. He has plenty of breaks."

"Lee asked me to help with training," I said hesitantly.

"You are quite talented," she said, sounding unsurprised. "I'm sure he has you in training, too, doesn't he?"

"Yes, but not with the others," I said. "How can he handle that many sagents?"

"Most of them are already primarily under their handlers' care," she explained. "They live in the complex nearby, but spend their days off with their new handlers getting to know them."

"Days off?" I repeated. "But it's training."

"It's going to take quite a while for you to adapt, Byul," she said, but it wasn't with any malice. She was just stating a fact, and I agreed. Everything was so different here, and not just the customs and food. The way they treated sagents was shocking and almost off-putting. I remembered what I had said to Lee before I knew he was my handler, about handlers not treating sagents like humans. In Destiny, sagents weren't human. We were objects to be used as much as possible before we inevitably broke. But here, sagents were considered human. They seemed to have similar rights to humans, perhaps even the same rights. It was due to Lee, I now knew, and based on Lee's earlier comments about almost being a sagent, I knew it was because of his past. I wondered at that. He had told me; had he told others?

"Do you know anything about Lee?" I asked cautiously, hoping it was appropriate.

"I've known him a long time," she said without hesitation. "What do you want to know?"

"Is it okay for me to ask questions about him?"

"He's your handler," she said. "It's natural you're curious. You can ask. If it's too personal, I'll tell you. I suppose you're wondering why he has microbes. Most sagents sense that pretty quickly."

I was surprised, but nodded. "He said he almost became a sagent."

"He's already talked to you about it?" she asked, sounding genuinely surprised. "He normally avoids the subject, but I guess it would help reassure you."

"What happened? He didn't want to talk about it so I didn't ask."

"What did he tell you?"

I briefly explained what he had said about the rival Family and she nodded. "That's the basics, but when you've been here a while you hear more details. Most of the yakuza know about him, and what he did. It's why he's so highly respected. He was the younger child, after all. He never would have inherited power, so if he hadn't acted as he did, it wouldn't matter that his father was head of the Family at one point. And the other clans wouldn't care about him."

"What did he do, then?" I asked.

"He was kidnapped by the son of a rival Family, as he told you," she said. "But they didn't inject him immediately, and they didn't do it to make him a sagent. They tortured him for days, trying to get him to betray his Family. They broadcast it to his Family, too, so everyone heard. There are still recordings that the heads of the Families listen to. It's a lesson in loyalty, they say, because he never broke, and he insulted the rival Family the entire time."

My eyes widened. That explained why he hadn't wanted to talk about it. I wondered what it would be like to be tortured without training. I knew how to handle it, but he wouldn't. Of course, I also would have broken instantly because that was part of my training. Well, not really breaking, but giving the appearance of breaking. If you didn't break, it just made it worse and I couldn't imagine what he had endured.

"Eventually they got tired of him," Mei said. "They injected him with enough microbes to mutate him. The process takes hours, usually. It's not instant. But they forgot that microbes also give people strength, and he killed all of them. His Family rescued him and drained his blood to rid him of the microbes. It doesn't always work, but they got to him before the change had set, and he was saved. There are other rumors, too," she added. "That an agency from Destiny was involved, that they were experimenting on him. That they were the ones who convinced the rival son to kidnap him in the first place. But they're just rumors. The rest is fact."

She eyed me. "He was twenty-one when it happened. I heard you're twenty-one, too. He'll probably be gentler with you than he normally would. Your situation has a lot of similarities to his."

I thought of the pain in his eyes when I confessed that I didn't want to be a sagent, and suddenly understood. It wasn't that I had caused him pain. I had stirred his memories, and they caused him pain. I was a little relieved that I hadn't hurt him, but then again, he wouldn't have been in pain if I hadn't reminded him of that experience so strongly. I wondered about the Destiny agency. Lee had said that they were experimenting on me by injecting me with so many microbes. Was that the same type of experiment he had been subjected to? Had the intent been to test him, not kill him, as the yakuza imagined? I wasn't sure, and couldn't talk about it with anyone because no one could know that my microbe count was above average.

Maybe Ananti, I considered. If I saw her again, I would ask. I had also never imagined that someone could lose a significant number of microbes through blood loss. I always worried about it when I bled, and was careful to keep my microbes, but I never thought I would lose more than a few. This sounded like he had lost a lot, enough to push him from an overdose into the safe zone. Did people in Destiny know about that? People didn't always survive Transition Day; if Destiny knew how to decrease the amount of microbes, was there a chance of saving them?

"I assume you know not to bring this up around him," she said. "It's not a secret, but he doesn't like to be reminded of it. Eric-san brings it up sometimes, to put him on edge, but no one else dares."

"Who's Eric-san?" I asked, trying to place the honorific. It meant respect, I was pretty sure.

"Eric Lee," she said. "The man in here earlier."

"Oh," I said. "Is that what he's supposed to be called?"

"What do you call him?"

"He told me to call him Lee-sama."

"Arrogant prick," she said, and I was shocked. I had never heard a sagent insult anyone, especially not someone in their agency. Sagents were insulted all the time, but it was our place to accept those comments. We were never to reply in kind.

"Sorry, Byul," she said. "But he likes to demand more respect than he deserves and that's a pretty arrogant title. Only Lee has the right to use the family name like that. If he wants you to call him that, though, you probably should. It's better to humor him, for the most part. Lee will talk to him and hopefully he won't harass you again."

"Or he'll harass me more," I said in a low voice, thinking of all the animosity and jealousy that must lay between them. Mei looked at me in surprise, and I realized I had spoken out of turn and implicitly insulted Lee-sama. I had to be more careful. She was so free with her speech that I was relaxing, and I couldn't relax. I had to be perfect at all times.

"Maybe you should go," I said rather abruptly. "I'm sure I'm keeping you from something."

"My job right now is to keep you company," Mei said. "Why do you want me to leave? Because you finally spoke your mind?"

I blushed. "I spoke out of turn. I can't let that become habit."

"I doubt you'd say something like that in front of a target, and even if you did, it would amuse them," she said. "Most targets appreciate humor and honesty, even if you have to manipulate it to your advantage."

I shook my head. "I'm sorry. I shouldn't have said anything, and I can't ever speak like that in front of a target. Maybe it's best if we don't talk."

"You're just getting interesting," she said with a mischievous smile. "And you can't kick me out. Lee wants me here. He wants me talking to you, too."

It was probably true. Lee would want me distracted from my thoughts and would have asked Mei to keep me busy, and that meant talking. She couldn't disobey, and neither could I. But I could watch myself more closely, and as Mei tactfully changed the subject and offered to walk me around the complex again, I agreed and vowed to watch my tongue. I couldn't lose control or let my guard down, and even though that was difficult here, with these strange people, it was part of my test. I wouldn't forget myself again.

CHAPTER 33

TRAINING

I took a deep breath and straightened my features. Lee was beside me, waiting for me to be ready to face the other sagents. I was allowed to take a moment to prepare. Even Acron allowed it sometimes. When sagents had to be perfect, we were able to take a moment first. But only a moment, because any more than that would be punished. I nodded at Lee and he opened the door and gestured me in.

Seven sagents were kneeling on the ground in a half-circle facing a bed, four women and three men. There were six yakuza behind them who must be their handlers, three men and three women. Two of them had dragon pins. Were handlers allowed to be high-ranking yakuza? Lee was, but he seemed like an exception. I bowed to the handlers, since they had power over me, and went to the center of the room with Lee. The bed was behind us. He hadn't told me exactly what we would be doing, just that I would be demonstrating some of the techniques he had seen me use on Sora and the judge.

"What a lovely sagent," one of the handlers with a pin said softly, in surprise.

I was pleased, as it was usually a good sign when other handlers were satisfied by me. Handlers were the only people who would admire me without trying to sleep with me, and I tended to have a positive view of handlers who weren't mine. Most sagents didn't hate their handlers, though the relationship

241

was adversarial to some extent. Acron was the only handler who might sleep with me. Most handlers respected the rules about sleeping with sagents. Of course, it made the knowledge of what he had done to me that much more painful. Only one handler broke the rules, and he only broke them for me.

"Remember that he's still in training, too," Lee warned. "Though I doubt he'll do anything wrong."

I wasn't sure whether that warning was intended for me or not. Was he warning me not to mess up, or was it a genuine comment to the others that I might not be perfect? It was training, after all, so perfection wasn't always required. It was for me, since Acron was always watching for my weaknesses during training, and when I was used in training later, but for most sagents, mistakes were allowed.

"My sagent is going to be demonstrating how to move into oral sex," Lee said.

That made sense. Most of the moves I made during that transition were ones I had discovered, not ones I had been taught. It made sense for Lee to want to teach those successful strategies to his other sagents. I didn't mind teaching them, and it probably meant I wouldn't have to have sex during this training, as it would likely stop before the sex. I was relieved. Most of the training I had been involved in relied on sex, and it was never pleasant.

Lee brought in a man who seemed to be the type of volunteer who helped with sagent training. It was a fairly desirable job and many people volunteered. Even though sagents in training didn't have the skills that trained sagents did, they were being taught to give pleasure and I had heard that even the worst sagent was better than most other experiences. Having volunteers also helped reduce the workload on sagents, since in the earliest lessons, trainees practiced on other sagents. That was where I was used, only the goal of the training I was used in was to hurt me. Volunteers were never hurt.

The man smiled at me eagerly and I glanced at Lee for permission before shyly smiling at him, keeping my eyes down but watching his body language for hints of what he would want in a partner. Lee leaned close to me.

"No preliminaries, just go from kissing down. Stop before you put him in your mouth, no matter what he wants."

I nodded, then Lee stepped back. The man sat on the edge of the bed, glancing at the other sagents and handlers nervously. I wondered if he had done this before. It took a certain type of person who didn't mind performing in front of this many people, especially since all of their reactions would be broken down in the training. But some people enjoyed it.

I took a few steps forward and lifted my hand towards him. He took my hand but didn't pull me closer. I wasn't used to being with shy partners, but I was certainly trained for it. In moments, I had him flat on the bed as we kissed. It was only a brief kiss, though, since that wasn't the focus. I began working my way down his neck. He was in Destiny-style clothes, luckily. I would have to learn how to do this with a kimono. I kept my body angled so that the sagents and handlers could see everything I was doing, as that was important. If they couldn't see, I would have to do it again. That wasn't a threat this time, but it often was.

Even as I let my tongue work along his belly, measuring his flinches and balancing his pleasure carefully, I made sure they could see. I was reacting as well, since Lee hadn't given me any instructions about my response. This was the typical response I would give, and I wasn't sure if that was part of the lesson or not. Because there was no foreplay before starting, I lingered more than I usually would to get the responses I wanted, and soon his hand was tangled in my hair as he moaned and pressed against me, and I skillfully kept moving down his body without letting him get what he really wanted. Right when I would usually give him what he wanted and take his cock in my mouth, I paused. The man tried to pull me forward and I backed up slightly, glancing at Lee for instruction. Lee gestured for me to sit up and I obeyed, letting my body start leaving its aroused state since that was no longer necessary.

The man moaned.

"You can't let him stop there," the man said, sounding desperate. He reached for me and I glanced at Lee, who approached and pulled me off the bed. The man rolled over, his back to the other sagents, and moaned again.

"Have some patience," Lee said to him, but he sounded sympathetic. Then he turned his attention to the sagents.

"Did you all observe carefully? What questions do you have?"

"Do they teach that in Destiny?" asked one of the women, sounding in awe.

Lee looked at me, and I realized I was supposed to answer. I wasn't sure what to say.

"You can answer honestly," Lee prompted.

"No," I said. "I figured that out myself."

The sagents and handlers looked impressed, and then one of the other sagents asked about the order of strokes I used on the chest. Lee looked at me to answer and I did, feeling unexpectedly shy. But of course I had to answer the questions. Lee hadn't taught it to me, and didn't know exactly what I was doing. There were several more questions. As I answered, Lee turned to the man on the bed and talked quietly to him, too quietly for me to hear. Two of the handlers asked me questions as well, to my surprise. I had never seen handlers participate in training before. They were focused on their sagents and making sure their sagents learned, not on learning things themselves. Then again, this was something no one else knew. Finally, the questions ended and Lee stood up. The man rolled onto his back. He was still hard and looked at me with desire.

Lee looked at the sagents, then at me. He drew close to me and spoke softly.

"Will you do that again? You'll need to go until his completion this time."

I nodded. That meant I didn't need to orgasm as well, which was easier. It wouldn't take long to give him pleasure after I finished demonstrating the moves again. I didn't mind. Lee instructed the sagents to observe again, and then stepped away. I went to the bed and this time, the man wasn't shy at all and yanked me closer. I began again, measuring his responses as I kept my body angled for them to see. Since the man was already aroused, my reactions were a little different. I tried to keep to mostly the same pattern so I wouldn't confuse the other sagents, but I had to respond to him. That was my primary goal. So my moves were different, to some extent, tailored to his motions and needs and highly aroused state. I let my body become just as aroused as last time.

This time, when I reached the end of touching him, I slid him into my throat and he moaned loudly. He thrust against me and I controlled him skillfully. I didn't want to rush him, but I didn't want to take too long, either. I gave him a few minutes before finishing him and he cried out as he orgasmed. I swallowed quickly, then withdrew from his body. Should I have swallowed? That was normal to do, as it wasn't appropriate for sagents to have cum dripping from our faces or to spit it out. I wasn't sure how the yakuza did it, though. Sometimes in training, you weren't supposed to swallow. Well, Lee hadn't specified, and that was what I would do in a real mission, so it would have to work.

This time, the man was fully satisfied and lay panting on the bed as Lee gestured me to stand beside him. Again, the other sagents asked me questions, mostly about the differences in what I had done. I could tell which sagents had little or no experience because they didn't seem to understand how to read their target's body. Most of them seemed to know exactly what I meant when I explained how I was adjusting to his needs, but two of them didn't. I glanced at Lee, unsure how to explain any further, and he smiled.

"You'll learn how to do that in time," he assured the sagents. "Any other questions?"

One of the handlers crossed his arms. He looked amused.

"How is he possibly still in training?"

"He's adjusting to the Drops," Lee said, and the handler seemed satisfied by the answer. I wondered, though. How long would I be in training? I would never have problems controlling my pleasure again, not since I had learned how to do it. Did Lee know I had fully mastered it? Was there anything else I needed to learn, or was it really just a matter of understanding the different culture?

Lee took my arm and pulled me to the side of the room, then escorted the man on the bed out of the room. Another volunteer came in. His eyes went to me immediately and my stomach sunk. How many times would I have to do this? But Lee pointed to the sagent who seemed the most experienced.

"Your turn," he said. The sagent stood up and glanced at his handler, who urged him forward. Lee came to stand next to me against the wall. "Watch carefully," he told me quietly. "If you see him make any mistakes, tug my sleeve and I'll stop him. You'll need to help him a few times, I expect. Do you object?"

"No," I said, relieved and curious. I had never been involved like this before. As the sagent moved a little awkwardly into kissing, Lee gave a correction and the sagent blushed before starting again, moving into it smoothly this time. They likely had no experience moving straight into things like this. Most sagents learned seduction before sex. The sagent did well until he got to the volunteer's abs, when he stroked the wrong direction with his tongue. I tugged Lee's sleeve, and Lee called for him to stop. The volunteer moaned softly, but didn't protest. Lee brought me forward and gestured for me to give the correction.

"You should do it clockwise," I said nervously, not used to giving instructions like this. "That's the way the blood flows there. You should be able to feel the pulse under your tongue. Try to speed it up with the motion."

The sagent nodded as Lee pulled me back to the wall, then had the sagent start from the beginning again. He was slower this time, more hesitant, and I could tell that this time, he was paying attention to blood flow. He did a good job and didn't make any other mistakes, aside from speed. I glanced at Lee, not knowing whether or not speed was something to comment on. Lee noticed and gestured for me to whisper to him.

"He's too slow," I said quietly, and Lee nodded.

"Wait for that," Lee said. I obeyed and continued paying attention, but the sagent did well. He stopped before taking the volunteer in his mouth, the same way I had stopped. But the volunteer wasn't nearly as desperate, because the strokes hadn't been fast enough to send the man's heart pounding.

"Good job," Lee said, and I was surprised. Lee knew the sagent had been too slow but was still congratulating him? "You've got a few things to work on," Lee added. But there was no mention of punishment.

Lee pulled me forward slightly. "What did you see wrong with it?" he asked me. I hoped I wasn't getting the sagent in trouble, but Lee wanted an honest answer.

"You were too slow," I said cautiously. "You have to adapt your speed to their heartbeat, and move slightly faster than that to keep their pulse increasing so they want more. If you're too slow, it still feels good, but they won't want anything else."

I gestured to the volunteer, who did look content without any other touching. The man had already lost his erection. The sagent blushed again and I hoped that wasn't dooming him to punishment. But neither Lee nor the sagent's handler mentioned punishment. Lee just nodded.

"We'll work on speed," Lee said. "I hadn't realized it was that important. Was anything else wrong?"

"No, you did very well," I said, hoping that counteracted any possible punishment, even though punishment still hadn't been mentioned. Lee smiled and squeezed my arm, then pointed to another sagent.

"You're up."

The first sagent moved back to sit down and his handler reached out to squeeze his shoulder. It was an odd gesture that indicated affection, which I had never seen between a sagent and handler before. Lee treated me like that, I realized. Did all of the handlers here treat their sagents with as much respect as Lee treated me? What a strange thought. Another volunteer came in, and I leaned back. This was nothing like the training I was used to. All I had to do was help these sagents learn, with no cost to me. I could handle this.

CHAPTER 34

ALONE

I collapsed on my sofa and stared at the ceiling. I was alone. After helping with training yesterday, I spent the afternoon and evening with Mei again. Sora contacted me several times to check on me, and I was getting used to it. He hadn't contacted me in a while, so he must be working right now. Lee had eaten breakfast with me and asked if I felt safe enough to be alone. He didn't mean physically safe. He meant if I was mentally capable of it. I was still mourning my family, but the pain was no longer as immediate. Nothing I did could change their fate. It was easier to just pretend it had already happened and they were already vanished, because if I kept dwelling on the fact that they didn't know it was coming, and imagining their reactions when they were vanished, then I would drive myself crazy. So I wasn't thinking about it.

This was the first time I had been alone in a long time, though of course I wasn't truly alone. One of the guards was here, unobtrusively stationed near the door. I shut my eyes and enjoyed the comfort of the sofa for a moment, then scooted to the chaise and reached for the remote. Mei had recommended quite a few movies and if I had a day to myself, I wanted to watch at least one of them. I picked out another adventure movie and grabbed a blanket to cuddle with. Mei had cuddled like this yesterday and when I asked if she was cold, she laughed and had me try it. I loved wrapping the blanket around me. It wasn't a temperature thing; it was a comfort thing. It was strange to be allowed such comfort.

There was a buzz on my chip and I glanced at it, smiling slightly. It was Sora, finally checking on me. I sent him a quick reply and returned to the movie. Having time to myself was strange, but I was adapting. I had spent my life talking about movies with people, but I had never really seen them before. My parents never took me to movies. I had seen a couple with friends, but it was always the movies they wanted. I had never been able to choose for myself, and have the freedom to watch it. There was another buzz and I glanced at Sora's response. Then I paused the movie and reread it. He wanted me to meet him, which I supposed made sense, but he wanted me to meet him in a different building. Did he not realize I couldn't leave? Another message popped up, assuring me that Lee had given me permission, as long as I went straight there. People would be guarding me once I left.

I considered, then asked why he wanted to see me. I trusted him, and I trusted Lee, but I wanted to know what Sora wanted so badly that I had to leave the podhouse for. There was a pause, then he responded that it was a surprise. Annoyed, I shut the entertainment console off.

"Sora wants me to leave the podhouse," I told the guard. "You'll go with me, right? He said I'd be protected, but I feel safer with you."

The guard didn't react in any way that I could sense, then I felt a tingle of microbes. It wasn't directed at me, oddly; it rippled outward and then seemed to bounce back. Was he checking with others to see what he should do? How much did the guards communicate while everyone thought they were mute? I felt the guard's response. He wasn't allowed to leave. He didn't want me to leave either, and though I didn't especially want to leave the haven of the podhouse, if Lee thought it was fine, then I would trust him.

"Thanks," I said to the guard. "I'll be back soon."

I felt reluctance from the guard as I went to the bathroom

to make sure I looked my best, then left the room. I wasn't entirely sure how to leave, since no one had told me how to contact the people in charge of moving rooms. Lee just made sure my room was attached to the right place every time I left. I looked around and went to the end of the hall where there was always a large room of some sort, whether the entrance, the medical rooms, or the gym. They were double-doors and the light flashed above them just as I approached. The door opened and Lee-sama stepped through.

His eyes latched on me immediately, hungrily, and I took a step back.

"You don't usually walk around alone," Lee-sama said. He had two people with him, both with dragon pins. High-ranking, but nowhere near as high as Lee-sama. Still, perhaps he would let me by, since there were witnesses.

I bowed low to the three of them. "I was trying to leave," I explained.

"You're running away?" Lee-sama asked with a chuckle. "You're not doing very well."

Blushing, I realized that wasn't the right thing to say.

"Lee gave me permission to leave. I'm meeting someone nearby."

"Where?"

I hesitated. "It's on my chip. I'm still learning locations."

"Slow learner," Lee-sama said, his brow crinkling. "Lee gave you permission to leave? That's unlike him. Are you sure?"

"Yes," I said. Sora wouldn't lie about that. He knew the danger to me.

Lee-sama studied me for several moments as I kept my eyes politely lowered. Finally, he gestured to the room behind him.

"The entrance is connected. Stay safe. It's dangerous for you."

"Thank you," I said, bowing again. The other two men stared at me curiously as the three of them continued down the hall. I went through the door into the entrance hall and gazed at the beautiful tapestry of the ocean. I barely noticed the dragon, so entranced was I by the rolling hills of water flowing across the bottom portion of the image. What would it be like to see that, to be there? I was jealous of the explorers who would return to Earth someday, when the microbes had all died off, and reclaim our planet. Life might not survive the assault of the microbes, but the ocean would still be there. That was what I wanted to see.

I broke my gaze from the ocean and went out the front door, hesitating only briefly before stepping out of the podhouse. At first, I saw no one and panicked, thinking no one was here to protect me, but then a group of men and women walked past with that smooth glide I knew meant they were yakuza enforcers. One of them looked at me oddly, and with an arousal that I could sense even across the street. The others ignored me, and I was glad. I knew the enforcers here wouldn't touch me, but I was still afraid.

I went down the street towards the building Sora indicated, checking the map frequently. The streets were mostly empty but every time I started to get nervous, another group of enforcers would come by. They weren't escorting me, but they were patrolling carefully and it reassured me.

The building was further than I expected, but in less than twenty minutes, I arrived. It was on the entire other side of the neighborhood. I had taken longer than I should have, I knew; a cat appeared on the street in front of me and I knelt like Lee had shown me, holding out my hand. The cat nuzzled me just like the first one. It might have been the first one, I considered. Could their coats change color? I wasn't sure.

I petted her for a long time, until she rolled over and ran just as quickly as the first cat had. Even though I had looked for dogs, I still hadn't seen one. Perhaps Sora would walk home with me and show me a dog.

It was an older building and almost looked abandoned, and I circled the block before approaching the door, wondering why Sora would possibly bring me here. I sent him a message that I'd arrived, not knowing if I should walk in, or knock, or wait, and I sent Lee a message, too, letting him know I'd arrived safely.

Something slammed into my shoulder and I jolted forward, nearly falling to me knees. My shoulder stung and it was quickly growing numb. How hard of a push was that? I looked back to see who had pushed into me like that but as I turned, I fell, my body growing weak and my eyesight growing blurry. I felt a message on my chip and I managed to key it. It was Lee, and the message flashed through my eyes.

Where are you?!

I couldn't respond, couldn't think, couldn't move, as my body went limp and blackness shrouded my vision.

CHAPTER 35

REMEMBERED PAIN

T he smell hit me first. I knew it. It wasn't just the physical scent; microbes mingled with the odor to rasp against my senses and my nostrils flared. Pain. Sweat. Blood. Fear. It was what I associated most strongly with my first agency. With Acron. Was this a nightmare? I had them sometimes, and they often started like this. The smell, then my own fear setting the microbes tingling, compounding the oppressive scent into an overpowering aroma that crippled me. It was starting already, and I felt so weak.

I became aware of my body next. I was tied up, sitting in a chair with one leg strapped to each chair leg and my hands behind me. Of course I was, if this were a nightmare of my first agency. It seemed like I had been tied up or bound more than I had been free. There was a thick cloth over my eyes, a gag in my mouth. My hands were locked behind my back in metal clasps that forced my fingers straight so I couldn't use my chip. That was new. My agency never bothered with that type of restraint because they knew I had no one to contact, no way to fight even with my chip. They controlled me. Why would I be dreaming up new ways for them to restrain me?

Someone took the gag out of my mouth and I gasped. That had never happened, either.

"Are you awake?" a cruel voice asked.

It was a good question. A tingle of fear shivered down my

spine. I couldn't be awake. This couldn't be real. This had to be a dream.

"No," I whispered.

There was laughter from at least two people. I reached out with my microbes to see if I could identify them, and my heart screeched to a halt. Acron. He hadn't spoken. He was on the other side of the room, I could tell. But he was watching me, amused by me, toying with me. And this wasn't a dream.

"You'll be punished for lying," Acron said, and I could feel him approaching. I stiffened in the chair that held me bound, but didn't want to react too much, for fear the punishment would be worse. Even so, he saw that instinctive reaction. I heard the air rush before his hand slammed into my cheek so hard the entire chair toppled, slamming into my right leg painfully. I didn't react. Any reaction would make it worse.

"At least you remember some things," Acron said, then grabbed my hair and hauled me back up. My eyes warmed at the pain, but I couldn't cry. I hadn't felt pain like this in a long time, but tears were not an option, not if I wanted to survive.

"Do you want me to remove your blindfold?" he asked, and I hesitated, wondering what the correct answer was. I tried to read him through my microbes.

"Yes, please, sir," I whispered, fairly sure I was right.

The air rushed at me again but I didn't move, didn't flinch, and no blow landed. Instead, I felt fingers untying the thick cloth and it fell from my eyes. Acron was to one side, and there was a man I had never seen before standing in front of me. And there, shackled to the wall across the room, was-

Sora.

I gasped, unable to stop myself, and another blow knocked me to the ground and silenced me. It was Sora. He was covered in blood and bruises, but it didn't seem like he'd been permanently damaged. He was gagged, but he was awake and watching me. Acron hauled me up by my hair again and pointed to Sora.

"If you disobey me again, he'll be punished with you. Understand?"

"Yes, sir," I said softly, but clearly. He wanted to hear my answer, so I couldn't mumble. Acron ran his hand through my hair gently, but the touch ignited fire in the follicles that ached from being yanked around so much. I sent my microbes to dull the pain, to heal the damage. I started healing my cheek and leg, too, though more slowly, as I didn't want Acron to notice. The pain subsided. Then a blade pierced my back. I only barely kept from reacting as the blade was dragged down, severing muscles and tissues and nerves and veins and right when I was about to faint from the pain, Acron withdrew the blade.

"Heal yourself," he said, and I sent all of my microbes to the task. He must have known I was using my microbes to dull my pain, and done this so I would have to focus entirely on surviving and be unable to spare anything for comfort. As I worked to bring the flesh back together, I knew not only that I would be able to heal completely without leaving a scar, but also that it would be hours before I was able to focus on anything else. I was completely helpless to him. As he liked it.

I felt hands on my wrists, and then I was free, though my fingers were still restrained. Acron came to the front and untied my legs as well. That was never a good sign. At least while I was bound, he could only do limited damage and I could hide my reactions better. When I was free, my entire body was exposed. I stood at his command. The cut in my back was perilously close to my left shoulder. I could still move my arm, but it was extremely painful and dragged my wound open again. If he made me use that arm, it would be even more hours before I healed. He was going to make me use that arm without question.

"I want you to kick your fellow sagent in a way that maximizes pain without causing damage," Acron said.

I mentally braced myself and obeyed. Sora screamed, and kept screaming after I returned to Acron's side. Acron watched me as Sora's screams finally subsided into groans and pants. Then Acron caressed my cheek.

"He hasn't learned yet, but he will," Acron said, and my heart chilled. "He's my sagent now. What is his name?"

"Smith," I said without hesitation, because hesitation would end Sora's life.

Acron's eyes narrowed. "That's not his name. Are you disobeying me so openly?"

"Smith is how he was introduced to me," I said, praying Sora wouldn't react in any way to contradict this. I couldn't look at him, but I could feel surprise in his microbes. I could also feel, to my relief, that he wasn't in nearly as much pain as he was pretending.

"You never learned his true name?"

"Sagents don't reveal their names," I answered. I hadn't lied to Acron yet but I would, to keep him from knowing Sora's name. I wasn't even sure why it mattered so much, since it was just a name, but it embodied the trust Sora had placed in me and I needed him to know that I would protect him no matter what, even if Acron forced me to hurt him again. He needed to know he wasn't alone, because I knew what it was like to be alone before Acron, and I wouldn't doom anyone else to it.

Acron studied me for a long time as Sora's moans grew farther apart. He was in pain, I could tell, but it was pain he could easily handle. He knew how to fake pain, even though I doubted he'd ever had to do it before. But why was he faking? It would only invite more pain. It was a stalling tactic, I realized. And it would protect me, to some degree. Because if Acron focused on him, he couldn't focus on me. But I could handle it, and he couldn't. Still, we might be able to make this work, to make it less painful for both of us while we stalled. Because I remembered Lee's message right before I fainted earlier. He didn't know where I was, but he knew I was gone.

"I'll ask you again, when you're more receptive to questioning," Acron finally said. "If you're lying, he'll be the one to pay."

I didn't shiver, couldn't shiver, but I wanted to. Acron knew how to break me. If I broke, would I remember to keep Sora's name a secret? Then Acron's eyes went to the other man in the room. He was a hulking man, with heavy muscles and pale skin like mine, hair a dusty brown. He seemed like backup and I wondered who else Acron had. He had to have a lot of protection to feel so confident. We were still in the Drops, I could tell. There were microbes in the air. But as Lee had once reassured me, the yakuza controlled the Drops. How was Acron arrogant enough to think he wouldn't be found?

"Call in the others and enjoy him for a while. Careful of his back. But use him thoroughly, with as much force as you see fit."

I stayed calm, wondering how many others there were. Acron turned back to me.

"You'll enjoy yourself with them," he commanded. "Every time they come, you come. If you're more than a minute ahead or behind them, you'll be punished."

"Yes, sir," I said. We had done this before. It was his way of preparing me for worse punishment ahead. He knew it would drain me of my resources, and with my microbes occupied with healing, it would take every single resource I had to control my body properly. By the end of this, I would be exhausted, in agony, and desperate. Then the pain would really begin.

Six men entered and I mentally braced myself as the first man pulled me into a rough embrace. This was going to hurt, and I was going to be weak, but I had done this before with seven men. It had been years, but I could still do it. I wouldn't fail, couldn't fail, because Sora would be punished with me. But as the men descended on me, I saw Acron release Sora from his shackles and lead him into another room. My heart screeched in fear, but there was nothing I could do. I just had to survive, and trust Sora to do the same.

CHAPTER 36
UNABLE TO HEAL

Five hours had passed. The men were finished. They had taken turns, resting so they could go again. I was mentally and physically drained and my back bled freely, blood mixing with semen to drip down my legs. I was standing, because that was what they wanted, but I wouldn't be able to stand much longer. I couldn't take any of this much longer. Not this many men, not this long. But none of them approached anymore.

Sora and Acron returned two hours into it. Sora was pale and in pain as Acron shackled him again, but he was alive and there was no permanent damage. Physical damage, that was. I could feel sharp pain radiating from him, even though I couldn't see any specific injury that would cause it. I couldn't pay too much attention to him, but I kept checking on him when the men rotated. Acron left for nearly twenty minutes before returning and lounging nearby, stroking himself as I remained absolutely silent and gave the men everything they wanted.

And now the men weren't approaching, and Acron stood. It was his turn. Somehow, having sex with him was far more painful than anyone else. It wasn't the physical aspects; no matter how violent he was, it wouldn't be worse than what I had just experienced. It was the sense of betrayal I still felt when I looked at him. He was my handler. He was supposed to protect me, care for me, treasure me. Looking at him was looking at my shattered dreams, my vanished childhood, the moment when despair first overtook me and I broke. It was almost more than I could stand as he approached me slowly.

"What is the sagent's name?"

"Smith," I said, my voice hoarse.

Acron stared at me, probably trying to measure my exhaustion and ability to lie. I had never lied to him before. Did he suspect me now? But he seemed satisfied and came up next to me.

"You're probably wondering why you haven't been rescued," Acron said lazily.

I had wondered that, though not much. There wasn't room for many thoughts when getting fucked like that. Now that he'd brought it up, though, a dark curiosity rose in me. Where was Lee? He should have found me by now. He knew I couldn't have gone far. Or had Acron moved me when I was unconscious? Even so, he had claimed to control the Drops and I believed him.

"He's abandoned you," Acron continued with a smirk. "I made him an offer, and he accepted it."

I stayed silent. Once I would have believed him, because it wouldn't occur to me that a handler would lie. But now that I knew how much of my life in Destiny had been built on lies in order to abuse me, I didn't believe him at all. Lee would never agree to anything with Acron.

Acron approached me and caressed my cheek, his hand trailing down my sweat- and cum-stained cheek to my neck. He shook his hand out and his smirk intensified.

"Sagents shouldn't look as disheveled as you do."

It was true, and I would be punished for it, but there was nothing I could do. He would punish me if I moved, so I couldn't wipe the mess off my body, and without a bathroom, I couldn't make myself up the way I needed to. I wondered if it would be better to be punished for moving, or for being messy. The punishments seemed about even, as I thought about it, and moving seemed more dangerous with him right here. I stayed still.

"You don't even care what the deal is?" Acron said, his eyes boring into mine. I didn't know what the right answer was, so I remained silent. It was almost always better to be silent than to speak. But as the air shifted and he slammed me to the floor, I realized this wasn't one of those times. I hid my pain as I lay on the floor and at his command, I stood. The motion had ripped my healing back apart again. More hours of healing, hours of pain. But I could still heal it completely. He would never risk permanent damage to me. I used the movement of standing to brush my face clean, hoping that was acceptable. He didn't comment on the gesture, so it must have been fine. When I was standing again, he stared at me. He wanted something from me. What did he want? If I didn't figure it out quickly, I was going to get punished. I thought about what he had been saying before knocking me down. That must be it.

"What is the deal, sir?"

It was so hard to think clearly through the pain, but I had to. Not only did my life depend on this, but Sora's did, too. I couldn't let anything else happen to him and I worried, because the pain I sensed from him sharpened every time he looked at me. Had I hurt him? Had Acron turned him against me somehow? Or did he hate me because this was my fault?

"If he interferes, you die and I leave with the other. He can't stop either of those things. If he lets me have you, then when I'm finished here, I'll leave that sagent," he said, gesturing to Sora. "He only gets one of you, and he's chosen his own sagent, not you."

My mind whirled. That didn't make sense, did it? Why would Lee agree to something like that? Maybe he would choose Sora over me, I could believe that, but not if both of us were hurt. If he were choosing Sora, why would he allow Sora to be hurt like this? That couldn't be the right deal. But he wanted me upset by the news, so I spared a few microbes to imbue my expression with shock and betrayal and not the confusion I actually felt. It worked, because Acron grinned.

"Are you upset? You should have known you could never escape me. You'll be punished for trying."

I barely stopped from shivering and knew a faint tremble

was visible, because his eyes narrowed. But it must have been small enough that he wasn't sure, because he didn't hurt me. My fear was mounting, though, and I didn't need my microbes to express that. No matter what deal was made, no matter what was happening, Sora and I were trapped here and Lee wasn't coming. Sora wasn't capable of surviving this. Only I was. That meant any escape was up to me as well. I was barely able to think, barely able to function, but everything depended on me. But as Acron took my hands – fingers still bound – and chained them to the ceiling, I didn't know what to do. I had never learned to fight. I had learned to run away, but even that didn't come easily. I needed to fight, but I couldn't let Sora get hurt.

Acron sprayed me with a hose and I remained as still as possible, though the water pressure was intense and nearly knocked me over. I rested some of my weight on my wrists. The metal dug into my skin as I let myself hang from the ceiling. It was easier that way, and it pleased Acron to see me so weak as the water blasted my skin. I could feel bruises worsening as he carefully aimed the stream of water at the places where the men had grabbed me, punched me, sucked on me. I shut my eyes and tried to focus even as the pain sparked and spread across my body. It was so hard to think. So hard to do anything other than stand here. But if I wanted to save Sora, I had to do something. What options did I have? What could I possibly do?

The water stopped and I hung there, water streaming down my body. I hadn't even realized there was a grate below me. Or maybe I had; I remembered it pressing against me painfully during the rape but it had just been one more pain, hardly noticeable. It was so hard to get my mind to focus on anything other than the pain, starting at the balls of my feet, aching against the sharp metal grate, to my knees, trembling slightly and unable to hold me up, to my ass, still bleeding, and my cock, manipulated into orgasm so often I knew it would take days to fully recover – days I wouldn't have – to my stomach, twisted and bitter with the flavor of cum still on my lips- I stopped thinking. Blocked out all thought. It was too much pain. Too much.

Shocking pain as Acron slapped me. I jolted back into consciousness, my body screaming in protest.

"You're not near your limit," Acron said in an angry voice. "Are you so out of practice? Is this all you can stand anymore?"

"I can take more, sir," I said, because that was what he wanted. I couldn't. I knew I couldn't. But I had to.

"Good," Acron hissed, and released the chains from my hands. I nearly fell to my knees and only just managed to keep standing. He didn't comment, which wasn't a good sign. That was something I should have been punished for. If he wasn't punishing me immediately, that meant he was saving up for a larger punishment later. Should I provoke punishment now to derail that, or accept the blessing of no additional pain for the moment and brace myself for later? I glanced up at him quickly and decided to wait. He was angry, even if he wasn't punishing me. Doing anything now would just make things worse.

Acron shoved me hard, unexpectedly, and I fell backwards and landed on the ground heavily. My back seemed to split with pain and I could feel that the skin had ripped open, and it wasn't smooth. Acron loomed over me and I held my hands to shield myself.

"Wait," I cried. "I can't heal myself."

"What?" Acron snarled, but he didn't attack.

"My back, sir," I said. "I don't know if I can heal it. It tore."

"Get up."

I obeyed quickly and he examined my back, tracing his finger along the slit in my skin. I could feel the smooth cut, and where it had ripped from the fall. I could feel his finger twist as he followed the bottom of the cut, jagged and uneven.

"Can you heal this?"

I shut my eyes and focused. My microbes were in overdrive, had been in overdrive for hours. They couldn't function at this level for much longer. I desperately needed rest. I needed medication. I needed a break from the pain.

"I can't, like this, sir," I said, my voice trembling slightly because it wasn't the answer he wanted. "I can't keep going and still heal this."

"But you can heal yourself, with the right resources."

"Yes, sir."

He turned me in his arms and stared deep in my eyes as if trying to tell if I were lying. I couldn't project honesty because I couldn't spare any microbes, but I was telling the truth. Hopefully, he could tell.

"You use your microbes to heal, don't you?"

"Yes, sir," I said slowly, worried because that smirk returned.

"Well, there's an easy solution to that."

I wondered what he meant as he went to the side of the room and searched through a stack of books, papers, and assorted items. Two of the men who had raped me pressed me against the wall, holding my arms tightly as Acron returned with a needle. I looked at it with a sense of foreboding. Acron's smile was terrifying and I stared at the needle. The liquid inside was clear. I didn't know what that meant.

"Do you know why you have so many microbes?" he asked, and I jolted. He had mentioned my microbe count. In front of people. People who didn't know. A trigger.

"We tested on you," Acron continued, oblivious to my sudden tension. Or maybe he misinterpreted it. "We tried it over a century ago, here in the Drops. Your yakuza handler, I believe. He couldn't adapt, but he survived. You adapted. What will happen when we give you more, I wonder?"

Then I realized what was in the needle and I heard Sora gasp. Microbes. He was going to inject me with microbes, and I was going to mutate. The trigger, I thought. I hated going into my killing mode, but he had unknowingly triggered it. I could. He had given me permission and didn't even seem to know it. It frightened me, and I wondered if I would return to normal. I would need to sustain it this time if I wanted to kill everyone here, and I worried I might kill Sora. But as the needle approached my arm, I had no choice. I tore my microbes away from their healing duties and twisted them, sparking the parts of them that I needed to change my perception.

CHAPTER 37
THE CHANGE

I heard Acron gasp but it was too late. I saw him as a target edged in red, and I yanked forward out of the grips of the two men and lunged at Acron. He dodged, barely, and stabbed the needle into me. I knocked it out but I could feel a surge of microbes in my body, imitating the current microbes. I could feel my body shifting, muscles forming where they hadn't been before. I was changing. It was different than the guards, but my body was changing and I was terrified. Should I withdraw now, when there was still a chance of recovery? But then I would still be trapped. No, I decided. I would kill everyone here and save Sora.

I tore the arm off one of the men who was still struggling to hold me, ignoring his screams and delighting in the rich scent of blood. I lunged at the other, snarling and knocking him to the ground. Driven by instinct, I leaned down and sank my teeth into his throat before ripping it out. The blood ran down my throat and it was sweet, not at all like I expected, sweet and filling and I wanted more. I saw a figure on the ground but it didn't feel like a threat so I ignored it. Where was the threat? Who was the threat? I hesitated, my mind fuzzy. I had to kill someone, and save someone. But who?

Someone knocked into me and I savaged them. I could sense others nearby. There was only one person still in the room with me and he wasn't moving, so I left, hunting the others. They were scattering, but I moved quickly, knocking them down from behind and ripping into them with my nails – my claws – and teeth. Two more. Then another. I lost count as the blood filled me. But not the one I wanted. I would know him. I didn't know how, but I would feel something when I found him.

I surged into a room filled with people but paused. They were different. Their scent was different. They had weapons but that wouldn't stop me if I was determined to kill them. But I wasn't sure I should kill them. Were they enemies? One of them stepped forward.

"Gabriel."

It was a name. A human name. Was I human? Was that my name?

"Gabriel, focus."

"There's no point," another human said, taking the man's arm and pulling him back. "He's too far gone. His mind is gone. You know that."

"He's not attacking," the man pointed out. "He's still there."

"Sometimes they don't attack," the other man said. "Sometimes they recognize us."

"You don't understand," the man said, sounding angry. "He's done this before. Not like this, but he's started to change and he's come back. He can do it again. Gabriel."

Again that name. I didn't know what was going on, what they were talking about. Was this someone I knew? People I knew? Was I supposed to recognize them?

"Gabriel, it's me," the man said. "Lee."

The name was familiar. A friend. Not the person I wanted to kill. I needed to find that person and kill him. I turned back to the door. No one in this room was hurting me so I needed to find the people who would hurt me, had hurt me.

"Gabriel," the man cried. "Don't leave. Listen to me."

I turned back, wondering what he could possibly say. Maybe he knew where the person I wanted to kill was. How could I ask him? There were ways to communicate. I couldn't think of them, but there were ways. He was using his voice to speak. Maybe I could do the same. My microbes were tightening my voicebox, I realized. I would never be able to speak. I loosened the grip of the microbes on my throat, forcing them into a different pattern. Other parts of my body shifted suddenly and I reeled, falling to my knees and quickly twisting my microbes back into a protective position. Speaking was less important than keeping myself safe, and killing.

The man approached me and I growled, but he ignored it. He ignored the cries of the other humans as well and crouched next to me, placing a hand on my shoulder. His touch was... familiar. I knew his scent. It was a good scent, with good memories. This was not the man I wanted to kill. Was this the man I wanted to protect? That didn't feel quite right, but I did want to protect this man now. He was in danger. I hadn't killed everyone yet. I needed to warn him. I slowly shifted my microbes again, loosening them so I could speak. When my body began shifting, I let it. I could take a moment of vulnerability in order to warn him.

"Acron," I whispered, not even sure how I knew the name. But it was the name of the man I had to kill. I remembered him. I remembered him hurting me and I had to kill him.

"You're safe, Gabriel," Lee said. I remembered Lee helping me. Holding me. Protecting me. "He can't hurt you anymore. I want you to return to your normal state. Focus on your microbes, Gabriel."

I considered. He hadn't said that Acron was dead. But he had said that I was safe, and I believed him. He wanted me to change my microbes and I wondered what I was supposed to change them to. I remembered that they hadn't always been like this. They hadn't always protected me like this. I felt Lee's microbes. Maybe I should make them like his. I concentrated on my microbes. They were vibrating with anger, aggression, pain, but I soothed them. I folded them back and as I did, I felt my body shifting again. I felt weak. Pain flooded my senses, and I wondered if it would be better to stay how I was to avoid the pain. But pain was acceptable if I was safe.

There was no real moment when my full consciousness returned, but at some point I became aware of how alien my thoughts were, and I realized what had almost happened. I had almost lost myself. I had almost become a killer, a monster. The second type of mutation that Lee had refused to talk about. An animal. My back ached and I sent my microbes to it, but I couldn't heal it. Not on my own. My microbes were barely functioning and my body was fading fast. Had Acron been killed? Would I have even known if I'd killed him? Was Sora safe?

"Sora?" I whispered, and Lee leaned forward and kissed my blood-streaked forehead.

"We're getting him now," Lee said. "You'll be taken care of. You're safe now. You're back. Just rest."

CHAPTER 38

RECOVERY

The world seemed different. My body ached and my mind barely churned to life. I couldn't open my eyes, just lie in what must be an exam chair. I could feel strong medicine being pumped into my body, and I could feel my microbes almost somnolent. Maybe that was the difference. Without my microbes, everything felt flat and dull. I struggled to rouse my microbes enough to scan my body. I needed to know if permanent damage had been done. My microbes resisted. They had never resisted me before. I switched tactics and instead of ordering them, I coaxed them. Pleaded with them. And they began to move. I had pushed myself too far, I realized as I felt the weakness of my microbes. I needed to protect myself better.

The scan of my body was satisfactory. I was severely injured. My back was still open, though it was healing. The bruises and minor cuts across my body were still there. If my microbes were functioning, they would be gone by now, but I didn't dare direct my microbes to fix them. I had done something when I forced my microbes to twist like that. Something about them had permanently changed. Or no… what was it?

Most of my microbes felt normal, I realized. Drained, but normal. Some of my microbes, though, felt almost angry. Resentful. They didn't like being in my body like this. What was happening? I thought back to everything that had happened to me. Awareness washed over me as I remembered Acron stabbing me with the needle, the microbes entering me – and immediately becoming twisted. Normally, that state of mind felt alien to me. My microbes didn't last long like that because it wasn't their normal state. But it was the normal state for my new microbes. They wanted me to be like that. They wanted the aggression, the hate, the blood. They weren't happy being passive like this, being ordered around and having to heal my body. Was my body really at war with itself? I had managed to return to my normal state, but would it last? And if I were ever accidentally triggered again, would I ever return, or would I be trapped forever? I shivered.

"He's awake," someone said, and I realized there were people around me. The medicine weakened and I slowly opened my eyes.

"Lee," I whispered, delighted to see him looking down on me. I had never been so happy to see someone in my entire life. Even seeing my sister's face when I was crouched in the family safe house, nearly at the point of chopping my hand off to stop the pain, even that joy was shadowed by this. But he wasn't the only one to care about. "Is Sora-"

"He's recovering well," Lee said.

"Acron?"

Silence, and Lee's lips twisted to a scowl. "He escaped. Barely. You got a chunk of him. He won't get far, and he'll be marked the rest of his short life."

I inhaled sharply as fear begin threading through my body. The angry microbes rejoiced because if I was afraid, I might change to protect myself. I shoved them down. There had to be some way to sort this mess out, to make them accept this form.

"What do you mean?"

"You took his arm," Lee said. "If he dies from blood loss, we'll find him, and if he managed to survive, well, he's not getting far. All five Families are scouring the Drops for him. He won't escape."

"Is Ananti here?" I asked, and she popped into my view. She looked incredibly relieved and though she was smiling, her eyes were rimmed with red as if she'd been crying.

"My microbes are strange," I said. "The new ones aren't adapting to this form. What do I do?"

"What do you mean?" she asked, taking a few steps to look at a monitor.

"The ones he injected me with," I said. "They want me to be in that form, not this one. I can't control them."

Lee hissed, his eyes narrowing. "Are you safe? Will you stay like this? Or will you change?"

"I don't want to change," I said with a shiver. "But they want me to. They're not content."

"Can you control them right now?" Ananti asked in a frightened voice. "Just a little longer?"

"Yes," I said. "They won't do what I want, but I won't change."

"Lee, should we try?" Ananti asked softly, and Lee sighed.

"I didn't want to. He's handling them so well."

"Apparently not," Ananti said. "Gabriel, we're going to drain some of your blood. It's dangerous, since your body is so weak right now. We know how to drain microbes at the same time. Not many, but hopefully enough. Would you be able to focus the new microbes so that those are the ones that are drained?"

I shivered. "They're mine," I said. "Why would I get rid of them? They're me."

"They're not who you want to be," Lee pointed out in a gentle voice. "Can you feel the needle in your arm? We're going to start flushing something through your veins that will force blood out of your body. Can you control your microbes enough to send them into the needle?"

I was silent, and I reached out to my microbes. Would the aggressive microbes leave? They didn't want to. They wanted to stay and they wanted to change me. They were part of me, but he was right; it wasn't a part I wanted. I could lure them out.

"All right."

Ananti came to my side and switched the tubes connected to my arm. She pressed on the needle almost painfully.

"Right here, Gabriel," she said. "Focus right here."

I nodded weakly. She counted down from three and I focused

my microbes on that needle, suggesting that if they traveled through the needle, they would find a body that wanted to become a monster. I felt a shiver through my body, something sucking out of me. I clutched my precious microbes and lured the others, projecting strength and violence if they went through the needle. But I clung to every single one of my microbes and where they were only a few of the other microbes left, I cried out for Ananti to stop. The sucking sensation ceased instantly. There were a handful of angry microbes left, but they seemed to recognize they were outnumbered as I released all of my microbes to flood through my body again. They faded and in moments, I couldn't even tell which were which.

Ananti was switching tubes again and watched me carefully. I realized I was breathing heavily, as if I had just run for hours. I slowed my breaths. I scanned my body and there was no resistance. My microbes were still exhausted, but they were functioning perfectly. All of them. I sent some to my back and let the rest continue to replenish themselves.

"Thank you," I said.

"Did it work?" Lee asked, and I smiled at him. It was a faint smile, but I was happy and wanted him to know.

"My body is under control again."

Ananti clipped an arm scanner on me and I instinctively pushed my microbes out of the way, then paused and let them flow freely. The scanner flashed red, and a minute or two later, Ananti took the results and let out a sigh of relief.

"Almost exactly what it was before," she said.

"Can I see Sora?"

Lee and Ananti exchanged a look and I tensed. Was Sora hurt? Lee had said he was recovering. But I remembered the sharp pain Sora had felt when he looked at me. Did Sora hate me now? He would likely never want to see me again. He wouldn't want me checking on him.

"He's still injured, Gabriel," Lee said. "He looks a mess. But he's healing quickly. It's just superficial bruises."

"He hates me, doesn't he," I said softly.

"No," Lee said firmly. "Why would you think that?"

"I could feel him hurting when he looked at me," I said. "And it was my fault he was hurt."

"I think he was hurting on your behalf," Lee said gently. "He said the most painful thing they did was make him watch what they did to you. He doesn't hate you at all."

"He doesn't?" I asked, bewildered.

"He's worried that you hate him."

"Why would I ever hate him?"

"It was his messages that lured you out of the building, into their hands. He blames himself. He said they attacked and disabled him, then used his chip without his permission. It's difficult to do, but not impossible. He read the messages as they were sent, read your replies, but couldn't control them. I'm just glad you thought to let me know when you arrived."

"I'm sorry," I said. "I know I shouldn't have left. I should have checked with you to make sure I had your permission."

"Well, even if you hadn't sent that last message, I had just found out you were gone. I would have started looking for you immediately."

"How? Did you notice I had left?"

"Eric did. He thought it was strange that you were leaving, even if you claimed to have my permission, and wanted to make sure you were safe enough. He checked with me just before I got your message."

"Lee-sama helped me?"

"You're part of the yakuza now," Lee said. "You're our family. No matter what he feels about you, no matter how he takes advantage of you, he'll always put your safety first. Everyone will."

"I didn't kill the wrong people, did I?" I asked softly, thinking of the people I had ripped apart and nearly devoured. I shivered thinking of my teeth – fangs – digging into the soft flesh of their throats, and the hot sweetness of the blood against my eager tongue.

"You killed the right people," Lee said. "All of them. Only Acron got away, and we'll find him soon. When you encountered us, you stopped. Do you remember that?"

"Vaguely," I said, shutting my eyes. "Like it was a dream. I wasn't really the same person. But I remember you. You talked to me. They didn't want you to."

"I exposed a lot of your secrets, Gabriel," Lee said. "I'm sorry. The yakuza who heard, who saw you like that, were isolated afterwards. We've emphasized how important secrecy is. They won't share it outside of the yakuza, I'm certain. No one will. But they might tell loved ones, or friends, and it may spread."

"What do they know?" I asked fearfully, trying to remember what exactly had happened.

"Your name," he said. "I'm sorry. It was the only way I knew to reach you. And they know that you became a Wolf, and recovered. No one – no one – has ever done that before. You were fully changed."

"A Wolf? That's what you call the other mutation?" I said. "I've heard of those. They're predators, right? Like cats?"

"They're actually a type of dog, but they are predators," Lee said with just a trace of amusement.

"Thank you," I whispered. "Thank you for talking to me. My mind was so strange. I wouldn't want to stay like that. If people know, it doesn't matter. Thank you."

Lee took my hand and squeezed it, and I felt his reassurance flood into me as his microbes sparked against mine.

"Acron said you made a deal with him," I said hesitantly. "I didn't believe it, the deal he described didn't make sense, but... why did you take so long?"

Lee's lips tightened. "It is true that we made a deal, of a sort. When I started looking for you, he sent me a message. He said if I tried to stop him, he would kill you and Sora. Instantly. So we had to move slowly, and make sure that everything was secure before we could move. He sent us images of what happened to you," Lee added reluctantly. "Videos. Some were streamed live, some weren't. Only a few of us saw. Me, Eric, Ananti, and a couple of others. We looked for hints as to your location and we found you, but we couldn't attack while you were so vulnerable."

He looked away, as if ashamed of that decision. "We were waiting. They were livestreaming it when you changed. When you attacked. We knew that was our chance. I was afraid I couldn't get to you fast enough, and you evaded us. We didn't want to split up and risk you killing us, and you were tracking down everyone else so well, we generally left you to it. We think Acron must have played dead to trick you into leaving before killing him."

"But you'll find him."

"Yes," Lee said firmly.

I sighed and shut my eyes. So Lee had seen what happened to me. I wasn't sure how I felt about that. On the one hand, I didn't want him to know my shame, but on the other hand, I had handled myself fairly well. Would he be impressed at how well I had done? Or would he notice all of the ways I had failed to obey?

"He said," I started slowly, looking at Lee. For once, I wasn't afraid of meeting his gaze. I wasn't afraid of anything right now. "He said they tested on me. On you. That was what happened to you, wasn't it? All of it."

Lee shut his eyes, appearing shaken, and I could sense his microbes easing the pain my words had brought. But I felt no regret for asking. Somehow, none of the usual rules of conduct seemed to apply. I wasn't bound in the same way. Was it because Acron would be dead soon? Or because being in his hands again had made me realize exactly how abusive he was, and how differently the yakuza viewed sagents? Lee wouldn't judge me for these things. I thought back on how he always seemed annoyed at my obedience, and I wondered that I had never seen it before. He was annoyed because obedience wasn't required, or at the least the blind obedience I had been taught, and he knew that as long as I followed those patterns, part of me was still trapped in Destiny.

"Yes," Lee said. "All of it. Except that I never changed. I was on the brink of it, but they found me in time. They drained my microbes as we drained yours, down to a safe level. The change never came. I survived."

I took a deep breath. Lee had survived, and so had I. I wondered how close the similarities really were. When Mei had said that a Destiny agency might be involved, I hadn't even thought to connect it to me and my agency. And they had streamed the assault on Lee to his family, just as they had streamed what happened to me to Lee. Did they know how doubly cruel that was, not just making him watch it, but making him relive that experience? Probably. Lee had helped me run away. Not from Acron, specifically, but he had still help me get out of Destiny. Acron probably hated Lee quite a bit. I shivered. Acron was alive, but not for long. I had to have faith in that.

"I know I have sick days in my... my contract," I said softly, forcing the difficult words out. I hated admitting weakness, because weakness led to punishment. But not anymore, not with Lee. "Can I use one?"

Lee let out a chuckle, then placed his hand over mine. "You're going to use more than one, Gabriel," he said. "Until you're fully recovered, you're not to do anything. And you don't need to push your microbes to heal yourself. You need to recover naturally. Don't push yourself."

"How will I pay it off?"

"This is my fault, Gabriel," Lee said sadly. "You won't pay off anything, because I should have kept a closer watch on you, and on Sora."

"It isn't your fault," I whispered, not wanting him to blame himself, but frightened to contradict him. Then again, the rules didn't apply, not really, so correcting him like this wouldn't end in punishment.

"There are a lot of people at fault," Lee said. "And Acron will pay for what he did to you. But you need to rest, and let me take care of everything. Take as much time as you need."

He stood up and I grabbed his arm. Once, I never would have grabbed anyone like that, let alone my handler. But things had changed. I had changed. And Lee didn't look upset. Shocked, but not angry. He came back to my side and took my hand in his.

"Don't leave," I said, and without a word, he sat next to me again. He probably had a lot of things to do, and there was Sora to think about as well. I shouldn't be taking him from his responsibilities. But he didn't argue, and didn't leave. He stayed there, with me, until my microbes faded from my awareness and I felt more safe and content than I had in my entire life. He was protecting me, and I was free.

CHAPTER 39

LEAVING SAFETY

Lee was still over me when I woke up, though he had probably left and returned. Ananti was monitoring me closely enough to be able to let him know when I would wake up so he could be at my side, and I was deeply reassured to see him. He stroked my face as I looked at him. I ached as I ran a quick scan of my body. Because I was barely using my microbes at all, my physical condition hadn't improved much. My back, the only place I had sent my microbes, was closing up, but I was still covered in minor injuries. I wondered how I looked, and if I would be punished for not healing myself faster.

Then I checked my thoughts. This was not Acron. This was not my first agency, nor even my second agency. I would not be punished here for things outside of my control. And Lee had specifically warned me not to heal myself quickly. That was my primary order to obey, and I was obeying it.

"I have news, Gabriel," Lee said, and I wondered why he didn't specify if the news was good or bad. "There's a group in the Drops who protects people from the yakuza. I believe you've met them."

I thought of the bed and breakfast where I had hidden from the yakuza after first deciding to stay in the Drops, and nodded.

"Acron went to them for help."

My heart chilled.

"They helped him leave?"

"No," Lee said, and I sighed in relief. "He told them a monster had attacked him, since he knew they would have heard rumors of the Wolves we keep. But they also know that Wolves aren't allowed to attack people without very good cause, and they contacted the judge, who has enough contact with the yakuza that they knew he would know what was going on, but not enough to be a threat. He contacted me, and I briefly explained the situation."

"Then where is Acron? He'll kill them if they don't let him leave."

"He was badly injured, and his arm was ripped off," Lee reminded me. "He's in intensive care fighting for his life. When the judge told them what had happened, they agreed to let him die."

"They're letting him die? What if he doesn't?" I asked, panicked at the thought that Acron would slip away and never be found until he struck again. I had ripped off his arm; when he found me again, he would not start out as gently as he had this time.

"They're letting him be executed," Lee corrected. "They would let the yakuza do it, but we can't enter their building. So I convinced the judge to do it for me. His people agreed. No one is allowed to attack a sagent like you so execution is a legal punishment, even if we don't go through the courts."

"Then they know what happened?" I whispered. "And how will we know he's dead?"

"The judge knows you specifically were attacked. The people who protect against the yakuza do, too. You had their prior protection, and I'm sure that's the only reason they're agreeing to this."

"But what if something goes wrong?"

Lee was silent for a moment. "I tried to argue that he needed to be brought under yakuza control to die, because you would always be afraid if you couldn't confirm for yourself that he was dead. They refused, but offered to let you come. To confirm his death."

"But you wouldn't be with me," I said slowly. "If Acron overpowered them, you couldn't protect me."

"It's not Acron I'm worried about," Lee said. "They have him under control, and I trust them. I also trust them to kill him, especially if they see you and see what he did to you. But I am worried about them. They might try to keep you there, or the judge might take you for himself."

"But I don't want to stay with them," I said. "I want to be with you. They'll understand. They let me leave last time, even though they didn't want me to go. I'll tell them I feel safe with you, and they'll believe me. They'll know I'm not lying."

It was true. If it was at the bed and breakfast, then they would have that strange field that prevented people from lying. They would have no choice but to accept my decision.

"I want to go," I added. "I need to see him die."

Lee nodded. "I thought you might want that. They can't legally hold him more than twenty-four hours. They're prepared to kill him, but the judge wants to avoid breaking laws if possible. He's already been held for most of that time. Do you have the strength to come with me now? I'll take you as far as I can."

I tested myself. I needed to see Acron's body in front of me, and understand that he was dead. I needed to feel his body cooling under my hand, or else I would doubt that he was really dead. I would always be scared that he might come back. I would never be safe. My body felt weak, but I coaxed my microbes awake. They didn't resist the way they had before. They were drained, but they would obey me just as they always did. I was grateful.

"I'm ready," I said, and Ananti and Lee helped me sit up. I got to my feet slowly. The aches in my body were increasing now that Ananti had taken out the tube giving me pain medication. She assured me that I wouldn't be in too much pain while I was gone, but it was enough. My mind was frayed from what Acron had done to me. But I didn't want her to know how much pain I was in, despite what she had given me, so I said nothing. If they knew how much this hurt, they might not let me leave.

Lee helped me into a loose kimono and I was grateful I wouldn't be trapped in tight-fitting clothing. Then Lee covered me in a hooded cloak so my face wouldn't be visible, and escorted me out. Slowly. I couldn't move very fast, dizzy from the aftereffects of the medicine and from the pain. Lee let me choose the pace, even though he should have forced me to keep up with him. He was different in every way.

There was a car waiting outside the podhouse, but I hesitated in the doorway of the building. Lee was with me, I assured myself. Last time I left, I was alone. This time, I was with my handler. Nothing would happen to me. Still, I flinched as I passed through the doors, and I wasn't able to hide it. Lee's hand tightened around me, but he said nothing. He wouldn't punish me for such an obvious loss of control. I wondered if I would be able to continue beyond where he could follow. I needed him at my side, but I needed to see Acron dead even more. And the people at the bed and breakfast would protect me. They already had. The judge would protect me, too. I had other people on my side against Acron. They wouldn't betray me.

Lee-sama was in the car already, I was surprised to see. Lee seemed surprised as well.

"Don't you have other things to do?" Lee asked, but there was no animosity in his voice.

Lee-sama looked at him, then at me. For once, his gaze wasn't dominated by lust and a need to control me. He appeared concerned, and perhaps even guilty, though I couldn't imagine why.

"You'll need protection," Lee-sama said.

"We can't go near. The judge has it under control."

"The judge may not respect you the same way he respects me."

I wondered if that were true. Lee and the judge seemed to have a working relationship, but then again, Lee had also sent a sagent against him. It was probably a very complex relationship, whereas Lee-sama's relationship was much clearer: he was the leader of the Dragon Clan and had to be obeyed. Lee-sama would bring additional guards, I was sure. The entire bed and breakfast would probably be surrounded by yakuza in case the judge turned on them and tried to keep me there, but perhaps the odds of that happening would drop if Lee-sama were there himself. I didn't mind if he came and I glanced at Lee, wondering what he would do. Lee was studying me, I realized, and when I looked at him, he nodded. He gestured for me to get in and I sat beside Lee-sama in the large car, with Lee on my other side. Lee-sama took my hand.

"I apologize for not stopping you," he said, and I blinked in surprise. Did he blame himself for that? "I knew Lee would never let you out, and that should have warned me that something had lured you out."

I responded automatically, reassuring him that he had don't nothing wrong, that he wasn't to blame, but inwardly I wondered. What if he had stopped me? What if he, at the very least, had forced me to confirm with Lee directly? Sora would be dead. If Acron realized his trap had failed, Sora would be vanished and killed. No, it was better that I was there. I knew how to handle that kind of treatment, and he didn't.

Lee-sama didn't look reassured by my words; he must be able to tell they were an automatic response and not genuine. The judge had been able to tell with me as well. I would have to ask Lee to help me train better so no one could tell I wasn't being entirely honest.

The neighborhood came into view and I saw a large group of clearly militant people. I tensed, thinking of the men who had raped me. Lee put his hand on my arm.

"Those are the judge's men," he said. "They're here to escort you. Do you feel safe enough? You don't have to do this."

"I'm fine," I said, because I couldn't show my fear. Lee and Lee-sama got out with me and we approached the people. The judge stepped forward. I was hidden under the hood and grateful he couldn't see me, because I was heavily bruised. My body ached, but I couldn't let it show.

The judge extended his hand and Lee and Lee-sama stopped walking at my side abruptly. We were about two blocks from the bed and breakfast. That was a long way to walk without Lee, and a large area for the yakuza to surround. Would they manage it?

Was I safe? I hesitated, and looked at Lee.

"They'll keep you safe," he assured me. I took a cautious step away from Lee, then another. The judge came forward, but didn't take my hand. He just offered it, and I took it. The judge led me into the mass of guards and we began walking. I glanced back to see Lee and Lee-sama looking frustrated. But they didn't seem worried, or at least too worried, so I tried to calm myself. The judge would protect me for now, and I would be back with them soon.

CHAPTER 40
FINAL JUSTICE

The judge took my arm as he escorted me towards the bed and breakfast. It was brightly lit, as it had been last time, and I was grateful for the hood that hid my identity and my injuries.

"Is that really you, Peter?" the judge asked, and I shivered. Did he doubt me? Did he think it wouldn't be me? And if he didn't think it was me, did he also doubt that Acron was a threat?

"Yes," I said. "It's me."

He didn't say anything else as we walked, and I decided that he must have been simply confirming, not expressing doubt. Soon, we were at the familiar bed and breakfast. The man and woman I remembered were there, standing on the steps. I wondered where Acron was being kept, and if he was secure. What if they let him escape? I hesitated again, suddenly wondering if Acron had planned this, if this were just an elaborate way to get me without Lee's protection. The judge's hand tightened on my arm and he pulled me to a stop.

"Do you feel safe?" he asked, just as Lee had. "I can take you back."

"No," I said, feeling a little faint. Acron was nearby, and I would have to trust these people for my safety. I didn't like having to trust other people. People had always betrayed me in the past. But not these particular people. So I kept moving forward. The man and woman led me into the house without a word, and

I felt the tingle of their shield as we entered the area where I couldn't lie. Once inside, the woman gestured to my hood.

"We heard you were attacked. But we need to ensure that it's you."

I slowly pulled off my hood, and they gasped. The judge, who was still holding me, let go of me abruptly. That couldn't be a good sign. They looked shocked, appalled, and I wondered how bad I looked. Lee hadn't given any indications, but he had probably seen me right after the assault, and I was sure I looked better than I had then. I couldn't meet any of their eyes.

"Did the yakuza do this to you?" the man asked sharply, and I did glance up at him, surprised.

"No. I thought you had the person who did this," I said, fear beginning to take root. But the man seemed to consider.

"I didn't believe what the yakuza said about him," he said slowly. "He doesn't seem like a threat."

"But I'm safe, right?" I asked, fear turning to panic. What if they were on Acron's side and had lied to Lee? I took a step back, and the judge grabbed me.

"You're safe," he said again. "My people have him secured. The owners didn't trust Lee about what the man had done. I'm in charge of security, and I do trust Lee."

I let out a breath, feeling some of the tension leave my body. This wasn't a trap. Of course the man and woman wouldn't trust the yakuza. But Acron was still secure.

"Where is he?" I asked, looking to the judge. "I want to see him."

Without a word, the judge led me down the hall. The woman walked at my side as the man went ahead with several of the guards. We entered a room, and I flinched. Acron was there, awake. Then I noticed the glass wall dividing the room. He couldn't get to me. There were guards on both sides of the glass and as the judge led me in, they aimed their weapons at Acron, who stood up and stared at me. I was stunned.

I had indeed ripped his arm off, but not cleanly. Most of his shoulder was left, though gutted from where I had torn the limb from its socket. Only the flesh was left and while it was wrapped with bandages, he looked horrific.

"You adapted," he breathed, still staring at me intently. I remembered what Lee had said about no one recovering from turning into a Wolf before. Was I going to be targeted even more, now that Acron knew? But Acron was going to die, I reminded myself. He wouldn't tell any agency, and no one would find out. I was safe. But as Acron's eyes narrowed, I couldn't help but shiver in fear. He noticed, and his remaining hand flexed as if longing to punish me. But he couldn't, because there was a wall separating us, and because there were people to protect me. I straightened. This was the most power I had ever had in his presence. I had never been protected from him before. It was almost intoxicating.

"You think you're safe?" he asked, shattering the feeling. "I'm not alone. We will hunt you down. You can't escape us forever, and you can only run away so many times."

I trembled and felt the judge's reassuring presence next to me. The man and woman were here, too, and they looked shocked by Acron's words. They were on my side, now.

"Kill him," I said softly, and Acron scoffed.

"You think you have that kind of authority? You're a sagent. My sagent. How dare you say such a thing?"

I took an angry step towards him, meeting his gaze squarely as I had never dared do before in my life.

"I'm not your sagent anymore," I said, trying to hold my anger to give me strength, because meeting his gaze like this was terrifying. "And I want you dead."

The judge signaled and Acron's eyes widened. He must not have realized they were planning on killing him, but as he turned to the guards in the room, it was too late. All of them fired, the bullets slamming through his body as blood splattered the glass wall. Acron slumped to the ground, coughing up blood, his remaining hand spasming before going still. He was dead.

"I want to touch him," I said, looking to the judge. "I need to know he's dead."

The judge nodded, then gestured to the guards again. One of them went up to the body and fired straight into Acron's head. To make sure he was dead, I knew, so that I could go close without any risk of him still being alive. It was gruesome, but I felt oddly vindicated. He was gone. I felt numb as the judge led me out of the room and into the adjoining one, where the body lay in a ruined heap of flesh. The head was entirely gone, but this was Acron. The arm was gone, but I knew him. I could feel the few microbes in his body, and I recognized them. I knew them intimately. This was not a fake, not a double. I knelt and touched him. He wasn't cold yet, but I could sense the chill starting to enter him. I could sense the lack of blood flowing through his veins, and I could see that nothing would ever bring him back. I was safe. For the first time, I was safe.

I let out a shuddering sigh, and felt weak. The judge, who was still holding my arm, helped me to my feet, and I collapsed into him. He held me tightly and I winced as his hand clutched right where my back was torn. He loosened his grip immediately. Acron would have gripped harder if he found somewhere that hurt me. And Acron was gone. Would everyone treat me with respect now? Lee did. The judge seemed to. The man and woman had, in the past. Was I finally considered a human? I thought back to all of my fears growing up, the fear of being a sagent that had always haunted my steps, the deep desire to be anything else. Acron had exploited that fear as well. He had exploited everything. And now, perhaps, the exploitation would end. But I remembered his words. He was gone, but there were others. I was safe, but not forever, and not from everyone. But being safe in this moment was enough, and as the judge helped me out of the room, I was filled with hope, a strange feeling I hadn't felt in years.

The judge helped me into a chair, and I realized the man and woman were right there as well. The woman sat next to me, cautiously putting an arm around my shoulders.

"You said your previous agency was protecting you," she said. "Were they protecting you from him? That's why you wanted to stay with them?"

"Yes," I said, voice trembling slightly.

"Are you sure you want to go back to the yakuza? You don't need protection anymore, do you?"

"I'm sure," I said. "I want to go back to Lee."

The woman seemed disappointed, as did the man.

"You don't have to be a sagent," the man said gently. "We can protect you. You can live a normal life."

"I would protect you," the judge added.

"I know what I want," I said. Once, those words would have been impossible. Even if I did know what I wanted, I never would have dared to say it. I would never make my desires known. Anytime I wanted something, it was taken away. If I desired someone, he was taken away. Not anymore. I wouldn't let it happen anymore. No one could take away what was mine, not anymore. And to my amazement, the three of them said nothing else to persuade me, nothing else to try to make me doubt what I wanted. They simply made sure I was strong enough to walk, had me pull the hood over my face again, and helped me to the door. The man and woman lightly embraced me, the woman kissing my cheek.

"We're always here if you need help," she said, and I thanked her. I didn't give my usual response, as it wasn't necessary. Only thanks were needed right now.

The judge kept his arm around my waist as the guards escorted us back to Lee and Lee-sama. The two of them were talking, it looked like, but as soon as we came into sight, Lee straightened and looked relieved. Had they been worried? Had they already been planning how to rescue me? The judge held me tight and just like the woman, he kissed my cheek.

"I'm also here to help, if you need anything, in any way," he said softly, and I thanked him, too. I hoped he knew how honestly I meant my thanks. And then the judge pushed me towards Lee, who was waiting just beyond my reach. I took several steps, and was enveloped into a hug. Lee-sama stroked my shoulder. They thanked the judge as well, and we got into the car again. I leaned against Lee, not afraid to show my weakness as we drove back to the yakuza section, and the podhouse where I was safe. I would ask to see Sora when we arrived, I decided. They would probably let me. I wondered if I would be going back to Ananti, or if I could return to my room. Given the ache in my body, I rather hoped I would get more pain medicine soon. I had never dreamed that I would be allowed to dull my pain, that I would actually expect such treatment from my agency.

We entered the podhouse and for a long moment, I stared at the rolling hills of water with the dragon soaring above. I was back. I was home.

THE END

ABOUT THE AUTHOR

Elizabeth James

Elizabeth James hails from Portland, Oregon and spent many hours of her childhood tucked away in the Gold Room of Powell's Books, reading science fiction and fantasy masterpieces and hidden treasures. She writes romance with strong elements of science fiction and fantasy as a result, focusing on LGBT characters.

THRALL OF DARKNESS

SCIENCE FICTION AND FANTASY ROMANCE PUBLISHER

Thrall of Darkness was founded because there is a shortage of good, quality literature featuring gay protagonists that does not reduce gay characters to stereotypes or dismiss them as secondary characters. Every story seeks to challenge the status quo by focusing on gay characters and combining drama, action, and sex into an addicting blend of fun-filled narrative.

You can find more information on Thrall of Darkness novels and short stories at thrallofdarkness.com.

BOOKS BY THIS AUTHOR

Demon Season

Taylor just wanted to bond with a regular demon during his first demon season, but instead he ends up with the prince of demons, an incubus! He fights through his fears of intimacy while battling past enemies as he and his demon come to a new understanding.

A Vampire's Desire

Kairos takes a job in an ancient vampire house knowing nothing about them and their society, and immediately falls in love with his boss, a powerful but cold vampire. As he tries to get closer, threats from a rival house threaten to tear them apart.

Tarragon Academy

Tarragon Academy is a college at the foot of a smoldering volcano surrounded in mist and mystery. First-year student Jamie is having a hard time adapting until he meets an upperclassman named Scott. Will Scott help him thrive in his new school, or does Scott have his own reasons for helping the beautiful young freshman?

Dragon Tamer

Luke has heard dragons all his life and when a dragon summons him to raise her dragonlings, he runs away to help her. But the world he enters is fraught with danger and he knows little of the outside world. As the dragons begin dying off and dragon tamers like him become scarce, a rival tribe kidnaps him and everything he knows is thrown into question.

First Prince

Wren is the beautiful yet rebellious first prince of Fontain, forced to move to the Imperial Palace as part of a treaty. Upon arriving, he receives a frigid welcome and realizes his stay will be fraught with danger. When he finds romance in an unexpected place, he realizes that his life may not be as dire as he imagined and pleasure can be found where it is least expected.

Prisoner Of Love

When Prince Tristan is captured in battle, he fully expects to be tortured and killed. But the torture turns to erotic pleasure as he learns that his enemy, Prince Ryan, is in love with him and has been planning his capture with meticulous care for years. Will Tristan hold firm to his principles, or will Ryan's forceful seduction overpower his senses?

Dark Offering

Nightmares are a nightly occurrence on the planet of Ylse, and they're strong enough to lure humans to be fed on by the creatures who haunt the night. Jarl is charged with risking the night to feed the colony. He comes across one of the creatures offering peace. Is the creature sincere or is this just a new way to lure the humans to their deaths on this inhospitable planet?

Bride Of Albis

Sam and his small crew of space-faring traders have their usual routine permanently shattered when they are kidnapped by pirates. Sam makes a deal with the head of the pirates: he will be sold as a slave in exchange for the freedom of his crew. But when he discovers that the pirate lied and sold his crew as well, he vows vengeance.

Seeking More

Seeking More is a collection of eight contemporary gay romance stories that range from the deeply emotional to action-packed, from hapless MFA students to couples on the brink of a new relationship. Each story is focused not only on steamy romance, of which there is plenty, but also on character development and an emotional connection between reader and character.

Eve Of Eternity

Sabine is a young woman searching for her identity while fleeing the powerful man trying to steal her heart and mind. She's almost under his control when she is kidnapped by a man with conflicting loyalties and a mysterious past who claims to kidnap her in order to rescue her. Will she break free from the men around her?

Treacherous A Dragon's Love

In the middle of the final battle against the great dragon Arostrath, a woman appears bound in golden chains. The King claims her as his reward but the youngest son has an unusual fondness for her that could cast the kingdom into ruin. Will his love for the beautiful and strange woman destroy the kingdom, or does her mystery hide the answer to all of their prayers?

www.ingramcontent.com/pod-product-compliance
Lightning Source LLC
Chambersburg PA
CBHW020301200626
46814CB00006BA/2020